Praise for Rosanna Ley

'A gorgeous story, full of heart'
Jo Thomas

'A wonderfully relaxing sun lounger read'
Sunday Express

'A real treasure to get lost in'
Tracy Rees

'Deftly written'
Kathryn Hughes

'Sun-soaked escapism'
Best

'Beautifully written, warm and romantic'
Rachel Hore

'Gorgeous'
Red Online

'A beautifully crafted slice of escapist fiction'
Heat

'A luminous, sun-soaked delight'
Woman's Weekly

'Beautiful, evocative writing'
The Sun

Rosanna Ley works as a creative writing tutor and has written many articles and stories for national magazines. Her writing holidays and retreats take place in stunning locations in Spain and Italy. When she is not travelling, Rosanna lives in West Dorset by the sea.

Also by Rosanna Ley

The Villa

Bay of Secrets

Return to Mandalay

Last Dance in Havana

The Little Theatre by the Sea

Her Mother's Secret

The Lemon Tree Hotel

From Venice with Love

The Orange Grove

The Forever Garden

ROSANNA LEY

The Saffron Trail

QUERCUS

First published in Great Britain in 2015 by Quercus Editions Ltd
This paperback edition first published in Great Britain in 2025 by

QUERCUS

Quercus Editions Ltd
Carmelite House
50 Victoria Embankment
London EC4Y 0DZ

An Hachette UK company

The authorised representative in the EEA is Hachette Ireland,
8 Castlecourt Centre, Dublin 15, D15 XTP3, Ireland (email: info@hbgi.ie)

Copyright © 2015 Rosanna Ley

The moral right of Rosanna Ley to be
identified as the author of this work has been
asserted in accordance with the Copyright,
Designs and Patents Act, 1988.

All rights reserved. No part of this publication
may be reproduced or transmitted in any form
or by any means, electronic or mechanical,
including photocopy, recording, or any
information storage and retrieval system,
without permission in writing from the publisher.

A CIP catalogue record for this book is available
from the British Library

PB ISBN 978 1 52944 315 8
EBOOK ISBN 978 1 78429 061 0

1

This book is a work of fiction. Names, characters,
businesses, organizations, places and events are
either the product of the author's imagination
or used fictitiously. Any resemblance to
actual persons, living or dead, events or
locales is entirely coincidental.

Typeset by Jouve (UK), Milton Keynes

Printed and bound in Great Britain by Clays Ltd, Elcograf S.p.A.

MIX
Paper | Supporting
responsible forestry
FSC® C104740
FSC
www.fsc.org

Papers used by Quercus are from well-managed forests and other responsible sources.

For Luke and Agata

Once, there was a girl who loved saffron. She loved its secrets, its mystery, the way it flowered in November when most plants were fading. She loved the wave upon wave of soft purple and green in the field, petals delicate as butterfly wings. She loved the urgency of the harvesting, the pulling of dusty red threads of gold in dimly lit rooms, voices murmuring and low singing while the pile of threads grew higher. She loved the aroma of saffron drying; its bitter and surprising scent. She loved the way it brought something special to a plate of food, sunshine to the heart. And, best of all, she loved its hint of magic.

She left the evening haze of the town behind her and began to trudge up the hill. It was one of those long, late-spring days that used to hold out such hope, when summer was something to look forward to rather than something to dread. But now at last the sun was setting and part of her journey would be in darkness. It didn't matter. She knew this pathway of old; it was as dear and familiar as a still-cherished lover. She could feel it. She knew exactly which way to go.

'Take care.' Tania had lifted her hand to wave. 'You sure you don't want me to call a taxi?'

She shook her head. 'I'd rather walk.' Walking meant thinking and, lately, she'd been doing a lot of that. Tonight, she'd had a couple of glasses of wine, too, and that was unusual these days. Perhaps she'd said too much. She'd got used to keeping her own counsel and it was unlike her to let it all out like that. She grimaced. Some of it at least.

The cliff wasn't easy. She paused to catch her breath. Below her, the last of the sun's rays illuminated a small shoal of mackerel leaping through the waves, slippery backs gleaming. And then they were gone. She watched as the sun sank lower, dipping into the horizon, its orange shadows darkening the water. She would take her time, she decided, on this journey back home.

She climbed the stile into the meadow. Last year, she'd seen a group of primary-school children here on a field trip, picking blackberries, their fingers stained red and blue, their teacher smiling as she talked to them about insects and birds. How heartening that had been. She had felt like congratulating the teacher on bringing these children back to nature; on encouraging such a love of the countryside in a world where people were spending most of their time indoors getting to grips with technology.

Bah, humbug. She was becoming a grumpy old woman. Perhaps she already was one. But things were changing. And now this . . . She shivered, although it wasn't cold.

She passed the tangled hedge of briars and brambles. And thought back. It was usually best not to. What had been done couldn't be undone. There had been a time when she'd imagined it would be different. But then again, perhaps it was like that for everyone. Everyone could think of 'a time'. *If I had done that differently, or that* . . . The course of events would be changed, perhaps for ever. Only they wouldn't be, because you couldn't play that game. There was no point.

She had recognized the finality of not replanting the saffron bulbs. Nell had known it, too. She had seen the knowledge in her daughter's eyes. She wasn't even sure why she had made it so obvious – she could, after all, have simply left the field as it was. But it was the fourth year. It was a compulsion. And so she had done what she always did. Let Nell make of it what she would. She had given her daughter a sign; it was all she would do for now. Nell must learn to read it for herself.

She came to the end of the meadow and climbed the second stile. The day was shifting towards its close; the final curtain. The sun had set, the redness in the sky was merging with the grey, and all the shapes she knew so well – of cliff edge and hedges, of wooden gates and dry stone walls – were blurring into the fuzzy shapes of twilight. The birds had stopped their flying and their chirruping. And the landscape around her, the landscape of Roseland, Cornwall, which she loved, was settling into the quiet of night-time, where the rustle of a creature in the undergrowth and the swish and scramble of the sea were the only sounds she could hear.

Nell, out of everyone, was innocent in all this. Whatever. And if *she* didn't need to know the truth then neither did Nell. What did it matter, after all, who belonged to who and who had done what? Every child was blameless when they came into the world.

The path here was narrow and close to the cliff edge. Below, in a tiny, rocky bay, the water sashayed through into the inlet, splashing on to the pebbles and larger rocks, drawing back with the tide towards the darkness of the ocean mass and the soft glow of the waning moon. She almost held her breath. Was there a sight more beautiful?

When you found out you were pregnant, she found herself thinking, *it should be the most glorious feeling in the world*. She put her hands on to her belly as if she could recall that feeling from more than thirty years ago, when she had been pregnant with Nell. *Glorious* . . . But that was in an ideal world. She looked out to sea. Her world had not been ideal, even then.

She sighed and walked on. And now? Around her now the darkness seemed to rest on the grass and the trees and the undergrowth; on the ocean and the rocks and stones below. The truth had always been a burden – even what she knew of it. And she didn't know it all. But that didn't give anyone the right to offload, and she wasn't about to offload now. That wasn't her way. Nell deserved better. She had not always done right by Nell. She had tried to protect her too much – she could see that. In the end you had to let your child go, no matter how you worried for her. And this was all she could do for Nell now.

She walked on, by feel, knowing exactly where she was from the familiarity of the path. And then it widened and she could sense rather than see the lane in the distance, a faint light from one of the cottages showing her the way. *One* way. Life was full of choices. There wasn't far to go now. And yet . . .

She moved closer to the cliff edge, drawn by the ruffled water, by the shimmer of the moon, by the hiss and the slap of tide on beach down below. She could see it and she could feel it. There really wasn't far to go now.

CHAPTER I

Five months later

She had been dreaming about her again. And that wasn't all. In those last seconds, just before waking; in those brief moments when you're not sure where you are, or sometimes even who you are, when a dream can seem your reality . . . Nell had seen the field of saffron. The flowers of the crocus bulb had just begun to bloom – it was that precious momentary pause before harvesting when the mauve coverlet seemed to have been gently drawn over the earth under an ice-blue late-October sky. It filled her vision, seemed to fill her world as it always had. Purple saffron.

But before she could catch it, before she could keep it, there was a swish of curtains and the vision was gone. It was morning. It was late October. But there was no saffron. Instead, there was her husband Callum, who had drawn the curtains and now stood by the bed carrying a tray and wearing a grin which seemed forced, perhaps because he hadn't worn it for such a long time.

Nell felt herself tense, though whether this was due to her dream, to Callum or because of the grief that still hung over her like a dark cloud, she wasn't sure. Her mother had died five months ago while walking along the cliffs sometime around midnight. She had gone and the saffron had gone, too. And Nell had lost her way.

'Wakey, wakey, sleepyhead.'

Nell opened her eyes wider and tried to smile reassuringly back at him. *I'm fine, really.* She'd done that a lot lately. But the truth was that she wasn't fine. And neither were they.

'Ta-ra! Breakfast in bed for the birthday girl!' His dark hair was still rumpled from sleep; she saw the determined shadow of stubble on his jaw. He was trying so hard to pretend.

'Thanks.' Her birthday. She'd almost forgotten. She was thirty-four today and this was her first birthday as a married woman. Her first birthday since the death of the mother she'd adored – which didn't bear thinking about, really.

So Nell pushed herself into a sitting position, grabbing a pillow to lean against. 'What a treat. How lovely.' The words seemed to echo around the room. Nell wondered if Callum found them as unconvincing as she did. But she didn't have the heart not to play the game he seemed to want to play. He was trying so hard. On the wooden tray was a mug of tea, a croissant on a plate, a big dollop of apricot jam beside it, a butter knife, a Japanese anemone in a slim vase and a fat cream envelope. This filled her with trepidation.

'Happy birthday, Nell.' Callum positioned the tray carefully on her lap (almost as if she were an invalid, she found herself thinking) and leant over it to kiss her lightly on the cheek.

When had they stopped kissing on the mouth, she found

herself wondering. Was it before her mother died or after? And did it honestly matter? He smelt of mint toothpaste and autumn leaves. 'Good dreams?' He smoothed her hair from her face and Nell closed her eyes for a second, thinking of another hand, a softer hand.

'I think so.' She decided not to tell him about the saffron.

It had been hard for them both since the death of her mother. *Why?* she thought, as she had thought so many times since it had happened. *Why did it happen that way?* And what had happened exactly? She had no idea. Her mother had been alone, walking along the cliff path in the middle of the night, for God's sake. And then . . .? So Nell didn't know how she had died, which added to the long list of other things she didn't know, other things which her mother had decided in her infinite wisdom not to tell her.

Nell realized that she was clenching her fists and that her shoulders were up to her ears. With a determined effort, she relaxed her muscles. It was bad enough not knowing things when her mother was alive – at least then she'd hoped she would tell her one day. But now that she was gone . . . This meant Nell would never know. And mixed up in this awful well of grief was the anger she felt against her for that.

Callum had done his best to support her. He'd held her in his arms when she wept – she couldn't believe there were so many tears inside her – he'd listened to her talking about the good times. He had stroked her hair, held her hand, soothed her brow, massaged her shoulders; done everything he possibly could. He had dealt with as much of the grisly administrative aftermath of death as was permitted. While Nell tried to make sense of it all.

In March, she had married him and her mother was still alive. By the end of May her mother was dead, and by mid-October she wasn't even sure if she and Callum would still be married by Christmas. What was going on? He was supposed to be her husband and yet it was her mother who seemed to have been the lynchpin that made Nell's world go round. Without her, everything, including her marriage to Callum, was flailing.

'Drink your tea, then,' Callum said, rather gruffly. 'Before it goes cold.'

'Sorry.' Nell took a deep breath. She must try harder, that was all. She couldn't give up on them without a fight.

Because Callum had always been worth fighting for, hadn't he? In Callum's well-ordered world – which was light years from the disordered planet Nell had grown up in – there was a right way to do things. You met a girl and you went out for drinks. This part had been easy; Nell had liked him from the first moment she saw him in the café where she made sandwiches and baguettes at lunchtime and in the evening ran around ragged to the tune played by Johnson, her boss, the head chef. Only chef. She'd wanted to get to know the tall, outdoorsy man with the warm hazel eyes rather better. In Callum's world, if this went well, you progressed to dinner (it had and they did), the cinema (a romantic comedy; he had laughed even more than she had), a music gig at the local arts centre – a local band who knew how to get everyone up on the dance floor – a walk along the cliffs from St Mawes to St Just, and a pub lunch. This would at some point lead to sex, although Nell had been seeing Callum for almost a month before the subject was broached – by Nell, in a 'what's wrong with me, anyway?' kind of fashion.

Callum had smiled at her, kind of strong and slow – boot-meltingly gorgeous, she had thought back then – and said, 'I just wanted us to take our time.' Which was lovely and, frankly, refreshing, in Nell's experience, where most men expected the full works after only a couple of dates. But when he leaned forward to kiss her – they were sitting in a crowded bar in Truro – and she felt the full force of him, as if he'd turned the intensity notch up by several dials, she had thought . . . *I don't need any more time.* And from the way he had made love to her that night in his one-bedroom flat near the river, gentle but with a rising passion that drew her irresistibly in, he hadn't needed any more time either.

That was about as far as Nell had ever got with any man. Sometimes it was her who finished things, sometimes him; sometimes it had simply petered out or never really got going in the first place. But it wasn't like that with Callum. They spent more and more time together. They both liked walking and cycling in the countryside and being outdoors, rain or shine. Nell enjoyed cooking and Callum enjoyed tasting the results. Their passion grew and they fell in love. The next stage for Callum was making a decision to share their lives. Living together, getting married.

'I don't know,' she'd said, the day he'd first suggested they move in together. They were eating pasta and drinking red wine at their favourite Italian café, and as usual Callum had managed to reserve the seat by the window. They had been together now for two years.

'What don't you know?' He was watching her closely; she could feel it. 'Whether or not you're ready? Whether or not you love me –'

'I love you.' She put her hand on his. She was sure of that much.

'Is it that you don't want to leave your mother?' he asked.

She wouldn't have put it quite like that. She would have said perhaps that she didn't want to leave her mother on her own, that she needed to get her mother used to the idea, that she wasn't quite sure how her mother would react. Or all of those things. 'Not exactly,' she hedged.

'Everyone leaves their parents one day,' Callum had pointed out, quite reasonably. 'It's what you do.'

Nell knew that. The words 'unhealthy' and 'unnatural' were hovering, though unsaid. But hovering was enough for them to emerge in a row, in the future, and so she wanted him to understand. It wasn't just a case of her saving up for a deposit to buy her own place, although that was part of it. It wasn't just how well they got on – most of the time. The usual conventions of life had not applied to her family. And there was just her mother; that was the way it had always been. Which meant that Nell felt responsible. Even so . . . 'You're right,' she said.

'But you're not sure how she'd manage without you?' he pressed.

'Sort of.' The truth was that she'd be more than capable. But they'd always been a team. The two of them against the world – or that's how her mother had always played it. And it was true, up to a point. So why had her mother always refused to talk about the past? About where Nell had come from? About who she really was? Team players wouldn't stay so stubbornly silent when one of the members needed to know something so badly.

'Is it because you're scared?' Callum's expression had softened. 'I'd look after you, Nell, you don't need to worry.'

But she wasn't a child . . . Just for a moment, she looked past him, out of the window into the street, where it had rained and the pavements were greasy and slick and a group of lads were standing around, smoking, laughing and drinking from cans of beer. 'Perhaps I should live on my own for a bit first.' Though she hadn't realized she'd spoken aloud until she saw his hurt expression.

'You're not sure,' he said. 'About us?' And he pushed his plate away, although he hadn't even finished his pasta, which was unheard of for Callum.

'I didn't say that.' And then she felt bad. 'I just think we should wait a bit,' she said. 'We're still young.'

'All right.' He rubbed at his jaw in that way he had and frowned. 'But you'll have to leave her some time, you know.'

Nell knew.

'Aren't you going to open it, then?' Callum went back to his side of the bed and, although he was already dressed – in blue jeans and a red-and-grey checked shirt – he unfolded himself back on to the bed beside her and grabbed his own tea from his bedside table. Hers was green tea with jasmine. His was Clipper Gold – strong and well-brewed.

Nell could tell he was excited. She felt her sense of trepidation grow.

'Have you got plans for today?' she prevaricated, sipping her tea, splitting the still-warm and crumbly croissant with her fingers, spreading some apricot jam.

''Course not,' he said. 'It's your birthday. And it's Sunday. You get to choose.'

Hmm. Nell would bet he'd already decided, though, what her choice should be. She lifted the white anemone in the vase closer, sniffed the delicate and wintry scent. She hadn't quite been able to catch the fragrance of the saffron this morning, though she knew it so well. Fragile petals sheltering fiery-red stigmata. The fragrance was alluring and almost impossible to pin down; a mixture of flame, honey and fresh hay. Could you experience a fragrance in a dream? Nell wasn't sure. She could unscrew a jar from the store cupboard in the kitchen downstairs and sniff the red threads of saffron inside anytime she liked. Savour their exotic aura, an elusive whiff of Moroccan spice roads and Persian palaces. But not the flowers – saffron flowers were far too transitory for that.

She thought back to the saffron she'd grown up with. They would harvest each plant when it was ready, gathering the crop in trugs to take inside. Her mother and Nell, and often a friend or two, would sit around the old and pitted farmhouse table where the plucking of the saffron took place every year. They would spread back the petals of each unopened flower as if it were an oyster sheltering a pearl and gently, deftly, tug the red, jewelled stigmata from the centre until their fingers were coloured slatey blue-grey on one hand from opening the petals and ochre on the other from pulling the threads. Meanwhile, the spent petals would gradually shroud the table as the precious tangle of threads gradually grew.

It wasn't easy work. The threads were delicate; they had to be pulled separately from the yellow stamen, the presence of which would dilute the batch; lavender petals would stick to their fingertips, stigmata would break, eyes would become sore. And the pile always grew so very slowly. But there was something about the dim light, the easy companionship between the women, the sharp scent of the saffron that started off like honey and then developed into something deeper, more musky, something much more potent that was, Nell found, its own reward, even when she wasn't much more than a girl.

The threads would be dried in batches on top of the Aga – Nell's mother had adapted a tray for this purpose. And they had to be dried quickly, before they turned musty and spoiled. So Nell's mother would watch over them, solicitous as a mother bird watching her chicks, spreading them out gently with her fingers until she was satisfied that they were fully dried and ready for storing. Their bitter-hay scent would drift from the kitchen into the rest of the house and on to their clothes. Faint stains of powdery yellow would appear on chairs, towels, pillows, as the saffron crept into their lives once more. And when it was over, Nell's mother would collect the leftover ephemeral wisps of purple flowers in her wicker basket and put them in a box in the airing cupboard to be used as what she called 'memory pot pourri' throughout the winter months. It was a reminder all right. As if they could ever forget.

Nell had grown up with the field of saffron in full view of her bedroom window in the farmhouse on the Roseland peninsula in Cornwall. Every four years her mother saw to it that the corms were lifted and moved to another site in the tradition of crop rotation so that land could be refertilized and the daughter corms which had crowded to the surface could be divided for replanting. That was how saffron fields grew. But the saffron was always in Nell's sight; she guessed that her mother had wanted it that way. And she watched the small saffron crop from the moment that the first papery, white, triangular sheaths protecting the tips of the leaves pushed through the soil to form a small tuft with the covering of the flower bud in its centre. Gradually, the leaves would grow. If the weather was good, a bud could become a fully developed flower overnight. And then the moment of glory when the temperature was perfect, the flowers finally unfurled and the long threads emerged and dangled, ready for the taking.

Saffron had been grown by their family for generations; her mother had often told her that. 'We have to work for our traditions to survive.' And she had become quite fierce as she said this, her eyes – such a dark shade they were almost indigo – burning with the passion of her words; her hands, floury from the dough of the saffron bread she was baking, dusting the dark hair which she pushed from her face as she worked. According to tradition, her mother used the whole saffron infusion rather than sieving it to get the very best flavour. Later, she would add currants, mixed peel, nutmeg and cinnamon. It doesn't need tarting up, her mother would say. Just a slice of golden sunshine and a little clotted cream. That fragrant yellow crumb. That hard-to-define saffron flavour. Heavenly. Nell could salivate just thinking about it.

'You, too, Nell. It's your legacy.' And she would turn around with a flounce, hair tumbling down her slim back, her brightly patterned skirt flowing with her as she fetched more ingredients from the larder. 'You have to keep it going, too.'

That legacy was an awful responsibility, Nell thought now, as she sipped her tea. Her mother should not have died – not so suddenly, and certainly not like that. Nell had been so terribly unprepared. She picked up the fat, cream envelope. 'Is this my present – or a card?' she tried to tease.

Callum raised an eyebrow. 'You'll have to open it and see.'

It would be both, she knew; she could tell. It had taken Nell a while to understand her husband – the way he ordered his life just as he ordered people's outside spaces. He was a landscape gardener and planner – and he did it the old-fashioned way. He liked nothing more than designing a garden space on paper on his drawing board, with a ruler, a pencil and the deep frown she always wanted to smooth away. And then he'd recreate it with lawn, with local stone, paving, decking and plants. And even while Nell sometimes longed for him to change his mind spontaneously, for his plans to dissolve into chaos, for something to turn out differently than he had expected . . . She was aware that it was this seductive sense of order that had probably attracted her to him in the first place. Callum – the living opposite of her mother.

Nell weighed the envelope in her palm. Callum had done his best to support her through her grief and her anger. But he had made it clear that what she now should be doing was moving on. How could you move on, though, when something inside you seemed to have died?

'We have to put the farmhouse up for sale,' he had said to her two months ago, when they were sitting in their cramped courtyard garden one sunny afternoon. 'It's ridiculous.'

'Ridiculous?' Nell hadn't liked the word. She had grown up there, lived most of her life there. She wasn't sure she could bear to sell it.

'It's been three months.' He'd got up from the bench and begun to pace the courtyard, as if he were trapped. 'It's just sitting there. Doing nothing. You have to face it. She's not coming back, is she, Nell?'

Nell felt the tears rise to the surface. Even after three months they were never far away. 'No,' she said quietly. 'She's not coming back.'

'And we could use the money.'

Nell hoped she hadn't heard him say that. But of course she had.

He came back to the bench and sat down beside her. 'We

could buy a bigger place. I could put some money into the business. We could even make plans for you to open your own restaurant. That's what you want, isn't it? What we both want?'

Nell said nothing. Her throat seemed blocked with an emotion she couldn't identify. Right at this moment, she couldn't say what she wanted.

'It's time, Nell.' He put his arm around her.

She wanted to rest her head against his shoulder. She wanted nothing more. She wanted to close her eyes and just let him take over. 'I don't know.' It felt like the conversation they'd had about moving in together all over again. But this time she didn't seem to have the strength to stand up for what she really wanted. It was her legacy. The farmhouse. The saffron.

'You're not your mother,' he said. 'You don't want to look after a smallholding, do you? I don't. I can't. You don't want that to be your life?'

Only it was. 'No.' Miserably, Nell shook her head. But . . . Her mother had been a tireless worker on the land – though when she could afford it she'd hired help. And there had been men – often there would be a man who would stay with them for months, working with her in return for a hot meal and shelter. These men had never stayed. By autumn, when the apples, pears and plums had been picked from the trees, when the fruit bushes had been harvested, when Nell's mother was making jam and preserving fruit and preparing for the winter months, that's when they left. Sometimes before; sometimes after the saffron. As a child, Nell never really knew why. One day they would be there, the next they'd gone. And it never mattered. Her mother was still smiling and singing and it was still just them, as it had always been.

But not any more. Callum was right. It was only five acres and a farmhouse; she had to look at it that way. There was the goat – already given to a family in the village who thought a pet goat would be a fun idea; they were from London, what did they know? And the chickens – sold to a neighbouring farmer's wife who lived down the lane. And there was the saffron.

'That place, that house, the land . . . It was Mum's world,' she tried to explain. And my world, she thought. For years, as a child, it was all she ever knew. Kept away from things on the outside that her mother thought could hurt her. Trapped, she thought guiltily. Or protected. It was a fine line. And she never knew why her mother had wanted to protect her so badly, what had happened to her that made her feel the world was such a bad place. Because she had never told her.

'I know,' he said. 'I understand how you feel, and I realize how difficult it is.' But he shifted away from her as he spoke, and she felt it. 'Leave it to me.' And she recognized the tone of his voice. It was the same tone he used with clients when he started to plan their landscaping. 'I'll get it all organized. You won't have to do a thing.'

Now, Nell slid her thumb under the seal of the envelope.

They hadn't sold the farmhouse, not yet, that was the main thing. It was up for sale, but it was still hers. For now.

She drew out the card. It showed a stick man kneeling in front of a stick woman offering her a heart. The stick man had dark hair and hazel eyes, like Callum, and the stick woman a mass of blond curls and blue eyes, like Nell. She wondered how many card shops he'd scoured to find it. It made her want to cry – again.

'Callum, I know things haven't been –' *so good between us lately,* she was going to say. Her mother's death had sent them on to different wavelengths and suddenly she wanted to acknowledge that truth between them, needed him to acknowledge it, too.

But he stopped her. He stopped her with a shake of his head. 'Don't, Nell. Not today.'

She hesitated.

A thin paper folder fell out of the card. Her present. Nell read the words inside the card – 'Happy birthday to my favourite chef.' She really mustn't cry again. She reached over and kissed his warm and stubbly cheek. If not today, she thought, then when?

'And . . .' Callum was waiting expectantly.

Nell was almost scared to pick up the paper folder. What if she didn't like it? What if he'd got it terribly wrong? It was bad enough having her first birthday without her mother – no one singing loudly in the kitchen, clattering pots and pans in the preparation of birthday pancakes, stomping around in her wellingtons because she'd just been out to feed the chickens, talking to a stray hen that had wandered into the house or the goat tethered in the yard. *Happy birthday, my Nelly!* Her mother's deep laughter. *My ray of sunshine.* Her mother had called her Nell because that's what her name meant in old English – light, ray of sunshine. She had been named after saffron.

Nell sniffed.

'Come on, Nell.' Callum squeezed her shoulder.

'OK.' She really had to stop this. Damn that dream. She opened the folder. A return ticket. A flight. She frowned. To Marrakech. 'Why . . .?'

'And . . .' Callum said again.

Nell realized there was another piece of paper. A sort of card receipt. She picked it up. For a cookery course, she read. In Riad Lazuli. In Marrakech. A five-day class studying Moroccan cuisine.

'What's this?' Though of course she could see. Callum had bought her a Moroccan cookery course in a riad in Marrakech. What she meant was – why? And how on earth could they afford it?

'Don't you like it?' Callum's determined grin slipped. 'I thought it would be the perfect present. You said you had holiday owing. I checked with the café.' His hazel eyes were still hopeful. 'I thought it would be an investment in your future. Our future. You've always said you wanted to learn more about . . .' His voice trailed.

'Moroccan cuisine. Yes, I have. I do.' Nell took a deep

breath. 'It's a wonderful present.' When he put it like that, it was almost the only present he could have given her.

Visibly, he brightened. 'You're sure?' He took her hand. 'You want to go? You're pleased?'

'Of course I want to go.' He wasn't to know that, since her mother had died, Nell had found herself more vulnerable than she'd ever known possible. He wasn't to know that it was hard to get up in the morning, hard to go to work, hard even to come home to her husband, without hearing her mother's voice. People lost their mothers all the time. They grieved, they got over it. It was life – and death. They didn't moon around thinking about chickens, women in wellies and the elusive scent of saffron. They went on with their lives; if there was a gaping hole, they skirted round it, they didn't fall in. They didn't keep their mother's Tarot cards wrapped in her favourite purple silk scarf and consult them daily for clues of what to do and how to carry on. They smiled, they tossed back the memories, they moved on. Callum wasn't to know, because she hadn't told him how bad it was. And he had made his feelings clear – he considered that it was time for her to at least start getting over it.

Nell wasn't sure which was the most daunting – the cookery course or staying in a riad in Marrakech. 'Wasn't it terribly expensive?' she asked.

He grinned. 'The flight was a steal. The cookery course – well, they had one place left and they'd slashed the price to get shot of it. Last-minute, you know. It isn't one of those posh riads. More sort of . . . um . . . backpacker.'

Backpacker. She nodded. With a name like Riad Lazuli it didn't really sound it. 'You're not coming with me, then?' she asked Callum.

For a second he looked past her, towards the back garden. But she could tell he was thinking of other people's gardens. 'I've got too much on,' he said. For a moment he sounded different, elusive. He came back to her, reached out and rumpled her curls. He hadn't done that for a while. 'This is for you, Nell. Just you.'

'Great.' To Nell, the word sounded mournful, but Callum didn't seem to notice. She looked at the date on the ticket. Pushed down the panic. She'd be leaving in three days' time. 'Thank you, Callum.'

'So . . .' Callum still looked worried.

Nell realized that, so far in their relationship, that's what she'd given him too much of – worry. She smiled her best smile, the one she kept in the top drawer. How could he know what she felt when she couldn't possibly tell him? 'It's perfect,' she said.

CHAPTER 2

'What did he get you, then?'

Nell glanced across at Sharon. 'Two crab baguettes,' she said. 'A cookery course. In Marrakech.'

'Oooh. Very nice.' Sharon grabbed the baguettes and sash-ayed across to the table in the corner.

Nell wiped her hands on her apron, turned to the next order. Beans on toast. Huh. When she'd done her first NVQs in professional cookery at Cornwall College she'd never envisaged this. And when she finally completed her founda-tion degree she'd been told that high-end establishments would now be more accessible for her, that she could climb the ranks and eventually become a chef. She looked around her at the Formica-topped tables and plastic chairs. Hardly a high-end establishment. It was all very well being qualified. But then you had to find a job.

'Is it, though?' she asked when Sharon reappeared, leaning on the hatch. She thought of Callum's elusive look. 'Is it a good sign for your husband to buy you a present that entails you going away for five days without him?'

Sharon laughed. 'In your Callum's case, yes.'

'And why's that?' Nell took out a couple of slices of bread

and popped them in the industrial-sized toaster. When she had her own restaurant, beans on toast would never make it on to the menu.

'Because he clearly adores you.' Sharon put her hands on her hips. 'And you don't know how lucky you are.'

Nell considered this. Not true, she decided. She did know she was lucky to have Callum. She couldn't imagine how she would have got past the shock of her mother's death without him. But an awful lot had happened that Sharon knew nothing about. And besides, Sharon was an incurable romantic.

'It's such a wonderful present.' Sharon was in full flow now. 'Imagine. Morocco . . . Blazing sunshine, fabulous markets, lounging around in a luxury riad –'

'I won't be lounging. I'll be working. Cooking – remember? It's not a luxury riad – it's more backpacker. And it's the end of October. It might not be that hot.'

Airily, Sharon waved these objections aside. She glanced over her shoulder to check the clientele were all still occupied. 'You'll have plenty of time off,' she assured Nell. 'It'll be blissful. I wish I was coming with you.' She nodded to a customer, scribbled on her notepad and swept off with their bill.

'So do I,' muttered Nell. She adjusted the hairband she wore to keep her curls from her face. On top of this perched the white hat Johnson insisted on.

The door swung open. Johnson strode through, as if summoned by her thoughts. 'Are we still doing lunches?' He glanced at his watch, shook his head sadly at the sight of the

20

baked beans. 'How many do we have booked for dinner tonight, Nell?'

He expected her to have such facts at her fingertips and frowned when she leaned over to check the reservation book. 'A table for four at seven and two tables for two at eight,' she reported. Not at all bad for a Tuesday night out of season.

'How symmetrical.' Johnson opened the fridge and squinted at its contents. 'Let's hope they all order one of the specials.'

Sharon brought over some plates and rolled her eyes at Nell.

And although she'd joked with Sharon, because that was how they got through their day, Nell found herself thinking, and not for the first time . . . Would she and Callum survive this – whatever 'this' might turn out to be? Her grief, she assumed. His need for her to move on from it.

They'd started arguing – arguments which led to him tearing his hands through his dark hair and stomping outside in his gardening boots to cut down more branches from their wayward spruce or to sweep the back courtyard. Arguments which left Nell feeling a bit like a wayward spruce herself. They hadn't made love for weeks – Nell wasn't prepared to calculate how many weeks. Callum was working longer hours, and so was Nell, and those hours didn't always coincide. He had started looking at her in a way that she could only describe as despairing. He had asked her to go the doctor, and she had refused; grief was a process and, whatever else, she did not need happy pills. He had started being over-polite. And solicitous. He had brought her breakfast in bed, for heaven's sake. He had insisted that they get on with marketing the farmhouse and putting it up for sale. And now he was sending her away.

'I'm just waiting for *my* Mr Right to come strolling in.' Sharon allowed her practised waitress-scan to graze over the clientele of the café on the waterfront. Nell looked with her, and chuckled. Two bikers, who must have lost their way; a middle-aged couple drinking cappuccinos, a misnomer since Johnson's café didn't actually have an espresso machine on the premises; and a grizzled walker, probably tackling the Roseland peninsula.

Sharon was referring, of course, to how Nell had first met Callum. He had come in here, one cold day in early spring, ordered tea and a cheese-and-onion toastie and simply stared at her. She'd seen him, through the deep hatch that separated the kitchen from the dining area, and fifteen minutes later she'd seen him staring at her again. Johnson had always said that a large hatchway which enabled their customers to see what was going on in the kitchen instilled confidence. Nell worried that wasn't all it instilled. The next day, Callum was there again, and the next he happened to be walking past when her lunchtime shift ended.

'I remember you,' he'd said, as if they'd met a long time ago. 'Can we go somewhere and talk?'

Nell hadn't been actively looking for a boyfriend. On the Roseland peninsula, most people were already familiar and the rest were tourists – grockles. She had met boys at catering college and done her share of dating. And she'd always supposed someone special would come along one day. But, so far, they hadn't. And in the meantime she had the café and she had her life with her mother in the farmhouse only a mile away. She had friends, like Lucy, who had trained with her at Cornwall College and was now living and working in Truro, and newer friends like Sharon. But, mostly, she had her mother.

She knew right away that Callum was different, even special maybe. He was doing some work on someone's garden, he said. Terracing and landscaping. Recreating. It was one of the big houses to the west of St Mawes with gardens which tapered down to the sea. Nell listened to the passion in his voice as he talked about the vision he had for the garden and, to her surprise, she found herself wanting some of that passion for herself. Callum was a breath of fresh air. He asked the right questions and looked at her in a certain way, a good way. But that, she reminded herself, was then.

Nell left the café after her shift and cycled back to the farmhouse, zipping along the familiar country lanes past the yellowing trees and hedgerows stumpy with the rotting remains of blackberries, head down and into the wind. It was like a test. It was one of those sharp days in October when winter suddenly seems close at hand. The musty air of autumn had acquired a definite chill that made her button her fleece right up to her chin. Home with Callum was another mile across the peninsula, but she'd got into the habit of stopping off here on the way, even though it wasn't on the way, not exactly. A bad habit, she told herself, swinging off the bike, grabbing her bag from the front basket and unlocking the battered front door with her own key. Soon, there would be no farmhouse – at least, not for Nell. The 'FOR SALE' sign was nailed to the fence like a rebuke.

Nell kicked aside some crumpled brown leaves, pulled open the stable door, stepped on to the cold kitchen flagstones and listened. Nothing. Well, what was she expecting? Her mother's voice? 'Hello,' she whispered. The silence was utterly complete, thick as a sea-fog.

Humming determinedly to break it, she filled the old kettle and reached for the herbal tea bags which were kept in an old Oxo tin. It was just, she told herself, that she wasn't quite ready to go home.

When the kettle had boiled, she poured water on to the tea bag labelled 'Harmonize', put the mug on the old farmhouse table and reached for her mother's Tarot cards, which had always been kept on a shelf of the pine dresser, wrapped in the purple silk scarf. Nell frowned, thinking of her question, and then slowly shuffled the pack. Obviously, it should concern Callum, her trip to Morocco, and her mother perhaps. Would her marriage survive her grief? Was she strong enough to do this? Could she see a cookery course in Marrakech as an investment in their future?

Her mother had always put more stock on the accoutrements. She would light a candle, burn some incense oil – lavender usually, but sometimes rose or patchouli. She would dim the lights (she always did her readings at night), put on some loose clothing (her kaftan or pyjamas), and sometimes soft, meditative music. Nell didn't do any of these things. She just focused. She wasn't doing a specific layout. She wasn't asking the Tarot to remind her of the past or predict the future. She just wanted to hear her mother's voice.

She blinked. The Sun seemed a good card to draw when you were going on a journey. And there were other obvious connections. The warmth of Morocco, the deep-yellow colour of saffron that bled from the flame-red stigmata, and even her own name, of course. Nell was determined to be positive. The Sun was an encouragement to leave shadows behind, but your shadow would always stay with you, wasn't that so? She listened, but her mother's voice seemed to get fainter, and Nell panicked. What if she couldn't hear her any more? What then?

She was relieved to draw the High Priestess as the next card. This was her mother. The woman of mystery. The High Priestess embodied feminine power and guarded all secrets. Nell's mother was the person Nell knew best in the world, and yet, who was she really? How well had she known her? Her life? Her past? Even her death? She knew how she had been after Nell was born – at least from when she had her own memories. But who had she been before that? Who was the young woman who had given birth to Nell? And who was Nell's father?

She left the cards and went to the dresser drawer to fetch the one and only photo album. In some ways, it had been her mother who had forced her hand when she had finally left home and moved in with Callum. One night when she wasn't seeing him they'd had supper together and Nell had got out the photo album. It wasn't something she did often — her mother never much liked it — but something Callum had said the night before had stayed with her and she was determined to get to the bottom of things.

'If we get married,' he'd said, taking her hand and stroking her thumb, '*when* we get married . . .'

She'd laughed, because he hadn't even asked her yet. 'Yes?'

'Who'd give you away? Your mum?'

'I suppose so, yes.' And since then she'd been thinking about it. It wasn't that she didn't want her mother to give her away. It was that she had no choice.

There were plenty of photos of her mother as a child, looking winsome and pretty in the old black-and-white snaps — sometimes in the fields around, in the yard, once on the beach and once — Nell's favourite — standing in front of the purple saffron field, laughing, as if the potent scent of the saffron had made her drunk with joy.

And then . . .

'What's all this, then?' Her mother had swept past her, collecting plates and cutlery from the table on the way. 'Feeling nostalgic?'

'No. I just . . .' She flipped the pages. Knew already what she would see. Nothing. It was as if her mother had simply disappeared. There were pictures of Nell as she was growing up — not many — taken by someone else probably, she could never remember her mother behind the camera; one of her mother's boyfriends who came and stayed with them for a while perhaps, or one of her friends from the village.

'Who was he?' she asked.

'He?' Her mother had her back to her and was washing up. Not just washing up. She had both taps on full blast and was squirting washing-up liquid as if her life depended on it. She was about as stubborn as they came.

'My father.'

She didn't reply. All Nell could hear was the water thundering into the bowl.

'Mum?'

'I don't know.'

The water was splashing on the floor now. Nell jumped to her feet and darted over, reaching across her to switch off the taps. Her mother was gripping on to the sink and staring straight ahead.

'Don't know, or don't want to tell me?'

'Both.' Her mother finally met her gaze. 'I can't go down that road, Nell. Not any more. I've told you.'

'But I need to know.' Nell willed herself not to give in. It was a bad thing, that much was obvious. Something that had hurt her, something that had made her want to protect Nell, keep her away from what her mother couldn't control – the world outside. And the last thing Nell wanted was to cause her mother more pain. But didn't she deserve to know the truth? Nell's mother had always held something back. And whatever it was, that's what was missing from those pages.

'I'm sorry.' Her mother picked up the cloth and resumed her washing of the dishes. 'But I can't.'

Nell wanted to scream. But what good would it do? 'Why not?' She ground the question out. But there was no point. She already knew the answer.

'It's too painful.'

'I'm sorry about that, Mum, but —'

'And you don't need to know.' She whipped around. 'Who brought you up? Who cared for you? Who'd give you the world? Anything?' She was trembling. Nell could see that she was trembling.

'That's not the point.' Why couldn't she see that? It made no difference who did what or who was the better person. The point was that it wasn't a competition and she'd never stop loving her mother, but . . . she needed to know, damn it. This was her heritage, her roots, her beginning.

'You can't keep harping back to things you know nothing about. You have to live in the present, Nell, not the past. And look to the future. It's the only way.' But her mother was shaking her head, and then she was crying and Nell ended up feeling bad, just as she always did. She walked out of the door.

When she came back in an hour later her mother was doing the Tarot cards and once again seemed serene and in control.

'I'm going to move in with Callum,' Nell told her. She wasn't going to dwell on the past any longer. She would do what her mother suggested. She would look to the future now.

And her mother barely flinched. 'You must do what you want to do, my love,' she had said.

But you couldn't really change what or who you were, and here Nell was again with the photo album, dipping into memories. She flipped the pages. Found the photograph of her grandparents, whom she'd never known. Her mother's father, upright, sepia and stern with a twirly moustache. Standing next to him, fair haired and sweet-faced, was Patricia, her mother's mother. They had both died young, her grandfather soon after the war and her grandmother just before Nell was born. It must have hit her mother hard – Nell understood that now. It was only since her mother's death that she had fully accepted her mother's emotional frailty. Accepted the possibility that, like Nell, she too had been lost and at times not known what to do.

Nell sighed. Woman of mystery, indeed. Callum had told her – more than once – what her problem was. 'You haven't accepted her death. You can't accept that she's gone.' And sitting here, looking at a raft of Tarot cards and a half-empty photo album, Nell suspected it might be true. She'd always believed that one day her mother would simply tell her everything she wanted to know. But she hadn't had as much time as she thought. Unless she had known exactly what she was doing the night she died. What if she had walked off the cliff on purpose? What then?

Callum had been delighted that Nell wanted to move in with him and immediately started making plans. She could move in to his one-bedroom flat as soon as she liked, he said.

But she had money saved so they could look around for a place to share, a small terraced house perhaps. And they would get married. Wouldn't they?

'Are you asking me?' Nell was still smarting from her mother's latest refusal to tell her what she wanted to know. 'Is this a proposal?'

'Yes!' And he had got down on one knee right there in the bar, people all around, and she had laughed and pulled him up again and said, 'Then you'd better see about getting me a ring.'

Nell's mother had been sanguine about the whole thing. She seemed to like Callum and she accepted all their plans without demur. She had some money she'd put by for Nell and she gave this to them as a contribution towards their wedding. Callum's parents, who had moved to Herefordshire some years before, also contributed, and Nell and Callum were married in the spring, the year after they bought their first house together.

Soon afterwards, Nell's mother had them round to supper one evening.

'I'm selling off some of the land,' she'd said as she and Nell were clearing up afterwards, both of them insisting Callum put his feet up in the sitting room as he'd had a hard day gardening, both of them secretly wanting more time together alone.

'Why?' Nell whisked around, tea towel in hand, and stared at her. She *was* the land.

'I can't manage it.' Their eyes met.

Was it true? It was hard work, Nell knew. She'd seen her mother half bent from the planting before now. 'I'll help you.'

'You don't have the time.' And then she was bustling past her, a pile of plates in her arms to put away in the dresser.

'But –' Her mother could get help in. She always had before.

She was right. Nell didn't have the time. And it couldn't be true. Her indomitable mother must be able to manage the land – she always had. So what was this all about? Was she talking about the saffron plot? The saffron was supposed to be Nell's legacy. Surely her mother couldn't be punishing her in some way?

Though as it turned out . . . perhaps her mother wasn't as indomitable as Nell had thought.

She had sold some of the land. She'd had the corms lifted, all of them, after last year's harvest, ready to replant in June, for it was the fourth year. But this year she hadn't replanted the saffron plot, and it was the first time. Outside, there were no saffron shoots growing sturdy and strong. There was no new growth, no new life, no bees falling asleep on the flowers while gathering nectar. Her mother had shown her when she was a child; she just pushed them gently off with the tip of her finger, so that they woke up slowly and flew away. Nell had thought that the saffron would always bloom. But this year it would not. Was that because her mother had known there'd be no one to harvest it? No one to keep the legacy alive?

Nell returned her attention to the Tarot cards. If she went to Morocco she could find out more about this secret spice which had meant so much to her mother. And perhaps in doing so some of her mother's mysterious past might be revealed along the way. High Priestess, indeed. 'Should I go?' she whispered. And as she turned over the next card, which was the Five of Cups, she could hear her mother's voice at last. *Let go of your loss, embrace change.* On the card, three of the cups were overturned, but two were left standing. Yin and yang. Loss is gain. And Nell knew she had to make this journey.

CHAPTER 3

Amy was organizing the main gallery space in preparation for the next exhibition, 'One Moment, One Weather', by a local artist, when she became aware of someone standing right behind her. And it wasn't Duncan.

'Oh.' Where had he crept up from? 'We're closed, I'm afraid.'

She turned back to the picture. It was more graph than painting and had been produced using some sort of weather map of wind speed and other meteorological data over an hour, every day for a month. Or something like that. Amy wasn't an artist, she was a photographer. She liked to think that she dealt with real subjects rather than imagined ones. And although she appreciated art and worked in this gallery in Lyme Regis, which supported local artists – and also local photographers, thank goodness – she couldn't help feeling that some artists were just a bit . . .

'Self-indulgent, isn't it?'

She turned again. She'd known he hadn't gone away from the smell. Nothing nasty, nothing fancy; just leather and what seemed to be the faint fragrance of grapefruit. Soap, maybe. He was tall – and since Amy was five feet eleven in socks, this was something she invariably noticed first about a man – he had almost-black, spiky hair which owed more, she suspected, to the whims of nature than to hair gel, and he was frowning, head on one side. Like a bird, she thought. Not a cute bird. More a bird of prey.

'Sometimes,' she said, 'it's best to keep your opinions to yourself.'

He raised a quizzical eyebrow. His hands were stuck in the pockets of his jeans. He seemed very much at ease.

Late thirties, she decided. A wild card. 'And I think I told you – the gallery's closed.'

'But do you really believe that?' Instead of scuttling away, chastened – and she had to admit he didn't seem like the scuttling type – he sauntered casually along to the next painting.

It was very similar to the last one. Amy wondered if she lacked the artist's sensitive eye. 'That we're closed?' She put her hands on her hips and refused to smile at him. 'Yes, I do. As you can see, I'm just setting things up. The exhibition opens tomorrow morning. At ten.'

'That we should keep our opinions to ourselves.' He sounded very serious. 'Do you believe that?'

Of course she didn't. Amy had often got into trouble for speaking her thoughts out loud. With her parents – who had, she guessed, always hoped for the kind of child who was seen and not heard, so that they wouldn't be disturbed from the all-consuming task of building up what had now become a hugely popular hotel in Lyme. With equally disappointed teachers at school, who had hoped that she would show signs of wanting an academic career – which had never happened. And of course from Duncan: boss, almost-friend, almost-lover. Could you have an almost-lover? Apparently so. Amy sighed. She supposed that she would have to do something about Duncan.

'Who are you?' she asked.

'Jake Tarrant.' He flashed her a quick smile. Dimples. A crooked tooth on the right-hand side. The man wasn't unattractive and no doubt was well aware of it. Which didn't give him the right to walk in here as if he owned the place.

Should she know the name? Jake. Jake Tarrant. Was he a local artist? Was he on the council? He looked as if he was meant to be here.

'And . . . how can I help you?' Amy decided to play safe. If he was meant to be here, he might be important – to the gallery and its future. And, quite apart from her own work, this was something Amy cared about.

'Ah, Jake. There you are.' At this point, Duncan strolled in, dressed in his usual gallery uniform of black trousers, blue shirt and navy blazer. His fair hair was thinning, and daily visits to the gym hadn't quite saved him from a slight paunch, but apart from that, he still had it – that smooth and confident way about him that generally got Duncan what he wanted.

So Duncan knew him. Amy tried to catch her boss's eye, and he avoided it. Which, as usual, told her quite a lot. Duncan was secretive by nature. He didn't spill out unnecessary information. He operated on a need-to-know basis. So if

Amy didn't need to know – what he was doing, who he was with, what plans he had or didn't have for the future, what made him tick – then she would never find out. But she had a feeling that this was something she should make it her business to find out about. Amy looked from one man to the other. She too had a gallery uniform – close-fitting tapered black trousers or maxi skirt, white blouse with collar, tailored jacket. But she tempered the smart look with a few choice pieces of big jewellery – today, a chunky copper bangle inlaid with turquoise and the two perfect globes of flecked turquoise ear studs. So Duncan had been expecting the visitor. She waited.

'Here I am, yes.' Jake Tarrant stepped forward, and they shook hands, friendly enough but Duncan slightly the more defensive of the two. This suggested 'council' to Amy, but Jake's faded blue jeans and ever so slightly scruffy leather jacket still made 'artist' the more likely. And the collar of the jacket, she noted, was turned up.

'So . . .' Amy fixed her gaze on Duncan. When she'd first joined the gallery she'd been flattered and seduced by those baby-blue eyes of his. *I love your work,* he'd breathed. *It's so fresh, so vibrant. I could offer you the occasional exhibition, of course, I'd love to . . .* And as it turned out, that wasn't all he could offer her. Drinks after work, the occasional candlelit dinner, receptions and previews, entry into a world of artists and photographers that made her feel she belonged. And in return? He was very convincing. He'd never been married and yet always had a glamorous woman on his arm – which

36

proved that Duncan had a seduction technique second to none. He'd been so good at making her feel special.

Whereas, in fact, Amy reminded herself, what they had wasn't special at all. It was easy, but was it right? They had no claim on each other or each other's time. They weren't going anywhere. She couldn't pretend that she was in love with him and she had no illusions about him being in love with her. Amy was in love with photography, and more than one man in the past had told her she was too strong, too opinionated and too difficult. Not Duncan, though, and perhaps that was why she couldn't quite bring herself to say goodbye.

As for the visitor . . . As Duncan's 'right-hand man', as he sometimes irritatingly referred to her, shouldn't she have been told who he was, rather than have to guess?

'Jake, this is Amy Hamilton. My right-hand man.' Duncan smirked.

'Hi, Amy.' Jake stretched out an arm and Amy felt her hand enclosed in his. The touch was warm, dry and brief. Grapefruit, she thought again.

'Hi.' She looked at Duncan enquiringly. *Tell me then, you bastard. Don't make me look stupid.*

'Jake is an events manager,' said Duncan.

'Ah.' The Moroccan project, she thought. And something tightened in her stomach. The year 2013 marked the eight hundredth anniversary of diplomatic ties being established between the UK and Morocco; yes, in 1213, good old King John of England had sent the first embassy to Morocco, which was recognized now as a starting point for the fruitful relationship between the two countries. There were 25,000 Moroccans living in the UK, the two countries shared a long history and the British supported Morocco's reform process. So the gallery had decided to hold a festival of all things Moroccan, which in turn had led to them being awarded some lottery funding. Since then, Duncan had sported an unappealing gleam in those blue eyes of his. More money, loftier ambitions. Amy couldn't help but notice it.

'And he's here to discuss some ideas.' Duncan glanced at his watch. 'Come through to my office, Jake.'

Amy frowned. And as Jake turned around she mouthed to Duncan, *What about me?* Even to herself this sounded a little petulant. But the Moroccan project was her baby. It had been her original idea – to organize an art and photography exhibition in the gallery to celebrate Moroccan culture, maybe throw in a workshop or two. So what was going on?

'Could you bring in some tea, please, Amy?'

She glared at him, but Duncan merely shot her a wink. *She'd give him some ideas.* 'And perhaps then you could join us.'

In the office Amy put the tray of tea and biscuits on Duncan's desk and sat down, uncomfortably close to Jake Tarrant, since there wasn't anywhere else. He had a notebook on his lap and was already scribbling something. Fine. Clearly, they'd started without her.

'Jake was just telling me some of his initial thoughts,' Duncan said smoothly.

'Oh?' Amy smiled sweetly at him. 'What were they, Jake?'

'A film screening, perhaps.' He shrugged. 'Morocco's big on film. It has an international film festival every year, in December. You're probably aware of that. I was thinking . . . art-house cinema? There's *A Thousand and One Hands* by the Moroccan filmmaker Souheil Ben-Barka. Or *Marock*? Directed by Laïla Marrakchi. That's controversial – and political.'

'And then there's *Hideous Kinky*,' suggested Amy.

'Ye – es.' He glanced up – perhaps to see if she was joking. She wasn't. 'We could have a cookery demo, too. A 'Travel to Morocco' information point – treks in the Atlas Mountains and all that. And an art exhibition.'

'By Moroccan artists?'

'Yes. Or artists influenced by Morocco.'

'Hmm.' He seemed to know what he was talking about. And his voice – which was growly but nice – held plenty of enthusiasm. But Amy kept her expression unimpressed. Had Duncan even told him about her photographic exhibition?

'Music . . .' Jake Tarrant's pen spun loopily over his notebook.

Amy watched, fascinated. 'Music?' she echoed.

'Moroccan hip-hop, Sufi, Gnawa . . . I've got a few contacts.'

Amy didn't doubt it.

'A week of events, you said?' Jake addressed this to Duncan.

'Ten days. Two weekends.' Duncan caught Amy's eye.

'We've already planned a photographic exhibition, which could be extended.'

'Photographic exhibition? That sounds good. Have you considered Moroccan street photography?' Jake looked interested.

'I'm going to Marrakech,' Amy said. 'So, yes.' She passed him his tea. 'Milk? Sugar?'

'Especially for this event?' Jake seemed surprised. He accepted milk but not sugar.

Perhaps, Amy thought, he wasn't accustomed to the word 'commitment'.

'Amy is a talented photographer,' Duncan broke in. 'We thought, since we had some funding, it would be a great opportunity to get some fresh and original architectural shots. And street shots, yes. The colour, the culture.' He made an expansive gesture. 'It's a rich landscape.'

'The photographic exhibition was originally intended to be the backdrop for the project,' Amy said primly. She passed Duncan his tea. When it was *my* project, she silently added.

'Good idea.' Jake nodded. 'A lynchpin. I like that. The photos could feature images of all the subject areas we're tackling.'

'Subject areas?' He made it sound like a college prospectus. And 'we'?

'Moroccan cuisine,' he said. 'Film, art. Weaving.' He stretched out long legs.

'Weaving?'

'North African rugs have a fascinating history.' Jake took a gulp of his tea. Everything he did seemed expansive; every movement, every gesture. Amy didn't think Duncan's office had ever seemed so small. 'The patterns are like a rural language of Berber symbols and motifs. Stories.'

Duncan nodded knowledgeably. Amy had a vision of herself in a souk in Marrakech, taking pictures of rugs while all around her market traders were hassling her to buy a different story. She blinked the vision away.

'Jake's suggested a weaving workshop,' Duncan said. 'A brilliant idea, don't you think, Amy?'

'Brilliant,' she echoed.

'And *zellige* for the kids,' Jake added.

'*Zellige?*'

'The art of mosaics and tilework.' He said this very seriously, his gaze not leaving her face. So why did Amy think that, somewhere inside, he was laughing at her?

'You've done this before then? The Moroccan theme?' Amy recrossed her legs and brushed an imaginary bit of fluff from her black, laced ankle boots. She'd known weeks ago that she should do more homework. She'd intended to, but her Great-aunt Lillian had needed more looking after since her fall, her mother had asked her to help out on reception when someone was ill and her friend Francine had asked her to do some babysitting. And then there was Duncan . . . She'd bought some books and planned on reading up on Moroccan design on the plane. It was very last minute, but Amy was a last-minute sort of person. She loved deadlines, they made the adrenalin flow.

'I've spent quite a bit of time there.' He shrugged. 'Made a few friends, you know –'

'Jake managed a similar series of events in London earlier in the year,' Duncan said. 'That's how I came across his name.'

And how come, Amy thought, it didn't occur to you to share that information? But she nodded. 'How lucky we are,' she said, 'to get such expert advice.'

'I'm glad you think so, Amy.' Duncan shuffled some papers on his desk. 'Because I want you to work with Jake on this one.'

Amy swallowed. 'You're not just advising us, then?'

'Deeper than decor,' Duncan said.

'Sorry?'

'Saturating the senses. There's far too much for you to do on your own, Amy,' he said. 'It's not just a question of ideas and experience. There's also budgeting, researching. Negotiating with suppliers. This is our chance to reach out to the community. Publicity, Amy. I want this to be big. And I've got too much on myself, as you know.'

Again, Amy noticed the gleam. Perhaps it had always been there and perhaps he used to hide it. Or perhaps she hadn't bothered to open her eyes wide enough to see. Special people were given respect; they were consulted, not merely relegated to making the tea. 'Fine,' she said. Though it wasn't. Being in overall charge of all gallery events and exhibitions, Duncan had his hands full, she knew, but this had never been a problem. Amy had been looking forward to managing this project alone. It was a challenge, yes, especially when the funding had come in, but she was perfectly capable. And she certainly didn't want to work with this man — who clearly knew it all, or imagined he did. How could Duncan have brought him in without telling her? How could he have given control of her entire project to an events manager?

At that moment, Jake Tarrant looked across at her. His eyes were the colour of rooibos tea — without milk. He knew, damn him. He knew that Duncan had gone over her head and he felt sorry for her. Which was even worse.

'I'm looking forward to working with you,' he said. He sounded sincere. 'Where are you staying in Marrakech?'

'In the medina. At a place called Riad Lazuli.'

'They're running a cookery course,' Duncan chipped in.

'You're doing a cookery course, too?'

'No.' Her mother would laugh like a drain at that idea, thought Amy. 'There's a local author who's writing a book about Moroccan cuisine,' she said. 'I've been in touch with her and her publisher and they'd like me to do the photos. I was hoping to tie it in with our project.'

'Plus, Amy might knock up a few decent tagines and bring them back with her if we're lucky,' said Duncan, chuckling at his own joke. Amy ignored him.

'When are you off?' asked Jake.

'The day after tomorrow.'

'Then perhaps you and I could have a chat tomorrow, before I go back to Bristol,' he said. 'Make some decisions about what sort of shots we need.'

'Of course.' Amy got to her feet.

'Good girl.' Duncan rose, too, reached out a hand and gave her a rather too intimate squeeze of the shoulder.

If he imagined that was the end of it, Amy thought, then he had another think coming. She had a lot she wanted to say to him – but she would wait until they were alone. And as for Jake Tarrant . . . As she left the room she glanced back at him once more. His tea-coloured eyes were curious – and thoughtful. And she knew what else he had seen.

CHAPTER 4

Amy decided to call in to see her Great-aunt Lillian. She felt too unsettled to go straight home to her flat, which backed on to her parents' hotel and had a perfect view of the sheltering arm of the Cobb – Lyme's curved harbour wall. It was Aunt Lillian who had paid for the flat's conversion; the deeds were in joint names – Amy's and Lillian's. Amy paid the mortgage; her aunt had provided the lump-sum deposit. Amy couldn't have done it without her.

She headed for the old town mill, a working mill until 1926, now restored to provide a café and studios for working artists. A few of the artists had exhibited in the gallery; what Amy liked most about Lyme was its involvement in the arts, from painting to photography to theatre. She walked on up the side of the mill, past the wheel and the leat, to the footpath running above the river on her left, the watercourse that fed the mill wheel. She could smell the distinctive and autumnal scent of the sappy plants that grew on the banks, some still flowering. And hear the water chuckle as it reached the wheel.

Her great-aunt had suffered her fall two weeks ago on the pavement outside her cottage, and when Amy had heard her wavering voice on the phone line she had immediately called the paramedics to take her into hospital for a check-up. Aunt Lillian had gamely protested her way through two days of tests before being discharged; Amy had collected her from the hospital and had been keeping a close eye on her ever since. She was fine, though, still spritely for eighty-five, though her eyes weren't as good as they had been, and she'd been told that there was little point in having the cataract operation she'd hoped for. Tests had shown that she was suffering from age-related macular degeneration – the kind that meant deterioration would be slow, steady and inevitable. Amy had to nag to get her to use her walking stick more often. She worried about her. She didn't want her falling again.

Amy walked along the Lynch, past Lepers' Well and up to Gosling Bridge. On the wall opposite, someone – apparently Banksy – had painted an origami heron with a goldfish in its mouth. Was it a valuable piece of art, or simply graffiti? The jury of Lyme residents was still out. She turned right. Her Aunt Lillian lived in a neat pink Georgian cottage with two bedrooms and a thatched roof.

Amy gave a sharp rap on the brass door knocker. Aunt Lillian was her long-time ally – in teenage battles with her parents about clothes, curfews and boyfriends – her comforter when her parents weren't available, which was quite a lot of the time, and the greatest admirer of her work. Her Aunt Lillian had magically appeared from America like a fairy godmother when Amy was ten years old. She had come over here after her husband's death in order to care for her sister,

Amy's grandmother Mary. She was older than Lillian and could no longer look after herself; there had even been talk of her going into a nursing home. But Aunt Lillian would have none of that. She moved into Amy's grandmother's house lock, stock and barrel and looked after her sister herself – until Mary died. And it wasn't just that, Amy reminded herself. Aunt Lillian had also saved Amy's family.

Amy peered through the window and rapped on the door again. This was no exaggeration. Her aunt had cared for Mary, she had supported them when things looked bad between Amy's parents, Celia and Ralph, and she had helped them out financially by investing heavily in the hotel in the days when it was little more than a down-at-heel B&B and in financial difficulties. And Amy fervently appreciated this, even if her parents didn't seem to have time to.

'They're very busy,' her aunt would say in their defence. But sometimes Amy wondered. Was that all it was? Or was there some other reason for her mother's unwillingness to acknowledge fully what Aunt Lillian had done for them?

'Don't you like Aunt Lillian?' she had asked her mother one time. 'Has she done something to annoy you?'

Celia Hamilton had shrugged. 'Who knows what really happened? Your grandmother was never easy. And guilt's a powerful thing.'

Why should Aunt Lillian feel guilty? And how did this answer Amy's question? She had no idea, and her mother had as usual been far too busy to explain. All Amy knew was that her aunt had bought Amy her very first camera for her

47

eleventh birthday. Not only that, but she had supported her seven years later when Amy had told her mother that photography was what she wanted to study.

'What can you do with photography?' Amy's mother had asked.

'I could work for a newspaper, or a magazine, or . . .'

'Go freelance,' Aunt Lillian had said. She turned to Celia. 'Why not? It's not so impossible. Anything's possible, if Amy wants it enough . . .'

Now, the door slowly opened at last.

Tiny, white-haired Great-aunt Lillian beamed. 'Amy. How lovely to see you.'

'How are you, Auntie Lil?' Amy examined her aunt's face for signs of weariness. Her eyes were a little puffy, but other than that she looked fine.

'I'm very well. Come in. I've just made tea. Would you say no to a toasted crumpet?'

Amy laughed. 'I don't think I would. Depending on what it was asking me to do, of course.' She bent to kiss her aunt's papery cheek, her face brushing against the wispy hair.

She was rather bent these days, and so thin that her bones seemed almost to jut through her fragile old lady's skin. But her blue eyes still held the bright beam of humour that had captivated Amy ever since her aunt had first arrived in Lyme Regis. She had adored her American accent, the soft and questioning lilt of her voice, her bubbling laugh and the clothes she wore. Most of all, she had loved the attention. Great-aunt Lillian had bought her sweets and comics and, before long, nail varnish and eye make-up. She had spoiled her unashamedly. She encouraged her to come round after school to the cottage she'd bought after Mary's death. She wanted to know how she'd spent her day, what books she was reading, what lessons she enjoyed and what her friends were like. But she never asked in a nosey, adult kind of way — ready to disapprove. She asked as though they were friends, as though she was really interested. From the start, Amy recognized the shadow of unhappiness that clung to her aunt, but she also saw that she could make it go away — at least for a while. And so she tried. She spent as much time with her Great-aunt Lillian as she could.

'Why did you come back here,' Amy had asked her more than once during their cosy times together, 'when you could live in America?' For, as a child and a teenager, that had seemed to Amy most definitely the best place to be.

'It's still home,' her aunt had said, though Amy knew that, as girls, she and Mary had lived with their parents in Bridport, ten miles or so to the east. 'You know, Amy, the length of time you stay in a place, that doesn't necessarily make it home.'

'But you must have made friends there. It must have been hard to leave.' Amy thought of shopping malls, cool hamburger joints and the pictures she'd seen of the New York City skyline.

But her aunt had shaken her head. 'There's nothing left in America for me.'

Amy's mother had told her often enough not to ask her

aunt so many questions. 'She's been through a lot,' she'd say, although her lips were pursed in that busy way she had. 'She's suffered a very sad loss. Whatever you do, don't mention it to her.'

But, 'Are you sad because your husband died?' Amy had asked her aunt, the first opportunity she had. How could she resist the temptation of such a secret? She knew that his name had been Ted, but her aunt didn't seem to have any pictures of him. Why not? What had happened between them?

Her aunt had shaken her head. 'No, I'm not,' she said. 'At least . . .' And then her face had crumpled and she'd turned away with a sniff. And Amy had felt bad about asking, after all.

'It's not your concern,' Amy's mother told her when she tried to pursue the subject with her instead. 'Honestly, Amy, why can't you ever just let things go?' And then she'd bustled Amy out of the way because she had to clean rooms and make beds and buy bacon for the breakfasts.

Why couldn't she let things go? Amy thought about this that night; in fact, she'd often thought about it since. Because she was curious, she supposed. Because a door had been shut in front of her and she felt the urge to open it. Because it felt unfinished, unresolved. Even as a child, Amy had needed closure.

Now, Amy followed her aunt into the living room, which looked out on to the street. It was inviting and warm from the heat of the mock gas fire she'd had put in a few years ago, when she had finally decided she was too old to manage an open fire. Privately, Amy had heaved a sigh of relief that one more hazard was out of the way. Her aunt's furniture was old-fashioned but comfortable: a sofa covered in a flowered, chintzy fabric; two armchairs with deep red cushions; a sideboard on which stood some framed photographs and a bowl of fruit, the postcard tucked behind it and almost out of sight; a coffee table with some squares of knitting, today's paper with a magnifying glass beside it – bless her; and a dining table positively laden with a teapot, sandwiches, a plate of crumpets and fruit cake. She looked as if she were expecting twenty to tea.

'You never know, do you, dear? I'll just fetch you a plate and a cup.' And she made her way through to the kitchen.

Amy scrutinized the photographs on the sideboard, as she so often did. She picked up the one of Lillian and Mary as young women, standing on either side of their mother – it had been taken during the war, Amy had been told, hence their mother's WVS uniform. Her grandmother Mary had certainly been the more glamorous of the two sisters back then. She replaced it carefully and picked up the one of her parents, Celia and Ralph, with ten year-old Amy and her grandmother Mary, gaunt and pale as she had been when Lillian came over from the States over twenty years ago. There were various pictures of Amy, too: at school, on the Cobb, standing still and straight and looking out to sea like the French lieutenant's woman (Amy always smiled when she saw that one), and one where she was standing in front of her first exhibition at the gallery – trying not to look quite as proud as she felt. There was a family gathering at the hotel to celebrate Lillian's eightieth birthday and one of Amy's parents' golden-wedding-anniversary party. And – of course – there was the photograph of Glenn.

Amy knew now about Glenn. She knew that he – not Aunt Lillian's husband, Ted – was the real sad loss that made her aunt's eyes stop twinkling, that wrapped the aura of sadness around her like a cloak. She didn't know the whole story – her aunt didn't like to talk about it – but she knew enough. Amy picked up the photo in its silver frame. He was about sixteen in this shot, epitomizing the innocence of youth, his hair, fair and fringed, brushing over the collar of the denim shirt he wore, his expression slightly troubled although he was smiling. The photographer had caught an intimate and revealing moment. Amy put the photograph back on the sideboard. She touched the corner of the postcard with her fingertip. She would love to have known Glenn.

Her Aunt Lillian had come back into the room and was standing watching her, plates and teacups in hand. 'Come on, Amy, dear. Leave him be. I'll pour you some tea.'

Amy went over to take the crockery from her. 'Do you ever wonder about him, Auntie Lil? About where he is now?' She must – of course, she must. She sat down at the table. Closed doors, she thought. *Why can you never let anything go?*

'Every day.' Aunt Lillian gave her a hooded glance. 'Not that it does any good, mind.'

Every day . . . 'But what if he goes back home?' Privately, Amy had often wondered about this, and now seemed as good a time to ask as any. People did, didn't they – even after many years had gone by. Back they wandered, like some prodigal son, returning to their roots, to the place where they had begun. Just like her aunt had once said – no matter how long you stayed in a place, that didn't make it home.

'Home?' Lillian looked vaguely around the room.

There were nets up at the window, but Amy quite liked the fact that you could see people walking by; the lives of Lyme bustling past, never knowing that you were watching them. Perhaps, she thought, this was because she was a photographer, wanting to peep in on other people's lives. Or perhaps she had become a photographer because she was a voyeur; because she *liked* to peep in on people's lives. Not in a bad way, she hoped. It was that curiosity again.

'Back to America,' Amy said. 'To his old home. Your home.'

'The neighbours know where to find me. I left an address with anyone he might contact.'

Amy helped herself to a crumpet. She buttered it and took a bite. It was oddly comforting; exactly what she needed after this afternoon's revelation, and Jake Tarrant. After he'd gone, she'd rounded on Duncan and accused him of going over her head.

'Amy, Amy, my darling, Amy,' he had said. 'Can't you see I'm thinking of *you*?'

'Really?' She stood by the door. She didn't know why she bothered.

'I don't want you to take on too much.' He frowned. 'I'm protecting you, can't you see that?'

Amy opened the door. 'By not telling me how things stand,' she said quietly. And she wasn't even sure if she was still talking about the Moroccan project, or something more personal.

'Don't be upset.' He took a step towards her. Any moment, she'd be in his arms and she'd lose her resolution to walk out of here. It didn't work, she realized, mixing your career with romance. Although what she had with Duncan . . . What had started with romance had slipped into convenience. They were there for each other – to provide gallery space, to make tea, for sex. What, after all, was the difference?

Amy pushed Duncan from her mind. 'But you don't think Glenn will ever go back to your old home, do you?' Amy didn't want to upset her aunt, but it bothered her.

'No. It's much too late for that, my dear.'

But why was it too late? Amy didn't understand. And she couldn't imagine why he'd never go back to someone like her Aunt Lillian, especially since she was his mother. But she'd like to find out. And more than anything, she'd like to do something to make her great-aunt happy. Anything. She'd done so much for Amy, for them all. She deserved to get something back. 'It's never too late,' she said. She took another large bite of her crumpet.

'It depends.' Her aunt sipped her tea. She seemed thoughtful.

'On what?'

'On whether or not I'm being punished. I sometimes wonder if that could be the reason he was taken from me.' She spoke as if she were talking to herself, as if she'd forgotten Amy was in the room.

'Punished?' What on earth did she mean? Why would she be punished for anything?

Her aunt looked up. 'There has to be a reason why he never came back,' she said. 'But it's not just that, of course. There's the rest of it, too.' She looked away, staring now into the flickering gas fire.

What did she see there? The past? And what was 'the rest of it'? Amy was intrigued. She was so used to the door being closed . . . But now her aunt seemed to want to talk. 'Why would you be punished, Aunt Lil?' Amy thought of what her mother had said about guilt and betrayal. What had Aunt Lillian done?

'Because I behaved rather badly, Amy.' She paused, still looking into the fire, her old, arthritic fingers working in her lap. 'No one can behave badly and expect to get away with it.' She sighed. 'That's why we have the forces of law and order. Ted was right in that respect. It catches up with us all in the end.'

'You? Behave badly?' It struck Amy that this was another subject that had always been out of bounds. Ted. Her aunt's husband. 'What rubbish.'

'Oh, but I did. That's why I had to come back to Dorset, you see. I had to make amends. To Mary. For everything.'

Amy stared at her. The more she discovered, the more complicated everything seemed to be. And yet this new revelation fitted with what Amy's mother had once told her. So what did her grandmother Mary have to do with it? Amy had never been as close to her grandmother as she'd been to Aunt Lillian. During Amy's lifetime, her grandmother had not been a well woman, and she'd never seemed very contented either. She used to complain – about everything. Amy supposed children didn't much like older people when they were like that, grandmother or no.

'Didn't you get on?' she asked. 'When you were girls? I expect you were very different?'

Her aunt laughed that soft, gurgling laugh that seemed to take her further back in time. For a second, she seemed to Amy to be that young girl in the 1930s. 'We didn't get on terribly well, it's true,' she said. 'And yes, we were very different.'

'I always wanted to have a sister.' Or a brother, Amy thought. At any rate, she'd never wanted to be an only child. She didn't know about being spoiled. That hadn't happened to her – at least, not until her great-aunt had come along. What had happened were too many days when there was nothing to do and no one to play with.

'Mary was four years older than me,' Lillian said. Her white hands, freckled with liver spots, fluttered in front of her for a moment and she clasped them together. 'It was a big gap in many ways. I suppose she'd got used to being the only one before I came along. And then she'd be asked to look after me, you see. She didn't always want to.' She smiled. 'Mary wasn't the type.'

Amy chuckled. 'I bet she loved you, though.'

'I don't know about that.' Her aunt's voice was wistful.

Was that why she had come back? Amy wondered. To try to gain her sister's love after all these years? 'She must have loved you.' Amy spoke with some assurance. She was confident that, if her parents had ever had the time to produce a younger brother or sister for her, she would have adored them.

'We didn't think about love, I suppose.' She sighed. 'Well, not in that way. She lived her life. I lived mine. She was prettier, popular, charming. I was . . .'

'What were you?' In Amy's eyes, Lillian had always been the more charming of the two sisters. But perhaps she was doing her grandmother a disservice; perhaps she'd been bitterly disappointed by life and had good reason to complain.

'I was probably a terrible nuisance.' Lillian shook her head. 'And some things never change.'

'But why did you have to make amends to Mary? It wasn't your fault that she wasn't very good at looking after you,' Amy asked. Any moment now, and her aunt would snap back to the present and close that door. Amy glanced across at the sideboard, at the postcard. 'What did you do that was so terrible?'

For a moment, her aunt didn't reply and her head drooped, almost as if she'd nodded off to sleep. But then she lifted her head and looked straight at Amy. It was a candid gaze. 'I made my sister very unhappy,' she said. 'It was cruel of me. Dishonest, even. I was selfish. I was young. But I should have known better.'

'But, what . . .?'

Lillian shook her white head as if to send the memory away. 'It's all in the past now,' she said determinedly, 'and I have to face it alone. More tea, Amy, dear? A slice of cake?'

Amy shook her head. 'No, thank you.'

'Why ever did we start talking about it?' Aunt Lillian put her head on one side and regarded Amy quizzically.

Enough, Amy realized. 'I don't know, Auntie Lil.' And she reached over to take her hand. But she did know. Glenn, she thought. And her little plan. 'I'll just clear up here,' she said, giving her aunt's hand a squeeze. 'And then I'll be off.'

By the time Amy emerged from the kitchen, her aunt was sitting in her favourite armchair, almost in a doze. Now, thought Amy. She went over to the sideboard and plucked the postcard from where it stood against the wall. Would her aunt notice it was missing? Probably. Her eyesight might be going, but she had the instincts of a cat. Nevertheless, Amy deposited the postcard in the front flap of her leather handbag.

'I'd better be going,' she said softly. Her aunt didn't deserve to be punished – whatever she'd done. She was a good person, a kind person. She deserved to be happy. Amy would like to do something for her in return for all that help she'd given them. And until you tried, you never knew. Any information would be useful. Amy could at least have a look, ask around – since she was going there anyway.

'I won't see you before I go to Morocco, Auntie Lil,' she said. 'You'll take care, won't you?'

If she did notice it was missing, she'd know where it had gone.

'I will, Amy,' she murmured. 'You, too, my dear.'

Amy bent to drop a kiss on her aunt's head. She knew that the postcard had a Moroccan stamp, even though there were no other clues regarding where it had come from. 'Don't worry,' she whispered. 'I'll come back to you.'

Her great-aunt nodded. 'I know you will, Amy,' she said.

CHAPTER 5

Essaouira, 1973

Glenn sat on the yellow-white sand outside his makeshift tent and watched the Atlantic waves pound the beach. It was a good surfing spot – but surfing wasn't really his thing. What was his thing? Well . . . he hadn't discovered that yet. He broke off a wedge of bread and ate it along with a handful of small, sweet dates. In the distance a lone camel sauntered lazily along the shoreline. Glenn was in Essaouira, western Morocco, and he was sure growing bored of travelling.

At first, once he'd left America and flown to Europe, it had been one hell of an adventure. He'd tried not to think about why he was there, about what had happened at home, about what might happen now he was away. Instead, he focused on the trip. He'd set off in 1969. He was doing what kids every-where wanted to do. He was seeing the world, hanging out wherever he wanted to hang out. He was meeting some really cool people. Jesus. It was a far cry from Vietnam.

He had taken an Icelandic Airlines flight to Luxembourg; travelled around a bit in Europe. From Amsterdam it wasn't a problem to get buses through to Istanbul. Transport was cheap, there were plenty of other kids making the journey and you could get all the info you needed from the under-ground press. He didn't feel like a tourist – though in a way he guessed that he was – and he loved it: hearing new languages, seeing new places, experiencing different cultures, waking up every morning in a different town . . . It was a true liberation. Even the most familiar things seemed strange and interesting, as if he were seeing them for the very first time. Travelling. You'd have to be crazy not to love it.

From the famous Pudding Shop in Istanbul he'd got lifts through to Pakistan, and from there rail travel was cheap right up to Kathmandu and Goa. Kathmandu was far out. It even had a road, Jochen Tole, nicknamed Freak Street after those who passed through. It wasn't just a load of hippie drop-outs who were making the journey, though. There were other travellers – overlanders – in the early seventies who were tak-ing advantage of open borders and better roads. Who could blame them for wanting to get a glimpse of a more exotic landscape? The weather was warm and everything else was cool. And as for Vietnam . . . In Nepal and India, it was easy to forget.

In the summer he stayed in the mountains of Nepal, where the hashish shops were legal and the best quality was there for the taking. And in the winter he went to Goa, where he camped on the beach. He drifted. It was too easy to live in a haze of heat and hashish and he only left in the end because he needed to get somewhere he could earn some money. Some of the other hippies and freaks got regular hand-outs from their folks; they sent funds through to a bank and there was no hassle. Glenn couldn't risk any of that. He kept his money in a leather pouch he'd bought in Afghanistan, attached to his belt. Next to his skin was the safest place. And it was safer still for no one to know where he was now or where he was heading.

But no one could drift around India and Nepal for ever. Glenn hitched rides to Spain and got a job working in a beach bar in Torremolinos for the whole of the summer in '73. It was a good scene. An endless beach sheltered by mountains, a great mix of German, Swedish, English, Americans, plenty of beautiful girls . . . But all the best things come to an end. He lost his job and at the end of September he went back to following the sun. It wasn't exactly an addiction – it was just that it was easier that way. He joined up with some guys heading for Morocco, took the ferry and went to Casablanca, then Marrakech. Marrakech was a riot – of souks and spices, colour and noise. It was fun but it was crazy. Glenn left after three weeks – and headed for the sea.

His first sight of Essaouira on the bus was the languid, moon-shaped curve of the sandy beach. After diving into the sea – how could he resist after that long and dusty journey? – he'd made his way to the harbour. He had dinner outside the fish shacks at the communal tables, where you just pointed to what you wanted, watched it being cooked and then ate with your fingers. Essaouira was breezy, white and bright. Seagulls wheeled overhead in the azure sky, waiting to swoop down to steal any scraps, their screeching only silenced by the muezzin's call.

There was an artist – a young German guy with long, shaggy blond hair who was sketching the fishing boats in charcoal and filling them in with electric-blue watercolour. Glenn chatted to him for a while. 'This seems like a good place,' he said. 'How long you been here?'

The German guy shrugged. 'A few months,' he said. 'Yeah, it's cool. Jimi Hendrix stayed here once. 1969.'

'Is that right?'

'Sure thing. Hendrix is like, God, man. You should visit Diabat, up the coast. It's a magic wasteland.'

Then the guy turned his attention back to his painting and Glenn walked towards the cobbled alleyways of the blue-and-white medina, checked out the number of music shops, the guys with dreadlocks and the girls in sandals and long, flowing dresses, the warm, dusky, laid-back vibe. No one seemed in a hurry, and Glenn liked that. In the archways below the Skala de la Ville, the cannon-lined ramparts along the northern cliffs, artisans carved from local *thuya* wood. Walls were whitewashed, with blue-painted shutters and doors; ultramarine, indigo, cerulean; blue all the way through, like the sea and the sky. And in the square, stray cats slept in the sun, raggedy children played tag and men stood in doorways in their *babouche* slippers smoking and drinking green tea *à la menthe*.

He explored the souks. The scents from the bazaars filled his head – mint, spices, the leather of the conker-coloured belts and slippers – and the vibrant hues of bedspreads and carpets washed into his mind. He came across the spice market, where Berber women gathered shyly to sell what they called *siwark*, a tree bark used to redden their lips. He wandered on to what seemed to be the Mellah area, a quiet maze of decaying mansions, atmospheric and appealing. And he wondered about the departed Jewish population. Where had they all gone?

That night he heard the Gnawa music for the first time. A band of guys wearing multicoloured, robes were doing a gig in Place Moulay Hassan, which was, he'd discovered, the name of the main town square near the waterfront. He soon learnt how important it was in the culture - Gnawa music played on traditional instruments; bass drums, iron castanets, tambourine and what he recognized from the music shops as the lute-like *guimbri*. It was Essaouira's hypnotic pulse; its living history. Men listened, rocked and swayed. Demurely black-robed women ululated wildly, hands held over their mouths, black eyes gleaming.

The following day, the guy from one of the music shops in the medina told him more – the mesmeric rhythms and chants were first developed by slaves brought to Morocco from sub-Saharan Africa. 'The sound of this' – he clicked the iron castanets – 'it is the sound of the chains.' That sent a shiver running down Glenn's spine, for sure. He could almost feel the slaves' heartache, their pain. There was more than one way of being enslaved. You could listen to that music and the rhythms seemed to seep into your very soul.

This town wasn't frantic, like Marrakech. It wasn't edgy

and Glenn didn't feel like everyone was trying to rip him off. It soothed rather than startled. He decided to stick around.

He met Howard on his fifth day. They were both camping on the beach and Glenn had had enough of it. It was autumn and the nights were growing cold. This was no Goa. The time had come for something more solid.

He approached a tent which was pitched less than fifteen metres away. 'Know a place to crash, man?' he'd asked Howard, offering him a smoke. Though clearly he didn't – otherwise, why would he be camping here on the sand?

Howard took the cigarette and examined it briefly, as if he thought it might magically turn into a spliff. It didn't. 'Funny that,' he said. 'I've been wondering about that very subject myself.'

Not so funny, though, Glenn thought, with the night temperature dropping the way it was. 'And?' He waited.

'Might be something coming up.' Howard had looked suspicious, even back then, his pale eyes narrowing as he stared towards the morning sun creeping over the hills behind them.

'Yeah?' Glenn leant towards him and lit a match, shielding the flame from the Atlantic breeze with his cupped palm.

Howard bent to take a deep draw. He was wearing a red-and-yellow skull cap, under which his hair was lank and fair, and a rough woollen jacket and jeans. And he was older than Glenn had first thought, his skin tanned and weathered. 'I know a guy.' He looked up at Glenn, scrutinized him from his tatty bush hat, past his tie-dye T-shirt and cut-off jeans to his bare feet. Glenn's desert boots still had some wear in them, but his plimsolls had gone by the wayside and he was living in flip-flops as much as he could. 'You American?'

'Yeah.' Though sometimes Glenn wished he could shake it off, that Americanness which seemed so linked with everything that had gone wrong. 'You're Australian, right?'

'Bang on, kiddo.' Howard drew in on the cigarette. 'This guy I know. He's Canadian. Crazy dude.' He laughed. 'But he knows of somewhere. He's been here for weeks. He's well into that Gnawa music, you know?'

Glenn nodded. Every night you could hear it wafting on the sea breeze, the beat of it a pulse as strong as the tide. Ganja music, he thought.

'Well, some musician dude's been living in this place, but he's moving on. Three bedrooms. Got any bread?'

'Some.' Glenn was cautious. His mother had been generous – God knows how she had stashed so much away without his father knowing – and he'd worked where he could along the way. But it cost to live, and cash was running low. Besides, when you were on the road it was best not to let anyone know you had a bean. The last thing he needed was to have his gear ransacked in the middle of the night.

Howard shrugged. 'I'll let you know later.' And he sauntered off towards the sea.

Glenn watched him. Howard stripped down to his underpants, pulled off the skull cap and walked into the shallows, splashing the water over his body, his face, his hair. When he emerged he looked like a drowned rat. 'You fight in Vietnam?' he shouted across to Glenn.

Glenn shook his head.

'Draft dodger?' And Glenn registered his sneer. What was his problem?

'War resister,' he corrected. 'Pacifist.' He held up both hands. 'No hassle, OK?' The Vietnam conflict was over at last. In January of this year Nixon had agreed a ceasefire. It was over, but the guilt of its legacy lived on – at least as far as Glenn was concerned.

'War resister.' Howard nodded. He eyed Glenn appraisingly and Glenn imagined his mental battle. What won would probably depend on how desperate for money he was. 'I'll let you know if the place comes up, man.'

'Sure.' Glenn went back to studying the waves. If not this, there would be something.

But that night Howard came over with another guy. 'This is Gizmo,' he said.

Gizmo? What the hell kind of a name was that? 'Glenn. Hi.' He lifted his hand. 'Good to meet you.'

Gizmo was short and stocky and sported dark dreadlocks and a blue bandana; the pupils of his dark eyes seemed dilated even in the darkness, and he was wearing faded jeans, a woollen jacket like Howard's that smelt like a dead animal, and a grin that looked like it was a permanent one. 'You wanna live in the riad, man?' he asked Glenn.

'The riad?'

'It's pretty run-down,' Gizmo said. 'But it's shelter, you know?'

'Who owns the place?' Glenn asked.

'Some rich old French guy. Word is he ain't never coming back.'

Glenn nodded. 'Sounds cool.'

Gizmo looked at Howard. Even back then he seemed in thrall.

'Wanna see it?' Howard had asked. And Glenn was in.

CHAPTER 6

The group was welcomed to Riad Lazuli in Marrakech with sweet mint tea poured from a teapot into decorative glasses from a considerable height – to aerate the tea, Nell supposed. She looked around the salon. Dusky, sky-blue-plastered walls, ivory and royal-blue geometric-patterned tiles, shimmering navy drapes that reminded her of the lapis-lazuli gemstone itself, deeply cushioned alcoves in mauves and lavender, a small plunge pool in the centre lit up by a Moorish lantern, a large kitchen off to one side . . . She felt a glow of warmth. The doors were wooden with intricate keyholes and bolts and decorated with gilt, and the creamy floor tiles were smooth as satin. This was just the haven she needed. And it wasn't backpacker in the least. Callum had chosen a winner. She began to relax at last.

Callum had taken her to the airport, determinedly cheerful, telling her what a great time she was sure to have, while Nell's stomach slowly churned. At Departures she nipped to the loo to take the Rescue Remedy her friend Lucy had recommended the last time they'd met up and Nell had confided some of her troubles. And when she came out again she hung on to Callum tightly for a moment. Why did she feel they were saying goodbye? Why did she feel so strongly that she was losing him?

He put his hands gently on her shoulders. 'You'll be fine, Nell,' he said.

'Yes.' She lifted her face for his kiss.

'You can do it.' He kissed her lips firmly. Her lips. 'You really can, you know.'

She wondered if he did understand how hard it was, after all.

'Yes.' And he was right – she had to do something to make things change. 'Bye, then.' She would do it, and she would enjoy it too.

Arriving at the airport just outside Marrakech, she reported to the driver holding a sign that read 'Riad Lazuli' and without further ado was whisked off to the ancient pink-walled medina in his taxi. The city walls were magnificent. At least ten metres high, they seemed to go on and on, with various towers and gates scattered at regular intervals.

'Riad Lazuli, it is in the centre of the medina,' the driver told her in broken French she could barely understand. 'A handcart is necessary for the next part of the journey.'

'I see.' Nell didn't, but she was intrigued.

They got out of the car, he took possession of a cart from a man standing nearby, launched her case into the centre of it and set off at a blistering pace. Nell followed, almost at a run, so she wouldn't lose him. How on earth was she to find her way around? The colours, noise and chaos were mind-blowing. The street was crammed with people in bright clothes; with market stalls filled with shoes, vegetables, spices; with mopeds and donkeys; and somehow they were all weaving a passage through. She'd never experienced anything quite like it.

Thankfully, after a few minutes they turned off into a quieter, narrower street, then off again into another. Soon they were negotiating what was little more than a narrow and dingy alleyway, the pink earthen walls rising high on both sides, the cobbles uneven and broken. The cart bumped and rumbled. The man muttered something unintelligible to himself and turned round to check she was still with him. She was. No way was she letting this man out of her sight. Some children were kicking a football around, their shouts breaking the silence. Nell concentrated on her breathing. It was like entering a timeless zone. She hurried on. She wasn't entirely sure if she found the high pink walls claustrophobic or restful after the bustle, noise and glare of the streets outside. The never-ending pink and brown should surely be stifling, but the walls seemed safe and porous; comforting somehow.

And at last . . . 'Riad Lazuli,' the taxi driver announced.

They were standing outside a nondescript, unnamed and unnumbered wooden door with a ringed hand of Fatima door knocker. He lifted this and let it fall.

The door was opened by a man dressed in a red-and-white loose-fitting tunic and baggy Arab trousers. 'I am Ahmed. I am happy to meet you,' he said. He took her suitcase from the driver and beckoned her inside. 'Come in, come in, please.'

He told her in a low voice how much she should tip the man, and Nell fumbled for the money in her purse.

She looked around her, signing the registration form as if in a daze. She was in a blue-walled salon and the decor was stunning. But before she had the chance to absorb her surroundings fully, Ahmed indicated that he would take her to her room.

She followed him up stone stairs which wound in a spiral right around the courtyard, the centre of the building, and into a small room with a high, ornate ceiling, a patterned Moroccan rug on the floor and a very large wrought-iron bed. There was a midnight-blue divan, too, loaded with shiny purple-patterned cushions glinting with gold stitching, and a low hexagonal table.

'You will be comfortable here,' he informed her. He opened a door on one side and indicated a small bathroom. 'Very soon, you must come downstairs, assemble with the others and take tea.'

Goodness. Nell unpacked a few things, combed her hair and reapplied her lipstick. That was about all she had time for. She'd hardly managed to catch her breath.

And now here she was, assembling and taking tea – the people sitting around her members of her group, presumably. The mint tea, *thé marocain*, green tea with mint, was sickly sweet but calming.

'English?' the middle-aged woman on the seat next to her asked. She was thin and spindly, with long, spidery arms.

'Yes.'

'Thought so.'

Briefly, Nell wondered what had given her away. Her frizz of blonde hair? Her slightly lost expression? The way she crossed her legs?

'And what do you do?'

'I work in a café.'

'Ah, a professional.' The woman gave her a knowing look.

'But I don't know much about Moroccan cuisine,' Nell added. 'I've never even cooked a tagine.'

The woman leant closer. 'I know nothing about cooking at all,' she confided.

'Oh.' What was she doing here then? Nell was disappointed. She'd envisaged being in a group of like-minded foodies, all swapping information and cooking tips. She imagined what fun she could have had if Lucy or even Sharon were with her. But they weren't, and Nell was on her own.

'And how did you become so interested in cookery?' the woman persevered. 'If I may be personal?'

Nell made a mental note to sit next to someone else next time. She sipped her tea. 'My mother encouraged me,' she said, in a voice she hoped conveyed that this was the end of the subject. *Not now* . . . But, despite herself, a vision of the farmhouse kitchen swam into her mind, her mother stirring something simmering on the stove, her young self up on a footstool at the big old table, helping roll out dough for ginger biscuits and mould coconut pyramids on a tray ready for baking. Her mother would encourage her to taste, too – and that was the most important thing about cooking. To taste and to adjust accordingly.

'What do you think, darling?' her mother would ask with a little frown. 'Should there be more coconut? More spice?'

While her mother was a good cook but a slapdash one, Nell became meticulous. It wasn't long before she started preparing entire dinners and, by the time she was twelve or thirteen, adapting recipes. *Wouldn't it be better if this had less tomato and a bit more stock? A dash of chilli could make this so much more interesting, don't you reckon? Why not put rosemary with the potatoes, Mum?*

With difficulty, she brought herself back to the present. Things were happening.

Ahmed cleared his throat and introduced their *dada* chef, Hassan, who spoke French, and their translator and course leader, Marion, who spoke both English and Italian. She would also take them to the souks tomorrow morning, Ahmed said, where they would learn some Arabic words for key items and be taught how to buy the ingredients needed for a tagine.

Smoothly but surely, Marion took over. 'The tagine is also the name of the dish which Moroccans use to cook it in,' she said. She picked up one from the table beside her. 'It is ideal for slow cooking,' she explained. 'Steam rises and condenses inside the conical lid here' – she pointed – 'and drips back into the food to prevent it drying out. The knob on the lid is equally functional. As well as being simple to lift with one hand so that you can stir with the other, it also acts as a spoon rest.' She demonstrated. 'Tagines can also be used to store bread, and the base can be used to serve fruit.'

'And if we don't have a tagine in our kitchen?' Spider-woman piped up.

'A good baking dish can be substituted' – though Marion's expression implied that it would be a poor substitute indeed. 'During the next few days, we will be seeking out native ingredients such as saffron from Taliouine,' she said. 'Olives and mint from Meknes. Citrus fruits from Fez. And we will be discussing the history of Moroccan cuisine.' She surveyed her audience through the thick lenses of her glasses. 'This kind of course is perfect to get under the skin of a country. Local food can teach you much about a society and its traditions. And what better way to evoke the memories of a trip than by learning to cook your own signature dish? To recreate the same mouth-watering smells that wafted through the markets and restaurants you visited?'

What better way indeed? Nell looked around the group. There were fifteen of them, men and women of different ages and nationalities, she guessed from the buzz of chat that had been circulating around the salon during tea. In addition to Spider-woman, there were two German women, probably in their thirties and clearly a couple, a young guy in his twenties who looked Scandinavian, an older man, a married couple – British – and an assortment of single women, one of whom was carrying a camera. She was tall and rather striking, with gamine good looks, and she was leaning back and observing the scene, a slight smile playing around her lips.

'Morocco – and Marrakech in particular – is a perfect destination for cookery classes,' Marion went on. 'Thanks to its diverse origins, its cuisine offers a large variety of dishes.' She pushed back a stray lock of greying hair which had escaped from her loose chignon. 'And all with a rich history.'

'What will we be cooking?' one of the German women asked.

'Tagines, couscous, pastillas . . .'

'Pastillas?' the German woman's companion enquired.

'A traditional Andalusi Arab dish. A rather elaborate pie made from squab, chicken or fish. Traditionally, it's served as a starter at the beginning of special meals.' Marion paused. 'We will be making bread, too. And briouats – triangular or circular stuffed pastries.' She glanced across at the chef, who was in the kitchen, only appearing from time to time to nod and smile or brandish his rather terrifying chef's knife. 'Besides a number of classical dishes such as the typical chicken tagine with lemon and olives, we will be discovering other recipes, which might generally be known only to Moroccans. For example, the tagine makfoul with caramelized tomatoes and onions, or the Tanjia Marrakchia.' She was really getting into her stride now. 'There is harira soup, which is often served with dates during Ramadan, and zaalouk, a delicious Moroccan salad made with aubergines and tomato. Not to forget the famous b'stilla, a pigeon pie with herbs, spices, lemons and almonds. That is aside from the considerable number of desserts.'

Gosh. Nell didn't know whether to give in to her hunger pangs or leave immediately. How on earth were they going to learn to cook all this in five days?

Their instructor/translator paused for breath. 'Tradition-ally, Moroccan recipes were passed from mother to daughter,' she informed them. 'Moroccan cuisine is essentially a family tradition, which explains how these dishes have kept their genuine character through the ages.'

Mother and daughter . . . Nell settled back in her seat. They had shared so much, and yet there was so much her mother had never told her. Why had she wanted to sell the land? What did she have to hide? And how exactly had she met her death that awful night on the cliff?

'Multiple influences on the cuisine can be traced,' Marion continued. 'An Arab origin dating back to the Abassids, traces of the Moorish in the sweet and sour notes of the tagines, Berber traditions in the couscous, Jewish and even Indian influences in the host of spices, such as cumin, cinnamon and ginger. It is a very mixed heritage. A marriage of influences and flavours.'

The woman with the camera, who was about her own age, Nell guessed, got to her feet in one fluid movement, put her eye to the viewfinder and took some rapid-fire shots of Mar-ion as she spoke.

Marion blinked and adjusted the scarf at her scrawny neck. 'I must introduce our photographer.' She shrugged in a way that seemed to indicate she'd rather there wasn't one. 'She is taking photographs for a Moroccan exhibition to be held in England. And there is also a cookery book, I believe?'

'There is.' The young woman smiled. She had a nice smile, thought Nell. Maybe she would be a kindred spirit. No one else, with the possible exception of the young Scandinavian, looked a likely candidate.

'So, if you are lucky, you might see your tagine in a book.' Marion let out a bark of laughter at her own joke.

'But if you'd rather not feature, that's fine.' The young woman spoke in a clear and confident voice. 'Just let me know. I'll be asking everyone for permission, in any case.'

'We have fifteen generous-sized workstations in our large kitchen.' Marion nodded towards the room in question, and the chef appeared, nodding, grinning and raising his dark eyebrows suggestively. 'But, where possible, we will also be using traditional cooking methods and tools. For example, we will cook over a wood fire.' She looked around the group and there was a general murmur of approval. 'This serves to remind us what Moroccan cuisine used to be like many decades ago, and how it is still practised in remote areas, far from big cities like Marrakech.' She bared her teeth in a wide smile. 'We are confident that you will leave this riad in five days' time fully understanding that couscous is not something you make in ten minutes from a bag.'

Nell could hear a phone ringing. She assumed an 'honestly, why don't people switch them off?' look, before belatedly realizing it was hers. 'I'm so sorry.' For a moment she couldn't even think how to switch it off, so instead she retreated through the shimmering blue curtains to the outside courtyard to take the call. It was Callum.

'Hello.' She refrained from telling him off for ringing her.

He wasn't to know she'd made an exhibition of herself answering his call.

'How's it going, then?' He sounded cheerful enough, considering his wife was away, she thought gloomily.

'All right. We haven't cooked anything yet.'

'Well, you must have only just arrived.'

'Mmm.' There was a tension in the way they talked to one another these days; she could feel it. Either they were trying to be polite or they were only one step away from bickering. And yet it used to be so easy. She shivered in the early-evening air, although it was still warm for the beginning of November. Around her, terracotta pots of oleander and bougainvillea continued to flower, and the heady scent from a trellis of winter jasmine was drifting her way. It was already quite dark and the walls of the riad loomed above her. In the summer they must live out here, she thought. It was the heart of the building. Although there was a canopy above it, it was still half open and she could see a luminous moon and the stars, so clear in the evening sky.

'Look, Nell.'

'Yes?' She felt a sudden sense of foreboding.

'The estate agent called earlier.'

'Oh?' Nell didn't want to think about the farmhouse, not now. She'd been hoping for a few days to herself – without the worries of home.

'They've found a buyer.'

'Really?' Nell frowned. Against Callum's advice, she had

insisted on marketing it for its full value; she had no intention of letting it go for less than it was worth. In fact, she thought now, she was still not sure she could let it go at all. So this was a surprise. And even more of a surprise was the timing. That a buyer should come along just as she went off to Morocco. It seemed a bit, well, odd.

'Isn't that great?' And was it her imagination – or did Callum sound a bit uneasy?

'Mm, well, maybe,' she hedged. She didn't want to, but she recalled that elusive look of his a few days ago, and the way she'd felt at the airport. Almost as if he'd wanted to get her out of the way . . .

'Maybe?'

She grasped her mobile more tightly. Her palm was damp, she realized. 'How much did they offer?' Offers could always be rejected. It happened all the time.

'The full asking price.' Callum sounded so pleased. Smug almost. She hated that. But why wouldn't he be pleased? she reasoned. When you put something up for sale you generally wanted to sell it.

'I'm not sure,' she said. She peered back into the room. To her relief, Marion hadn't waited for her and was still chuntering on about the history of Moroccan cuisine. She could catch up from one of the others later. What she really wanted to know about was the history of saffron. Where had it come from? How had it come to Cornwall? What mysterious quality did it possess that made it so special? Callum was her husband. And she still loved him – didn't she? So why did she feel that he was intruding on all that?

'What do you mean, you're not sure?' His tone changed.

'I'd like to meet them first.'

She heard him sigh. 'It isn't an interview, Nell.'

'I know. But I still want to meet them.' She put her mental foot down. She would not be pushed into this. She didn't expect Callum to understand. But she couldn't possibly let the farmhouse go to someone she hadn't even met.

'So what on earth shall I say?' He sounded rather cross now. Well, tough, thought Nell. Let him.

'I'll be back in five days. Say that we need to think about it.' She kept her voice firm. Whatever was going on – if something was going on – he needed to know that she meant what she said.

'But, Nell . . . If you'd only let me –'

'Please.'

'It's the full asking price.'

'I know.'

'They could back out.'

'I know that, too.' Inside, people were moving around and she could smell food, a tantalizing fragrance of the lemons, olives and chicken that had been mentioned earlier. 'Look, I have to go.' She didn't want them to start eating without her. And she didn't want to be having this conversation. Not now.

'All right. I'll try to stall them.'

'Fine. Bye.' Nell switched off her phone. A buyer for the

farmhouse, her mother's farmhouse. Already. And Callum was determined to sell . . . But she wouldn't think about it, not yet. She wouldn't think about Callum either or whatever it was that was happening to them.

Back inside Riad Lazuli, Marion looked at her and let out a pointed 'Ah.'

Nell caught the amused glance of the female photographer. She looked nice. Maybe later she'd try to talk to her, find out more about this Moroccan event Marion had mentioned. And, in the meantime, dinner was on the table. Chicken tagine with lemons and green olives steaming in its conical pot. And Nell couldn't wait to get stuck in.

CHAPTER 7

Amy was thrilled to be in Marrakech. It was so colourful, so vibrant, so alive; it was hard to put down her camera for a second and she didn't know what to look at first – there was so much.

As soon as they'd finished their delicious breakfast of crêpes and honey, eggs, fresh figs and yogurt this morning, Marion, well-informed but with a dubious hairstyle and dress sense, had taken them to the jumble of fruit, vegetable and meat markets to buy ingredients for that day's dish. Stalls were heaped with watermelons, capsicums, red onions looking as if they'd just been pulled from the earth, courgettes with blossoms intact and sweet-smelling oranges. Dried apricots gleamed like miniature suns. Live chickens strutted in cages; a stallholder sliced cutlets from a fresh rack of lamb. In Marrakech it seemed there was a place for everything – from the leather workers at Souk des Sacochiers, where they made bags from animal skins or templates for *babouches*, to the wrought-iron makers at Souk el Haddadine. And they had whisked past them all, Marion leading the way like a Scout leader, Amy's camera clicking.

Marion indicated the street food. The fragrance of cumin and garlic was thick in the air, combining with the scent of pastry frying. 'Here we have bissara. Fava-bean soup.' She pointed to a bulbous earthenware pot full of thick yellow liquid simmering over a charcoal brazier. 'And briouats.' The group nodded knowledgeably.

'And note the donkey-drawn *carossa*,' Marion added, as a cart laden with mint leaves passed by. 'In Morocco, the old traditions are respected; there is no need for them to change.'

Amy wondered why Marion had first come here and why she had never left. Had she fallen in love with a Moroccan acrobat in the square perhaps? She scrutinized their leader as she forged ahead. Perhaps not. Morocco, she guessed, had a way of getting under your skin.

Afterwards, when their heads were pounding from the haggling, the shouting, the clatter of cart wheels on the cobbles and the braying of donkeys, and with their baskets full of fresh produce, they'd trailed after Marion back to the riad, all of them looking somewhat overwhelmed, and Amy had left them there, setting out again to capture some more of the street life of Marrakech.

It was indeed an overwhelming city. It took hold of you and threw you into its bustling centre and you almost felt you could drown in the barrage of voices, the wail of the muezzin call to prayer, the pure intensity of the colours and the smells – of spices and mint, musk and rose. There was just so much of everything. Amy imagined her portraits as life-size stills, forming the centrepiece of her exhibition. The people of Morocco; around them their food, their architecture, their flora and fauna, their culture.

She had been bursting to escape from the confines of the group and now, at last, she was free. She took some action shots of the raggedy kids with dark, matted hair and cheeky grins who played football in the pink labyrinthine alleys of the medina, tossing them some coins in token of her appreciation but waving away their offers to take her to the square, the riad, the Gardens . . . Back in the souks, among the men sprawled on mats and cane chairs, she captured on camera an old man with a lined and leathery face and a white beard like Methuselah's who was sitting with his feet in a bucket of water. She even got some shots of a group of shy women with henna-patterned arms, though unlike the men, who grinned, waved and did their best to get in the frame, most of the women were resistant to being photographed. They spread their hands over their faces, they shook their heads, they turned away. And of course she had to respect that.

She took mind-blowing close-ups of the tall cones of spices – turmeric, paprika, cumin and ginger – which must be re-erected constantly to reach such a pinnacle of perfection, she imagined. There were also bundles of cinnamon sticks, heaps of star anise and fragrant dried rosebuds, nutmeg and liquorice root. And more . . . Enamel bowls of cured olives, jars of the menthol crystal that was said to cure allergies, blocks of richly scented amber and white musk and mountains of green mint tea. Personally, Amy could have done with a mug of rooibos. But the fact was that Marrakech was a complete explosion of sensuality. She experimented with the patterns made by row upon row of rugs, carpets, throws, bedspreads, hanging like bright flags on lines outside the market stalls. The colours, the architecture . . . The sunlight and the smells . . . Even in November. There was no end to it, really. Amy wasn't following the list Jake Tarrant had given her, though. She was following her creative nose.

They'd met for a coffee at the Town Mill café to discuss her trip and, rather irritatingly, he'd seemed just as relaxed as he had been the day before, his long, denim-clad legs stretched out in front of him, feet crossed. Nice boots, she thought. Stripy socks. Today, he seemed very much in charge.

'I wanted to check we were singing from the same song sheet.' He pulled the notebook he'd been writing in yesterday out of his battered leather briefcase and brandished it in the air.

'Oh yes?' Amy moved her coffee a bit closer to her, and out of range.

He put the notebook on the table. 'A Moroccan event isn't just about photographs of the Atlas Mountains and some cookery workshops.'

'Of course not.' Amy was stung. Is that what he'd thought?

'It has to go deeper.' He leaned forward, a note of passion in his voice that surprised her. 'There's been a real sea-change in Morocco's cultural orientation, you know, Amy. They're looking at us in a new light these days. As far as they're concerned, the English language is now *la vraie langue du progrès*. The true language of progress.'

Amy raised an eyebrow at that. 'Another excuse for the British not to bother learning any other languages, then,' she remarked.

'Perhaps.' He conceded this with a crooked smile. And dimples.

'But the British are getting rather keen on Moroccan culture, too,' she pointed out. It worked both ways.

'They are.' He nodded with enthusiasm. 'There're all kinds of educational and business links currently being developed between the two countries.'

'Really?' Amy sipped her coffee. It was strong and mellow – just as she liked it.

'Which are bound to create stronger links between them.'

'I'm sure you're right.'

'So what we're looking for . . .'

Amy thought about what she was looking for. She was looking for the character of the place, what made it operate the way it did. As far as she could tell, it was the strict customs of religion that decided how Moroccan society was run – the repression of its women, for instance. Its history, which was responsible for its diversity. And the heat and landscape that dictated what the earth produced. It was a sunshine place and yet a dark place. Suppression meant that corruption could flourish, that people could be controlled, that –

'Are you listening to me, Amy?' He had torn his hands through his hair and it was sticking up at all angles. Amy was amused at first. And then she caught the glimpse of his sadness.

'Of course,' she said again. 'We don't want any old tourist shots. I agree. I'll just go over there and see what comes up.'

He frowned. 'Perhaps some planning would be useful, though? As I was saying, I've made a list to help you.' He plucked a sheet of paper covered in close typescript from the briefcase and handed it to her.

She glanced at it briefly and put it in her bag. 'OK. I'll have a proper look at it later.' She didn't mean to sound offhand. It wasn't that she didn't take her job seriously. Far from it. But she didn't want to be restricted to certain geographical locations or ideas. She didn't want to follow Jake Tarrant's photographic guidebook. She wanted to wander. She wanted to get lost. She wanted to go into people's houses and have a glimpse of the real Morocco – see the way they actually lived.

'We'll have to work closely on this, Amy.' He was leaning forward again and looking at her intently. A bit too intently. Under the leather jacket he was wearing a blue cotton shirt and a thin sweater. She found herself looking at his hands; they were hardly ever still. No wedding ring.

'Fine.' She finished her coffee and got to her feet. She could tell him that he should trust her, that she wasn't an idiot, that she knew what she was doing. But why should she?

'I know you weren't expecting an events company to come swanning in . . .'

'Really,' she said, 'it's not a problem.'

He seemed about to say something else and then changed tack. 'While you're away, I'm going to be organizing the workshops we discussed. And the film screenings.'

'OK.' And I, she thought, am going to Morocco to see how it really is. Never mind that he was probably a nice man who cared, never mind that he was sad about something. She still wasn't about to let him dictate what pictures she should take. She wasn't that kind of photographer. She preferred to work alone.

She was just using her zoom to take some shots of the storks nesting on the towers and bastions of the ruins of the El Badi Palace, the broad fan of their black tail feathers a perfect contrast to their white chests and backs, and their sharp orange bills against the crumbling pink walls, when she caught sight of one of the women from the Riad Lazuli cookery course. She was being escorted across the square. Amy frowned. The boy with her was young, gangly and looked pretty innocent, but enough people had warned her about Marrakech tricksters to put her on her guard. As far as Amy was concerned, the more innocent they seemed, the more likely they were not to be innocent at all.

She hurried across the square. She'd cut them off. She had already noticed this woman with her wild frizz of blond hair and a big – if wobbly – smile. She reminded Amy of someone, but she couldn't think who. She looked bubbly and yet sort of subdued at the same time. Her eyes would light up and then grow shadowed. Sadness again. Amy would quite like to photograph her, but she hadn't yet even had the chance to talk to her, and today there were plenty of other things to focus on.

'Hey!'

They'd stopped, and he was showing her the storks. They were a good omen, Amy had heard. Everyone liked them. Dutifully, the woman was nodding and taking a photo. She was like a lamb being taken to the slaughter.

'Hey!' Amy shouted louder.

'Oh, hi.' The woman turned. She seemed pleased to see her. 'Sorry, I can't remember your name?'

'Amy.' She held out her hand.

'Nell.' She smiled. 'I'm . . . er . . . This is Kamil. He's taking me to the Mellah quarter.'

'Oh?' Amy examined him close up. He was rather awkward looking and had a shock of dark-brown hair. And he didn't seem pleased to see her, which only confirmed her theory. He must have thought his luck was in. 'Why?'

'The best spices are there,' she said. Bless her. 'At the fairest prices.'

'Really?' Amy folded her arms and looked at him.

'Yes, of course,' he blustered. 'You must come and see.'

'Kamil lives there with his family,' said Nell. 'He has to go there now – for dinner. They always eat together.'

'Come,' he said.

Uh huh, thought Amy. 'It must be hard to make a living here in Morocco,' she said to him conversationally as they all three walked on. 'But at least you have the tourists.'

'Oh.' Nell looked at her. 'You mean . . .?' She glanced anxiously at her guide, who was now walking a step or two ahead.

He turned. 'I show you best place to buy,' he said. 'Fair prices.'

'This not tourist Marrakech,' Amy whispered to Nell behind her hand. She had heard countless traders saying this to tourists all day.

Nell looked doubtful.

He glanced over his shoulder. 'This not tourist Marrakech,' he said.

Nell turned to Amy. 'Am I being an idiot?' Her eyes widened. She stopped walking.

'No.' Amy linked arms with her. Clearly, she needed looking after. 'Come on then, show us,' she said to Kamil, who stood waiting for them just ahead. And to Nell: 'It's fine, just be on your guard.'

They followed Kamil through a narrow opening in the crumbling wall of the city that led to the Mellah, the Jewish quarter, and a busy street of stalls that looked remarkably like all the rest she'd seen so far. He stopped, apparently at random. 'All the prices are the same, you see.' He pointed to the pyramids of spices. 'This is how you know they are fair.'

A man emerged from the shop. Kamil shook his hand. 'I do not know him,' Kamil said to Amy and Nell. 'But I can tell he is honest man. Maybe the most honest in Marrakech.'

He had some work to do on his technique, Amy thought. She exchanged a glance with Nell.

The trader looked suitably modest. 'I show you many things,' he promised.

'Any minute, he'll be offering us mint tea,' Amy whispered.

'Come in, come in, I will take photograph, I will make tea . . .'

Fifteen minutes later they emerged, giggling. He had made tea and it was delicious – not mint tea but something richer and sweeter made with vanilla and rose. He had offered them everything in the shop from turmeric powder to argon oil, all at the very best prices, and he had tried unsuccessfully to demonstrate the stress-relieving effects of a musky amber massage bar on Nell's neck and shoulders.

'In our country we might leave our shoulders uncovered,' Amy had told him reprovingly. 'But that doesn't mean we allow them to be touched by strangers.'

But they had escaped only a few euros poorer, proud owners of some fennel sticks (Berber toothpicks), a terracotta pumice (Berber body scrub) and a clay pot which when wet would leave a deep-red pigment behind (Berber lipstick). Fair dos, thought Amy. The shopkeeper clearly wasn't happy and it wasn't enough of a haul to share with his young accomplice, but it was high time they realized they'd do better out of tourists if they stopped trying to rip them off all the time.

'How come you're not at the riad, anyway?' Amy asked Nell as they finally found their way out of the Mellah maze. 'I thought you were all going back there to cook after you'd been to the souk.'

'We did,' said Nell. 'We spent a couple of hours in the kitchen with Hassan and then we were given some time off to explore.' She looked at her watch ruefully. 'And I'm due back five minutes ago.'

'No problem. Here's the square already.' Amy led them towards the far corner and down the narrow streets, directions she had memorized earlier. Three things she'd inherited from her father – his height, good spatial awareness and a sense of direction. And you needed all three in Marrakech.

Nell followed her. 'How did you know it was a scam?'

Amy shrugged. 'That's what they do.'

'All of them?'

'Most.' She laughed. 'But remember – they don't have a lot, and they think we're all incredibly wealthy.'

Nell looked disappointed. She was clearly a romantic. 'Look,' said Amy. 'It's a great city. Colourful, lively, atmospheric. Fantastic architecture. Yummy food.'

Nell nodded.

'But it's best to walk around like this.' She demonstrated, camera and bag held close to her chest, looking neither to left nor right and walking fast and with purpose.

Nell laughed, as Amy had hoped she would. She had a nice laugh. The sadness didn't suit her. Amy wondered what had happened. A love affair gone wrong? A disappointment in her job? Whatever it was, Amy felt the urge to make it better, couldn't help herself.

'Tell me about the event you're organizing. Where's it to be held?' Nell asked.

'Lyme Regis.' Amy told her the background. But she didn't mention Jake Tarrant. The list he'd given her was burning a hole in the pocket of her jacket. So far, she hadn't looked at it once. But she had thought about the man. Interesting, quirky, a bit of a know-all. She wasn't sure if she liked him but he'd certainly had an effect. 'And you?' she asked.

'Well, I'm here to cook.'

'Down here – see the antique shop, that's your landmark.' Amy pointed down the alley. 'First left, second right, third door along on the left. Is that all?'

'Is what all?'

'Are you just here for the cookery?' She was sure there was something else.

Nell stopped walking so abruptly that Amy almost bumped into her. 'No. My husband bought the course for me as a birthday present. He thought it would help me forget.'

'Forget?' She was walking again now, but more slowly, along the sandy alley. Around them the tall, salmon-pink walls of the medina seemed to close in and everything was once again in shadow.

She turned back to face her. 'My mother died,' she said. 'Very suddenly. I mean, she wasn't ill or anything. She just . . .'

'Oh, I'm so sorry.' Amy reached out, put a hand on her shoulder. 'I didn't mean to pry. I always say too much without thinking first. So people tell me.'

Nell shook her head. 'It's OK,' she said. 'Well, obviously, it's not, but . . .' She straightened her shoulders. 'Cooking helps me forget – at least for a while.'

'That's good, but –'

'Here we are.' Nell spoke in a bright voice but Amy wasn't convinced by it and she felt bad. But she was right. This was the small wooden door to the riad. Nell lifted the hand of Fatima and let it fall and, almost immediately, Ahmed opened the door wide for them to enter. 'Good afternoon,' he said. 'You would like tea?'

Nell and Amy exchanged a smile.

'Maybe later,' said Nell. 'Thanks, Amy.' And with a quick squeeze of Amy's arm, she hurried off to join the others.

Amy had an idea. She pulled the postcard from her bag. The picture on the front showed an old arched door, painted blue, the paint flaking, revealing brown wood beneath. Above the arch, carved into the pinkish stone building blocks that made up the portal, was an emblem, a flower with eight petals, two symmetrical branches entwined underneath. The stone walls on either side of the door were old and crumbling. The door was very slightly ajar, revealing discoloured, ancient black-and-white floor tiles. There was no clue on the back of the card regarding where the photograph had been taken; just the scrawly writing. And the Moroccan stamp.

'Ahmed,' she said. 'Do you know where this is?' She had already asked Marion last night, and the taxi driver who'd brought her from the airport. Neither had been able to help. And Amy had seen nothing like it during today's exploration of the city.

He frowned. 'I do not think it is Marrakech,' he said at last.

Amy had suspected as much. She supposed it was too unlikely that she would have picked the same city to visit as Glenn. 'Any idea where it could be?'

He shook his head. 'I am sorry, no.'

'Fez? Casablanca?' She didn't have time to travel all around Morocco.

Ahmed shrugged. 'I am sorry. I do not know.' He regarded her with his serious, dark eyes. 'But I am sure you will find what you are looking for,' he said. '*Insha' Allah.*'

'*Insha' Allah?*'

'If God wills it,' he explained. 'It is presumptuous to assume that fate will allow you to do everything. Fate is not the controller. Neither is man. God is the being who decides.'

'Sounds quite convenient to me,' Amy murmured. She tucked the postcard back in her bag.

'It is.' He flashed her an unexpected grin. 'You must agree to all social engagements, of course. But if you cannot make it . . .' He shrugged.

'. . . it isn't necessarily your fault,' Amy finished for him.

'Exactly. It gives you a . . .' He frowned. 'How do you say it?'

'A get-out clause?'

'Yes.' They exchanged a conspiratorial glance and a chuckle.

'OK if I take a few pictures of the riad while no one's around?' Amy asked.

'Certainly.' He bowed his head in head in assent.

Whether God willed it or not, Amy wouldn't give up her search. She'd keep trying, for her aunt's sake. Nothing ventured, and all that. Despite what her mother thought.

'There's no point taking that with you,' she had said when

Amy had shown her the postcard the night before she left. 'Even if you find out where it is, he won't still be there, will he?'

'He might be.'

Her mother gave her one of her brisk hugs. It was clearly time to go. 'Darling, be realistic. It was sent over thirty years ago. That's a long time. He didn't want to go home and he didn't want to be found. What do you think you can do that a private detective couldn't?'

Amy shrugged. She had no idea – yet. Her aunt had been desperate when she'd put a private detective agency on to tracing her only son. But who could blame her? 'The personal touch?'

Her mother opened the front door. Amy had called round to say goodbye and found her poring over her accounts book, although it was almost 9 p.m. When would she slow down? When would she have done enough?

'See you in a week or so, Mum,' she said. She wanted to say more, she often wanted to say more – but she wouldn't.

Her mother nodded. 'Take care, darling. You're sweet, and I know you only want to help. But you have to face up to it, you know. He's moved on – in one way or another.'

'Dead, you mean?' Amy paused on the step. She was glad her aunt wasn't around to hear this theory.

'It's possible, isn't it?'

'Or he feels he can't go back home,' Amy said. 'For some reason?' She waited for her mother to fill in the gap.

'Whichever.' No help there then.

'Do you know why Aunt Lillian feels guilty?' Perhaps it was a family secret, but if so, wasn't it about time Amy was let in on it?

'I have an idea.' Her mother shook her head. 'But I don't know for sure.'

'And will you tell me?' *Why can you never let anything go . . ?*

She shook her head. 'There's nothing to tell. What's past is past. Lillian's been good to us. She adores you. I wouldn't want to stir things up, even if . . .'

Even if?

'. . . if he is still alive, he doesn't want to be found. And he could be absolutely anywhere.'

'I have to try, though, Mum.' Amy must remember. If not for her great-aunt, she wouldn't be going to Morocco at all – at least not with a camera slung over her shoulder.

As Amy took a few shots of the interior of the riad, the secluded lapis-blue niches lit by the coloured glass of Moorish lamps, the decorative tiles and the *zouak* – the brightly painted wood of the panelling and furniture – part of her mind concentrated on the task at hand and part drifted back to thinking about why she had taken up photography in the first place. She had wanted to capture things, how they looked in certain lights, at certain times of day. It fascinated her how objects, places, people could change when they were in light and when they were in shadow. Photography was an expression, a way of touching the world: her way – with the mind, the eyes, the heart.

She had seen pictures of whole rooms decorated with *zouak*

panelling from floor to ceiling. They were stunning, though here at Riad Lazuli the effects were far simpler. She focused on the light shimmering from the Moorish lantern on to the ice-blue plunge pool strewn with rose petals. A nice touch. The pool was backed by indigo-and-cream geometric tiles, and above this a faded lilac *tadelakt*, the grainy paint-wash on plaster favoured by Moroccans she'd been looking at in a book on the plane coming over. It was similar to Italian stucco, she supposed, a sort of sand and lime mix, polished with a rough stone and black soap before being painted. This one was old and had become veined like marble. Amy looked more closely at the tiles. Why were they always geometric in design? Was the art – of ceramics and weaving – an escape from real life? A way of drawing attention away from the physical world and on to pure form, to order? She was beginning to understand already that one of the precepts of Moroccan architecture was to induce a sense of peace, to create a haven from the chaos outside. And here in Riad Lazuli, it really worked.

Amy had soon found that there was a lot to learn about photography – even before she continued her photographic studies with a BA at Kingston University. Then she had realized the power of the photographer. Not only could you create visual scenes from versions of reality, but you could record them for ever. You could use them to persuade, to influence, to send out a message. How powerful was that? The photograph of an image would recall small details to mind long after most people had forgotten everything. And a photograph could inspire an emotion many decades after that emotion was first felt. She wasn't interested in digital enhancing. To her, what existed in reality would always be more fascinating. But she was interested in storytelling and she was interested in atmosphere. And Morocco had both.

Amy replaced the lens cap on her camera and put it away.

Anything's possible. This was what her aunt had said to her mother when Amy had first said she wanted to be a photographer. And this was the mantra Amy had tried to make her own. She might be able to find some clue about what had happened to Glenn all those years ago. Anything was possible.

Amy pulled Jake's list from her pocket. She scanned it. Go here, do this, take these shots . . . This was supposed to be *her* project, *her* exhibition. She screwed the paper up and threw it in the bin discreetly tucked behind the desk at Reception. She was the one who was here. And she needed to keep her creative independence. So sod Jake Tarrant. She didn't really care what Duncan thought. He should have consulted her before he brought the events manager in. She would keep to her own rather more spontaneous agenda. And she would face whatever consequences that might bring.

CHAPTER 8

Paris, 1974

The deal had been done and a fair amount of pastis consumed. Tomorrow they'd be heading back to Essaouira and the Riad La Vieux Rose. Glenn had been against this trip – Christ, he and Howard had argued long into the night. It was too soon. It was setting a precedent. It wasn't what he wanted. But in the end he had to admit defeat. Where else would they get the money?

'What are you gonna do, man?' Howard had said, mouth curling. 'Go back home?'

Glenn hadn't told him – but it was as if he knew.

Glenn left Gizmo stretched, snoring and out for the count on the banks of the River Seine. Beside him was some old bloke fishing; his ancient bike with the wicker basket ready for his catch leaning on a tree behind them. Apart from him and Giz, there were just a few student types sitting around reading and chatting. Gizmo would come to no harm. This was Paris – a little dingy, but bohemian; a place where you could live and let live. Glenn could imagine staying here if he had the funds. It was pricey. But the city had been bloody useful for them – in providing said funds. Howard had been right. They were inconspicuous. They were freaks, hippies, travellers, call them what you will – and plenty of people called them other names besides. But, generally, no one bothered them.

Glenn was keen to explore. He cut down away from the river and soon came to the narrow rue Mouffetard, a lively and bustling cobbled street crammed with tall, shuttered buildings – some of them faded and worse for wear – and what seemed like real Parisians going about their business. Down the hill, an open-air market was in full swing; vendors shouted, laughed and waved their produce in the air, competing with one another for business. There were vibrant fresh flowers still touched with dew, piles of lusciously gleaming fruit, long sticks of fresh French bread, and seafood displayed in shallow ice buckets. Glenn wandered from stall to stall. The sweet, sharp fragrance of langoustines and crab mingled with the floral overtones, with crusty bread and ripe, runny French cheeses. He bought a baguette and some Brie and ate it as he walked further down the road.

He passed a young guy in an open embroidered shirt and faded blue jeans sitting in a doorway playing his guitar, busking; the tatty straw hat in front of him contained a few francs and a lot of centimes. There was a butcher's shop and the inevitable *boulangerie* on the corner. What a great neighbourhood. It felt so real. This was close to the heart of '70s Paris, but it still had an old and rustic feel in the blistered painted façades, the old-fashioned decorative shopfronts in mahoganies and golds, the high doorways and fan lights and the ancient engraved street signs, wall sculptures and lanterns.

Glenn reached the small square at the bottom of the road. He finished up his baguette, wiped his mouth and fingers on the thin paper serviette it had been wrapped in, retraced his steps and dipped inside a bookshop. He could never resist them, and this one was about as different from a bookshop back in the States as it could be. The shelving rose practically to the height of the ornate and dusty ceiling and the space between the shelves was narrow. Was there an English section? Glenn had a sudden longing to read some poetry, to flick through one of the books that he'd studied at Wisconsin. He thought of his copy of Salinger's *Catcher in the Rye*, accidentally left in a room back in Turkey a few years ago. It all seemed such a long time ago, too long. He was homesick, he realized, with a jolt. Christ.

In the foreign-languages section a girl stood, engrossed. She was neither tall nor short, but she was slender and wore indigo-coloured jeans, a lilac cheesecloth shirt and a string of red love-beads. Her long hair hung past her shoulders and halfway down her back. What really stopped Glenn in his tracks, though, was the air of stillness that seemed to surround her. Maybe it was because she was engrossed in whatever she was reading. What was she reading? It seemed suddenly imperative to know.

Glenn took a step closer, but she didn't respond. He glanced at the shelves. There was some English poetry – he saw a thin volume of the Romantics and one of Alfred Tennyson. Yeats. Ah, Yeats. He plucked it from the shelf and leafed through, the familiar words only half absorbing him because he could smell the scent of her. Rose and vanilla. She smelt like *thé royale*. He smiled. 'Excuse me. *Pardonnez-moi?*'

She glanced up. Her eyes were a perfect almond shape and dark as chocolate. Her mouth was a little too wide. Her skin had a light olive sheen. She looked French. But she was in the English section, wasn't she?

'*Oui?*' She sounded French, too. She didn't look unfriendly but she didn't smile.

Glenn braced himself. In his travels he'd long got over any embarrassment in talking to people he didn't know. It was what you did when you were travelling alone. And she was pretty, very pretty. 'Do you speak English?' he asked. 'I was just kinda wondering what you were reading.'

'*Pourquoi?*' She cocked her head slightly to one side.

Okay, so she was definitely French, but she spoke good English, too. She must do – she'd understood him, hadn't she? 'Why? Because you were so . . .' He searched for the right word. '. . . rapt.'

'She does that to me.'

'She?'

'Emily Dickinson.' She handed him the book. She was reading 'There's a Certain Slant of Light'. 'Do you know her work?'

'Sure.' So she was English but spoke fluent French. Glenn found he wanted to impress her. ' "Presentiment – is that long Shadow – on the Lawn. Indicative that Suns go Down –"' he said.

'"The Notice to the startled Grass/that Darkness − is about to pass −"' She sighed. 'It's beautiful.'

And so are you, he found himself thinking. *And so are you.* 'Do you live here?' he asked her. 'In Paris?' Dickinson had it spot on. Presentiment was a shadow all right. You couldn't pin it down but it sure existed.

'Sort of,' she said. 'It's a long story.'

'I'm not short of time.' He grinned. Hoped the old American charm hadn't been completely washed away by the troubles and adventures of the road. He hadn't used it much in Morocco. All the chicks there not hidden away for religious reasons were already hooked up with some other dude.

She laughed, tucked her hair more neatly behind one ear. 'What about you? Do you live here?'

'Nope. Just passing through.' Force of habit made him look around to check no one was listening, which was crazy, because who would be listening in an old and dusty bookshop in downtown Paris? 'Right now I'm based in Morocco,' he said. 'The west coast.'

'Ah.' Her eyes gleamed. 'The hippie trail. The Marrakech express.'

'Well.' He shrugged. 'It's a cool scene.'

She nodded. 'I've been in Paris for three weeks.'

'You sure speak good French.' *Yeah, Glenn, like three words.*

'My father was French. My parents lived here when they were first married. Before the war. Then he went to fight and *Maman* was interned in the most appalling conditions, until the authorities found out that she was pregnant and released her. That's when she went back to England.' She laughed. 'Why am I telling you all this?'

'I'm Glenn.' He held out a hand. 'Because you're friendly? Because we've experienced an instant rapport?' He raised an eyebrow. 'Because of a slant of light that's a bit like the shadow of presentiment?' God, he was good. He hadn't lost his touch, no way.

She hesitated and then smiled again. 'Bethany. But you don't have to give me all that bullshit.'

Ah. 'Sorry,' he said. 'Couldn't resist.'

'It's OK. I'm glad you like her, too.'

'And are you buying the book?' He closed it gently.

Her expression saddened. 'Not today.'

'Then perhaps I could . . . um . . .?'

'Oh, no.' Her hands fluttered as she went to take the book from him and put it back on the shelf. 'Really. I . . .'

'I insist.' And he once again took charge of the book and strolled over to the proprietor's desk, where the man sat lounging in an old cane chair. '*Monsieur. S'il vous plaît?*'

The old man glowered at him, opened the worn cover and pointed to the price scribbled in pencil on the inner sheet.

Miserable old fart. Glenn pulled out a five-franc note. 'Let's have a coffee to celebrate,' he said to Bethany. He gave her the book.

'OK. Thanks.' She eyed him curiously as they walked out of the shop. He estimated that he was six inches taller than her. If she stood in front of him and bent her head slightly he could kiss the top of her head, no worries. 'You're an unusual kind of guy, aren't you, Glenn?'

'I sure hope so.' He hadn't done anything like this before. It was pretty random, pretty personal, too. But hell, he'd wanted to buy her that book and now he didn't want to let her go. At least not until he'd found out a bit more about her. Like what she was doing in Paris and where she was planning to go next. Home to England? He sure hoped not.

It turned out that Bethany had come to Paris with a girlfriend called Suzi. Suzi had run out on her after two weeks – having fallen madly in lust with a French guy called Claude who had swept her off on an adventure to Marseilles. Bethany rolled her eyes when she came to this part of the story and Glenn found himself wondering how cynical she was. Too cynical for love? Not that love was in the offing, but making love certainly was. Her body was the sort he was convinced would be soft and warm and up for it. And her mind was pretty interesting too.

Bethany had almost run out of money, she told him. She had a job washing up in a dingy café near the Panthéon further up La Mouff, as she called this neighbourhood, but she hated it and the man who ran the place kept trying to grope her whenever no one was around. 'So I s'pose I'll have to go home,' she said. She pulled a dejected face.

'You don't want to?' He wondered what was at home. A controlling father? A complaining mother? Maybe a suffocating hometown that made her want to scream? 'Don't you get along with your folks?'

'Oh, Mum's OK.' She fiddled with her teaspoon. 'People think she's dead interesting. But where I live – it's a dump, nothing's going on, everyone's so straight, you know?'

Glenn nodded. He knew. All around the world, Western kids were saying the same thing. They all wanted to escape the confines of home, to be a free spirit, to have a taste of a different sort of life.

She sighed. 'And besides . . . Who goes off travelling for three weeks? It's so embarrassing. I was hoping to get to Thailand, to India. To . . . well . . . somewhere. Not just France.' She looked around her in despair.

'Do you meditate?' he asked her. It wasn't quite a random question. Since the Beatles had done it, loads of kids wanted to visit the mystic East and find a guru in India. And there was that sense of stillness about her which had first attracted him. He guessed she was a bit of a free spirit.

But she looked surprised. 'Yeah. But that's not the reason I want to go to India. I just want to travel, to see something of the world. Hit the road, you know? Well, everyone's doing it, aren't they? Look at you. And you're American.'

Glenn decided that now wasn't the time to tell her about his history. About why he had left his home and country, and why he couldn't go back. Even so. He felt bad about his mother. Felt he'd let her down. He'd never forgive himself if anything had happened to her, but he knew the best way to keep her safe was to stay away, not even write to her. At least then the old man would have nothing to punish her for.

They were sitting in Le Vieux Chêne – the old oak, as signified by the oak tree sculpted on its façade – which was, Bethany had told him, Paris's oldest bar and a place where revolutionaries used to meet in the nineteenth century – until it was transformed into a *bal musette* dancing club a few decades later. The revolutionary history Glenn found easier to believe than the dancing one; the place was full of kids his age and younger, students and travellers drinking coffee and red wine and smoking, and there was a feeling in the air – of animated conversation, of laughter, the buzz of youth. She was wrong: not everyone was doing it. But most of them wanted to.

'Have you been to India?' she asked him.

'Sure.'

'Wow! How was it?'

'It was pretty cool.' Though he wouldn't say it had been spiritually enlightening exactly.

She looked wistful. 'Paris was supposed to be just the beginning. You're so lucky.'

'But you don't want to travel on your own?'

'P'raps I'm not brave enough.'

Already Glenn was feeling strangely protective towards her. 'It's different for a girl,' he agreed. Especially for a girl with no money. It could be dangerous, and he didn't want to think about that.

'Yeah, it is.'

'You could come back with me to Essaouira,' he said casually. It was safe enough now. They'd got rid of all the stuff and they had enough dosh to keep even Howard happy.

He could sense her silently assessing the situation. Like, could she trust him? After all, she didn't know him from Adam. 'What do you mean?' she asked finally.

'Just as friends.' Who did he think he was kidding? 'It'd give you a chance to see Morocco at least. And Spain on the way through.' It wasn't so unusual to hook up with another traveller like this. People did it all the time. It was no big deal. *Yeah, Glenn, remember that. It's no big deal.*

'Wow!' She cradled her coffee. Seemed to come to a decision. 'Really? Wow.'

'It's nothing much.' Glenn tried to look modest. 'The place we're living in, it's like a small commune, that's how we try to run it.' Or how Howard tried to run it, he found himself thinking. The guy was a bit of a control freak, it had to be said.

'And there's a spare room?'

'Well, no.' He had to be honest with her. 'But you could bunk in with me. For the moment, anyway. And . . .'

She leant forwards and kissed him softly on the lips. 'That's cool,' she said.

'Honestly?'

'Whatever happens happens. I like you. It's a good start.'

Yeah. It was a good start. Glenn liked the feel of that kiss. He liked getting the scent of her up close as well. He glanced at his watch. 'Shit,' he said. 'We'd better go find Gizmo.' It was four hours since he'd left him on the banks of the Seine.

Bethany stared at him. 'Who the hell's Gizmo?' she said.

'Ah, well . . .' He scraped back his chair. It wasn't easy to describe Gizmo. 'He lives in the riad too. In Essaouira. He's part of the commune.' He tossed a few francs on the table.

'Right.' Bethany looped her patchwork bag over her shoulder. 'But Glenn . . .'

'Yeah?' He led the way out of the café. He hoped Giz wouldn't create a scene when Glenn introduced Bethany into their equation. He could just imagine him: *What d'you wanna complicate things for, man? She's just a girl. You don't know a thing about her.* But Glenn already knew everything that mattered. Call it instinct. Call it presentiment. He knew Bethany would turn out to be a good thing.

'If you're living in Morocco, what are you doing in Paris, anyway?'

The following day they spent most of the morning preparing a butternut-squash couscous with saffron and a zaalouk aubergine and tomato salad under the watchful eye of Hassan, Marion flapping through their ranks like a bird on the wing, making a comment about preparation here, adding a historical note there. Then it was time for questions.

Nell had been waiting for her chance. Grinding the threads, preparing the saffron into an infusion for cooking, had given her such a warm glow. And smelling the familiar scent, edgy yet sweet, had transported her back to the farmhouse in Roseland once more. Her mother had always maintained that saffron, like grapes, picked up flavours from the soil, and Nell was sure that their saffron was honeyed and gentler than the variety they were cooking with here. But they were both special.

'Why do we grow it, Mum?' Nell had asked her once. No one else seemed to, although all the local bakeries sold saffron buns. 'Have we always grown it?'

'Your grandmother did,' she said. 'And her grandmother before that. For as long as we know. Once upon a time most people grew a little saffron, but then most people stopped – for a while.'

'Because it was hard work?'

Her mother smiled. 'Very probably. Fashions change, people didn't want it.'

Privately, Nell found this hard to believe.

'Cheaper and easier alternatives came along.' Her mother gave her a knowing look.

Nell knew how she felt about cheaper and easier alternatives. *Grow fresh, make from fresh, be natural, don't cut corners . . .*

'But that didn't stop our family.' She looked proud of this fact. 'Sometimes you just have to stay true to what you believe in, Nell.' Her eyes had grown misty. What had she believed in? Nell thought she knew. She believed in love and family history. She believed in the Tarot and in destiny. She believed in nature and the countryside. And she certainly believed in the strength and power of saffron. But what else was there? What else was closeted away in her past, never to be believed in again?

'And they always grew it here?' Nell asked her. 'They always lived here?'

'For as long as we know,' she said again. That's what made it a legacy. *Stay true to what you believe in.* Nell believed in the saffron, too. Which was why it was so hard to accept – that soon the farmhouse and the land around it, the little field of saffron, wouldn't belong to her family any longer, if Callum had his way. *The full asking price . . .* It almost seemed like a conspiracy. Get Nell out of the way and then sell it – quick. *Then she'll have to get over it.* But whatever problems there were between them, Callum wouldn't do that to her, would he?

She'd consulted the Tarot last night. The reading had been dominated by the Moon card. The Moon was a tricky one. Nell had stared at the image and focused hard. The Moon's light was dim, the pool at the bottom of the card representing the subconscious mind – which meant uncertainty and that she must trust her instincts. Something might be hidden, not yet out in the open. All the facts had yet to be revealed. So she must tread carefully and avoid making hasty decisions. Because drawing the Moon could be a warning.

Now, she raised her hand and took a deep breath. 'I wanted to ask you about saffron,' she said. This seemed like a good opportunity. Saffron had filled her mother's mind – at least throughout every October and November, during the blooming, harvesting and drying processes. And often during the winter months, too, when a pinch of saffron in a rice pilaf or a chicken stew could somehow add that missing touch of sunshine from the summer past. Just a few delicate threads were all that were needed to turn an ordinary meal into something rather extraordinary. So surely saffron could tell Nell something about her mother? *What was the bad thing that happened? Why could you never tell me what I needed to know? Why did you do it that way . . .?*

'Yes?'

'Can you tell us more about the history of saffron? How it's grown in Morocco? What recipes it's used in?' Nell knew that it had often featured in English recipes from the sixteenth to the early eighteenth century, and that it had been superseded in Britain by 'new ingredients' such as vanilla, cocoa and cane sugar, which was when most people stopped growing it. Later still, artificial food colouring would have been cheaper and easier to use than saffron, and the arrival of synthetic chemicals would have made it redundant as a dye. *Stay true to what you believe in . . .* But surely the time was ripe for an English revival?

'That's rather a lot of questions.' But Marion sounded pleased.

'Whatever you can tell us,' Nell amended. She was sure she wouldn't be disappointed. At least as far as food was concerned, Marion was a walking encyclopedia.

Marion beamed. 'Many people believe it originated in the Orient,' she began. 'And it's certainly true that cultivation was widely spread in Asia Minor, far before the birth of Christ. But in fact it was first grown in Crete. And I believe I'm right in saying that one of the first historic references to the use of saffron comes from Ancient Egypt, where it was used by figures such as Cleopatra as an aromatic and seductive essence.' She coughed, slightly embarrassed.

Nell suppressed a giggle. Saffron as an aphrodisiac? Her mother hadn't told her that one.

'In classical Greece it began to be used as a dye and possibly for its healing qualities,' Marion went on. 'And the Berbers of Morocco, who also used it in cooking, took saffron to Spain during the Muslim conquest of the eighth century. So you can see that it has a long history in this country, too.'

And in England, thought Nell. Saffron had certainly got around.

'The word "saffron" derives from the Arab word *zafaran*, meaning "yellow",' said Marion. '*Zafran* – as it is called here in Morocco – is essential to our cuisine. You probably realize that already. It is the taste we love. But it is also the colour.' She looked around to ensure they were all still with her. 'It can be used in a tagine, in rice, in couscous, as we have seen today, in sauces and in soups.' She raised her arms in the air as if to thank the heavens for the spice. 'Saffron is an ingredient imbued with an air of exoticism, sensuality and beauty.' She looked around her audience once more. 'We will be cooking with it again. It's a special ingredient, and valuable, too, so there are many imitations.' She touched her nose and nodded knowledgeably. 'Beware in the souks. Not all *zafran* is true *zafran*.'

'Isn't it more highly priced than gold?' put in one of the German women.

'Comparing by weight, yes, it is.'

'And where is it grown?'

'In Morocco it's grown on saffron farms.'

Nell's interest quickened. 'Where are they? You mentioned Taliouine?'

'Yes. The most famous are situated there in the foothills of the Sirwa Mountains. Most of them are still family owned. But there are others nearer here. It's possible to make a day trip from Marrakech,' she said. 'Many people do.'

Possible to . . . And it was the beginning of November. Chances were that the saffron was being harvested even as they spoke, and it could go on for a few weeks. It was too good an opportunity to miss. But this course didn't include any trips to saffron farms and neither did they have enough free time. It was tempting. But how could she possibly fit in a visit to a saffron farm?

'There is a myth attached to saffron,' said Marion. She turned to Nell. 'If you are interested in the spice, you may already know it, my dear.'

Nell shook her head. 'No, I don't.' Her mother had never told her any myth. But she couldn't wait to hear it.

'The legend tells that a handsome youth, Crocus, set out in pursuit of the nymph Smilax in the woods near Athens after he saw her dancing with her friends in a glade.' Marion smiled indulgently. 'He neglected his friends and his family. He was bewitched by her.'

They waited for her to continue. Nell wondered if Marion had ever been bewitched by anyone. She couldn't imagine it somehow; she was far too practical.

'Smilax was flattered by his amorous advances at first, but all too soon she tired of his attentions. He continued his pursuit; she resisted. She longed to be free to laugh and dance and swim with her friends.' Marion sighed, as if she might be secretly longing for the same things herself. 'Finally, she grew so fed up that she cast a spell on the poor youth and transformed him into a saffron crocus. Its radiant orange stigmas were said to hold the glow of an undying and unrequited passion. He became a small purple flower with a heart of golden fire.'

There was a brief silence in the room and then someone said, 'Goodness.' Someone else laughed and someone else again began to clap. 'What a great story. You're a mine of information, Marion.'

Marion laughed and blushed to the roots of her hair.

But Nell was thinking of the men who used to live with them at the cottage. None of them stayed for long, but each one seemed to be almost bewitched by Nell's mother, with her Tarot cards, her easygoing ways and her sense of fun. Each one would stay and do some jobs in the farmhouse in return for his keep, and each year, come autumn, he would be gone. My God, she thought. Her mother was Smilax!

'You're married,' Amy said.

They were in the hammam, steaming their bodies clean, just as the women who lived in this city did it, not under a shower for five minutes with a few blobs of gel, but in a way that truly deep-cleansed the pores, the way these people considered necessary. To get really clean you had to sweat it right out, apparently. There were still public washhouses used for the ordinary morning wash. This, then, was more of a ritual. It had been Amy's idea.

'We have to try it,' she had said after lunch, when Nell had been considering lazing on the sun terrace at the top of the riad with a book; it was sunny and sheltered and surprisingly warm for the time of year. 'We have to get under the skin of the country – literally.'

And Nell had remembered that Marion had said something

like that about the food, too, and so half reluctantly she had agreed to come along. It would be an authentic experience, and she could read a book in the sun some other day.

'Yes, I'm married.' Even to her own ears the words lacked conviction. Nell thought of Callum. Did he still love her? Did she still love him? There was so much she wasn't sure of. But what she did know was that he couldn't accept the sadness in her life, the current chaos of her mind. *He didn't really know her.* The thought crept up on her through the heat and the damp and the steam. They were married, but he didn't really know what went on inside her.

'But don't you find it hard to be yourself?' Amy's voice was muffled in the steam. It competed with the sound of running water, the clatter of buckets – for you had to take not only soap but a bucket of hot water and a bucket of cold in with you – and the disembodied murmur from the other women in the hammam, gossiping in their sing-song Arabic voices.

'Myself?' Nell felt herself beginning to relax. It was almost impossible not to. In here, she wondered if she could lose herself. Just let it all slip away . . .

'Isn't it hard to keep your own identity? Hard to do your own thing – you know, your cookery and stuff – when someone else is around all the time?'

Nell knew exactly what she meant. She closed her eyes for a moment. Allowed the sensuality of the hammam experience to drift over her, to reach her very core. 'Sometimes I think there are so many bits of me,' she said. She opened her eyes again. Something about being here in the positively slovenly heat, feeling the grime of the city sliding from her skin, was making her say more than she usually would. It was an intimate situation – to be naked in a steamy room with a woman you hardly knew, not to mention all these other women, whom she knew even less. It was revealing – even though superficially she could see so little in the fog of heat and dim light. Perhaps she was getting rid of much more than the grime from her inner pores?

'There's the bit that's passionate about cooking,' she went on. 'There's the bit that still belongs in the farmhouse I grew up in with my mother . . .' Her voice wavered, but she plunged on. 'And there's the bit that's married to Callum.'

'So you're saying he only has part of you?'

'Sort of.' Nell wasn't quite sure how to explain. And she didn't know how substantial that part was either. She used to think it was a big slice. But it seemed to be diminishing rather than growing stronger. 'Sometimes I feel as if I have a secret self,' she mused.

Amy nodded, as if this made sense to her. Her head was thrown back and her eyes were closed. Her short dark hair was damp and clung to her scalp, her face glistened with per-spiration. 'Does it matter?' she asked. 'Is it enough?'

Nell decided to be honest. 'I used to think so,' she said. 'Now . . . I'm not sure.' She thought of how long it was since she and Callum had made love. She hadn't told anyone about that, not even Lucy. It wasn't right, she knew it wasn't right, and she didn't want Lucy to tell her so. And it also wasn't right that she and Callum hadn't even talked about it. Did he still want her? Did she want him? She glanced towards the walls of the building, which looked like smooth concrete. They, too, were sweating, glistening with water droplets; the only light filtered in through the green squares of glass in the ceiling. Callum was still an attractive man. She was still a sexual woman. But since her mother died, she just hadn't felt it. What had happened to her? Had her grief made her emotionally dead?

'Hmm.' Amy stretched her long, slender body and yawned languorously. 'That must be why I'm not married.'

'Never even been tempted?' Amy was a striking-looking woman. Not pretty – her features were too strong for that – and not beautiful. Her nose was perhaps too long, her forehead too broad. But her high cheekbones and intelligent eyes gave her a look of class and confidence and there was a quirk of humour to her mouth. Nell had been right. She was a kindred spirit. Lucky Nell. A Moroccan cookery course and a new friend. She, too, stretched, and surrendered herself to the wet mist of heat. She felt as if she were floating. It was another world entirely from the steam room at the gym.

Amy had also insisted they both have a massage. This had involved what seemed like a lot of cracking of joints followed by a violent body scrub with a rough cloth from a very large lady. They had sluiced water over one another and were now repeating the steaming process for the last time. Already her cleansed skin felt silky and soft, but Nell wasn't looking forward to the icy water that was apparently in store for them at the end.

'Not really. I frighten them all away.' Amy laughed, but Nell caught the vulnerability behind her words. 'I'm tall. I'm opinionated.' She opened her eyes. 'Hey, you don't think the two things go together, do you?'

Nell laughed with her. 'No, I don't. You're strong. I wish I had half your strength. Since Mum died the way she did . . .' Nell tailed off. Despite the heat of the hammam and the pleasure of unburdening, she didn't know her quite well enough for that – not yet.

But Amy reached out and squeezed her hand. Her touch was warm, damp and reassuring. 'You'll find your feet,' she said. 'You've got to give yourself time to grieve. To start again without her – as your own woman.'

'Mmm.' Amy didn't know the details, Nell thought. And yet still, she seemed to understand. Her own woman. She hadn't managed it so far, and she had no clear idea of how to begin.

CHAPTER 10

Jake had told her she should visit the Saadian Tombs to see the architecture and mosaic tiling, but the following day was so crisp and sunny that Amy decided instead to visit the Majorelle Garden, designed by the French artist Jacques Majorelle in the twenties and thirties. It gave her a definite sense of satisfaction to be veering off the path he had laid for her. Perhaps that was her problem – she'd always been a rebel.

She had just stepped into the walkway lined with tall, majestic bamboo gently quivering in the faint breeze when her mobile rang. It was an unknown number. She answered it, sitting down on a bench for a moment. The polished tile walkway stretched in front of her like a promise; the curtain of bamboo planting was elegant and lush; and the sky peeped out above it, clear autumn blue.

'Hello. Amy?'

She recognized that growly voice. She wondered if thinking about him had somehow conjured him up. And, if so, she should stop. 'How did you get my number?' This was her second thought. If she didn't much like him, was it because he was interfering with her work? Or was it for some other reason?

'From Duncan. Is it a problem? Can you talk?' His voice had been warm at first, but she heard it change. She supposed she hadn't been very friendly.

'Sorry,' she said. 'You just took me by surprise, that's all. How's everything going?'

'Great. Later this morning I'm having a meeting with one of those artists I told you about. And we've already set up the cookery workshop.' She heard the enthusiasm in his voice. He'd certainly thrown himself straight into the project. Duncan would be pleased.

'Sounds good.'

'And how are things your end?'

'Fine, fine.' Amy suddenly couldn't remember a thing from the list he'd given her – apart from the Saadian Tombs, that was. Perhaps she shouldn't have thrown it away. 'I'm in the Majorelle Garden. It's stunning.'

'Good.' He didn't sound too impressed. Perhaps he thought it was too much of a tourist thing.

'And I took loads of street shots yesterday. The city's amazing.'

'Yeah. I loved it, too.'

'You've been to Marrakech?' But, of course, he'd said he'd spent time in Morocco; he would have visited this city.

'I certainly have.' He laughed. 'That's how I knew what to suggest you looked for.'

'Ah.' Amy wondered if she'd jumped to conclusions about him. Had he simply been offering his expertise, trying to help?

'And I've had another idea.' She could picture him pacing up and down, tearing his hands through that spiky hair. Or leaning back in his office chair and stretching out his legs. Or making loopy notes in that damned exercise book of his.

'What about?'

'The music.'

'Oh, yes?' She remembered him mentioning this at their first meeting.

'I'd opt for Gnawa. They call it trance music. It's very big over there. One place is particularly renowned for it.'

'Trance music?' She wasn't too sure about that.

'I thought you could go there, have a listen, talk to some of the musicians, see if any of them might be interested in coming over for the event.'

His enthusiasm was contagious. Amy was beginning to realize just how much of an event Jake wanted this to be.

And he was still talking. 'They might even have a contact in the UK. What do you think?'

At least he was asking her opinion. Amy could visualize a gig on the waterfront, or in one of Lyme's pubs. Or perhaps the Marine Theatre might be interested. They could easily link in another venue. 'It sounds like a good idea.' She couldn't tell him, but she also had her own agenda to find time for. 'What's the name of the place?'

'Essaouira.'

'I've heard of it.' She frowned. 'Vaguely. Where is it exactly?'

'It's on the west coast. Jimi Hendrix stayed there once. It's a beach resort with a difference.'

'It sounds a bit touristy,' Amy said pointedly. The last thing she wanted to do was trail off to some coastal town with big hotels and no atmosphere, just to listen to some trance music. And it would take far too much of her allotted time. 'Can't you just listen to some of them on YouTube and then send them an email?'

'I think it would be a good idea to go there.' Jake sounded as if he meant to get his own way. 'You could do a small detour, couldn't you?'

'I only have a few more days.' And she didn't want to waste it in a beach resort. 'I'd rather spend a day or two in Fez,' she said. 'Or even Casablanca.' Those cities sounded more like the kinds of places Glenn would have gone to. And much more interesting from the point of view of the project – photographically speaking.

She heard him sigh. 'Amy . . .'

'I've got to go.'

'Hang on a minute, Amy.'

'Sorry. Bye.' She ended the call. Essaouira? She wasn't completely at his beck and call, whatever he might think. If he wanted to go there so much, he should go himself.

Amy wandered on down the walkway, through the tall palms, past the brightly painted urns of cobalt blue and powder yellow filled with cacti and honey-scented jasmine which bordered the tiled fountains; over narrow blue trellised bridges and under wooden pergolas of hot-pink bougainvillea and trailing vines. She paused by a lake of floating water lilies, took some shots of the water rippling through sunlight and shadow. It was the end of the flowering season, but this place was still a tropical paradise. She'd never seen such vibrant waves of colour.

There was an art exhibition and a café; all the buildings were of Moorish design and all painted blue and yellow. Amy drifted into one of these to find some old posters of Yves St Laurent collections of the seventies, the word 'Love' intertwined with images of snakes, hearts and the female form. *Love* . . . Had Glenn been a bit of a flower child? she wondered. Had he got lost wandering around the world? Was that why he had never come home? Yves St Laurent had owned the gardens since 1980, and his ashes had been scattered here when he died, according to the information she read. It was a good place. Amy took so many pictures . . . At this rate it would be almost impossible to decide which ones to choose for her exhibition.

All the blue in the garden made Amy think about the faded blue door pictured on the postcard, and she took it from her bag to look at it once more. That was why the place was so anonymous. Blue seemed to be the national colour of Morocco. It was everywhere. And as for the flower carved above the portal . . . she'd seen plenty of similar carvings here in Marrakech, not of flowers particularly, but of animals and strange runic designs. Viewed as a whole, it was an unusual image – the door was so old, the carving so emblematic, the tiles and crumbling stone so evocative of a lost era . . . And yet it could be anywhere.

She thought of the day her Great-aunt Lillian had first told her about Glenn. She had picked up his photograph in her aunt's living room. 'Who's this?' she had asked.

'My son.'

'You've got a son?' Ten-year-old Amy tried to work out what relation he would be to her. Cousin? Second cousin? Uncle? He would be her mother's cousin, she thought. 'I didn't know that. Where is he now?'

Her aunt had stared out of the window of the cottage in Lyme as if she hoped he might stroll down the street at any moment. 'I have no idea,' she said.

Amy had frowned. Her aunt's sadness made her feel so helpless. And how could you have no idea of the whereabouts of your own son?

'He left home when he was twenty-one years old,' her aunt elaborated. 'There were lots of reasons.'

Amy wondered what they were. 'And what happened?'

'He never came back.'

Amy had stared at her, uncomprehending. She could understand him leaving. But why would he never come back?

'He travelled around a lot,' her aunt said. 'He couldn't write to me. There were reasons – too complicated to explain to you now, my dear. But he did write to me once. He sent me this postcard.' And she had showed it to Amy.

'Is it from another country?' she had whispered.

'Yes.' And her aunt turned it over to show her the stamp. 'Morocco.'

Amy had studied the handwriting as if it would give her

some clue. It was large and untidy. But she had no idea where Morocco might be.

Dear Mom, it said. *Just to let you know I am fine. Hope to see you again one of these days. Love.* And then his name, scrawled: *Glenn.*

And now? Would Glenn – if he were still alive – ever guess that his mother had moved back to England to care for her sister? And could she really have been cruel to Mary? What had she done? She was such a gentle soul; so generous and kind. Amy couldn't imagine.

She was just having a coffee and thinking about returning to the riad for lunch when her mobile rang again. Couldn't he leave her alone for five minutes? She smiled. She wouldn't change her mind. She might be working with the man, but her itinerary was her own affair.

But she saw immediately that it was Duncan. 'Hello, sweetheart,' he said. 'How goes it?' Dulcet tones. Dulcet Duncan, she found herself thinking.

'I suppose he asked you to ring me?'

'He?'

'Jake Tarrant.' Even the name sounded threatening to her peace of mind.

'No, why? Has something happened?'

'No.' Apart from the fact that she wasn't being trusted to do her job, apart from the fact that she wasn't being consulted, apart from the fact that ignoring his pathway and being set on her own meant she had to get it right.

'I just phoned to see how you were,' Duncan said. 'Look, Amy, I know I should have told you about Jake —'

'You should, yes.' Amy felt her shoulders tense. These conversations on her mobile were undoing all the relaxation and de-stressing achieved in that hammam yesterday afternoon. And she had felt so good — even the final shower of icy water had been exhilarating.

'But I knew you wouldn't like it.'

'Even so,' she said.

'Even so. You and I, Amy . . .'

You and I . . . In truth, there was no she and Duncan. She was a distraction for him, a bit of fun and friendship, nothing more. And he was a diversion for her, a way of persuading herself that she had her life under control; that everything was going well. Who needed a man in your life when you had a career you were passionate about? Who needed someone to come along and take control and make demands until your very identity was under threat? Amy had no intention of being trapped, of losing the things that made her what and who she was. She thought of her conversation with Nell. It clearly wasn't working for her, was it?

'We have a special relationship,' he went on. 'It's important to me.'

'But so is the gallery,' said Amy.

'Well, of course, so is the gallery.' She heard his tone change.

'Don't worry, Duncan,' she said. 'I want the best for the gallery, too. If I'd known you wanted the Moroccan event to be so big, I would have understood that we had to bring in an events manager.'

'You would?'

'Of course.' *But you should have told me.* She couldn't believe he didn't get that.

'Good girl. That makes me feel so much better.'

If he said 'good girl' to her one more time, Amy thought that she might scream. Here and now, in this tranquil setting of tropical green and cobalt blue, she would just open her mouth and let it out. Loudly. 'But about our special relationship . . .'

'Yes?'

Duncan had never made any promises. He had never let her think that there might be more. Had she wanted more? Maybe she thought she did at first – women were always supposed to want more. But the truth was that she'd been drawn to Duncan because he was what he was – smooth, sexy, self-obsessed; too tied up with work to want to control her, too selfish for love. He'd never been relationship material, and she knew it. Duncan was safe. Unthreatening to her peace of mind. She had imagined he was exactly what she wanted. But she'd been wrong. She wanted more. 'From now on I'd like to formalize things.'

'Formalize things?' He sounded confused.

'I work for you, Duncan, and I work with you. For now.' She'd give him that to think about. 'But, in the future, I'd like to be consulted about anything that affects me, and I'd appreciate it if you treat me as an employee rather than . . .' Words failed her. '. . . anything else.'

'Oh. You mean . . .?'

'Exactly,' she said. She shouldn't have let it happen in the first place. Francine had said as much, and she was about the only person Amy had told, the only friend she knew wouldn't judge her. Keeping this from her had been the last straw. That and the expression in Jake Tarrant's rooibos-tea-coloured eyes.

There was a pause. 'Perhaps we should talk about this when you get back, Amy, my sweet,' he said. 'You sound upset.'

'I'm not upset,' she insisted. Though she was, a bit.

'But why? There's no one else. We're not hurting anyone.'

And there never would be anyone else if she let it drag on. Which wasn't a problem. What was the problem was that her relationship with Duncan made her feel dishonest – as if she wasn't being true to herself. It was Nell and the hammam that had led her to this conclusion. Nell's raw emotions – about her mother's death, about her husband. She was in trouble, but at least she wasn't pretending. 'I don't want to discuss it any further,' she said in her firmest voice. 'Goodbye, Duncan.'

Amy looked around her at the broad palms and the trickling fountain. And she felt a load lift from her shoulders. Nice. Another kind of freedom.

CHAPTER 11

Lillian took the X53 to Bridport. It was a cold day and she had to wait at the stop by the clock tower, where a wicked breeze could catch you as if it fully intended to whip you out to sea. But Lillian kept out of it, and besides, she was well wrapped up.

She'd been back to Bridport several times when she first returned to Dorset. It was her childhood home, and when she came back to England from America she'd fully intended making her home there once again. But once she saw how poorly Mary was, once she took in the state of things here in Lyme with Mary's family – her family . . . Well, she decided she'd better stay close.

Lillian saw the bus coming and got her bus pass out of her bag and ready, making sure to put her gloves in her bag first – they were soft brown leather and a present from Amy; she didn't want to lose those. After that, she supposed, there was little reason to go back there. There was a big supermarket – but what use did she have for that? There was a buzzing antique and vintage market – but she was vintage enough herself not to require one of those, thank you very much. And there was her history. That *was* something she needed – sometimes.

Lillian took her place in the queue and climbed on to the bus, making sure she held on to the rail with a firm grip. She'd been more careful since her fall — with her failing eyesight, she had to be. Her independence had been hard won; she didn't want to lose it now. She showed the bus driver her pass and briefly mourned the days of conductors who had time for a cheery conversation as they punched your ticket and swung and clattered up and down the spiral stairs. Upstairs, she decided, taking a deep breath and launching herself up on to the first step. She headed for the front seats. It was worth the climb for the view.

Lillian settled herself, put her bag on her lap and waited for the bus to tackle the hill. She loved Lyme Regis, too. She gazed out of the window at the countryside, which was finally accepting that it was winter. The trees had mostly lost their leaves, the undergrowth had grown sparse, the flowers had all but disappeared. There were still blackberry stumps in the hedges, but they'd mostly rotted or been eaten by birds. There were some bright holly berries too and she even spotted an occasional red campion. But it was a winter landscape, and it would be several long months, she thought, with a small shiver, until spring.

Lillian had kept a diary once. She'd started it when war was declared, although she was still only a child. She understood more than they thought, though. She understood that there was a need for a record, for something more permanent, with the world becoming more fragile, more precarious, more anxious. But the world had also become more exciting — especially when the GIs came to Bridport.

She chuckled at this thought and turned it into a cough when she saw the woman on the other side of the aisle giving her a sharp look. Mustn't let anyone think she was talking or laughing to herself – Heaven forbid. At this, Lillian almost chuckled again but managed to hold it in. She settled back in her seat. She'd kept the diary right through to when the troops left the town – she hardly missed a day. And then she started writing to him instead, and she had no need to keep the diary any more. She'd destroyed it a long time ago, before she even went to America; it was part of her girlhood, her old life. She'd have no need of it, she thought, once she became a woman.

They were lucky in Dorset – everyone said so. There were no serious air raids and hardly any bombs, though Father insisted they erect their own Anderson shelter in the back garden – with the help of the local Boy Scouts – and they had to run there sometimes when the siren sounded, whether dinner was on the table or not. Lillian hated the cold, corrugated-steel building, but Father said it was their lifeline and that they could sleep in it if necessary, although they never did.

Lillian had seen a German bomber, though. Two planes flew in from the sea one Sunday when she and Father were crossing West Allington Bridge, so low that she could see the swastikas, and one let loose a load on East Street, destroying a row of houses there. She'd never forget the wail of the siren, the crump of the bombs, the shattering of glass. Father pulled her down, and they stayed there for several long moments after the explosion. They were shaking, both of them. Some-one said the Jerries had been aiming for Gundry's; someone else said the railway station. But what they got were houses. And people. Just ordinary people. Lillian sighed. After the bombing, the crater that was left filled up with water, and Lillian saw boys with jars and nets fishing for tadpoles. Despite everything, she'd had to smile.

They weren't as short of food as many – or so Mother kept telling them. Bridport was a rural town, so there were farms all around where farmers grew crops and kept animals. They had a garden big enough to grow all their own vegetables and some for their neighbours besides. Everyone shared what they had. 'Dig for victory,' they were told, and they didn't need telling twice. They grew potatoes, runner beans, sugar-snap peas, purple flowering broccoli, beetroot, cabbage and onions. They kept chickens for eggs and when they stopped laying they made a handsome Sunday lunch. Lillian's mother was good at making a little go a long way. There was a milk factory in Beaminster. And there were rabbits – everywhere. There was fishing off West Bay for mackerel and conger eel. 'We won't starve,' Mother said. 'Don't you worry.'

They had to keep to the blackouts – you could be fined for an infringement of the rules – and Lillian found this gloomy and depressing. There were fundraisers and concert parties, though, put on by the Blackout Brighteners and others. As a family, they often played cards or sat around the wireless set with their cocoa to listen to music and comedy, like, *It's That Man Again* with Tommy Handley, which was Lillian's favourite.

'Designed to boost the spirits,' Father said. And he was probably right. On a more serious note, Father liked them all to listen to the regular news bulletins in the evening, and sometimes a speech by Winston Churchill or an address by the Queen to the women of Britain, who were being encouraged to do their bit to help the war effort. And they did.

Mother was a member of the Women's Institute and worked for the WVS organizing transport, distributing pamphlets and emergency food rations, caring for old people and casualties. Unlike most men in Bridport, who worked in the rope and net industry, Father was an engineer in an aircraft and maintenance factory outside of town, but he still had to do Fire Guard duty of up to forty-eight hours a month. He hadn't been called up because of his occupation and because he was already forty-two years old. And then there was Mary. At eighteen, she was just too young in 1943 to be conscripted. She worked in the same factory as Father, helping to make aircraft parts.

Lillian remembered the day the GIs marched into town. How could she forget? She was in Bucky Doo Square and they walked right past her towards the White Lion and the house opposite, which was to be their billet. Handy for a pint of Palmers beer, she couldn't help thinking, even then. It was November 1943, and she didn't know it – not then – but they were coming to be part of the D-Day invasion the following June. Probably, they didn't know it either. They must have wondered what on earth they were doing here in this God-forsaken place, where it was damp and cold and everything was rationed and where children followed them around, shouting, 'Hello, Yank,' and hoping for gum or sweets to be thrown their way.

It was a few weeks later that Lillian met Ted. What did people say about them? Overpaid, oversexed and over here? Certainly the GIs, with their smart, well-tailored khaki uniforms, made their own soldiers look scruffy. The Americans all looked like film stars. Lillian had no idea how her father had come across this particular GI or why he was in their home about to share their dinner. She couldn't imagine what he would think of their little semi-detached house with the stained-glass panel in the front door, the French windows that led from the dining room into the garden, the simple rugs on wooden floors, the lino in the kitchen and bathroom. But she knew what she thought of him. She was bowled over. What she saw was someone tall and broad-shouldered, with warm brown eyes, a firm, shadowed and cleft chin and dark-brown cropped hair. Her very own Rhett Butler. She almost swooned.

'Pleased to meet you,' she stuttered when Father introduced them. Why was she trembling like this? Why was she so short of breath?

'And I'm sure pleased to meet you, Lillian.' His voice was deep but soft as velvet. 'I've brought you all some cookies as a small thank-you for inviting me to your house today. Here.' He gave her the packet of biscuits he was holding and shot her a broad smile. And then she saw him register what – or who – was behind her, and she saw his expression change. Ted had seen Mary. And, like every other man before him, he was instantly smitten.

Lillian sighed and, like she always did, made way.

'Goodness me.' Mary was regarding Ted in that way she had, her eyes teasing. 'What do we have here?'

'Ted . . . Meet my elder daughter, Mary,' said Father. 'So, girls, we're fortunate that these brave American soldiers have come over here to help us win this war. It's our job to make them feel welcome and appreciated. To give them a taste of British family life.'

'And have you been welcomed?' Mary asked him. 'Have you been appreciated?' She moved over to the fireplace, where there was a coal fire burning, and flashed a look back at him. Her eyes told him that she could manage both single-handedly. She laughed, as if the whole thing were a joke anyway.

Lillian could see that he was entranced by her. And who wouldn't be? Her sister Mary was eighteen years old and beautiful, slender-waisted but curvy in all the right places. Lillian looked down at her own skinny fourteen-year-old body. Shouldn't she be growing a little more – in those places? She still looked like a boy. Whereas Mary . . .

Although there was clothes rationing and they were all supposed to 'look better on less', very few managed it like her sister. Tonight she was wearing a floral-print frock, a woollen jacket and rayon stockings. Lillian guessed that she'd swiftly got changed when she realized a handsome stranger had come to dinner. Her lips were a rosebud of crimson, her skin was creamy, her cheeks had a blush of rouge and she smelt of

Mother's eau de cologne. Her hair was dark and lightly curled and her eyes were dark as violets. She looked like a film star, too, thought Lillian miserably. They were a perfect match.

'Thank you, Lillian. I'll take those.' Her mother whisked the biscuits away from her and took them through to the kitchen, where, no doubt, they would be rationed out for the days ahead. Lillian looked after them longingly.

Meantime, Ted had taken off his cap. 'It's a friendly town, Miss,' he said to Mary. 'We sure don't have any complaints.'

'Call me Mary,' she said. 'Sit down. Tell me everything.' Her voice was at once both feminine and confiding. Lillian vowed to practise this tone tonight before bed. *Tell me everything*, she whispered silently to herself.

'Everything!' He laughed – loud and hearty – and the family laughed with him.

They were all aware, Lillian thought now, that no one knew everything, and especially not a GI billeted in Bridport. He was waiting. They were all waiting. Everyone knew something was going to happen, but no one quite knew what. There were exercises that went on, training for something. There was a sense of a build-up, but no one knew what they were building up to.

'How do you like our food, for a start?' Mary asked him.

'Well, now . . .' He sat on one of their barley twist chairs, put his elbows on the white tablecloth Mother had spread on the table. 'Some of the boys complain about the Brussels sprouts and the cabbage' – he grinned – 'but you won't hear that from me – no, ma'am.'

'Would you like a cup of tea?' Mother asked him, and Lillian saw him try not to wince. She guessed that English tea wasn't to the taste of GIs any more than sprouts.

'Thank you, ma'am,' he said. 'You're an angel.'

She laughed and brushed away the compliment, though Lillian could tell she was as charmed as they all were. 'It must seem very strange to you boys.' Mother shook her head. 'This country, the people, our different customs, and so on.'

'Your roads are pretty narrow,' he admitted, 'and it sure ain't easy to find our way around with no signposts and all these little lanes all over the place.'

Father nodded. 'All the signposts have been taken down,' he confirmed. 'Got to confuse the Nazis, you see, lad.'

'Yes, sir.' Ted nodded.

'Are you planning on keeping us safe from now on?' Mary's voice dropped almost to a whisper. 'Can you do that?'

'I sure would always do my best to fulfil that obligation.' He winked, and Mary laughed again, until their father shot her a glance of disapproval. 'It would be a privilege.'

'So you say.' Playfully, Mary tapped him on the arm. 'But how do we know it's true? After all, you might be big and strong, but you can't stop the bombs falling, now, can you?'

'Believe me, I would if I could.' Already he was eying her with the admiration Lillian had observed in others before him.

Men fell in love with Mary all over the place. It was utterly unfair. She already had a whole queue of them. There was Tony, a pilot, who took her out to lunch at the British

Restaurant whenever he was on leave; Michael, who was in the navy and 'positively yearned' after her – so she said; Tristran, who was on a special secret mission somewhere that no one was supposed to know about . . . And that wasn't even counting any of the local farming lads like Johnnie Coombes who hadn't gone to war for one reason or another. It was more than enough for any girl. And yet Mary always seemed to need to add to the number. In fact, Mary seemed to want any male attention she could get. And she had a recklessness in her eyes, a sense of devil may care in her words that somehow suited these times of war.

'Hmm.' Again she assessed him from under her lashes. 'Then I rather think that you and I shall get on, GI Ted.'

He grinned. 'I sure do hope so. And I also hope you'll do me the honour of accompanying me to the dance next Saturday?'

He was a quick worker himself, Lillian thought. She saw her father's expression as he got to his feet, switched on the standard lamp and returned to the table.

'Dance?' Mary sounded as if she had no prior knowledge of such an event. As if the weekly dance wasn't something that she spent the rest of the week planning for.

It was a lost cause, Lillian realized.

Mary had always been the golden girl. She knew how to manipulate their father and she knew how to please their mother. How did she do it? Yes, she was prettier, cleverer and more confident than Lillian. But she had something even more intoxicating – she had a sparkle of life about her. She was like champagne. You wanted to taste it and then you wanted more.

When Lillian was younger, she had idolized her sister. But Mary had little time for her. When she was supposed to be looking after her she simply took her with her to meet whatever boy had taken her fancy that month, and Lillian had to hang around, ignored and feeling a nuisance.

And now? Lillian stared at the oatmeal-coloured wallpaper with its flower-patterned border under the picture rail, at the bevelled mirror above the fireplace and the framed paintings of long-gone English landscapes on the walls. At anything rather than Mary and Ted. She could hardly eat her mother's rabbit casserole, although it was delicious and no one else was having any trouble. She half listened to the talk winging around her. Father talked of war and aircraft; Mother talked of her work at the WVS; Ted talked about America and how different things were there from here; and Mary listened, laughed and flirted. Was she interested in him? It was hard to tell, since Mary flirted with everyone.

When he left that night, he brought out more gifts. He was clearly a generous man. He presented Mary and Lillian with chocolates and their mother with a large tin of coffee.

'Heavens,' she said, looking at it suspiciously. 'Thank you, Ted.'

Lillian mumbled her thanks and took her chocolates up to her room, where she could watch Ted's departure and practise talking like her sister.

Mary saw him out, closing the door behind them to

protect the black-out, a torch in her hand, the beam shining downwards so that they could at least see where they were walking.

Lillian peered past the net curtain and into the night, the lights out in her room, her door shut behind her, watching them linger by the garden gate. Mary was talking softly, her hand resting on his arm, and then he said something and Lillian saw her nod. She was agreeing to go to the dance. She just knew it.

Most times, Lillian couldn't wait to hear Mary's stories of the weekly dance, which lately had featured the jive and the jitterbug, brought over by the GIs, who performed it with the British girls, somewhat controversially, according to Mary. 'All the old bags moan about it,' she had confided to Lillian. 'It's a bit loose.'

'How does it go?' Lillian had begged for a demonstration but Mary was already bored with her audience.

'You'll see one day,' she said. 'When you're sixteen.'

The bus was coming into Bridport bus station. Lillian realized she had daydreamed the journey away with these memories of the past. She took her gloves from her bag and pulled them on, doing up the clasp of the bag and listening for the sharp click. *When you're sixteen.* It was only one more year and a few months. And now, of course, it was so very long ago. But, at the time, the prospect had seemed like worlds away.

CHAPTER 12

Morocco, 1974

When they arrived at the riad, Glenn tried to see it through Bethany's eyes. He remembered only too well his first sight of the interior.

'Wow!' He'd turned to Gizmo and Howard and known his excitement shone in his eyes. Not very laid-back of him. But the place was so cool.

'Riad la Vieux Rose,' Gizmo had announced as proudly as if he'd built it. 'Some groovy pad, huh?'

Like most riads, from the outside it had seemed like nothing special. It was situated in the heart of the medina, within a maze of narrow streets which were as interlinked as a spider's web. Just a plain wooden door with a rose emblem carved above it. And as Gizmo put the key in the lock and pushed hard, the smell was fusty, as if the place were damp and no one had lived there for years. But inside . . .

The door opened into a wide living space full of old furniture in varying states of disrepair. Chaises longues, damp and matted cushions piled on top of wooden benches, a massive, pitted old table, rickety chairs. That musician guy who had dossed here before clearly hadn't bothered doing much. The wooden shutters were hanging off their hinges, the ceiling, although high and ornate, was badly cracked and stained with damp, and the coloured lanterns and lamps were dirty, some of them broken. There were wooden pillars, some of which had been daubed with graffiti and love and peace signs, though underneath you could see the red and gold of the brightly painted wood. The floor was filthy, and the tiles chipped. But Glenn could make out some of the intricate patterns in the cracked glaze. It looked like some ancient crimson-and-yellow runic design. It was pretty spectacular.

'Wow!' said Bethany.

Glenn grinned. The place looked much the same now, though they'd shifted a lot of the furniture and cleaned the floor. 'The kitchen's through here.' He led the way over some wooden planking that formed a walkway where the tiles were a bit dodgy.

'Yeah, like I'm interested in the kitchen.' Bethany rolled her eyes, but followed him anyway.

He laughed. It had been a tip when they first moved in, but they'd set it up now so that there was running water and they could cook tagines and heat water for baths on the old brazier. There wasn't electricity, but they had candles and oil lamps. Hell, it was a whole lot better than camping on the beach. 'Come upstairs.'

He led the way into the courtyard and up the wrought-iron spiral staircase. Upstairs was where the riad came into its own. Crumbling stone columns supported an upper courtyard with three rooms leading off it. Flaking white-painted ironwork edged the windows like lace.

'Through here.' He showed her his bedroom. Their bedroom.

'It's fab.' She dumped her bag on the floor tiles, sank on to the bed and draped herself suggestively on the worn satin coverlet. The ornate wrought-iron frame had been here when they first moved in, and Glenn had managed to buy a second-hand mattress. One of the guys he'd worked for had given him the quilt and a faded rug for the floor. He had put up some curtains and scrubbed the red-and-yellow tiles until they shone. There was a chest of drawers, a tallboy-cum-wardrobe and a sink over on the far side of the room, next to a massive cast-iron bath. The walls were tiled with mosaic work below battered cedar panelling.

'It's like some sultan's palace.' She stretched out and closed her eyes.

But Glenn wanted to show her the upper terrace. It was the riad's *pièce de résistance*. 'Come on,' he said.

Bethany opened her eyes and sat up. 'Why is it called the Riad of the Old Rose?' she asked.

'Did you see the emblem?'

'Uh huh.'

'It's the town's emblem. The six-petal rose of Mogador. That's what Essaouira was called back then. A whole bunch of houses have it carved over their entrances.'

'Nice.' Bethany climbed off the bed. 'How long have you been here?'

'Seven months or so, I guess. It's not so easy to leave.'

'I can imagine.'

Apart from the amazing space of Riad La Vieux Rose, Essaouira had proved to be one of the easiest places to live on a low budget. It wasn't always pretty, but it was real. Glenn had learnt a lot on the road. It wasn't all about hanging out in cafés discussing Jean-Paul Sartre or the lyrics of Leonard Cohen. Sometimes you couldn't even afford a cup of coffee. It wasn't all about writing poetry or dancing on the beach around a driftwood fire either, although he had done all these things. It was more than that, and less. It was often about scratching a living. With his reasonable French and speaking English, Glenn found that he could get some casual translating work, and the odd bit of teaching English as a foreign language came along, too. Here, if you had long hair and wore flared jeans and tie-dye, no one seemed to care. Moroccans were polyglots – they spoke in a constantly changing mix of Berber, Moroccan Arabic and French – and maybe this cosmopolitan quality extended itself into a welcome for everybody. It was the kind of place where you could be accepted, where you could hang loose, enjoy the warmth, the vibe and the music, and slowly become part of the community.

This, at any rate, was the side of Morocco he loved. There was a darker side, a political side, which he was aware of from the talk in the cafés, though Gizmo and Howard just didn't want to know. But Glenn had always been political, and old habits died hard. King Hassan II clearly had a conservative and firm grip on the country. He was known for being suspicious of those around him and ruthless against anyone who dared oppose him and, recently, there had been not one but two attempts against his life – one resulting in a coup lasting several days.

The whole thing made Glenn uneasy. For one thing, there were close and continuing ties between Hassan II's government and the CIA, who had helped to reorganize Morocco's security forces in 1960 – and Glenn was more than aware of his own dodgy position as far as the US authorities were concerned. And, for another, Hassan's fear of discontent had resulted in the 'Years of Lead' or *Zaman al-Rusas*, as the more political guys in the local cafés referred to them. Dissidents had been arrested, executed or simply 'disappeared'. Newspapers were closed down and books banned and burned. Opposition politics was a life-threatening activity in Morocco during the low points of the Years of Lead. Harassment of dissidents was commonplace and several outspoken anti-government activists were jailed and tortured or died mysteriously.

It wasn't, then, the ideal place to hang out for a pacifist and war resister like Glenn. Draft dodger, Howard would say. But what was a guy to do? The truth was that Essaouira's laid-back vibe made the political scene pretty easy to ignore. And so, that was more or less what Glenn did. This wasn't his country. He wouldn't get involved. He was in enough of a mess as it was.

As for the riad, Glenn, Gizmo and Howard weren't a match

made in heaven. Howard had seemed OK at first, but the truth was, he could be a miserable bastard, and Gizmo was solid crazy even for a freak, but he was also a survivor with a heart of gold and Glenn liked the guy. Even Howard could be a laugh – and he could always get hold of the best Moroccan kif. The deal between them was unspoken, but it fell into place from the start when the plumbing wouldn't work and Glenn and Gizmo just looked blankly from one to the other. They didn't have a clue. Howard did the practical stuff. Basically, he mended anything that was broken. So Glenn and Gizmo were left to share the chores: cooking, cleaning, laundry, those were their domains. And it worked out just fine. They cleaned the courtyard and the terrace by swilling buckets of water around, and they hung clothes, rugs and bedding on the balustrades and windowsills to air. They took turns to shop at the market and fish stalls and whoever cooked didn't have to clear up. Simple.

But, come the winter, things had taken a turn for the worse. Gizmo couldn't always go out busking, so he was broke; Glenn lost his translation work when the guy he worked for left for six months in the south of France; and Howard . . . well, Howard was just generally pissed with it being winter.

'We need to sharpen up.' He'd paced around the riad from dilapidated room to dilapidated room, examining draughty windows and broken doors. 'We've got to do some maintenance. Jeez. Take a look at this dump.'

'Yeah, but the rent's low, y'know.' Gizmo was as close at his heels as a friendly spaniel.

Howard turned on him. 'D'you wanna survive the winter, or what?' he said.

'We can keep warm.' Glenn was good at collecting driftwood. He walked for miles sometimes and they had a good stash. The brazier would heat the kitchen at least.

'We need more bread.' Howard slammed the door of the kitchen so that it rattled on its rusty hinges. 'I need to buy stuff.'

'I'm broke, man.' Gizmo pulled a sad face. 'No can do.'

'Then we've gotta do a deal.'

'What kind of a deal?' Glenn didn't like the expression on Howard's face. Scheming. And he didn't want to do any deal. Dealing drugs – even in Morocco, which was pretty much renowned for it – just wasn't a cool idea. He'd left America to avoid jail. He wasn't about to get banged up in some other country instead. No way.

But Howard insisted, and Gizmo supported him – like always – and no amount of arguing would change his mind. Howard had contacts – surprise, surprise. He knew how it could be done. He even had a run-down Seat 124 which he'd bought in Spain when he'd had a bit more bread. It was a simple matter to obtain hashish in Morocco. And everyone wanted it in France and the UK – to name but two countries. 'Morocco's all about trading,' he said. 'That's where it's at. Everyone does it. Everyone understands.'

'But how risky is it, man?' Gizmo asked. 'Me and the cops, we sure ain't good friends. I don't need no hassle, no way.'

He made the noise of a siren, so strikingly real that Glenn

nearly jumped out of his skin and Howard snapped at him. 'Shut the fuck up, this isn't some joke!'

'But –'

'Forget the cops,' Howard said. 'Strewth, man, what you should be worrying about are the drug barons. This here's a rich industry. And it's getting bigger all the time. They won't want us treading on their toes. You'd better believe it.'

Glenn stared at him. And this was supposed to make him feel better?

'Stay loose.' Howard clamped a hand on his shoulder. 'We'll keep it low key, small time. We ain't gonna get greedy. That's the trick, mate. Don't get greedy.'

Glenn didn't feel remotely greedy. He was so ungreedy he didn't want to do it at all. But it seemed he had little choice in the matter.

They all put in the last of their money and Howard bought the stuff.

'Hey, doncha think we should just –' Gizmo's eyes were alight.

'Forget it,' said Howard. 'This is business. And this is good stuff. We don't need to try it.'

Two of them should go together, they decided. Three would attract attention and be too threatening; one wouldn't be able to watch his own back. Two was perfect.

And it had gone OK. This time. They'd done the deal and made some money, and Howard had made the riad water-tight and ready for winter. They had enough food, they had enough beer and they had enough ganja of their own. The trouble was that the following spring Howard had wanted to do it again . . .

Glenn led the way up to the terrace, where there was a broken fountain and an ancient fig tree and where you could relax and listen to birdsong and the plaintive call to prayer. He knew Bethany would be knocked out. Howard had set up a grill on a flat stone up there, and Glenn often took a bucket down to the harbour to pick up sardines or mackerel, bringing them back to barbecue on the roof terrace. Howard had rigged up a sound system, too, using an old Sony cassette player and some speakers he'd managed to acquire. 'We gotta have sounds, man,' Gizmo had said. 'Birdsong just ain't always enough.'

Gizmo was up there already with Howard, who looked like he'd hardly moved from his habitual prone position on the mattress under the makeshift orange tent he'd created from a mangy old bedspread, which provided some much needed shade in the summer and protection from wind in the spring and autumn. He'd fixed the fountain, though, and it was dribbling water, albeit inconsistently, from its spout on to the cool and cracked blue tiles below.

'G'day, Giz,' Glenn heard him say. 'How'd it go?'

'Perfect, man.' Gizmo dangled a pouch in front of him.

It had been a bit hairy as far as Glenn was concerned. He'd half expected the car to conk out, though Howard was always confident in its abilities, but lucky for them it had made it. The borders and customs were dodgy, too – Gizmo might look like a freak but, weirdly, he also had an innocent look about him. There'd even been a police roadblock but the police had just shrugged and let them right on through. It was probably like coffee time or praying time or something. Glenn didn't want to do it again, though. They shouldn't push their luck. They'd have to find another way.

Howard grabbed the pouch from Gizmo and pushed himself up to sitting. He was about to empty it on to the low table next to the cushioned mattress. Then he clocked Bethany. He pulled the skull cap he wore through winter and summer further down his forehead and frowned. 'Who's this?' He tucked the pouch into the pocket of his cut-offs.

'Bethany, meet Howard.' Glenn performed the introductions.

'The last of the Three Musketeers?' Bethany quipped.

Howard winked at her but didn't get up. 'Didn't they tell you?' he said. 'I'm number one.' He looked from her to Glenn, and his eyes narrowed.

Bethany regarded him in that still, thoughtful way she had. 'It's a nice place you have here.' She looked around her, at the ancient and rusted iron chairs casting their shadows on the tiles, at the old fig tree and the dribbling fountain, the crumbling balustrade and the rooftop view of the medina. The sky above. 'Like a separate world. A safe haven.'

Glenn knew exactly what she meant. It was that feeling of being in an open space with the quiet of the dusty walls around you, looking up into the great expanse of the sky. You were in the bustling medina and yet there was a sense of tranquillity, of privacy, of containment. Everything in the riad happened in its centre. It was all about the solid walls protecting the heart within. It was a kind of security.

Howard shrugged. 'Everyone's escaping from some shit or another.'

And was it Glenn's imagination? Or did he give him one of those looks again?

Knowing Howard wouldn't have any food, they'd brought some with them – just cold stuff – and Glenn went down to the kitchen to get it together. They had beer, too. Glenn felt a warmth running through his veins. It was good to be back.

'So where did ya meet your friend?'

Glenn looked up. Howard was lounging in the doorway, a thin spliff held loosely between his brown fingers. He pushed his fair, matted hair from his eyes.

'Paris.'

'Paris! Jeez, man. And you and her, are you, like, together now? Just like that? Huh? When you just met her in Paris?' He drew sharply on the spliff, like he was angry or jealous or something.

'Pretty much.' Why was it such a big deal? They'd slept together – literally – squashed in the back of the car, and they'd kissed, long, passionate smooching that was never going anywhere. Not in the back of the car with Gizmo in the front. But he knew he wanted her.

Howard frowned. 'Does the little lady know what you were doing there?'

'Nope.' Glenn tore the bread into more manageable hunks and put a generous wedge on each plate. He didn't like

Howard calling her that. 'Little lady'. Bethany had asked him and he'd made up some story. He didn't like deceiving her, but he had the others to think of, too, and they'd sworn to be discreet.

'And would she be planning on staying, would you say?'

'Yeah. For a while.'

'Strewth, man.' Howard balled his fist and half turned away.

'What?'

'You could have asked.' He let the roach end of his spliff fall on to the kitchen floor and ground it under his boot.

Glenn stopped what he was doing. 'Is it a problem? Because if it's a problem we'll find us some other place.' He was mad. Why couldn't Howard just cool it? What was so bad about having a girl to stay? He might as well still be living with his parents.

'No worries.' Though Howard shook his head. 'We'll give her a trial period. See how it works out.'

'A trial period?' Glenn couldn't believe what he was hearing. 'Jesus, man. What is it with you, huh?'

'We're a community, mate.' Howard lowered his voice. 'It's a delicate balance, you know?' He picked up a plate. 'We're a democracy, yeah? We consult. We vote. We decide. Right?'

Glenn shrugged. Howard's rules. Maybe he *was* jealous. Maybe what he needed was a woman of his own. A woman of his own. It was a good thought. Glenn went up to the terrace to find her.

CHAPTER 13

Although the cookery course was pretty much full on, the organizers seemed to appreciate the fact that here they all were in a fascinating city and that they needed at least some time off to explore. This afternoon they had three whole hours, so Nell and Amy decided to go shopping. 'It's how women bond,' Amy said, laughing. 'And this is Marrakech. I hope you've got plenty of room in your suitcase.'

Nell had. As she had already discovered from their food-shopping trip, the northern part of the old city comprised mostly overlapping souks, each devoted to a different trade. Heading north up rue Souq as-Smarine, they were soon overwhelmed by copperwork, carpentry, and dyeing on their left; jewellery and leatherwork on their right. The main arteries of the medina were wider, the veins more narrow, some covered with bamboo or rushes for shade. Nell was grateful for that. The beating of the sun was like a weight on her head. There was just so much noise, so many people, such little space. She felt on edge, as if anything might happen.

They paused in Rahba Kedima. 'It's the former slave market, apparently,' Amy said, consulting a guide to the city she'd picked up earlier. Nell shivered. It was a sharp reminder of the city's turbulent history. Today, though, only carpets, sheepskins and the rough, brown, hooded djellabas worn by many Moroccan men were for sale. Heaps of spices were also laid out on the ground, along with cosmetics and potions.

'To charm the djinns,' the vendor, who was sporting a large black turban, told Nell when she took a closer look.

'Djinns?'

'Spirits.' He shot her a gappy grin. 'Black magic.'

Nell was tempted to ask more questions – she supposed the Tarot might be regarded by some as a kind of black magic – but there was too much to see and they reluctantly dragged themselves away from the heady fragrances of musk, amber and frankincense, back into the sunshine; into the intense light and sharp shadows.

They drifted from the main streets, into the labyrinth of alleys and courtyards, the tangle of souks, peering in at silversmiths, woodcarvers and cobblers at work, listening to the sales patter: 'Come and look, see, it costs *si peu*, *si peu*, nearly nothing'; following their noses and wandering down any street that happened to entice them. There was even a souk for the dyers: strips of cloth in royal blues, dusky pinks and bruised purples hung in rows above their heads, the rich colours filtering the sunlight. Amy got out her camera. 'This place is like a living theatre,' she murmured.

They began their serious shopping in the Souk des Sacochiers, where the leather workers made bags and satchels and where they spent a long time discussing the merits of goat versus cow skin with a vendor whose opinion swung depending on which bag Amy seemed most interested in. She finally decided on a traditional traveller's bag in soft tan with metalwork and proceeded to haggle. She was very good at it. Finally, she simply shrugged and walked away.

Nell followed her. 'Have you changed your mind?'

'No.' She grinned and, sure enough, the man came flying out of his shop, bag in hand. 'I give you best price of 2,000 dirhams' had evolved to a sorrowful 'You rob me, lady,' as Amy finally claimed the bag at a fraction of the asking price.

'How on earth do you do it?' Nell asked.

'Simple.' Amy winked. 'You decide how much you want to pay and then stick to it. I read somewhere that you can get anything for around a quarter of the asking price.' And then when she saw the expression on Nell's face: 'Don't worry – he's still making a good profit.'

Nell toyed with the idea of buying Callum some pointy *babouches*. He'd like them. But . . .

'Has something happened?' Amy asked her. She was very observant, perhaps a bit too observant. 'Have you two had a row or something?'

They certainly had. And it had left Nell feeling more unsettled than ever. Callum had phoned a few times, but he always seemed to end up talking about the farmhouse, hassling her about the sale. She had got to the point where she didn't even want to take his calls – which couldn't be right. And then this morning, before breakfast . . .

'The estate agent's phoned me again, Nell,' Callum said. 'He's got back to the buyers and they're unwilling to wait.'

'Not even for a few days?' Nell thought of the Moon card. This only confirmed her feeling that she should trust her instincts and not make hasty decisions. 'Why not?'

'Because they've got other properties to see, I expect.' Callum sounded as if this was obvious. And he also sounded very fed up. Nell wasn't sure what to do. Selling the farmhouse meant a lot to him. It meant they could move on, buy a place where Nell could run her own business, maybe put some money into his landscaping concern, or pay off some of their mortgage. And it would mean that at last Nell would say goodbye – to her childhood, to her mother. She knew why it mattered to him. But what about what mattered to her?

'They've probably sold their own place and want to move on. People do expect a quick decision, don't they? That's normal. They don't want to hang around.'

Waiting for some silly ditherer to make up her mind, Nell silently added. But of course he didn't say it.

'That's up to them.' Nell could feel her stubborn streak growing even more so. 'If they decide against it, there'll be other buyers.'

'Nell!' She heard his frustration. 'Do you really mean that you'd let this offer go, just because you haven't met them? Haven't approved of them?'

Nell didn't much like this side of Callum. 'Actually, yes,' she said.

'Why?'

'Callum . . .' She tried to explain. Again. 'The farmhouse

has been in my family for generations. It's now been entrusted to me. I can't let it go to just anyone.'

'For Christ's sake . . .'

'That's just how it is,' she snapped. She took a breath, a pause; it wasn't his fault; none of it was. 'It's only a few days. If they're the right people, I'll know.' Would she, though? And was she simply prevaricating? No doubt this was what Callum thought. What would happen if she didn't agree to sell? Would he ever forgive her?

'And if they're the right people and we lose them?'

And I lose you . . . 'We won't,' she said. 'If we lose them, then they weren't right.' And she knew she wasn't just thinking about the potential buyers.

'The estate agent can't understand it,' Callum said. And neither could Callum, that much was obvious. Nell knew that his logical brain would never accept her fatalistic approach. 'He thinks we're crazy. He wants to know what the hell's going on.'

Nell bridled. 'And who is he working for exactly?'

'I'm going to tell him to go ahead.'

She gripped her mobile more fiercely.

'You can meet them when you get back. And if you think they're not right for the place, then we'll back out if we really must.' He paused. 'But only if there's good reason to. We can't risk losing them, Nell. It's madness.'

'No,' she said. 'We're not going ahead. Not yet.' Impasse.

He sighed. 'It's my decision, too, Nell. We're married, remember.'

But for how much longer? The thought ploughed into her head. 'It's my house,' she said.

Her declaration hung between them like the sword of Damocles.

'Isn't it a joint enterprise?' he said mildly after a few seconds had elapsed. 'When you're married? Don't we share our worldly goods?'

Not the farmhouse, she thought. He was trying to make light of it, but she knew she'd hurt him. She couldn't help it. He had pushed her and she'd responded. 'Not the farmhouse,' she said out loud.

'I see.' His voice was cold suddenly, and she hated that. 'At least we know where we stand. I'll phone the agent and tell him what my wife has decided then, shall I?'

'OK,' she said. *When you're married . . .*

'But if we lose them and we don't find another buyer,' Callum said, 'don't come running to me for sympathy, Nell.'

'I won't.' She tried to sound brave, but the sadness was there. How many sadnesses, she wondered, could you take, before your love fell apart?

When she'd finished relaying the gist of this to Amy, her new friend only nodded and squeezed her arm. Nell was glad Amy didn't say anything against Callum, glad she didn't try to give her any advice. She hadn't known her for very long, but Amy had already become important to her. Maybe even a friend for keeps.

She bought the *babouches* for Callum in any case. 'Think positive,' Amy whispered. They were bright yellow, like sunshine, and Nell had to put them away quickly in her bag, because she didn't want to look at them.

Amy bought a stripy, multicoloured bedspread and two cactus-silk scarves, one for herself and one for Francine; rosewater for her aunt and argan oil for her mother. For her father she found a small leather wallet for carrying credit cards. Nell also bought a scarf for herself and one for Sharon, as well as some soft leather hand-stitched shoes in olive and purple.

Finally, they'd had more than their fill of the souks and the sales pressure, not to mention the coughing, shouting, hissing and kissing noises that were apparently what passed for flirting in Morocco.

'Let's go out for a drink after dinner tonight,' Amy suggested as they made their way back to the main street. 'I need to take some after-dark shots in the square.'

You had to get lost in Marrakech — it was practically compulsory — but Nell was impressed by Amy's sense of direction. Already they were back in familiar territory. Nell remembered what Marion had told them about Marakesh and Jemaa el-Fna. That the square was the hub of Morocco's ancient storytelling tradition. That for over a thousand years storytellers had gathered there to recount ancient folk tales, often using actions to make the fables into living theatre.

'Why not?' Nell agreed. It could be fun. After that disturbing confrontation with Callum, she felt like letting her hair down. She was always grateful to get back to Riad Lazuli after an hour or two of sensory overload on the streets of the medina. It was comforting, a perfectly tranquil haven in which to retreat from the noisy bustle and hassle outside. The storm and the calm, she found herself thinking. An oasis. But she'd also like to experience some of the nightlife of Marrakech.

'Ahmed told me about this bar,' Amy said.

'Oh yes?' In Marrakech there weren't many bars. And quite a few of the restaurants had a no-alcohol policy.

'I'll get the directions.'

They walked back towards the riad arm-in-arm. As they passed a spice stall, Nell stopped abruptly and pointed to a small pyramid of red-gold positioned between a larger heap of ginger and another of paprika. The tangled pyramid seemed to shimmer in the late-afternoon light. 'Saffron threads,' she said. 'My mother always grew it, every year, and her mother before her.' Instinctively, she bent closer to catch the sharp and addictive scent. 'This year she didn't replant the bulbs.' She turned to look at Amy. 'It was the first time. That's what makes me think . . .'

'Think what?'

Nell shook her head. She couldn't say it.

'What, Nell?' Amy's voice was gentle.

But still, Nell couldn't reply.

'How did she die, Nell? You never said.' Amy drew her into the pink alleyway by the antique shop; their landmark. Suddenly, all was quiet, apart from a man pulling a handcart at the far end. 'You said it was sudden? Was she taken ill? Is that it?'

'We live in Roseland,' Nell said. 'It's in Cornwall.' They continued up the alley. The man with the handcart disappeared around the far corner, and now they were alone. The high pink walls of the medina protected the inner life, thought Nell, just as the women's veils protected their faces. Amy was right. The souks and the bazaars and the Jemaa el-Fna were part of a living theatre. And this was real life, backstage.

Amy nodded. 'I know it. And?'

Nell drew breath. She hadn't intended saying any of this. It was just seeing the saffron glimmering in the sun like that. 'It happened around midnight, they think.'

'What did?'

'She was walking. She often just went off walking. I don't know where she was going or where she'd been. She was on the cliff path. She went too close to the edge . . .' Nell faltered.

'Too close to the edge?' Amy stopped walking. 'You mean, she fell?'

'Yes, she fell.' Except that she could have jumped. Would she have jumped? To kill yourself seemed such a selfish act to Nell. It showed such a lack of thought and compassion for those who were left behind. Would her mother have been so selfish? Could she have possibly been so unhappy, so desperate, that she would have jumped? Nell didn't like to think so. But if she hadn't jumped, if it had just been a tragic accident . . . Then why hadn't she replanted the saffron bulbs this year?

CHAPTER 14

Dinner that evening was mechoui lamb. Nell had informed Amy that, traditionally, it was cooked either in a pit in the ground, or on a spit over a fire, as Hassan and the cookery group had prepared it today, and eaten with salt and cumin on the side for dipping. It was delicious. When the last of it had disappeared from her plate, Amy sat back in her chair and sighed with pleasure. How lucky was she to be part of this? But she and Nell had things to do, so after waiting a respectable half an hour to be sociable and digest the feast, they slipped away from the rest of the group to go out into Jemaa el-Fna at night.

It was a balmy evening, and the stars were sharp and clear in the velvet sky. '*Bonjour!* Hello! Hello!' The children begging in the alleyways tried to offer them directions. Amy gave them some fruit she'd purloined from the dessert. But she already knew the way.

At night, the main square was quite another creature. The first thing the two women heard was the music: the clashing of cymbals, the throbbing of drums, the cacophony of voices talking, laughing, singing; filling the wide, open square, which was lit up with the soft glow of candles and the gleam from lanterns on colourful stalls. The square was crowded, as always; it was Moroccan at its core, but there was a multicultural feel, too – from the tourists of all nationalities, from the young people dressed not only traditionally, in long robes, but also in jeans, even though the girls still wore silk scarves around their heads – sometimes with a baseball cap on top. Amy managed to sneak a photo. The men wore the usual djellabas and leather-thonged sandals, or jeans and jackets, also skull caps, or even a straw hat or fedora.

The feel was that of a circus arena. The intensity was awe-inspiring. Amy and Nell paused for a moment to drink it all in, but it was risky to stay still for too long – you might have a snake draped around your shoulders or a monkey deposited in your arms before you knew it. The darkness was scented with the smells of open-air cooking, of meat being grilled and roasted; of frying, of pastries, of smoke rising and incense hanging heavy in the night air. There were bowls of steamed snails, fried whitebait and lamb kebabs with harissa sauce. Stalls sold dates, figs, fresh orange juice, *citron* and *pamplemousse*; the oranges, lemons and grapefruit piled high in pyramids. There were henna tattooists, musicians and story-tellers – all performing, all vying for attention, trying to draw passers-by and their money into their inner circle.

Amy couldn't resist the snake-charmer. The words *Charmeur de serpents* were written on the snake-box, and she showed Nell the accompanying drawing of a rather ominous skull and crossbones. The *charmeur* himself had long, white hair braided to his shoulders and wound through his ruby-red turban; his thick beard hung down past his chest. He wore a rough linen shirt with a striped robe on top. And as he played his flute-like instrument, the snake slowly uncoiled, winding upwards obediently, tongue flickering.

They bought orange juice and, although they were still full, they couldn't resist trying some spirals of deep-fried dough sprinkled with spices and sesame seeds. Scrumptious. Amy licked her lips. And there was a dancer. They stopped to watch her. She was dancing alone, languorously, as if in a trance, waving her arms, her hips circling, her limbs fluid as she moved into the beat.

Everything seemed upfront and open, but when she looked more closely Amy could see small clusters of men, heads together as if involved in some clandestine night-time meeting; old men watching the proceedings but strangely apart from it all as they smoked their hubble-bubble pipes; gangs of youths scanning the crowds. Amy was taking lots of shots but, as she did so, she became aware of a sense of otherness, of menace lurking in the shadows. She shook it off. She was being over-imaginative. This was a stage. As she and Nell had already agreed, it was just theatre, and theatre could be scary because it wasn't real.

Nevertheless, she took Nell's arm. 'Let's find the bar,' she suggested. Nell didn't seem too fazed by their surroundings, but Amy had known she was vulnerable and now she knew at least part of the reason why. Did Nell think her mother had committed suicide? She must do. How hard that must be to live with. Amy didn't know Nell well, but already there was a bond between them, and Amy's heart went out to her. They were both looking for answers here in Morocco. And female friendship, she was prepared to trust.

Despite this bond, they'd clearly experienced very different upbringings. While Nell had been sheltered throughout her childhood, Amy had been left to go her own way. Not that she held any resentment towards her liberal parents. But it must be nice to have had such a close relationship with your mother – even though now Nell had lost her. Had it happened because there were just the two of them? Even so, Amy appreciated what her own parents had done, what they'd wanted to achieve and how hard they'd worked to get there.

As they retraced their steps through the square, Amy thought back to when she was seven years old, to the day they'd moved into the hotel in Lyme; of her parents' excitement. Her father, trying to be practical, rushing around to get things sorted, doing repairs in the bedrooms, adding a lick of paint where it was needed, putting up a shelf here and there, adjusting the settings on the boiler. 'Everything's going to be different now, love. You'll see.' He had looked so happy, so confident. Amy hadn't seen him look like that in a long time. She'd felt a rush of love. 'Oh, Daddy!' Felt the warmth of his arms as he hugged her. He wasn't a man for showing his emotions, not at all touchy-feely; it was almost as if he didn't dare let himself go. Her mother was dashing around, too – her eyes all sparkly and eager. 'What do you think, darling? Do you like it? It's a fresh start for us. This is your new home.' And Amy could see that it meant a lot to them.

She had shot from room to room, exploring, getting the feel. Gradually, she slowed down. She liked the fact that there was a view of the harbour and the Cobb, even though there were a few houses in the way. She liked the maze of rooms – only eight bedrooms for guests, but even that seemed a lot. But most of all she liked what it had done for her parents.

They were living in the flat to start with, which was small and poky, and her father didn't have much time left over to do much to it. But Amy didn't mind. It was too important to get sorted, to start bringing in the guests, her father said.

And her mother agreed. 'We'll be busy from now on, darling.' And she had given Amy one of her brisk hugs. As if they hadn't always been busy.

Before this, they'd run a small B&B in Bridport, but her father had still had his day job; he taught in the local primary school, and oh yes, they'd always been busy. But some time ago he'd started taking days off sick, and then weeks, and the next thing Amy knew, Mum had said he was giving it all up and that they were moving to a different place, a bigger place, and that they would be running it together. It was too stressful, she said, being a teacher. With B&B or a small hotel, guests came and went, but you always knew where you were.

'You might have to be on your own a bit more,' her mother told Amy once they were installed in Lyme. 'But you're a big girl now. You'll just have to manage. We all will. You'll make new friends at your new school. And it's just at first. When we can afford it, we'll get more staff in to help us.'

Amy had nodded. She didn't mind being left to her own

devices. She was used to it – though she'd always longed for a sister to share things with. A new school was a bit scarier, but she was quite looking forward to that, too.

But the business hadn't gone as well as her parents had hoped. There was a lot of competition from other bed and breakfasts and hotels in Lyme Regis and they'd put so much into the mortgage that they didn't have any spare for all the things they kept saying they had to do.

They started arguing. Her father became grumpy. He began to look anxious again and Amy noted the furrow in his brow and the sagging around his eyes. He was always tired. He started snapping at them both and he went out for long walks and sometimes even to bed in the afternoons. Her mother's voice changed. It became more strident and demanding and clearly irritated her father. They argued about the hotel, they argued about the flat, they argued about him not doing his full share. They argued about Amy's grandmother, Mary, who was becoming increasingly frail, and they argued about money. They talked about giving it all up, moving away, even – horrors – about getting divorced. Amy heard them at night – their bedroom was next to hers – even though they tried to keep their voices down. 'What about Amy?' her mother would say. 'What about Amy?'

Amy didn't know what was going to happen. The future was uncertain, and she was really frightened now. She couldn't concentrate at school and she didn't want to go home. She even thought about running away, but she had no idea where to go.

And then Great-aunt Lillian moved back to England, to Lyme. She seemed to assess the situation immediately. She took things in hand, and the family were so desperate, they simply stood aside and let her. She put money into the business: 'I *insist* . . .' And persuaded them to make a few changes. 'I can't think of a better use for it,' she told Amy's mother. And when they tried to argue with her: 'That's what they'd do in America.'

Thinking back, Amy was astounded that they'd let her do so much. She even persuaded Amy's parents to see a marriage guidance counsellor, and she took over the healthcare of her sister, Mary – though no one argued with her over that one. And, gradually, slowly, they all started smiling again. Amy met a girl called Francine, who had just moved to the area and soon became her first special friend in Lyme. Her Aunt Lillian bought her a camera for her birthday. Her parents occasionally even held hands. And that was why, to Amy, her aunt was like a fairy godmother with a magic wand. Somehow, since she came into their lives, everything had become all right again.

The rooftop bar Ahmed had told Amy about was magnificent. On the second floor there was an open terrace with outdoor infrared heaters which looked out towards the Badi Palace and the Mellah quarter; there were tables set for dinner, but also cosy, dusky-pink alcoves with cushioned seating and lanterns sending a soft glow over the curtains, the tablecloths, the highly polished wooden floor. Around them, winter jasmine had been wound through the trellising, its perfume filling the air.

The place was buzzing, and it was hard to find a seat, so it was no surprise when, after half an hour, they were joined at their table by another party – an English guy, in his late thirties, Amy guessed, and another man of about the same age, who looked Moroccan, although he was in Western dress. At first, they merely nodded hello and continued their own conversation, but when there was a lull the Englishman, who, Amy noted, had been speaking in what seemed to be a fluent mix of French and Arabic, smiled at her. 'How long have you been in Marrakech?' he asked.

'Only a few days. And we're leaving soon.' Amy sipped her white wine and smiled at Nell. She didn't want to leave; she was enjoying herself far more than she'd expected to.

'You are tourists?' asked the other man. He spoke English, but with a strong, guttural accent.

'Sort of.' Amy told them a bit about the event they were planning at the gallery. 'And Nell's doing a cookery course,' she added. The two men seemed nice enough; there was no reason not to be friendly.

'Ah, the delights of Moroccan cuisine.' The Englishman sighed. 'I sometimes think that's what's kept me in the country so long.' He glanced at his companion. 'Eh, Rafi? What do you think?'

'I am sure of it.' The other man laughed. He was watching Nell appraisingly.

'How long have you been here?' Amy was curious. The

Englishman was very well spoken. He certainly wasn't just a traveller; he must work here in some capacity.

'Ten years.'

'Not just travelling through then,' put in Nell.

'I *was* just travelling through,' he said, 'but one thing led to another and then another and . . .' He shrugged.

Rafi added something in the language they'd been conversing in.

He laughed. 'He says I chose the way at my crossroads,' he said. 'The Arabs have strong beliefs about these things.'

Amy nodded. 'And not just about crossroads,' she murmured.

'But when you get to a crossroads . . .' At first, Nell seemed to be talking to herself, but then she looked up at the Moroccan man. '. . . how do you know which way to go?'

It wasn't hard to guess what she was thinking about. Or who.

'You go with your heart,' he said. His eyes were very dark, almost black in the dim light. And then he smiled, a flash of white teeth that broke the sudden tension around the table.

'But what do you think of Morocco? Of Marrakech?' The Englishman directed his question at Amy. She looked past him into the night sky, the stars like glittering sequins, the moon almost full and shimmering blue-white. What could she say? She had such mixed feelings. 'It's fascinating. The colours, the street life, the performances. But . . . it's not a great place for women, is it?'

'You don't think so?'

'Half the time they're covered up and not allowed out; they can't speak to anyone who isn't known to them or female; and they're not even allowed to learn another language or to drive.' She and Nell had been discussing it. Amy liked to think of herself as an independent woman. This was a chauvinistic society, and she didn't fit in.

Rafi turned to Nell. 'You are very quiet. Do you agree?' He eyed her seriously.

'Of course.' She looked straight at him and then quickly away. 'The way women are treated is abhorrent to us, you see. We've been brought up so differently. It's hard for us to understand.'

The Englishman picked up his wine glass and swirled the contents around. 'It's true that, here, women have a different status.'

'A second-class status,' said Amy.

'Perhaps.' He offered them some wine from their bottle of white in the cooler. Their glasses were almost empty and so both nodded their thanks. 'Women might seem to be invisible, inaudible, powerless. But . . .'

Rafi interrupted him sharply but, again, not in English.

'He says they do have power,' the Englishman translated. 'In the home.'

In the home. Amy exchanged a look with Nell. She put down her glass. 'That's not enough for women any longer. Sometimes they need to be heard outside of the home. They want more.' She thought of Nell's husband, making her feel bad for being reluctant to sell her own inheritance. She thought of Duncan, blithely assuming that it should be Amy who made the coffee and kept them supplied with loo paper and other necessities. And she thought of Jake, assuming control of what had been her project, not trusting her to do her job without interference. So was it any better in their culture? Or were they all just paying lip service to the idea of equality?

'I admire your spirit.' Rafi fixed her with his intense dark gaze. 'But the women here, they have their own strength, they rejoice in their difference.'

'Perhaps because they have no choice,' retorted Amy. She picked up her glass and took another sip. The wine was slightly acidic but refreshingly citrussy. She thought about her own choices. She had chosen a relationship with Duncan. She'd taken the easy option. But she wouldn't be making those kind of choices any more. Next time – if there was a next time – she'd be braver.

'I'm Matt.' The English guy held out a hand. 'And this is Rafi.'

Amy and Nell introduced themselves.

'What I like about this city,' Nell spoke up, with a little smile at Rafi, 'is the mix of people and cultures. Arabs, Berber, French . . .'

'You are right.' Rafi nodded. 'When the Romans came to Morocco they called its people "Barbarians", which became "Berbers". They prefer to be called Amazigh.'

'Free men,' put in Matt. 'Marrakech was fought over for

many years between the Muslims and the Berbers – even before the French came along. They all wanted it because of its prime position on the trading route: oranges, spices, nuts, grains, dates, animal skins, precious metals – you name it.' He smiled.

'And saffron,' Nell said softly.

'Saffron, yes, of course,' said Rafi. He looked thoughtful.

'And you might approve a little more of the lives led by the Berber women,' Matt went on. 'They don't have to cover up – at least not to the same extent. They have a lot more freedom.'

Its history could tell you so much about a place, thought Amy. Religion was such a strong cultural influence here; the Koran was the bedrock. And perhaps it needed to be, because of the number of battles, because there had always been so many others trying to take their land.

'Do the Moroccans still resent the French protectorate?' Nell asked Rafi.

'Why should we?' He shrugged, but his black eyes glittered. 'The French, they gave us roads, railways, cafés . . .'

'And more bloodshed,' added Matt.

Amy was curious. He seemed to have so completely made this place his home. 'What really made you stay here?' she asked.

He seemed to consider. 'I went into business with a Frenchman who was living here. And with Rafi. And here I am still. Sometimes that happens in Morocco. It has a way of keeping you. It's hard to explain.'

'What are the other cities like?' Nell asked. 'Are they all as manic as this one?'

'Fez is our most historic city,' said Rafi.

'Like going back to medieval times,' added Matt.

'It is the soul of Morocco,' said Rafi. 'Sometimes we are scared of what Marrakech has become.'

Nell smiled and nodded as if she knew exactly what he meant. And Amy wasn't sure if she was imagining it, but there seemed to be a bit of a spark between those two. She hoped that Nell would keep her head. Her marriage might be in trouble, but she was still hanging on in there. A dalliance with an attractive Moroccan stranger might be an appealing prospect, but it could also be dangerous.

Matt was still talking, apparently unaware. 'Casablanca's more westernized, more dynamic, more modern. And Agadir . . .' He pulled a face.

'Has been ruined by tourists, I know,' said Amy. That was one place she certainly wasn't interested in visiting.

'But for me, Marrakech is still the pulse,' said Matt. 'I love it.'

Once again Amy wondered. Maybe . . .? It was worth a try. She pulled the postcard out of her bag. 'Do either of you have any clue as to where this might be?' she asked. She just had a feeling.

Matt examined it carefully. 'I don't remember ever seeing this place,' he said at last. 'What about you, Rafi?'

He, too, stared at it intently, then shook his dark head.

'Is it important?' Matt laughed. 'I expect you've realized

by now that there are a lot of old doors and crumbling walls around here.'

Amy felt a stab of disappointment. But she was probably expecting too much. Matt was right. It *was* just an old door and some crumbling walls. Except . . .

'There is a town where the doors and shutters, they are all painted blue,' said Rafi.

'Really?' Amy exchanged a glance with Nell. 'What's the town called?'

'Essaouira.'

Essaouira. Amy couldn't believe it.

'It is a coastal town.'

'West coast,' Matt added. 'Not touristy, though. More of an old hippie hang-out.'

Old hippie hang-out. Jimi Hendrix, she thought. She'd been offered a legitimate excuse to go there and she'd turned it down. Because she'd jumped to what might have been another wrong conclusion? 'How likely do you think that this is in Essaouira?' she asked – before she dropped everything and raced over there. And lost face with Jake, she added silently. But in her heart she was already convinced. Glenn had gone there as a traveller in the seventies. Hippie hang-out sounded just about right.

Matt drew a tablet out of his leather bag. 'Let's have a look for that flower emblem.' He switched it on and started tapping. Amy sipped her wine and waited. *Essaouira . . .*

'Looks likely,' he said at last. 'Here.' He showed her a

picture of another carving – not dissimilar to the one on the postcard. At least, it was another flower.

Rafi let out an exclamation. 'But of course,' he said. 'The rose of Mogador.'

Amy saw these words written under the picture on the screen. 'Mogador?'

'It is the old name of the town,' said Rafi. 'Essaouira was called Mogador. And this is its rose.'

They left the bar soon afterwards and wandered back into the serpentine alleys of the medina – dark and deserted at night, apart from the odd scavenging cat looking for scraps of food. There had been a shift in atmosphere; the darkness seemed really sinister now. Nothing in this city, thought Amy, was quite what it seemed.

'What did Rafi say to you?' she asked Nell. He had drawn her to one side when they got up to leave, the two of them speaking in low voices.

Nell looked embarrassed. 'He asked me out to dinner.'

'He doesn't waste much time.' They walked on. 'And . . .?' she enquired.

'And it wouldn't be a good idea,' said Nell.

No doubt she was right. Someone like Rafi would only confuse the issue for Nell. Nevertheless, Amy sensed something different about her new friend as they found their landmark and entered the pink passageways of the inner medina once again.

'Where did the postcard come from?' Nell asked her. And

so Amy told her the story, her voice soft as they made their way back to the riad.

'Does that mean you're going to Essaouira to look for him?' she asked when Amy had finished and they arrived back at Riad Lazuli.

'I think it does.' Amy lifted the hand of Fatima and knocked. There was nothing to stop her. And, at last, she thought, she was getting somewhere.

CHAPTER 15

Lillian supposed she should think about doing some house-work, but thinking was about as far as she got. Her visit to Bridport had tired her more than she'd expected and vacuum-ing had never held much of a thrill. When she was married – now *then*, she'd had to make an effort; it was more like a job. But those were the days when women's roles were more clearly defined. It was enough to be a housewife and mother – more than enough. Nowadays, it was different. Young girls like Amy – well, not so young any more, she sup-posed; Amy was a lot older than Lillian had been when she'd left to go to America to get married – felt more strongly about their careers, their personal fulfilment. Was this a good thing? Lillian thought of Mary, of Celia. She supposed so. Although . . .

Bridport wasn't a big town, not really, though it had always seemed so when she was a child. But there was a lot to see. She'd had a coffee in a café in the bus station, which was, rather eerily she thought, set out like an American diner – and she'd seen more than enough of those, thank you very much. And then she'd set off to see some of the old places. The pub that had been called the White Lion, the white house opposite where the troops had been billeted, the car park in East Street where the bombs had destroyed all those houses, the square and the old cinemas. Each building brought back a certain memory, some more keen than others. Perhaps it was a good thing she wasn't living here in Bridport, Lillian thought. She wasn't sure that she'd be able to cope with having the past at such close quarters.

After the dance on Saturday, after the family had been introduced to Ted Robinson, the dashing GI, Mary hadn't said much at all. Lillian knew Mary would be seeing him, though; she sensed it.

One evening a few weeks later when her sister was getting ready to go to the cinema – with a girlfriend, she'd told Father – Lillian crept into her room. Mary was sitting at the dressing table putting a dab of red on each cheek. She'd added almond oil to an old stub of lipstick for this purpose. She raised a perfect half-moon of an eyebrow when she saw Lillian.

Lillian sat down on the satin-covered pink eiderdown on her bed. 'Where are you going?' she asked innocently. 'The Lyric?'

'The Palace,' Mary came back, quick as a flash. Both cinemas were busy these days; they changed their programmes twice a week and, since the Americans had come, there could be queues right down the road.

'Are you seeing Ted?' Lillian asked outright.

'Ted?' Mary's dark-blue eyes were far away as she gazed into the mirror. She blended in the rouge on her cheeks.

'Ted who came to dinner.' How many Teds were there? And there was none, Lillian reckoned, who was a patch on him.

Mary eyed her in the mirror. 'I might be.' She snapped open her lipstick and lined a perfect bow. Girls were encouraged to wear make-up more than ever these days, though, as yet, Lillian wasn't allowed. It was another thing that lifted morale, she supposed, though whether it was the morale of the men or the women, she wasn't sure. At any rate, she couldn't imagine her sister without her 'red badge of courage', though she hardly needed it; Mary even looked good in the baggy overalls she had to wear in the factory.

'Tonight?' Lillian held her breath.

'Ssh. Don't tell.' Mary put a finger to her lips, not touching them.

'Do you like him?'

Mary blotted her lipstick with a hanky. 'Of course I do, silly.'

'But do you *like* him?' Lillian wanted to shake Mary sometimes, she was so casual. She simply had no regard for the men's feelings. Normally, this didn't bother Lillian too much. More fool them, she'd think. But this was Ted. And anyone could see Ted was special. It wasn't just the way he talked – though Lillian loved that sexy drawl; and it wasn't just his smile – the flash of white teeth, accompanied by a cheeky wink. He was so different from anyone she'd met before. And the twinkle in his eye had stayed with her; he haunted her dreams.

Mary observed her once again in the mirror. This time her eyes were cool. She picked up her hairbrush and began to tidy her hair. 'The GIs are the most thrilling thing to happen to this town – even a child like you must be able to see that.' She took a kirby grip from the cut-glass bowl on the dressing table and began to re-pin. 'It really has been utterly drab here since the war started.' She smiled a secret smile to her image in the glass. 'Until now.'

'The GIs?' For Lillian, there was only one GI, although you couldn't but be aware of the rest of them, strolling around town as if they owned the place, drinking in the pubs, laughing with the children, chatting up the girls in the shops, in the streets, in cinema queues – wherever they had the chance. They put the British boys in the shade.

'They're so terribly attractive.' Mary sighed. 'So romantic. So . . . self-assured. A girl needs a bit of glamour in her life, you know, Lil.'

Lillian nodded. She knew.

'When everything around you is so frightfully dull . . .' She put down her hairbrush and frowned into the mirror. 'To be on the arm of a GI . . . it gets you noticed.' She relaxed her face and gave her nose a final dab of powder. 'Perfect,' she announced. She blew a kiss to herself in the mirror.

Lillian tried to imagine being on Ted's arm. The thought made her feel quite weak. Not because she wanted to be noticed, but because – and she admitted it now to herself for the first time – she had fallen head over heels in love with him. He had walked into their home and he had captured her heart. These past days since he came to dinner, she had spent ages walking up and down in front of the white house opposite the pub where he was billeted; hoping, praying, that she would see him, that he would recognize her, that he might speak to her . . . Mary didn't have to do that, of course. He would always seek out Mary. And now she was seeing him, going out with him, even kissing him, maybe. Lillian shivered.

'And then there are the nylons.' Mary was running her hands lightly over her legs now. She was wearing stockings with a faultless seam – and it hadn't been drawn on. 'And the chocolates. The silk scarves. All the little luxuries we've had to do without.'

'Is that why you're seeing him?' Lillian glared at her. 'To get nylons and chocolates?'

'Of course not.' Mary twisted around to face her. 'And what do you care? Do you have a pash on him yourself, is that it?' She laughed. 'Oh, darling, now I see why you're so interested.' And she got up from the chair, stretched and smoothed her skirt over the curve of her hips. 'Don't bother yourself, little sister,' she said. 'You're just a baby. Ted wouldn't be interested in a child like you. I can guarantee that much.' And off she went with a giggle, a flounce of her shoulders and a flamboyant toss of her hair.

Lillian watched her go. She felt more miserable than ever. And the trouble was that Mary was right.

Even so, Lillian thought now, even so . . . She'd switched the radio on earlier and wished she'd chosen a music station.

Something classical and soothing. The man speaking – holding forth, she'd call it – was a politician and he had a self-satisfied drone which was irritating rather than compelling. She was also conscious that she'd dropped off more than once (from boredom, no doubt) and that really wasn't the thing. Not in the middle of the afternoon.

Lillian decided not to think about what had happened next – not now. She'd thought of it often enough and, hopefully, she'd paid her dues. Instead, she thought about springtime.

When spring came and the troops started mustering, it was clear that something big was in the air. There had been times when it wasn't possible to go down to the beach at West Bay; they were often carrying out training exercises such as Exercise Yukon, which she'd heard discussed by her parents. Otherwise, everything continued as normal or at least wartime normal. As for Ted, Lillian's feelings hadn't changed and she was terrified she wouldn't get the opportunity of seeing him again, of speaking to him. Because of what had happened. Because of what she had told him; what she had done. And because one day soon, she knew he would be leaving.

Of course, she felt guilty. It hadn't been her place. She had let her emotions take over, allowed her heart to rule her own common sense. But whatever she had done, she knew that she had to see him.

And then her chance came. It was a rainy day and the American troops were lined up along West Street, in front of the White Lion. The landlady was taking out jugs of her home-made elderberry wine and doling out glasses of it to help keep them warm.

Lillian saw him. They were all there. The road was full of trucks and jeeps and soldiers. 'Ted! Ted!' she shouted.

She saw his face light up. And she saw the moment he realized it was only Lillian and that she was on her own. 'Hey, Lillian.' He smiled and winked. 'How you doing, Duchess?'

'I'm very well,' she called back, though her heart was beating rather fast. 'And you?'

He laughed. 'I'm just fine, little lady. Just fine.'

Lillian grabbed her chance. 'Can I write to you?' she shouted.

'What's that you say, honey?'

'Can I write to you in America? Can I be your penfriend? Can I write and check that you've come back safely from the war?'

She heard the other men laughing and teasing him – 'Hey, Teddy, you've made a conquest there' – but she kept her eyes fixed on his and she hoped he would see the earnestness there. She had only spoken to him a few times. But in those moments he had brought a sparkle to her wartime life, a glimpse of another world, more exciting and more liberated than the one she lived in. Mary was in the past now – Lillian wouldn't even think of that. Ted had been hurt, but he could trust Lillian. She had his welfare at heart. She gave a damn about love.

He seemed to hesitate. Then, 'Sure. Why the hell not?' He grabbed a piece of paper from his pocket and scribbled something down. The trucks were beginning to move. He put the paper in a half-empty packet of chewing gum and threw it towards her. Lillian caught it. She opened it carefully. She had his address. She hadn't lost him. Not yet, anyway.

Later, she learnt of the invasion of Europe. Later, she learnt he had gone to Omaha. But, for now, she kept the thought of him wrapped and closeted in her heart.

CHAPTER 16

Morocco, 1974

'How did you first get involved?' Bethany asked him one day. 'With the peace movement, I mean?' It was summer, and she had been living with him at the riad for two months. It had been the best two months of his life, Glenn thought now.

He had told her what he had told Howard when they first met on the beach – that he was a pacifist and that he'd objected to the Vietnam War on moral grounds. But he knew what Bethany was really asking. *Was it because you were a coward? Was it because you were scared to go over there and fight?* He knew, because he'd asked himself the same question God knows how many times – and he'd seen it in his mother's eyes.

His mother. He pictured her sweet face. Her clear blue eyes, her neat features, the flicked curl of her hair. She'd been scared for him all right. She hadn't given a damn about the Vietnam War . . . Well, hey, that was unfair. Perhaps she had. Perhaps she'd been political in her time, though she'd never let on. But back in 1962 she was more concerned with the war waging in her own household. Her husband and her son, locked in combat. Most of the time, the tensions were bubbling under the surface like a live volcano. But they were all aware of them. So she didn't join in the discussions that could make the thing erupt. Once, his mother used to laugh; but she hadn't laughed for a long time. She stayed, anxious, on the sidelines; determined to keep the peace.

'From arguing with my dad,' he told Bethany. That was how he had first got 'involved', as she put it. He'd been naive. But he'd recognized – even at the age of fourteen – that he was his father's polar opposite. And he'd wanted to rebel, even though he wasn't sure at that age what he was rebelling against. Rebel without a cause? Glenn allowed himself a wry grin; James Dean had captured the feeling in that movie all right. He could still feel that kid's desperation, his need to holler, 'I can't do anything right!' But Glenn had a cause. His cause was to fight against everything his father stood for; it was the cause of youth.

Glenn was fourteen when he first entered Central High School, Philadelphia, as a freshman. It was a new world and he loved it. He got into reading, and soon he was devouring books like J. D. Salinger's *Catcher in the Rye*, with its themes of teenage angst and alienation. His cause was underlined. It wasn't just him, he realized. There were others.

He didn't know the background of Vietnam, though, not at the start of his freshman year. His father was always banging on about other wars – the Cold War, the Korean War, the war he himself had been involved in – the Second World War. Glenn listened, but a lot of it swam right over his head. It was old stuff, ancient news.

'What was he like?' Bethany asked now. 'Your father?'

Glenn allowed the picture of his other parent to jigsaw together in his mind. Tall, dark, upright. With what they call a military bearing. Beetle brows and a frown that was never far away. His eyes were brown, like nutmeg, with orange flecks. 'Arrogant,' Glenn replied. 'The old man had high expectations. He sure made me feel inadequate anyhow.'

It was the arrogance that had first made his hackles rise. His father's arrogance. The arrogance of America. What was it with his father's generation and war? Glenn used to wonder when he was fourteen. The world seemed to be laid out in front of him to taste and he couldn't see the point of wanting to destroy any of it. Was it about power? At school, he'd learnt about the formation of the United States of America. He understood why his father was proud of the constitution; of what they'd achieved. Hell, he was proud, too. But he watched the news on TV and listened to what older guys in school were saying and he wondered, weren't they in danger of getting carried away? Didn't some American politicians seem to think their country was responsible for the democracy of the whole goddamn world?

'Maybe it would have been easier if you'd had a brother,' Bethany said. 'Or a sister. To spread the load of those high expectations, I mean.'

'*You* don't have a brother or a sister.' Glenn rolled over to face her.

'I did have.' Her almond-brown eyes seemed huge in the soft light of the red-and-blue lantern by the bed. He thought of the day they'd met in the bookshop in Paris; remembered the stillness about her that had first attracted him. He had never thought she'd fit in so well; hardly dreamed that she would stay so long.

She had soon proved herself surprisingly independent. She found a part-time casual job cleaning in a small hotel on the waterfront and she had taken over the cooking from Glenn and Gizmo. They weren't complaining – she did a much better job. She swam in the Atlantic Ocean most days and she practised yoga on the beach, and sometimes on their roof terrace if Howard and Gizmo weren't around. She strolled around the streets of the medina in a floppety hippie hat she'd bought in the souks her first week here, her patchwork bag slung over her shoulder, her paisley skirt billowing in the breeze, her slender arms already tanned, and it seemed she had a friendly word and a smile for everyone. Sometimes she brought back doughnuts strung on a palm frond and they dipped them in mint tea for a tasty snack just as the locals did. But she brought Glenn more than this. There was a spiritual quality about her that calmed him. She was like a burst of summertime. Glenn felt a burden gradually easing from his shoulders, a sense of freedom lifting him towards the sky. And it was thanks to this girl. There had been quite a few hippie chicks on the road. But he'd never met anyone like Bethany before.

'You did have?' He traced a finger down her cheekbone. The line of it was perfect. At first he'd thought her mouth too wide for her to be a beauty. But he'd since changed his mind.

'I had a brother.'

'What happened to him?' He moved away slightly so he could catch her whole expression, so he wouldn't miss a thing.

'He died.' She didn't blink. 'He was only a baby. He contracted leukaemia.'

'Oh, Jesus, Bethany . . .'

'We loved him, though.'

'Sure you did.' He stroked her dark hair. He'd often wondered what it would be like to lose a sibling, to lose a child. It sucked, he knew that much. When he was a teenager, boys were already being sent to Vietnam, and it wasn't too long before everyone knew someone who had lost a son or a sweetheart.

When Glenn was growing up no one talked much about Vietnam, although the conflict was already in full swing. There was so much more going on. Other wars – Korea and the Cold War. Racial desegregation, the start of the Civil Rights Movement, NASA and the Mercury Seven, the first US astronauts and *Sputnik* 1 . . . Vietnam was low on the radar. His father, though, was big on all military campaigns and, even before any troops went in, he often talked about how the US were providing funds and advice on reform and military training to South Vietnam.

When Glenn had asked him why, he laughed. 'Don't they teach you anything in that school of yours?' he'd said. 'Because they're anti-commie, that's why.'

Back then, Glenn didn't even know what it was to be a communist. But he soon found out. In his freshman year at high school, he came into contact with a certain teacher, a young radical called Brad Stoneleigh, and made a new friend, Al, who had new ideas, absorbed from a liberal upbringing very different to Glenn's. It was an exciting time. He was learning about the world. And things were changing. This was still a new decade. The sixties. People were responding to their charismatic president John F. Kennedy. He had new ideas, too. Nothing would ever be the same again.

'What *did* he believe in?' Bethany asked him. 'Your father, I mean.'

That wasn't hard to answer. 'He believed in war.' Glenn lay back, head in hands, looking up at the once ornate ceiling of their bedroom, now crumbling into disrepair. 'I believed in peace.' Though it struck him now, thinking of his determination to be everything his father was not . . . Was that the reason for his pacifism? He sure as hell hoped not.

'Your father was pro-war?' Bethany echoed. 'Even pro-Vietnam?'

She was English – she didn't get it. But Glenn felt like saying, Who wasn't? Certainly at the start of the sixties most Americans supported the Vietnam policy and weren't afraid to say so. Until, at least, things turned really nasty. 'Especially Vietnam,' he said instead. McCarthy had a lot to answer for – thanks to him and others like him, communism was seen as an evil. *The* evil. And when Glenn's father talked about communism – which he did, often, and in disparaging terms – boy, did he bristle. His shoulders tensed, that clean-shaven jaw of his twitched, and he'd give his newspaper such a sharp flick to straighten the pages, you'd think there was one of his 'dirty commies' hiding inside it.

The historical situation in Vietnam, Glenn learnt from those he began to hang out with at high school, was complicated. The struggle for independence after the Second World War had left two governments, North and South, and a country that was divided. North Vietnam was as communist as they came.

'He was scared shitless of communism,' Glenn explained to Bethany now. 'People still are. One falls and the others follow. Dominoes, you know?'

'Dominoes?'

He made a gesture of a row of dominoes sliding into one another and falling down. They even called it the domino effect. 'He thought it had to be contained.' Now, there was a word. "Contained". What did that mean? Shut it in a box, hide it away and pretend it no longer exists?

'Is it right to fund and encourage a war in a tiny downtrodden country just because we're scared?' he'd asked his father over breakfast one Sunday.

'We're not scared, son.' His father's voice was calm and measured and held just a note of scorn. 'We're American.'

'But you're talking about a war, Dad.' Glenn wished he could get through to him. 'A war where innocent people get killed and most people don't even know what they're fighting for.' He had been shocked when he had read about the level of violence in Vietnam. Did the American public know what was going on? Did his father?

'And what would you do, if you're so darned clever?' his father asked.

Glenn was aware of his mother; restless, anxious, moving over from the kitchen sink, where she'd been washing dishes, ready to intervene, her hands clasped in that nervous way she had. 'Ted . . .'

'Withdraw,' said Glenn.

His father's expression darkened. 'Allow the bloody commies to take over? Is that what we've fought for? Hell, what about American honour? What about the future of our country? *Your* country?'

'Isn't it a bit early in the day for discussing politics?' Glenn's mother had protested. 'Can't we sit down to a family breakfast on a Sunday morning before we go to church and just talk pleasantly about . . .?' She seemed to be mentally searching for a topic. '. . . something else?'

Glenn loved his mother, but he'd already learnt that you couldn't, and shouldn't, sweep everything under the carpet. Things had to be said. Otherwise, how would anything be changed? Sacrosanct family Sundays . . . Images flickered in his head. Going to church, doing the chores, mowing the lawn, talking to the neighbours, family dinner. It was all so damned safe. It made Glenn want to scream. He'd discovered a new thread to life in debates at high school. And he wanted to run with it.

His father moved a clean plate that was still on the table to one side. There was something in the action that seemed somehow threatening to Glenn. 'We've made a goddamn commitment.' His father's voice rang out, proud and true. As if he were running for President, Glenn found himself think-ing. 'America has made a goddamn commitment.' He got to his feet and stood, towering over Glenn, it seemed. 'And we were right to do so.'

Glenn took a deep breath. 'Wrong, Dad.'

He saw his mother grip the back of the chair. He stood up, too. On level ground, he thought. Almost. He wasn't as tall as his father – not yet. But one day he would be. Even now he wasn't so far off.

'Wrong, son?' His father glared at him; black beetle brows drawn into a frown. 'What d'you mean, *wrong*? Care to rephrase that?'

Glenn felt that they were all holding their breath. 'With respect, sir, Eisenhower had no right to intervene in an internal debate about another country's government.'

'Is that so?' His father's eyes glittered.

'That's what I think.' No one had the right to dictate how others should live their lives, what they should believe in. And, suddenly, Glenn realized something. He wasn't repeat-ing what Brad or Al or any of the other guys had said. He wasn't parroting what he'd read in any pamphlet. This was Glenn speaking. This was what he believed.

His father swore, low, under his breath. He ran his fingers through his short, dark crew cut. Glenn recognized that he was near to the edge. And he almost wanted him to step over. 'Oh, it is, is it?' His father clenched his fists. He took a step closer to Glenn. Would he take a swing at him? Was that what he'd do?

'Yes, sir.' Glenn gritted his teeth and held firm, though he felt himself sway.

'Ted.' His mother took a step towards his father, but he put up a warning hand to stay her. And inched back, his breathing shallow.

He gave his son a level and thoughtful gaze. 'You've a lot to learn, boy,' he said. 'You don't know everything, though you think you do. Fact is, sometimes a stronger force has to intervene and do what they know to be right.' He nodded, as if satisfied he'd had the last word, turned on his heel and walked out of the door.

'We can't withdraw because we can't lose face.' Glenn realized that he was trembling. 'That's the truth. What kind of strength is that?'

'That's enough, Glenn.' His mother swiftly crossed the room and took his hands in hers. 'Leave it. Don't get drawn in. Let him be. That's all I ask.'

So often as a child, Glenn had buried his head in her breast and felt her warm arms wrap around him. She had given him comfort and support and asked for nothing in return. But now . . .

It was his turn to take her in his arms. She felt so small, so defenceless. She'd washed her thick, dark hair ready for church and the ends were flicked into a delicate wave. Her hair smelt of lime, of her shampoo. 'I don't know, Mom,' he whispered in her ear. 'I don't know if I can.'

★

'He drew me in,' Glenn told Bethany now. 'Into politics, into thinking about war and what we were doing there in Vietnam. And then I got some of the answers I was looking for at high school.' He looked at Bethany, at the smoothness of her brow, at her eyes, which seemed to hold a sense of peace he'd only ever dreamed of. He'd imagined he knew so much. And he'd wanted, more than anything, to prove his father wrong.

Once he was drawn in, there was no going back, not for himself, not for his mother's sake, not for the sake of any elusive family harmony. He was growing up. And his world, the world of his generation, was light years away from the world of his father.

CHAPTER 17

The course at Riad Lazuli was coming to an end and Nell felt sad. She and Amy had come here to the Saadian Tombs on this, their final day – her choice; Amy had seemed unusually reluctant – but Nell could sense her friend's growing anticipation to be gone. For Amy, it wasn't nearly over. She couldn't wait to get to Essaouira, on the next leg of her journey, to find what she was looking for. Even if she found nothing, she would at least have tried. And Nell felt a fleeting stab of envy. What was *she* looking for? She had thought she had some idea, but now she wasn't so sure.

She had loved this time in Marrakech, she had so enjoyed meeting Amy, and the course on Moroccan cuisine had surpassed her expectations. She'd quite fallen in love with the food of this country – with the slow and deliberate cooking, the precision in the use of delicate spices, the mix of the sweet and the sour. But how far forward had she come in her quest to find out more about her mother's life? Not very far at all, she conceded. And as for her marriage . . . In saying what she'd said to Callum, she had taken an irretrievable step away from him. She had separated herself on a practical level, just as they were separated on a physical one. What next?

She had to admit that the encounter with Rafi in the bar last night had taken her by surprise. Here was an attractive man from another culture who seemed to get what she was about, who seemed to understand her on some deeper level without her having to explain. What did that say about her relationship with Callum? And Nell had responded to Rafi. Perhaps she wasn't as emotionally dead as she had thought. Perhaps his attentions had been flattering and simply acted as a trigger. Because she might have told him that it wasn't a good idea to meet for dinner, but the truth was that she'd been tempted. What did that tell her about her marriage?

The Saadian Tombs near the Kasbah Mosque were a rather glorious mausoleum built for Sultan Al-Mansur in 1603 from Italian marble, mosaic tiles and gilded wood panelling. They had been walled up by one of his not so admiring successors until their discovery in 1917, so Marion had informed them at lunch when they'd told her where they were heading. Nell watched as Amy pulled out her camera. No doubt, she was less interested in the history and in the hundred or so members of Saadian royalty apparently buried in graves within the grounds than she was in the magnificent vaulted roof, the colourful *zellige* tiles, the delicate Arabic script and the elaborate carvings which she was currently photographing with a resurging enthusiasm.

'He didn't tell me it was this good,' she muttered.

'He?'

'Oh, just a colleague at work.'

Uh huh. 'Have you had to change your flight back to the UK?' Nell asked her. 'Because of going to Essaouira?'

'Oh, I've got a couple more days. I've left things as they are for now. I'll go with the flow.' Amy continued taking shots of the mosaics.

And they *were* rather lovely. Nell had noticed that the patterns were either geometric or abstract. Some radiated from a central star shape, some were floral, others a beehive pattern, like a honeycomb. She stood back a little to admire the effect.

'So many ancient techniques passed down and perfected through the generations.' Amy shook her head, as if wondering at the marvel of the workmanship. 'And all created to remember someone by. It takes your breath away, doesn't it?' Amy had stopped taking photographs. Now she was just drinking it all in.

'Mmm.' Although you didn't need this kind of splendour to remember someone. Nell found herself once more thinking about her mother and saffron. What must it be like, she wondered, simply to go with the flow? Amy's plans were so fluid, so flexible, and hers seemed so staid in comparison. Perhaps, rather depressingly, that was all part of being married. You had another person to consider – and she wasn't even doing terribly well on that front. She and Callum hadn't talked since that last conversation. But they would have to sometime. They would have to decide what to do. And she felt the pain of imminent loss like a punch in the belly. Too much loss, she thought.

'Yeah, so I'll see how it pans out in Essaouira before

I decide about the flight,' Amy returned to their previous conversation.

'But when are you leaving Marrakech?'

'Tomorrow morning.' Amy turned to grin at her. 'I couldn't miss tonight's grand feast.'

Nell glanced at her watch. 'Which reminds me. I must get back.' Thank goodness for cooking. At least when she was cooking she could forget – for a while.

For their final culinary challenge, they were all preparing an individual signature dish under Hassan's guidance. She was making a chicken tagine with fennel. She had chosen fennel because not only did she love the unique taste of it but the vegetable was in season and she preferred to cook with this factor in mind. It was a relatively simple recipe, but still time-consuming when you were making it for so many people. And although she'd done most of the preparation, she still wanted to allow plenty of time for the final stages, to get the delicate flavour just right.

'Why don't you come with me?' Amy's eyes gleamed.

'Where to?'

'Essaouira, of course.' She took Nell's hands in hers. 'It would be an adventure. You deserve an adventure.'

'Oh, I couldn't.' Though Nell smiled. An adventure sounded fun. And her mother would approve. She had certainly had her share of adventures – even though she'd kept quiet about some of them.

'Why not?'

'My flight's booked for tomorrow afternoon.'

'You could change it.'

'And Callum's picking me up from the airport.'

'You could ring him.'

Yes, but what would she say? That she was heading off for an adventure – when their marriage was quite clearly on the rocks? That she wasn't ready to go home? That instead of missing him – though she did – coming here to Marrakech had made her doubt their relationship, seriously consider whether or not they had a future at all? Nell shivered. 'And I have to get back to work. Real work. In the restaurant.'

'Ah.' Amy turned back to the tombs. 'OK. It was just an idea.'

Later, at Riad Lazuli, Nell went upstairs to get changed for dinner. But instead of going into her room she passed by the latticed windows and took the stairs that led to the upper roof terrace.

The sky was shifting into icy blue tinged with pink in preparation for sunset and the swallows were circling, rising, darting above the rooftops of Marrakech. She could feel the tremble and flutter of their wings as they arced and soared above her. Nell rested her hands on the balustrade. She looked out towards the twelfth century Koutoubia minaret, standing tall among the pink medina rooftops with their cypresses and lilac, their bougainvillea and fig trees. She could even see the Atlas Mountains, high and hazy in the distance beyond the flat, cocoa-brown plain and the palm groves outside the city walls. The pink of the medina was growing deeper now, turning almost salmon as the sun dropped and the yellow late-afternoon light hit the roofs and the walls.

Nell was pleased with her dish. Hassan had tasted it and he'd been complimentary, too. She'd been worried that he would disapprove since she had adapted the traditional recipe slightly. She'd always done this; it was part of her long-standing relationship with food, going back to when she first cooked in the farmhouse with her mother. In this instance she had added saffron and ginger to the delicate blend of fennel and coriander. It added, she felt, a touch of sweetness, since the preserved lemon could make the recipe rather acidic. But it also added an edge. It lifted the flavour while maintaining its subtlety.

Hassan had frowned. Then: 'You have flair,' he pronounced.

'Thank you.'

He spoke to Marion and asked her to translate.

'He wonders what you will do with your skill?' she asked. 'Are you already a professional chef? He thinks you must be. You pick things up very quickly. But you like to add something new, something of yourself.'

'I don't know any other way to cook,' Nell told him.

Marion translated. He nodded. 'It is the best,' he said. He spoke again in Arabic.

'The best way to express your own creativity,' Marion supplied.

Nell was flattered. She had a high opinion of Hassan's qualities as a chef, too. She had been lucky to have such a patient and thorough instructor. And he had given just as much attention to everyone, no matter how inexperienced or skilled. 'And yes, I do work in a restaurant,' she added, 'but I'm hoping to open my own place eventually. That's my dream.'

When Marion had translated this, Hassan nodded. 'You will do it. *Insha'Allah*,' he said. *God willing.*

The sun was dipping lower and the light was deepening into red and grey. It had been another surprisingly mild day— Marion had told them that, in November, the daytime temperatures here could vary between fifteen and twenty-three degrees Celsius – but as soon as the sun went down it grew chilly and you had to wear a sweater. Nell could see snow on the high peaks of the mountains. Marion had told them that it melted only in high summer, so already it had returned.

And so must she. Nell thought of the farmhouse. She hadn't had time to do the cards in the past few days. She paused as this realization sank in. It was a bit of a shock; she had practised Tarot on and off for years and had done a reading almost every day since her mother had died. Here, though, every day was a whirlwind. There was breakfast on the terrace or in the pink salon downstairs, depending on how warm it was, followed by cooking instruction and prac-tical lessons, interlaced with Marion's historical anecdotes, and then lunch. And as soon as she was free for a couple of hours, there was Amy, flying here, there and everywhere, eager to devour every new sight and experience and capture it on camera. More food preparation followed. And then there was dinner. By the time Nell went to bed at night, she was exhausted. But she slept deeply and well on a feathery pillow that smelt of cinnamon, and it was a sleep that was more refreshing than any she'd had for a long time.

She was living. Nell looked up at the swallows, heard their distinctive whistle as they flew hither and thither. They were living, too. Playing, she realized. Or so it seemed.

As the sky was transformed into a brilliant orange, Nell felt tears come to her eyes. Maybe it was this place, or just these few minutes of being alone. Her mother had died, but Nell wasn't ready to stop hearing her voice. She wanted to know more about the woman who had given birth to her – yes, even about the bad stuff. It was part of her mother's story, and so it was now part of them both. And if she found out who her mother really was . . . perhaps then she could finally accept that she had gone. And maybe even why she had done what she did. Because Nell hadn't finished with living, not for a long while yet.

It began with a high note. The muezzin, the call to prayer through first one megaphone in the medina and then another, starting from different places at different times and then combining, picking up drama, building to a climax. Nell had become familiar with it and yet it still took her by surprise. It was a wailing, at once both plaintive and hypnotic, sad and compelling. The language meandered; it was a chant, a drone that was designed so that it could not be denied. She closed her eyes and listened.

The twilight sky, the echo of prayer lying still in the air, was so breathtakingly beautiful that Nell couldn't leave the rooftop terrace until the sun had finally set, streaming like shot silk across the sky and the medina. Until the sky was darkening into night-time.

Down in her room, she quickly got changed into a soft jersey pale-blue maxi-dress and went down to see Ahmed in Reception. The blue of Riad Lazuli, she found herself thinking, was a deep, almost celestial blue. Like the gemstone the riad was named after, it was studded with golden pyrites which shimmered like stars.

She noticed that Ahmed wore a gold ring on his little finger. The lapis inset within the band was tiny but perfect.

Ahmed smiled as he saw her looking. 'It is the stone of friendship and truth,' he said.

'It's beautiful.' And they had captured the colour so well in the decor of the riad's interior.

He bowed his head. 'And what can I help you with?' he asked.

'Would it be possible to use your computer?' she said. 'I wanted to see if I could change my flight home.'

'Ah.' He didn't seem surprised. 'I can help you with that, of course. You want to stay longer in our country, is that it?'

'Yes,' she said. 'I want to visit a saffron farm.'

'Good idea.' Amy was behind her, grinning from ear to ear. 'Tell you what. You come to Essaouira with me and I'll come with you to the saffron farm. I reckon they're in the same general direction. Deal?'

'Deal,' said Nell. There was her mother and there was Callum; the dead and the living. It was only another few days at the most. She would do what she could about her mother first. She had to. And if Callum couldn't understand that need, then so be it. After that . . . she would worry about what she was going to do about her marriage.

CHAPTER 18

The following day, Amy and Nell said their goodbyes and took a taxi from Riad Lazuli to the bus station, handcart to the city walls included.

'Damn it,' said Amy, after they'd bought their tickets and joined the people waiting outside.

'What?'

'I'll have to call him.' He ought to know where she was heading – this was supposed to be a work trip, and Jake Tarrant was, apparently, in charge. She found him on her contacts list, where she'd placed him after his call when she was in the Majorelle Garden. Under 'Rooibos'.

'Amy?' She heard the surprise in his voice. Maybe even a note of pleasure, but she could be imagining that.

'About Essaouira,' she began.

'Yes?'

It wasn't easy. Amy exchanged a glance with Nell. Thank goodness she was coming with her. She was a great companion, and Amy was looking forward to spending more time with her. A friend for life? It certainly seemed that way.

'I've changed my mind,' she said to Jake.

'Oh?'

'In fact, I'm waiting for the bus to Essaouira right now.' She winked at Nell.

'So you want to check out the music there?' He sounded somewhat taken aback. He didn't need to know about the blue door, Amy decided.

'I thought it made sense, yes.'

'OK. Ah.' He paused. Seemed about to say more. 'What changed your mind? Did Duncan –'

'No.' She really didn't want to talk about Duncan.

'Only I didn't mention it to him. In case you were wondering.'

'I wasn't.' Amy stepped to one side to allow a woman past. She was carrying a baby strapped to her back and a large bag on her arm, and herding two children in front of her. Her husband walked beside her; his responsibility seemed to comprise of holding the bus tickets.

'Amy, I wanted to talk to you,' Jake said. 'I've been thinking. Maybe we got off on the wrong foot.'

You could say that.

'You and I are working on this event together, as a team. We need to collaborate.'

Collaborate. If Amy were to offer to help the woman . . . How would her husband react? Would he be embarrassed? Angry? Would he even notice?

'Duncan brought me in, I know. But this project . . . it's our baby. Yours and mine.'

Yours and mine? Amy ignored the heat of the morning sun on her forehead. The flush seemed to be filling her entire body. But she was far too young for the menopause, and it wasn't that hot, not really. And this project used to be *her* baby. She had to remember that. She hoisted her bag further up her shoulder. But she mustn't bear a grudge. She must move on. And, to give him his due, it sounded as if Jake wanted that, too. 'Well . . .' She pictured him in her mind's eye. Spiky hair, dimples, crooked tooth, those boots . . . She smiled. Caught Nell giving her a curious look and quickly turned the smile into a frown. 'Yes, I suppose it is,' she said.

'The relationship between you and Duncan . . .'

'What?' She really was frowning now.

'Oh, come on, Amy.' He laughed. 'I'm not stupid. I admit I was surprised. A woman like you . . . But it's none of my business.'

'No, it's not.' And what did he mean – *a woman like you*? 'But, just for the record, it's a past relationship.'

'Past?'

'Yes. As in no longer current. *Finito*. Ended.' And never had a decision felt more right.

'I see.' Though he sounded as if he didn't believe her.

'And . . .' Why was she trying to justify it to him? For goodness' sake. Her love life – or lack of it – was her own affair. The gallery was her own affair. And Duncan's. Who did Jake Tarrant think he was? An events relationships counsellor – brought in to re-establish harmony? 'Never mind,' she said. 'I have to go. The bus is coming.' On cue, it screeched into the depot in a cloud of pink dust and everyone surged forwards, a human tidal wave.

'I was just going to say that your relationship has nothing to do with me,' he said. Rather curtly, she thought. 'I'm not interested in personal stuff. I just want this Moroccan event to be a big success.'

Not interested in personal stuff? He needn't worry – neither was she. 'Presumably, that's what Duncan's paying you for,' she said, equally coolly.

'And about Essaouira. I need to tell you something.'

Amy picked up her case and followed the rest of them to the side of the coach, where the driver was flinging the bags haphazardly into the luggage hold. 'What?'

'The thing is, Amy –'

'Tell me when I get back.' She'd had enough. 'I have to go.'

On the bus, Amy watched the countryside shift from roadside stalls selling plants and ceramics and leafy orange groves just outside the city to a more desert landscape, the pink-brown earth broken up from time to time by tall palms, olive groves and bamboo. There were settlements, too – the sleepy villages often looked like nothing more than a collection of shacks, but there was always a mosque and a café, donkeys and trailers, men sitting around, working with wood or metal and boys sorting cartloads of fresh mint.

The road was good and the bus fast; during the two and a half hour journey they overtook scooters, clapped-out Mercedes taxis and trucks – usually laden with building materials or crates of melons. Later, Amy saw sheep and goats on the plains and a woman with a swathe of hay on her head leading a bullock. Meanwhile, throughout the journey, the backbone of the country, the rose-tinted Atlas Mountains, remained soft and unfocused in the near-distance.

Amy became aware that Nell was watching her.

'Do you like him?' she asked.

'Him?'

'Whoever you were talking to on the phone just before we left. Jake Tarrant, wasn't it?'

Amy gave her a look. Just what was she implying? 'He drives me crazy,' she said. 'And, before you jump to conclusions, that's not in a good way, OK?'

Nell shrugged. 'Maybe that's because you want him to pounce.'

Pounce? Against her will, a vision of Jake flashed into Amy's mind. Pouncing. She gritted her teeth. 'I certainly do not,' she said.

Nell grinned. 'Not even a bit?'

'Well . . .' He was attractive, she'd give him that. And he hadn't been too smug when she'd told him she'd changed her mind about Essaouira. He was intelligent. Interesting. And the sadness she'd glimpsed in him drew her – just a little. What was it, she wondered, that made her so drawn to people who looked sad? 'He's unhappy about something,' she added. 'I don't know what.'

Nell tucked a blond curl away from her face. 'I expect you'll get to the bottom of it.'

'Who says I'm going to try?' But Amy couldn't help laughing.

Nell laughed with her. She seemed cheerful enough now, but last night during the banquet – which had been a huge success, with lots of different and authentic dishes to taste and try – Amy had noticed her slip out, probably in order to make that phone call to her husband. She'd come back twenty minutes later, slightly red-eyed but with that same determined, wobbly smile. After that, Amy had taken pictures of the group – she'd already taken some of the food before they'd demolished it – and when she looked for Nell later, she'd gone up to bed.

'How did Callum take it?' she asked her now, as they were driven through the desert landscape, the dust flying. 'What did he say about your change of plan?'

'He said that he isn't sure who I am any more.' Nell stared out of the window.

'That's a bit extreme.' She had only changed her itinerary by a couple of days. What was so wrong with going off to look at a saffron farm – especially when saffron had always been such an important part of her family history?

'Maybe it is.' But Nell didn't seem too sure. 'Or maybe he's right. Amy, how can you tell if someone really knows you?'

Oh, dear. Amy thought of Duncan, and she thought of Jake. She was certainly no expert. But . . . She put her arm around Nell's shoulders and gave her a quick squeeze. 'You just can,' she said. 'In time.'

CHAPTER 19

Morocco, 1974

It was autumn and the wind was getting that chill again. They still ate supper up on the roof terrace, but now they wore jackets and took blankets up there with them. There were no more summer picnics on the beach with the purple brocade cushions washed and re-stitched by Bethany, the little tripod brazier Glenn had picked up for a song, the tea kettle and whatever foodstuff goodies Bethany had prepared for them. He'd loved those picnics, when it was just the two of them watching the waves, the heat of the sun visibly quivering over the sand, the occasional camel being led by the reins, reminding them that this was Morocco. And that they were here, living the dream.

Glenn wondered how Bethany would cope in the winter. She was such a sunshine girl. He was tempted to suggest they leave and go to India, take their chances, travel overland, as he had done before. But they didn't have much money; they lived hand to mouth as it was, and at least they both had work here. Bethany was still cleaning in the hotel and was planning to put in a few weeks crop-picking at a place just out of town. Glenn had found a job teaching English to the children of a

217

well-off French family who lived in a villa on the outskirts of the town. Howard didn't seem to do anything much, as far as Glenn could tell – though he always got money from somewhere. And Gizmo was still busking down by the harbour. He didn't make a lot, but sometimes people felt sorry for him and bought him lunch or a strong Arabic coffee, which seemed to keep him going. The four of them weren't exactly a family, but they were a small community. It was working. Since Bethany had joined them, it really was working. And Glenn didn't want to split their little unit up – at least not yet.

'Where were you when it happened?' Howard asked him one night in his lazy drawl. Was he trying to catch him out? Glenn often thought Howard was aiming to show him up in front of Bethany.

'It?' Up in the sky, the swallows were doing their class act. Glenn was conscious of the soft thrum of their wings, their distinctive call as they formed chaotic patterns in the sky above. Swooping, diving, running out of power and stalling in mid-air. Soon, though, they'd be moving on down to the Sahara Desert and then past the Equator, maybe to the Congo.

'Kennedy's assassination, man.' Howard sounded shocked. 'I thought that's how you Yanks always said it – you know – *Where were you when it happened*?'

Glenn shrugged. It was true enough. People still talked about it. People still asked that question. Even in a hippie commune in Morocco.

Gizmo started playing his guitar, softly. He had taken to wearing loose Arab trousers and tunics these days. With his dark dreadlocks and bandana and the banana-yellow *babouches* that most of the Arabs wore, he could be taken for a Moroccan himself. He was strumming the chords of Leonard Cohen's 'Bird on the Wire'. Glenn had listened to the *Songs from a Room* album constantly when it was first released. The lyrics were indelibly printed on his mind; it was so associated with his leaving. He, too, had tried in his own way to be free.

'In my room at home, reading.' It was a Friday lunchtime and, normally, he'd be in school, but he'd been off with flu and had only got up that morning. His father was home, too, from the bank, on his lunch break.

'What happened?' Bethany eyed him gravely. She always wanted detail. It wasn't enough to know where you were when it happened. Bethany needed to know what you were thinking, what you were feeling, how it had affected your life. The entire emotional picture – that was Bethany.

'I heard a cry from downstairs.'

Gizmo stopped playing and handed Glenn the skinny spliff he'd picked up from the ashtray.

Glenn took a drag. 'Then silence.'

'You can't hear silence, man,' Gizmo said. 'That's not possible. Silence is just there.'

Glenn looked at Bethany. 'You can.'

She nodded. 'You can.'

'Only relatively speaking, man,' Gizmo groaned.

Howard said nothing. He just sent his pale gaze humming from Bethany to Glenn and then back again. Like a bloody husky. God only knows what he was thinking. He was pretty much a closed book. Since his initial protest, he hadn't said a word against Bethany. The deadline for her so-called trial period had come and gone without mention. Glenn supposed Howard had accepted her. And she cooked for him, didn't she?

'What did you do?' Bethany sat perfectly still.

Glenn shrugged. 'I ran down the stairs, hanging on to the banister. I was still spun out from the flu . . .' But it had been such a cry – and from both of them.

'And?'

'My folks were just standing there.' In front of the black-and-white television set, eyes wide, strangely united, frozen to the spot.

Bethany nodded.

'All Mom could do was point at the TV.' But Glenn soon found out for himself. Kennedy had been assassinated as he rode in the presidential car down a street in downtown Dallas by a guy called Lee Harvey Oswald. Lyndon B. Johnson had been sworn in before the plane took off back to Washington that same day.

'It was a shock, man.' Gizmo paused in his playing. 'Freaked me right out.'

'Sure was.' Glenn passed on the spliff. Some of the more political guys in school had said that Kennedy wasn't what they needed in America, that for all his fine rhetoric about peaceful solutions to build stability, he had done nothing to bring the Vietnam conflict to an end. But . . . Glenn was only fifteen. He wasn't sure what America did need. Kennedy was young and energetic and had at least given them all hope. To see him assassinated . . . Glenn was horrified. Everyone was. And it only intensified the strength of his increasingly pacifist views. Was this what they had come to? A citizen of America shooting his own president?

'Your father must have been really upset,' Bethany said.

His father. Even Glenn had been surprised at the depth of his father's mourning. The Sunday following the assassination, the three of them had watched the live TV coverage as Lee Harvey Oswald was transferred from police headquarters to the county jail. They saw the pistol being aimed and fired at point-blank range, and they heard the shot.

'Good man.' Glenn's father clenched his right fist and smacked it hard into his left palm. 'Good man.' Later, they discovered the assailant was a nightclub owner named Jack Ruby and that Oswald had died two hours later at Parkland Hospital.

They watched Kennedy's funeral on the TV, too. Jackie Kennedy and the president's two brothers lit an eternal flame. Little John F. Kennedy Jr, whose third birthday it was – and who would, Glenn guessed, be forever traumatized – gave a salute to his father and, for the first and last time in his entire life, Glenn saw his own father weep.

'Yeah, it was an emotional time,' he said now. He blinked. Christ, and here he was crying himself after all these years.

Bethany reached out to put a cool hand on his arm. She often wore a kaftan or djellaba like the women of Morocco – though she never hid her face. 'It helps me understand the place, the people,' she'd told him. 'I want to feel what they feel.'

'What *do* you feel?' Glenn asked her.

'I feel like a different person.'

Glenn had smiled and told her he knew what she meant, but the truth was, he didn't want her to be a different person. He loved the one she already was.

But that was Bethany. A few days ago she'd met an old woman in the artisans' quarter and had come back with her hands hennaed and bandaged with strips of cloth. They'd all laughed at her and told her she was crazy, but when she eventually unwrapped the cloths her hands were decorated with the most exquisite deep-orange markings Glenn had ever laid eyes on. 'It's beautiful,' he'd told her, running his fingertips gently over the henna.

'Black-magic woman,' Howard had added, raising an eyebrow.

And now, once again, Glenn saw Howard clocking their connection. What was it with the guy? What the hell was his problem?

'Do you think Kennedy would have put a stop to the conflict, if he'd lived?' Bethany asked.

'A lot of people thought so.' Though this was easy to say. Regardless of Kennedy's promises, the war in Vietnam had gone on. And as Diem, the puppet leader, lost more and more ground in South Vietnam, the only American response was more funding, more aid, more helicopters.

Glenn hunched up his knees and wrapped his arms around

them. The sun was going down and the sky was mottled with pink and grey. Dusk. They'd have to get hold of some more fuel for the fire; maybe he and Bethany should go down to the beach and look for driftwood before it got dark.

Those high-school debates seemed like worlds away now. About Vietnam, about America. As a country, they were relatively new. They hadn't been exploring or colonizing for centuries; they had never been an empire. Was that why Americans always felt they had something to prove?

'Once Kennedy was gone, the mood of the press changed even more,' Glenn told Bethany. 'I can remember being in the common room, reading a battered copy of *The New York Times* . . .'

'Woohoo, *The New York Times*.' Gizmo flailed his arms around wildly, dreadlocks flying, and they all laughed.

'What did it say?' Bethany wrapped her scarf more tightly around her neck.

Yeah, he thought, he'd take her down to the beach. They'd run along the sand, the salt wind whipping her hair, and he'd hold her until she was warm again. 'They criticized Diem for his blatant ineptitude . . .'

'Blatant ineptitude – yoo woo, college boy,' jeered Gizmo.

Glenn threw a cushion at him. Howard just smiled that cool, lazy smile of his.

'It was clear as bloody day to everyone that he wasn't winning the war. No one liked Diem's brother Nhu, and no one liked Nhu's wife.' Glenn chuckled. 'They called her the Dragon Lady.'

'No Nhus is good news,' muttered Gizmo.

Bethany laughed. There was a spark in her eyes that drew Glenn. He couldn't imagine that spark ever not drawing him.

'D'you wanna go down to the beach and look for driftwood?' he asked her.

Howard shifted his position on the mattress. He stretched out his legs. He looked bored.

Bethany got to her feet and held out her hand.

Living at the riad was hardly the lap of luxury. But life, thought Glenn, was pretty much perfect. He'd heard about the amnesty programme brought in by Ford last month. Did that mean he was no longer a political refugee? He supposed so, although he didn't know the exact terms of the amnesty. Some kind of community service, he guessed, for maybe up to two years. Just another kind of imprisonment . . . Anyway, he couldn't imagine going back home – not yet, anyway. Why would he? They were living here in the moment. The stars were lighting up the dark curtain of the sky and he was with the woman he loved. He couldn't imagine anything that could possibly go wrong.

CHAPTER 20

'Let's go in here.' Amy ducked into the shop she'd spotted, the windows of which were plastered with posters of Jimi Hendrix, Bob Marley and Cat Stevens. It was a tiny den full of records, music memorabilia and old musical instruments. They should know about Essaouira's heyday; they seemed to be still living in it.

Ahmed had booked them into another riad – how could they stay anywhere else? Amy had said – though they'd insisted on a budget one. And it was dilapidated, but charming. They would be here in Essaouira for two or three nights. Depending.

So far, Amy liked the place. It was very different to Marrakech – open and airy, with a wide curve of sandy beach which would be appealing in the summertime but was bleak and windy in November, despite the camels with colourful saddles they spotted in the distance. The medina was smaller than the one in Marrakech, and far less manic. It was just as vibrant, though, Amy thought. Even romantic. And the traders in the souks under the cloistered arches of the main street weren't as pushy; people in general seemed friendlier. It was less of a tourist hotspot; more real.

This morning they'd walked to the harbour, where a fleet of blue fishing boats was moored. Fishermen dressed in a variety of djellabas, jeans, corduroy trousers and oilskins were crouching, mending huge trawling nets and lining the walkways, shouting, pointing and beckoning to tourists and onlookers; others were passing buckets of fish in a human chain to be stacked, iced and crated. Beside their stalls were pails of sardines, langoustines and wriggling eels, pots of octopuses, spider crabs and ponderous lobsters; the plastic crates and trestle tables were loaded with John Dories, skate and rainbow-scaled dorados glittering on heaps of ice. Some of the locals were coming with their own buckets to pick up their fish for dinner. Gulls screeched and swooped overhead, looking for pickings. But even the men didn't like Amy taking photographs – either that, or they expected her to pay for the privilege – so she kept it low key. Which was rather a pity, since the fishermen were interesting, too, with their wizened faces, white beards and sea-stained clothes.

But they were looking for the blue door. They made their way along the honey-coloured ramparts, past a row of cannons, where the wild sea crashed on to black rocks, and walked through to the large open square where a stage was being erected for the gig that night. 'GNAWA MUSIC', proclaimed a large banner above and, to confirm it, Amy saw a lorry emblazoned with the words 'Touareg Prod' in the process of being unloaded by its crew. Clearly, then, the Gnawa scene was still a big attraction here. Trance music, Jake had said. Jake. She wondered what he had been about to tell her.

But whatever it was, it would have to wait, because she certainly wouldn't be phoning him again. If she wanted relationship counselling, she had Nell . . .

The man serving in the music shop was laid-back in his approach to customers and clearly not in a hurry to get on, so Amy told him about the Moroccan event they were organizing in Lyme. He spoke very good English.

'We were wondering if any of the Gnawa bands ever came to play in the UK?' she asked. Well, Jake was. 'We can't afford a huge fee or anything, but if they happened to be already on tour . . .'

'Ah yes. It is possible.' The proprietor, sixty if he was a day, began to rummage in the drawers of an old desk, pulling out leaflets and scraps of paper. He scribbled down names and email addresses for her on another sheet. 'Why not?' He nodded his head energetically. 'You can contact them. Here.'

'Thanks.' Amy took the sheet of paper from him. Or Jake Tarrant can, she thought. It would give him an opportunity to demonstrate his administrative expertise. She smiled grimly.

'Can you tell us a bit more about the music?' Nell was asking the man in the shop. 'What are these?' She picked up a pair of black iron castanets. There were quite a few scattered around the shop, all different sizes.

Amy thought about Nell's question: 'How can you tell if someone really knows you?' She had been talking about Callum, of course. *How could you?* Amy wondered now. Was it from the way they'd understand what you wanted, the way they might second-guess you, know what you were thinking, what you were about to say? She supposed that was it. Your special person should understand you that well, shouldn't he? He should *get* you. But she was no expert. The truth was, she'd never experienced having a special person for herself. And the thought was scary – she wasn't at all sure she wanted to. Because if you had a person like that, you'd depend on him. And you could lose him, too.

'This is the *krakeb*,' said the music-shop man. 'Gnawa music is a mixture of ancient African, Berber and Arabic religious songs and rhythms. It is a prayer and a celebration of life.' He demonstrated how to hold the castanets between the fingers and thumbs. 'You want to try?'

'OK.' They both had a go. It was surprisingly difficult, though Nell was better at it than Amy. At least Nell's attempt sounded faintly musical.

He showed them the lute-like *gimbri*, which looked a bit like a wide cricket bat with three strings for plucking, and the bongo drums, which could be patted with the palms of your hand or brushed very gently. 'It is ritual music,' he said. 'The music is often combined with chanting in Arabic or Gnawa.'

'What do they chant?' Nell asked.

'The message will be spiritual or religious. A message with the power to heal,' he said.

'But who are the Gnawa? Originally, I mean?'

'Descendants from the black brotherhoods of slaves taken and transported by traders along the caravan route,' he said.

Amy remembered Rafi telling them about the caravan

route, and how Marrakech had grown to be so important for trade. She guessed that Nell remembered, too.

'Originally, their purpose was to serve as guards to Morocco's sultans,' he went on, 'but it is said that when a mystical musician healer named Bilal cured Mohammed's daughter Fatima by singing her a song, their role changed from guards to musical doctors. Or those who heal the soul.'

'And where does trance come into it?' Amy asked. She liked the idea of healing the soul. It seemed like a journey. But was it the power of the history behind it – or was it the ganja they were probably all smoking?

'A very good Gnawan musician can use the *krakeb* to make sounds that place the audience into a trance.' He picked up the castanets as he spoke and moved his arms to the clacking beat, beginning to sway.

It was all Amy could do to stay upright. She blinked.

'You must hear a Gnawan song.' He selected a disc from a rack on the wall and slotted it into a CD machine on the shelf.

The music began with a wail and a strangely insistent string melody and continued with the clacking of the castanets and the beating of the drums. One singer led the song, others joined in with the refrain; a cymbal kept up a clashing accompaniment and a tambourine jangled in the background. It was almost impossible not to sway from side to side, to resist the intensity of the rhythm. One phrase seemed to be repeated over and over. Perhaps that was how they achieved trance, Amy thought. And it went on and on. Surreptitiously, she glanced at her watch. Fascinating though it all was, she had other fish to fry.

'A song may last up to several hours,' he said. But he smiled mischievously and switched off the machine. 'You like to buy a CD?'

'Of course we will.' Amy handed over some dirhams. It was the least she could do after all the information he'd given them. 'And may I ask you one more question?'

He bowed his head in assent.

'Do you recognize this place?' Amy produced the postcard from her bag once more.

He frowned. 'It may be here in this town, yes,' he said.

'Do you think so?'

'Or it may be in some other town.' He shrugged. 'Who can say?'

Someone, Amy hoped.

'But you had a lot of travellers here?' Nell asked. 'In Essaouira? In the sixties and seventies?'

He looked old enough to remember. Amy noted that Nell had avoided using the word 'hippie'. But the shop was a real hippie den – what with the pictures of sixties musicians, the old albums, the dusty gramophone and the motley collection of instruments from drums to castanets to tambourines to guitars.

'Yes, yes,' he said. 'Many people come here for the music, the sun, the sand.' He grinned. 'And the ganja.'

'Not just Jimi Hendrix then,' joked Nell.

The man put his hands together as if in prayer. 'Hendrix,' he said. 'He brings many people here still. He stayed down the coast, in Diabat. You must visit.'

'I think a relative of mine was here in the seventies,' said Amy. 'He was the one who sent this postcard. His name's Glenn Robinson. I don't suppose you've come across him?' It was a long shot. She should have brought the photo of Glenn with her; it might have helped. When that had been taken, of course, he'd been little more than a boy, and though she'd looked at it so many times Amy doubted she'd recognize him herself now even if she were to bump into him in the street. And, anyway, her aunt would never have parted with that precious photograph of her only son. 'He's American,' she added.

'Ah, American.' He nodded. 'We have many English, many American. Sometimes they camp on the beach. Or live in the old riads.'

'The riads?' Amy was surprised.

'The run-down riads. Some of them have been empty for many years.'

'Were there many of those around in the early seventies? Are there many now?'

He shrugged. 'Of course. Essaouira, it is a shifting town. It flows like the ocean and the wind. People come, people go. There is a riad like this along the street. Number 21.' He pointed. 'You must go and see.'

They did. When they got there they could see that number 21 was pretty much derelict, though it must have been beautiful once, judging by the carving around the old door, the decoration on the portal.

'Look!' Nell pointed. The emblem of a flower had been carved in the centre of the portal, though, due to time and erosion, it had crumbled and lost some of its definition. But . . .

'The rose of Mogador,' Amy said. She pulled out the post-card once again.

They both scrutinized it, looked back at number 21. It was the rose emblem, but it wasn't *the* rose emblem. And although the door had once been painted blue, like so many of the doors and shutters here in Essaouira, it wasn't *the* blue door.

They had lunch – fresh sardines – at a café in a cobbled and cloistered courtyard that was sheltered from the wind, and continued exploring in the afternoon. Amy had spoken to lots of people but, predictably, no one had heard of Glenn and, although there were lots of young hippies around, there didn't seem to be many of the older variety. She realized that she would have to give up. They had navigated their way around the entire town and they hadn't found the door. And even if they found it – what then? Glenn would hardly be liv-ing on the other side of it. It was a picture on a postcard; it didn't have to have any personal connection to him other than his sending it to his mother all those years ago.

'We've tried our best,' she said to Nell when they stopped at another café for a cup of eye-wateringly thick Arabic coffee.

'So what next?'

'We'll go to the saffron farm.' One particular farm had been earmarked for Nell by the owner of the riad and, as it was November, there was a bus going there in the morning for a day trip. Many people wanted to see the crocuses in full flower; it was quite a spectacle, and would, Amy hoped, make a good centrepiece shot for her exhibition.

They left the café and began to make their way back to the riad. In a narrow backstreet filtered by the shadows of the afternoon sun, they stumbled on another hammam. 'Look at this.' Nell drew her attention to the information board. 'Orson Welles did some filming here for *Othello* in 1949.'

'Another celebrity,' murmured Amy. Jimi Hendrix, Cat Stevens, Bob Marley and the rest, all lured by Essaouira's charm. Was that what had drawn Glenn here? she wondered. What had he been like? What had he been looking for? And why hadn't he ever gone back to his family? Back to America?

But Nell was pulling at her arm. 'We have to look in here.' She seemed very determined, so Amy followed her, past a sign reading 'ANTIQUES' and into what seemed to be an ancient riad. It drew them in further, through the pitted wooden door and into a narrow and musty passageway with wooden beams above it which opened out into a large court-yard full of ancient urns and statues. They began to explore. It was a fascinating collection – a true treasure trove of antique furniture and *objets d'art* arranged on three galleried floors, each rectangular room leading out from the centre and loosely themed: one room laid and hung with carpets and rugs on the walls and stone floors, one of religious artefacts, one of books, tapestries and paintings, and so on. The riad must have been a stunning place, though it was now well past its splendour date. The sculpted plaster was cracked and flaking, the pillars crumbling and the tiles broken; bits of timber propped up walls, a pile of rubble gathered dust in one corner and glazed lanterns lurched from the walls. A massive palm tree had grown through the centre of the courtyard up to the rooftop and beyond. It stood framed against the clear blue sky.

'And it's got a fabulous view.' They had walked right to the top and were looking down at the streets of Essaouira. Amy could see the minaret and, in the distance, the ocean, the waves curling into the shore. She let her gaze wander down into a quiet backstreet below, where some men were unloading a truck. She blinked. 'Nell.' Amy grabbed her. 'Look down there. Do you see what I see?'

There was a cobbled street and some half-derelict buildings. And just in front of the delivery truck . . .

'It's the blue door!' Nell gasped.

CHAPTER 21

Of course, Lillian had known immediately that Amy had taken the postcard. Bless her. Lillian knew she'd look after it. Considering Glenn was her son, Lillian had little enough of him.

When she'd first received it, when she'd seen it lying there on the front doormat, she'd snatched it up, greedily reading the few words he'd written, holding it to her breast . . . She knew she should destroy it. Just to be safe. But, in the end, she couldn't. The postcard held his last touch. Of course she couldn't.

Now, Lillian opened the top drawer of her bureau, where she kept her most treasured possessions. Not that there were many. Ted had destroyed her letters to him, every one. Just as she had kept his, every one. Why had she bothered? Why did she still treasure them after everything that had gone on? Lillian picked them up, ran her fingertips over the smooth surface of the top envelope, the one he'd written when . . . She looked out, away from the letter, towards her sitting-room window and the town street outside her net curtains. She had kept them because of what they had meant to her then. But she didn't want to read them now. She didn't want to be reminded of what might have been. Because it was never meant to be, and it never was.

Instead, she made her way over to her favourite armchair and lowered herself down. She thought of *her* letters – the ones she'd written to his home in America when she knew he wasn't there, when he first left Bridport and she didn't know where he was going, only that he was going to fight in the war, only that he was leaving, probably for good. Lillian had a place for writing her letters back then. She wrote them in her bedroom, where she was least likely to be disturbed, kneeling on a cushion on the floor and leaning on the windowsill. That way she could look out and remember how it was when the GIs left that day, how it was when he'd said he'd write to her. It also gave her a good vantage point. It warned her when her mother was coming home, or Mary. She didn't want anyone to know about the letters. Especially Mary.

Dear Ted . . .

At first she couldn't think what to write, so she wrote about Bridport and people she knew. And then she looked back at what she'd written. Boring, boring, boring . . . And when would he even receive the letter? She scrunched the page up into a ball. She had to do better than that. Why would a man like Ted be interested in people in Bridport? She was supposed to be showing him what she was really like. And what she was really like wasn't all this. It was about how she wanted to get away.

Her fountain pen flew over her mother's creamy-white writing paper.

Nothing ever happens here. It's so quiet, so predictable, so . . . She searched for the word . . . *humdrum. I always know what is going to happen – we all do. Sometimes I think I'll go mad with the sameness of it.*

When the war was over, she wouldn't be staying here in Dorset. Lillian stared out of the window into the grey street. She would get a job, or travel, do something with her life.

How should she sign it? 'Sincerely' seemed far too formal. 'All the best' seemed too impersonal, even optimistic – considering he was fighting in a war. She decided on 'Fondest regards, Lillian'.

She read it through once, immediately thought of a hundred ways she could make it more interesting, and sealed it in one of her mother's envelopes quickly, before she could change her mind. This was already her fourth attempt.

That afternoon Lillian went to the post office, the letter burning a hole in her pocket. She queued up. 'A stamp for America, please,' she said importantly to Daphne Hudson, who was behind the counter.

'Oh, yes?' Daphne scrutinized first the letter and then Lillian. 'What's this, then?' She shifted her bulk on the stool she sat on, raised her eyebrows in enquiry.

And that was it exactly. Lillian fidgeted uncomfortably under her gaze. You couldn't do anything in this town without everyone knowing about it. 'I'm running an errand for someone,' she said. And she leaned closer. 'It's a secret.'

'Ah.' Daphne nodded. Her whole body vibrated under her dark-brown dress. 'It'll be for your Mary, I reckon. One of them GIs.'

Lillian watched as she weighed the envelope. She opened her large book of stamps and leafed through the pages. 'You should tell her from me that she should use airmail envelopes.' She plucked one from a box beside her and passed it across the counter. 'You write on it instead of using a separate sheet of paper. Then you fold it.'

Lillian picked it up. It was blue and flimsy. 'Oh,' she said. 'Thank you.'

Daphne chuckled. 'Cheeky lot, them GIs, eh? Brightened up the town, though, didn't they, duck? For a while, anyway.'

'Oh, yes.' Lillian nodded. *For a while.* 'But you won't –'

'Say anything?' Daphne turned around and put the letter on the counter behind her. She put a finger to her lips. 'Oh, no. Mum's the word, eh?'

'Mum's the word,' repeated Lillian. She walked out of the post office. She'd write again next week, she decided. And this time she'd use the blue airmail paper. She could hardly wait.

In May 1945 it was over. Lillian and her family listened to the king's speech in disbelief. But it seemed to be true; it really seemed to be true. Even Mary, who was now engaged to be married to Johnnie Coombes, after weeks of whispered conversations with their mother and a decision to name the day just as soon as it could be arranged, seemed back to her normal self.

And then it was VE day. Shops had rosettes in the windows and there were flags and bunting everywhere. Bonfires were lit, there was a street party down the road, they opened the pier at West Bay and there was dancing like Lillian had never known. Lillian got caught up in the frenzy of celebration. A woman flung her arms around her in the street and a young farm lad whirled her round and kissed her full on the lips.

Lillian still wrote to Ted, though not as often. And she never heard back. But she could still picture him, his twinkly brown eyes and cropped hair. The uniform, the cheery 'Hi, Duchess.' And she couldn't help wondering, *Where is he now?*

CHAPTER 22

Morocco, 1975

'Happy birthday, Glenn.'

He opened one eye. She was wearing her loose cotton robe and Moroccan leather flip-flops and carrying a tarnished metal tray. On it was a small, silver-plated teapot and two tiny decorative glasses. He hiked himself on to one elbow and watched her as she placed it carefully on the low table, every movement languid, her long, dark hair falling forward like a fan.

'Come here, you.' He held out his hand.

'*Thé royale.*' She smiled. 'To celebrate.'

'Wow! A whole lot better than champagne, babe.' They sold it in the bazaar; the green tea contained fresh mint, star anise, liquorice, cardamom, cloves, vanilla and tiny rosebuds. They didn't treat themselves to it very often; when they did, they used it over and over until it tasted of nothing but dusty hot water.

She sank on to the worn satin coverlet of the bed next to him and he pulled her closer. Her skin smelt of the musky scent she wore, her hair was soft and fell across his face, tickling his mouth as she kissed him. 'I've got something for you,' she said.

'I sure hope so.'

'Wait a sec.' She pulled away and, reluctantly, he let her go.

She padded over to the other side of the room, and he watched her as she retrieved a brown carrier bag from under a pile of their clothes. He smiled. She came back, holding the bag in front of her like an offering.

'What's this?'

'Open it and you'll find out.' She laughed.

Inside was some tissue paper and then . . . He drew out a thick red woollen scarf and a shoulder bag patched together with different fabrics, the peace sign sewn in black next to a pink-and-white daisy. He laughed. 'Groovy . . . Did you –?'

'Make them? Yes, of course.'

'Amazing.' He wound the red scarf around his neck, pulled the shoulder bag over his head and on to his shoulder. Apart from this, he was naked. 'What do you think? Do they suit me, huh?'

'You look great.' Her eyes shone. She grinned, went over to pour the tea.

She'd opened a window and untied the sash. An arc of sunlight was lighting up the dust motes and creating a shadow on the grey stone floor. The breeze billowed the muslin curtain. Springtime seemed to enter the room like a promise. 'My best birthday,' he murmured, watching her pour the golden liquid into the two cups. He pulled off the scarf and the bag, placing them carefully on the bedside table. How had she managed to make these without him knowing?

She paused and looked over her shoulder. 'You haven't had your birthday yet. Only the first five minutes, anyway.'

'I know it already.' He laid back and stared up at the ceiling. 'Hey, I'm here with you, aren't I?'

'You are.' She brought him the tea. He sat up and she placed the glass in his hands. 'And I'm here with you.'

He kissed her forehead.

'But you must have had lots of good birthdays.' She settled back on the bed again, her bare brown legs curled under her. 'What about when you were a child?'

'Yeah, sure, they were cool.'

Glenn remembered his mother's sweet face as she carried the birthday cake into the dining room where he and his pals were romping around playing whatever birthday games they played, and which usually ended up in some good-natured rough and tumble. His mother. It had been six years. Sometimes he could hardly believe that. Would he ever see her again?

'And at uni,' Bethany went on, 'when you were doing all your political stuff, what did you do on your birthday, then? Go out drinking? Get laid?' She laughed, softly.

Glenn remembered his sophomore year at the University of Wisconsin. He'd gone there in the fall and, towards the end of the winter semester, his parents had come to take him out for his birthday. That year, spring didn't seem to hold out the hope it had before. There was too much uncertainty. It felt like they were all teetering on the edge of some sort of apocalypse. Glenn had got heavily involved in campus politics. And the more involved he got, the more activist he became.

'My folks came up to see me that first year,' he told Bethany. 'It was a total disaster.'

She sipped her tea and looked at him over the rim of the cup. 'What happened?'

'The usual.'

Glenn had shaken hands rather awkwardly with his father – upright and military, as ever, in his grey suit, collar and tie; clean-shaven, with that damned crew cut of his. And he'd hugged his mother. She looked real nice – she was wearing a little pill-box hat in robin's-egg blue and a close-fitting navy outfit that showed she hadn't lost her figure. But she looked tired. He remembered she had looked tired. The skin around her eyes was bruised and dark, and her rich, brown hair, though still neat and flicked up at the ends, had lost some of its lustre.

'Well, son,' said his father, 'how's it going?'

As they sat down, ordered dinner, ate their starters and drank a beer – orange juice for Glenn's mother – he filled them in on how he was doing at college. He was studying American Literature and the Literary Imagination. His marks were only average; the subject held his interest, but there was a lot happening on campus that had little to do with the literature programme. 'Sports?' his father asked hopefully.

Glenn shrugged.

'Have you met a nice girl?' His mother smiled. Her hands were clasped in front of her.

Glenn could see that his father was disappointed and his mother was desperately trying to be proud. 'Politics, I guess,' he said. He'd received an official letter from his draft board when he started at Wisconsin. He was classified 2-S, 'which you will keep until you graduate'. Education had given him deferment. But what about those guys who couldn't afford this sort of education? What about the black guys on street corners who wouldn't have the choice?

His father looked away. His mother gave a little – not very encouraging – nod.

In his birthday card was some money.

'We didn't know what to get you,' his mother said.

'You could start off with getting a decent haircut.' And his father laughed that sharp, humourless bark of his.

The waitress brought out their steaks.

Glenn put his hand to his hair. It was long and wavy and he liked it that way. 'Most of the kids have long hair,' he said mildly.

'And dress like tramps,' his father added. He got stuck in to his meal, slicing the rare meat neatly with his knife so that the blood oozed.

Glenn looked away. He'd put on a clean t-shirt and his jeans weren't that bad. He glanced down at his sneakers. Some caked-on mud and the laces were a bit frayed. That was the trouble with parents. They were obsessed with appearances. What really mattered was what was going on inside. Why couldn't they see that?

'Now, Ted.' Glenn's mother, forever the mediator, laid a

hand on his arm. Glenn noticed her worn wedding ring of narrow gold – apart from tiny pearl studs in her earlobes, it was the only jewellery she wore.

'And smoke pot all day.'

Here we go, he thought. Of course they smoked pot. Everyone smoked pot. It was how you relaxed, how you got a bit deeper into the things that mattered. His father was so straight he'd die rather than not know exactly where he was heading.

'Ted.' Glenn's mother sighed. 'It's our boy's birthday.'

Glenn shrugged. It usually only took his father ten minutes to wind him up. He was used to it. He picked up his fork and steak knife. He wasn't going to let the old man spoil his appetite.

His father simply ignored her. Nothing new there, then. 'You must have heard about these damned fool protestors,' he said, finally placing his knife and fork in a straight line in the centre of his empty plate. 'These students. Long-haired freaks, so-called peaceniks – thinking they know it all. Don't want my son tarred with the same brush, now, do I?'

Glenn stared at him, fought to stop the hackles rising. Didn't he know the truth? Couldn't he hear what Glenn was telling him? Did he really not know that his son was one of those long-haired student protestors? One of the freaks? Last year, a thousand students from Yale had marched in New York City, and colleges just about everywhere were holding anti-war lectures and debates. Glenn was part of it. And he wasn't in a minority any more.

'You think we should still be there then, Dad?' He kept his voice level. 'In 'Nam?' If there were no soldiers, Glenn thought, there would be no war. But there were, and the war was escalating. Ground troops had been sent in to protect American bomber bases – into the jungle, where they probably wouldn't even be able to tell the difference between the Vietcong and some innocent peasant farmer, for Chrissake. Glenn had read Bernard Fall's *Street Without Joy*. He had prophesied how it would be.

His father clenched his fist then slowly opened it again a finger at a time. 'We're doing what's right, son,' he said.

'Right? How can a war against humanity be right? Don't you see –?'

'I see you've got no faith in your country, son. And I see that nothing's changed. You haven't had any sense knocked into you.' His father's voice vibrated with emotion. 'You're still what you always were.'

Despite his previous resolution, Glenn had lost his appetite. He pushed his plate and his half-eaten steak away. Sometimes, he didn't know why he bothered. But it was part of the protest, wasn't it, the fight? It was up to them to make people like his folks understand how it really was.

His father began to scan the dessert menu.

'Have you finished, love?' His mother eyed Glenn's plate anxiously. 'Aren't you hungry?'

'I'm done.' He wasn't in the mood for this – not any more.

Glenn's mother looked from one to the other of them in despair. 'Every time,' she murmured. Bad luck for her, Glenn supposed, to have two men in her life with such opposing views.

Glenn rested his hand on hers. 'Sorry, Mom.'

'I should have made a cake.' His mother smiled weakly. 'Maybe they'll put some candles on our dessert for us.'

Something in her voice got to him. She was right. It was his birthday and he should at least make an effort to keep the peace. So with a last reluctant look at his father – why did he always want to fight him? – Glenn swallowed his anger and chose his dessert. Nothing had changed. Why would it? His father was still blind and his mother was still clinging to the illusion that they were a proper family, a family who could have dinner and celebrate together. A farce, he thought. That's what it was. Because they were all pretending. They weren't facing up to what was really going on in Vietnam. Apart from the protestors, no one was. And no one, he thought, would give a damn about birthdays out there.

'You did what you could.' Bethany took his glass and put both glasses back on the tray. 'You protested, you marched, you refused to go to war.'

'Yeah.' They had marched and held up banners, stuck flowers into the gun barrels of riot police, they had pro-claimed peace not war, love not hate. But what good had it done?

'And here I am.' He reached across, untied the belt of her robe. He didn't want to think about that any more. He didn't want to feel guilty about any man who might have taken his place in the ranks and got himself killed, he didn't want to think that he could have done more; been braver, made a difference. Not now.

'Here you are,' she agreed. Her hands stroked his face, moved to his neck, his shoulders. 'Here we are. And you mustn't be sad about birthdays. Not on your birthday.'

He groaned. He was twenty-six years old. His mother would be wondering where he was. He should write to her. Let her know he was alive. A postcard, at least. The old man wouldn't make her pay for a postcard, would he?

His mother's tears, his father's frown, Vietnam and the politics of America. He had left it all behind, and here he was with the woman he loved, living hand to mouth in a communal riad in western Morocco. Everything had changed, and yet nothing had changed. He was still preaching peace, not war. He was where he wanted to be. And yet, as he held Bethany in his arms, as he felt her cleave towards him, her eyes half closed with desire, her skin soft and tanned and smelling of musky rose, all he wanted to do was forget.

CHAPTER 23

'You're running away.'

This was what Callum had said to her when Nell told him she'd extended her trip by two days and was coming here to Essaouira. She glanced across at Amy, who had been deep in thought ever since they'd found the blue door. Nell squeezed her hand and was rewarded with a faint smile. They were walking side by side back to the riad. Nell knew that Amy was bitterly disappointed, and she couldn't blame her. Against all odds, they had found the door, which clearly belonged to a very old building, probably a riad. But it was impossible to tell for sure.

They had rushed out of the antiquey riad and taken a couple of backstreets to get to the place they'd spotted. But the door was locked and barred, and all the shutters were tightly closed. Amy had paced up and down and even knocked on the neighbouring doors, but her questions were met only with blank stares. The doors and the shutters looked as if they'd been shut up for decades. A long time must have elapsed since anyone had glimpsed the black-and-white tiles of the floor inside. The paint on the door had flaked way beyond the point it had reached when the postcard photo had been taken, and the stucco had crumbled even more. But there it was – the carved emblem of the rose of Mogador above the portal of the blue door, in a little-used backstreet on the outskirts of the medina in Essaouira.

They stayed there for half an hour or more. Now that she'd found it, Amy seemed reluctant to leave.

'What now?' Nell had asked at last. 'We could come back with an interpreter? Maybe someone from the riad –'

'There's no point.' Amy seemed to have made up her mind. 'We've found it. But what does it prove? Nothing, really.'

'That Glenn was in Essaouira?' It seemed unlikely that he would have bought the postcard anywhere else.

'Probably. But that's about all. And it was a long time ago. He could have spent only a few days here, for all we know.'

Nell supposed that she was right. Even so, on the way back to the riad she insisted they call into the music shop to get the owner to ask around. Amy shouldn't give up hope – not yet. But it was beginning to seem as if the trail had begun and ended with that blue door.

You're running away. Callum had sounded sad rather than angry when he said this to her, and this had made Nell feel guilty – until she remembered some of the things he'd said, the way he'd tried to take over, his lack of sensitivity about the farmhouse, his inability to understand.

'No, I'm not.' It didn't feel like running away. Running, yes, perhaps. But running towards something, to find something, not running away.

Nell had drawn the High Priestess in the Tarot again this morning. The woman of mystery, the card Nell had always associated with her mother, which made her feel closer to her than ever. She usually appeared in a reading when you needed to listen to and trust your inner voice. And, in this particular spread of the cards, she often indicated that life was changing, too. Things that once seemed certain could no longer be taken for granted. Some mysteries might become clearer.

'Are you running away from me?'

Nell held her breath. 'I'll be back in a few days,' she said. That was all she could say for the moment. *And then we'll see . . .* She just needed more thinking time. Even Callum knew she had to run somewhere; that she couldn't stay as she was, as she had been.

'I'm not sure who you are any more,' Callum said.

His words had slipped inside her; they'd been dancing in her head all the time they'd been in Essaouira. Perhaps, Nell thought, she was only just finding out herself.

Last night, after they arrived here, they had eaten fish mqualli tagines in a local eatery – the fish and shellfish here were excellent – and Nell had particularly wanted to try it, as she hadn't come across it in Marrakech. As they were eating, she had tried to analyse the ingredients and, when they'd finished, Amy persuaded her to have a chat with the chef. 'Go on,' she said. 'What do you have to lose?'

'All right.' Nell realized that she had a lot to learn if she was going to bring her new idea to fruition.

'Mqualli' was a term that referred to sauces made with

ginger, saffron and oil. 'But in this classic dish, it is *les poissons*,' the chef told her in his broken French.

'Fish?'

'Eel.' She didn't know the word, but he showed her by means of the fish tank in the restaurant. 'But you could use this, or this.' Swordfish, whiting or dorado, she surmised.

'It is layered with *les pommes de terre, les tomates et les poivrons rôtis*.' Potatoes, tomatoes and roasted peppers. But Nell knew there was more.

'Chermoula,' he said. 'Olives and preserved lemons for zest and flavour.'

Nell was already accustomed to the way lemons and olives were used in Moroccan cuisine. But chermoula?

To her embarrassment and secret delight, he beckoned her through to his kitchen, where she got a few cheery waves from members of the staff who were busily stirring sauces, boiling rice or washing up. She seemed to be a novelty. The chef opened a fridge and showed her a jug half filled with liquid. He held it out for her to sniff.

Mmm. 'Strong,' she said. '*Très bon*.'

Chermoula, he told her, indicating certain spices on the shelf, was a marinade for fish and the foundation of a number of Moroccan fish dishes; it was made with fresh coriander, garlic, paprika, cumin, salt, ginger, cayenne pepper, lemon juice and . . . of course, saffron.

'Thank you so much,' Nell said. '*Merci beaucoup*.' There was nothing as good as talking to the man in charge.

★

'We don't have to go the saffron farm tomorrow,' Nell said to Amy. It was unlike her friend to be so quiet. Nell was concerned. 'We can stay in Essaouira for a while. Just to see . . .'
What? If the blue door should suddenly open? She wondered what on earth she could say to Callum if she delayed her return any longer. And what about Johnson? He wouldn't like it one bit. Spontaneity was all very well, but you had to be responsible, too.

'No need.' Amy knocked on the door of their riad, and the girl came to let them in.

'Would you like some tea?' she asked politely.

'No, thanks.' Amy was already making her way to the stairs.

'For the visitor?'

'Visitor?' As one, Nell and Amy swung around. Through the archway, Nell could see a man sitting, legs stretched out in front of him, looking relaxed, as if he belonged here. She didn't know him, but –

'What on earth are you doing here?' Amy's voice rang out clearly.

And Nell knew who it must be.

CHAPTER 24

It was easier, granted, to stay in the armchair than go to switch the kettle on for tea. It was easier to switch on the telly and escape into the inane antics of some game show than it was to read a book – especially now that her eyesight wasn't what it was. As for the past . . . Lots of things were easier than thinking about the past – at least when you suffered from a guilty conscience, some might say. But even when you were old, you shouldn't necessarily take the easy option. It wasn't good for you. Lillian braced herself and pulled herself out of the armchair. She still had a life to live. Mustn't let things slide.

In the kitchen she filled the kettle and checked the bread bin. There were a couple of slices left in the loaf. One small sandwich: that would do it. Not cheese – that would give her nightmares, but a thin slice of ham perhaps, with some tomato. She got out the bread board and her knife. Amy had tried to get her to buy it sliced, but it wasn't the same. Young people didn't really understand that, for morning toast, you needed it quite thick but that for sandwiches it should be wafer thin. And it might sound silly, but that breadknife with the green handle which had been Mary's and, before that, their mother's, was part of Lillian's independence. Take that away and . . . She still sliced the loaf vertically, just as her mother had done. And that was another thing.

When you were young, you couldn't imagine being old. She spread the butter thinly. *A little of what you fancied . . .* When you were old, days ran into one another, with little sense of purpose, she'd found. Lillian fetched a tomato from the fridge and began to slice it cleanly. She missed that sense of purpose. She'd lost it when Glenn left and then again when Ted died, though it had come back soon enough when she realized that now there was a chance of finding him . . . After that, she'd found a new sense of purpose in coming back to Dorset, too. She laid on the ham, then the tomato, then the other slice of bread, so thin you could almost see through it. She had always had it. *Until now . . .*

But at least Lillian had Amy. Lillian hadn't told her, though, about Mary. She couldn't bear it if Amy were ever to look at her that way . . . Amy made things so solid, so real; Lillian blessed the day she'd come over here, the day she'd met and befriended her great-niece. Lillian missed her. Celia had called in yesterday, but it was just to check up on her, she could tell. She had stayed for a quick cup of tea, but Lillian had noticed her glance at her watch, not once, but twice. She'd be needed back at the hotel, of course. She was always busy – the irony being that Celia's work ethic had paid Lillian's investment back – and some.

The other thing about old age, of course, was that people felt a responsibility towards you – and this made Lillian feel uncomfortable. Duty and responsibility always had. Ted, too, had been a stickler for duty; this was one of the reasons he could never share Glenn's views on pacifism and Vietnam. Duty and responsibility came first with Ted; they always had. And this wasn't necessarily a bad thing. He had been a loyal man; a man who did his duty. And he expected that loyalty in return, which was why . . .

Celia had looked around, bright and bird-like, asked if anything needed doing.

Lillian had told her no. 'I miss Amy, though,' she'd added. And, 'I expect you do too.'

'Me?' Celia seemed surprised by the question. For a moment she seemed to shift into another mode; from businesswoman to mother. Her eyes took on a note of wistfulness which Lillian hadn't seen there before.

She's your daughter, Lillian felt like saying. It was none of her business, not really. She had seen many things when she first came back to England, one of them being that Amy's parents had little time for the girl. But she'd also seen that Celia and Ralph loved her – that wasn't the problem.

'Yes, I do,' Celia told her. 'Even though she hasn't been gone five minutes.' She seemed to consider. 'It's just that –'

'You're so busy,' Lillian replied. Somewhat crisply, she knew.

'Yes.' Reminded of this, Celia had got to her feet and picked up her cup and saucer and Lillian's cup and saucer from the table by the armchair. The look of wistfulness had disappeared. She took the crockery into the kitchen. Lillian could hear her rinsing things under the tap.

'There's no need,' she called through. 'I'll do them later.'

'No problem.' Celia came back into the room – so quickly that she couldn't have washed up properly, Lillian found herself thinking. Which was the problem with doing things quickly, of course.

'I should go.' But Celia looked around vaguely, as if, just for a second, she was searching for a reason to stay.

'How's Ralph?' Lillian asked. She recalled how utterly dire the relationship between Celia and Ralph had been when she'd first come back to England. Really, she had held out little hope. But she supposed Ralph was one of the reasons why Celia was as she was. She might have been content running a small B&B in Bridport, but Ralph couldn't cope. Lillian could have told Celia that a man who couldn't cope with the stress of teaching might have similar problems taking on a hotel and a large overdraft in Lyme Regis, too, but she hadn't been around at the time to do so. Fortunately, it had worked out for the best – she hoped. Celia had risen to the challenge and dragged her husband along with her.

'He's fine.' Celia's eyes clouded over. And Lillian knew this was so. Ralph was fine. The hotel was making money; he could do a few jobs in the morning and play golf in the afternoon. His wife had taken on all the worries. Why wouldn't he be fine?

'And everything's going well with the hotel?' Lillian asked. Not that it was any of her business any more. Celia and Ralph had bought out her investment, which was as it should be. They had no need of a sleeping partner now, and why should they listen to the views of an eighty-five-year-old woman? Nevertheless, it was another purpose in Lillian's life which had now come to a close. *One down . . .* 'Plenty of guests?'

'Quieter until just before Christmas,' Celia said. 'But it was one heck of a busy summer.'

Lillian nodded. 'But if you ever wanted to give more time to other things . . .' She let this thought hang. '. . . you could always get a manager in. In the future, I mean. Delegate.' She watched her.

'Oh. Well, yes.' Celia frowned. 'I suppose –'

'Though it's hard,' Lillian nodded, 'when we've always had to do it ourselves. We think no one else can do it like we can.'

Celia laughed. 'Very true.' Her expression had softened, just since she'd been here. Lillian wondered, as she'd often wondered, how much Mary had told her daughter, how much she knew. Lillian had come back over here to care for Mary, but Celia had never welcomed her with open arms. She'd only accepted her help – her interference, as she probably saw it – because she needed it so desperately.

'But thank you for coming, my dear,' Lillian said. 'I appreciate it. With Amy being away and everything.'

'I should come more often.' Celia's face took on the habitual expression of harassment once again.

'No, no.' Lillian rose to her feet and took a few steps across the room. She put her hand on Celia's arm. 'There's no obligation,' she said softly. 'I know you probably promised Amy. But I'm fine, as you can see. You're welcome to come any time you want to, of course. But never feel you have to.'

And Celia had given her a long look, as if she were seeing her for the first time somehow. 'Thanks, Auntie Lillian,' she had said. 'I'll remember that.'

The kettle made a *harrumph* sound and the vibration turned to a shrieking whistle which made Lillian jump, even though she'd been waiting for it. She switched off the gas and the kettle shuddered. She made the tea. Cut herself a small slice of fruit cake and put it on a plate. She carried the black tin tray carefully through to the sitting room and put the tray on the table in front of her armchair. But before she sat down she went over to the bureau and opened it.

One pressed cream rose in a creased white paper bag was all she had left of Mary's wedding. She found the bag, carefully lifted out the pressed flower and held the delicate dried rose in the palm of her hand. That's what happens to us all, she thought. We start off fresh and vibrant and we end up dried to a crisp. She chuckled. Strangely, though, the cream rose had held on to its beauty, because it had been pressed at the height of its glory. She'd had the whole bouquet once, of course.

Lillian had been surprised at the speed of Mary's wedding to Johnnie Coombes. She had even wondered . . . But despite looking a little pale and out of sorts, there appeared no reason for a shotgun wedding. So perhaps it had been love? Perhaps what happened with Ted had taught Mary a lesson – and stopped her from breaking men's hearts. Lillian had no idea, because her sister never told her. Lillian had never been Mary's confidante and that was one thing that hadn't changed.

Mary did, however, ask Lillian to be her bridesmaid. Johnnie had a sister, Edie, and she was to be the other. Neither of them, Lillian thought, was likely to outshine Mary, though she knew it was ungenerous of her to be thinking this way. Indeed, Mary looked pale but radiant on her wedding day – dressed in a simple white satin dress with a veil, satin slippers, white lace gloves and carrying a bouquet of cream and red roses. Heaven knows where they'd got it all from, but Lillian supposed friends and neighbours had all chipped in; everyone had something to lend or donate.

'Are you happy?' Lillian asked her, as they made the final preparations back at the house. Mary's hair was dark and shining, her lips were red, her skin positively glowed. Lillian searched her sister's expression. She couldn't escape the feeling that she didn't know Mary, not really.

'Of course I am, silly.' But Lillian saw the look in her indigo eyes in the second before she turned away to pick up her bouquet. And it was not one of a bride on the happiest day of her life.

Mary said and did all the right things. She repeated her vows clearly and she smiled at her bridegroom as he did the same. She held out a slender white hand for the ring to be put on her finger and she closed her eyes when at last they were pronounced man and wife and Johnnie bent to kiss her. She laughed as they walked back up the aisle, looked adoringly up at Johnnie for the photos, kissed and hugged her guests. No one could have played the part better. And as her new husband proudly held the passenger door open for his new wife, for they were about to drive away into their married life, Mary had turned and looked straight at Lillian.

'Catch, little sister.' And she had thrown her the bouquet. Was it Lillian's imagination, or had that look said, 'Better luck than me'?

Lillian put the rose away, back in the paper bag where it had lain all these years since. She hadn't been able to keep the bouquet, but she had pressed just this one cream rose between the pages of Father's encyclopaedia. This rose had gone to America and, like her, back it had come.

With this rose, memories of her sister could flood into her mind. And many of them were uncomfortable memories. Lillian thought she knew why Celia had never welcomed her into the family quite as warmly as Amy had. Mary must have told her at least part of it. And yes, it was true that Lillian had done wrong. But back then, Lillian hadn't known the full story; Mary hadn't told her what was going on, she had been kept in the dark. She had tried to make amends. What more could she do?

Lillian sipped her tea. There was one thing, perhaps.

CHAPTER 25

To Nell's surprise, Amy seemed angry to see him. She must have taken it harder than Nell had realized. Either that, or there was a whole agenda that Nell wasn't aware of.

'Ah, well . . .' He started to get to his feet.

'Checking up on me, are you?' Amy's arms were folded. And she was glaring at the poor man. Jake Tarrant. It had to be.

'Certainly not.' It was his turn to look angry now – or at least affronted. 'I tried to tell you on the phone but you practically cut me off –'

'Mint tea?' asked the girl on reception.

Amy and Jake ignored her.

'Can I get you a glass of –?'

'Yes, please.' (Jake)

'No, thank you.' (Amy)

They spoke at the same time. Fine, thought Nell. She took an executive decision. 'Yes, please,' she told the girl. 'That would be lovely.' Mint tea was supposed to have calming qualities.

'I didn't cut you off.' Amy looked sulky now. But she took a few steps closer. 'The bus was coming.' She glanced at Nell for corroboration. 'Wasn't it, Nell?'

'Yes.' Nell nodded. She knew whose side she was on – should it be necessary.

'And you could have phoned today. At any time. To warn me,' Amy said pointedly.

Jake narrowed his eyes. Amy hadn't said how attractive he was. Well, not conventionally so, perhaps. Oddly compelling. And at ease with himself. Or at least he had been until Amy had unleashed her emotions in his direction. Now, he just looked shell-shocked, poor man.

'I didn't know I had to warn you,' he said coolly. 'We're colleagues, aren't we?'

'Yes.' Amy sat down and Nell sat next to her. 'But you may as well admit that you were trying to catch me out.'

'Catch you out at what?' he asked mildly.

'At . . .' Amy floundered.

'At not doing her job properly,' provided Nell, who was getting the gist. Amy didn't want Jake to know about the blue door.

'Exactly.' Once again, Amy folded her arms.

The girl from reception returned with mint tea in a pot and three glasses on a silver tray.

'Thank you.' Nell indicated that she should put it down on the table in front of her.

Jake sat down opposite Amy. He frowned. 'Why should I want to do that?' he asked. 'I've got no reason to think you're not doing your job properly. And it's your gallery putting on the event.' He gave her a look. 'Yours and Duncan's,' he amended.

Amy looked as if she might explode. 'Then why *are* you here?' she countered.

'Because I love the country. Because I fancied taking a weekend off. Because I'm in the middle of organizing a Moroccan project for your gallery. Because you told me you had no intention of coming to Essaouira and I wanted to organize some music for the event.' He stretched out his legs and leaned back in his seat. That seemed like a lot of plausible reasons to Nell. But how would Amy react?

'Right,' she said, with some sarcasm.

'If you want something done' – he shrugged – 'do it yourself.'

'Which does imply you don't think me capable.' Amy was like a terrier, Nell thought. She just wouldn't let it go.

'You said –'

'I did tell you –'

Again, they spoke together.

Nell decided to pour the tea.

'I did tell you I'd changed my mind about coming here.' But Amy's voice was quieter now, more accepting. She wasn't looking at Jake, though. She was looking beyond him, towards the busy street outside. Perhaps she was still thinking about the blue door.

'I'd already booked my flight,' he said.

Impasse. They stared at each other. Nell was so fascinated by the interaction between these two that she kept pouring and jumped when she realized mint tea was overflowing from the glass on to the tray. Hastily, she began mopping it up with a paper napkin.

'Besides,' he said. 'Like I said, I've got a thing about Morocco.'

He might as well have added, 'and I've got a thing about you.' Couldn't Amy see that? Nell sighed as she passed them both a glass of tea. Amy still seemed suspicious. Clearly not.

'Well, we've made some contacts.' Amy put her tea back down and pulled her notebook out of her bag. Nell was impressed at how effortlessly she could switch into business mode. 'I was going to email you.' She eyed him disapprovingly, as if he had deprived her of a valued task. 'But you can take them now.' She handed him a sheet of paper. 'We're off in the morning.'

'Off?' He sipped his tea, tucked the list she'd given him into the pocket of his jeans.

'We're going to visit a saffron farm.' She seemed to be waiting for him to question this. He didn't.

'I'm hoping to take some shots of the crocuses in full bloom.'

'Sounds good.' He nodded. 'And will you have dinner with me tonight?' he asked. 'Both of you? Maybe we could listen to some music later.'

'All right.' Amy could sound a little less grudging, thought Nell.

She thought fast. 'I have a bit of a headache,' she said. 'I was thinking of having an early night. But you two should go out.'

Amy whipped around. 'Since when?' she demanded. 'You were perfectly OK earlier.'

It had come on, Nell thought, listening to the two of them pretend there wasn't any chemistry between them. 'Well . . .'

'You have to come,' Amy declared. 'Otherwise, I'm staying here, too, so I can look after you.'

'No need,' Nell conceded. She knew when she was beaten. She found herself meeting his ironic smile. So he didn't know how to get through to Amy any more than she did.

'Meet you here at seven thirty?' Jake raised a twisty eyebrow.

'Perfect,' said Nell. She could hardly wait for a whole evening of this.

'See you then.' Jake got to his feet and swung out of the room with a long, loping stride. Nell watched him go – she couldn't help it.

Until Amy elbowed her hard in the ribs. 'What are you staring at?' she hissed.

'Nothing.' Nell put on her innocent face.

'Trust me,' said Amy. 'He's difficult. And he's not what he seems.'

'Mmm.' But Nell was certain of one thing. Amy was looking a lot more cheerful now.

CHAPTER 26

Morocco, 1977

'I don't want Bethany to have anything to do with it,' Glenn said. It was a hot day and he was sweating – but maybe not just from the sun beating down through the bush hat he was wearing. Maybe at the thought of what might happen to Bethany. It was July, Bethany had been here for almost three years and she knew nothing about the runs they'd done in the past – one or two when she was still a relative newcomer; since then just one, when she was away working on a nearby farm.

That last one hadn't been a good one. Howard knew a guy who was a board shaper, and he'd made them a special pair of surfboards for the trip. It was ingenious. But Howard reckoned the fewer people who knew, the better. Howard and Gizmo had done the run, but it hadn't gone well. They'd made plenty of dosh, but there'd been a roadblock, they'd been questioned for ages and Howard had ended up having a row with one of the policemen and been bloody lucky he wasn't arrested. How they hadn't found the stash, God only knows.

'Fact is,' Howard had said when they returned, 'they're

cracking down on it, man, they're getting to know all the tricks.' And he'd sighed as he counted the bread. 'Reckon we'll have to give it a rest for a while. Make this lot last. Find another way.'

But now he'd changed his mind. The trouble was that it was easy money – if it went smoothly. It was a temptation. And Howard was broke.

'And why would that be?' Howard asked now. The three of them were sitting around the table. Howard was rolling a joint. He had long fingers and dirty nails and was wearing his usual summer uniform of frayed denim cut-offs and a yellow T-shirt. And the red-and-yellow skullcap, of course. When he'd announced that they had to do another run, that they needed the dough, Glenn had disagreed. But, as usual, he'd been overruled. Howard liked to think he was in charge around here. He didn't seem to get that, in communes, you didn't have anyone in charge – that was the point.

And now he was saying that Bethany had to be part of it. Glenn could feel himself tensing up. He didn't like it.

'She's not involved.' She wasn't here at the meeting, was she? She was inside, in the kitchen, cooking their supper – chicken with couscous, tomatoes and prunes. Glenn felt his stomach grumble. He was hungry.

'Why not?' Howard sprinkled tobacco on the cigarette papers he'd sealed together. He rolled the shreds between his fingertips and Glenn could smell the sweet pungency of it mingling with the steam from Bethany's tagine. 'She lives here, don't she?'

It was true that they'd agreed originally that everyone would take a turn doing the run and that they'd do it in pairs – different pairs each time. Variety, they'd decided, was the way to stay free, remain undetected. It was patterns and it was conformity that sold you down the river; that's what people were looking for. But that was back in the day. It was before Bethany came here. Things had changed.

'I'll take her turn, then,' Glenn said. 'And my own.'

'No shit, man.' Gizmo adjusted the knot of his blue bandana. 'If you go together, then that means there'll only be one of you. Far out . . .'

'She's a girl.' Glenn reached for his tea. They'd run out of beer, of course. He knew it wasn't easy to make any dosh around here – but there were ways, relatively legal ways. Translating, working in restaurant kitchens, cleaning in hotels, crop-picking at nearby farms. He and Bethany didn't have a lot, but they had work and they'd never starve.

'You don't say,' drawled Howard. 'What's that got to do with it? Does that give her some sort of privilege, man? Being a girl?'

Privilege . . . Glenn looked away.

'Equal rights, dude,' agreed Gizmo.

'And who does the run is everybody's business.' Just for a second, Howard looked up and Glenn felt his pale-blue eyes bore into him. Christ. He lived with the guy, but he didn't like him. He was cold as bloody ice. 'It gives us more cover, don't it, having a girl on board.'

'Good point, man.' Gizmo nodded and looked hungrily at the joint Howard was taking his time over.

Howard unwrapped the foil and lit a match, putting it to the lump of brown hashish. He crumbled a corner with his fingers and sprinkled it evenly over the tobacco.

'She's not doing it.' Glenn tried to stay calm. It was too risky. He wouldn't take the chance. She was only here because he'd brought her here. He wanted to protect her, dammit.

Howard smelt his fingers and then licked them. 'Maybe we should ask her, yeah?' He cocked an eyebrow at Gizmo.

'Yeah.' Gizmo chuckled. 'We should ask her. Hell, why shouldn't she have a say?'

'Ask me what?' Bethany stood there, hands on hips, a smile hovering around her mouth, her face glowing from the heat.

'Nothing,' said Glenn.

Howard rolled the joint. He licked the paper and looked up at Bethany as he did so. 'If you're one of us,' he said. 'If you're part of the group. Or just a hanger-on.'

Bethany glanced across at Glenn and he saw the uncertainty in her eyes. It made him mad. 'Leave her alone,' he snapped. 'She doesn't want to know.'

'Cool it, man.' Howard twisted one end of the joint. In the other he inserted a thin roll of cardboard. He put in his mouth and lit the other end, breathed in. The sweet and heady scent filled the air. They all seemed instinctively to breathe in with him, even Bethany. 'Do you?' He offered her the joint, a faint smile twisting at his mouth. 'Do you wanna know, Bethany?'

They were in a rut. Glenn knew they were in a rut. They should have left before this. A few times he'd suggested they leave, but there always seemed to be a reason to stay. It was easier to stay. 'Where would we go to?' Bethany had said. 'Back to grey old England? No, thanks.' And Glenn couldn't contemplate going back to America.

No sooner had Jimmy Carter been inaugurated in January this year than he'd introduced full amnesty for those who had dodged the draft. That should have made Glenn feel good. Now, he could go back home. His mother, he was sure, would be expecting him to go back home. But it left two issues in his mind. One, if you asked for a pardon, you were admitting you'd committed a crime. And two, he would have to face the guilt he felt for running away in the first place, for letting his mother down, for not protecting her, for not going back the second he could. So. 'We could do a bit more travelling?' Glenn suggested.

'But where would we find such a cool place to live?' said Bethany.

Glenn was aware that she loved it here. She loved the food and the spices; the warmth and the laid-back vibe. The history of Essaouira had reached out and drawn her in. She loved that the city of Mogador, as it was then known, had been built by the Phoenicians in the sixth century. 'Wow!' she said. 'My mother would be so interested. She's always said our family had links with the Phoenicians.'

'Really?' Glenn listened to her talking eagerly about the ancient Phoenician site – how it was used as a trading post and a watchtower, how a purple dye used on royal robes in Europe was extracted from a species of shellfish found nearby, and the more recent cultural history concerning what he privately called the Hendrix myth and the Living Theatre.

Bethany hadn't been here long before she insisted on dragging Glenn and Gizmo to Daibat. She couldn't believe they hadn't been there and she couldn't believe Howard didn't want to come.

'There's nothing there,' Howard had told her. And, privately, Glenn agreed with him.

Bethany rolled her eyes. 'We should go and visit in the spirit of pilgrimage,' she said. 'I can't believe you guys. And there's the café.'

'The café?'

'The Hendrix café. And "Castles Made of Sand", that was inspired by the ruins of the Borj el-Berod watchtower, you know.'

Glenn didn't want to tell her that the song had been recorded two years before Hendrix's visit. That's if he had ever visited. He guessed he had. Probably stayed a couple of hours, long enough to get the myth going, for Essaouria to milk it for as long as they reasonably could. As far as Glenn could tell, the people of Essaouira had never recovered from the famous visit and the stories were growing more remarkable with every month that passed by. But Howard told her, anyway.

'Well, it's obvious, isn't it?' Bethany said. 'There's "Purple Haze" as well, don't forget. Don't tell me that's a coincidence.'

'Coincidence?'

'The purple murex shells,' she said. 'Come on, guys. He must have come much earlier. In secret.'

Howard laughed, but he wouldn't be shifted. And when they got there, it was a windswept and desolate wilderness. It would have made a great film set for an old Western, Glenn thought grimly, taking off his hat before it blew away. They found the watchtower, a decaying former fortress slowly sinking into the water to the south, but the wind was blowing the fine sand in their eyes and even Bethany could find nothing much to see, apart from a couple of camels. They found the garishly painted café with its Hendrix pictures and proclamations. But there were no customers, only one member of staff – sleeping on a wooden bench – and nothing to eat or drink. Some café, thought Glenn. It was time to leave.

Glenn had looked out for other places to stay in the town, but there was nothing around – at least nothing that didn't cost. So here they were, still. Perhaps the time to leave had been and gone.

'Of course I want to be involved.' She didn't even look at Glenn. She took the joint from Howard and inhaled deeply, held it for several seconds in her lungs, exhaled. 'I am involved.' Only then did she send a defiant glance Glenn's way. 'I'm here, aren't I?'

He sighed, felt his shoulders slump.

'Far out,' said Gizmo.

'I like your spirit.' Howard's gaze was appraising and Glenn hated it.

He felt his fists bunch together. And then he thought of his father. With a huge effort he unclenched his hands, spread out the fingers, forced his shoulders into a casual shrug.

Bethany sent her clear-eyed gaze his way. 'Glenn?'

'Up to you,' he said.

'So what's it all about?' She drew up a rickety chair and passed the joint on to Gizmo.

'It's my turn to do the next run,' said Howard.

'Since when?' snapped Glenn.

'Since I volunteered.' Once again the pale-blue gaze met his.

'Run?' Bethany looked confused. Glenn's heart went out to her.

'This is how it goes. We all put in some bread and I buy a stash from a guy I know.' They were all watching her, waiting for a reaction.

She shrugged.

'Two of us take it to France. Sell it. Bring the profits back here.' Howard sat back.

'France?' Her eyes widened. She looked at Glenn. 'That's what you were doing in Paris that time?'

He nodded. 'But we haven't done it in a while,' he said. 'And you don't have to be involved.'

'If you're scared,' Howard added.

Bethany took a deep breath. 'I'll take my turn,' she said. She glanced at Glenn. 'It's only fair,' she added.

He shook his head.

'And am I right in thinking you're pretty good at the lingo?' Howard asked.

'Yeah. I speak French.'

'Perfect.' Howard's eyes gleamed. 'So you're ready to take a turn when the time comes?'

'Sure.'

'I'm the number one.' Howard smiled slowly and licked a shred of tobacco from his thin lips. 'And I suggest we have a vote here and now to see which of you lot come with me.'

'OK.' Bethany nodded. She closed her eyes, lifted her face up to the sun.

She just didn't get it. 'I'll do it,' said Glenn. 'I'll come with you.'

Lazily, Howard turned towards him. 'So Glenn is proposing ah, Glenn. And Gizmo . . .'

'Huh?' He blinked, came to, passed the joint on.

'You're proposing . . . ah?' His gaze rested on Bethany, whose eyes were still closed.

'Our little lady.' Gizmo grinned. 'You got it, Howie. Great cover.'

'Let's vote. All those in favour of Glenn raise a hand.'

Glenn raised his hand. He was the only one.

'And Bethany?' Howard grinned.

He and Gizmo raised their hands.

'You didn't vote, Bethany,' said Howard. 'You abstaining or what?'

She nodded, looked confused.

'Then you're gonna be coming with me.'

Glenn got to his feet. His appetite had left him. Why was he even trying to protect her? He'd been protected himself – by his mother when his draft papers came in, and before that by his college education. What good had it done him? It had only made him feel more guilty – that other kids were being drafted and sent to fight in a war that no one wanted to be part of. He'd felt privileged. And he didn't want to exercise that sort of privilege. It wasn't right.

'Where are you going, baby?' Bethany asked.

He shrugged. 'Nowhere.'

He left the riad and walked down to the sea, past the blue-and-white harbour, the fishing boats stacked up on the beach. He kicked at the sand and stared out into the Atlantic Ocean. At least here there was a breeze. And he needed to cool down. He couldn't get rid of the feeling that Howard had orchestrated this whole damn thing.

Shortly after that birthday dinner in Wisconsin with his parents, twenty-five thousand protestors had marched on Washington – Glenn among them, his father's words about freaks still ringing in his ears. It had been unlike anything he'd known before. A young Quaker guy holding his baby daughter in his arms had set himself on fire outside Secretary of Defence Robert McNamara's window in the Pentagon; that's how strongly some people felt about the war. The baby had been snatched to safety but the papers had sure made a meal of it. And by the end of 1966 so many men had been sent in that press and TV networks went, too, and the progress of the Vietnam War was viewed by American families on the early-evening news. No one could pretend any longer.

Glenn watched a small posse of camels moving across the sand in that determined but ungainly way they had. In the distance, a small blue fishing boat was heading for the harbour; he'd been out late. Most of the catch was brought in on the morning tide; the harbour would be drenched with sea-water, with the shouting of fishermen selling their wares, the bargaining, jostling townspeople, the rich scent of fresh fish and the more sickly stale entrails picked up by the gulls.

And so the war had dragged on while Glenn continued with his education. Sometimes it felt as if the war – even though he wasn't an active part of it – *was* his education. It had taught him what to believe in – even before Martin Luther King and the Civil Rights Movement got involved in 1967, even before guys were burning their draft cards in public demonstrations and protests were getting more violent by the day. Not everyone was content to stand around singing Dylan's 'Blowin' in the Wind'. Things were changing. That year, almost a thousand draft dodgers were caught and punished; thousands more were going to Canada to escape it. What did you do when you received an order that was morally bankrupt? Men were beginning to say no.

Things were heating up at Wisconsin, too. In October 1967 three hundred protestors blockaded a chemistry building, Glenn among them. Wisconsin was big on engineering and Dow Chemicals were recruiting prospective new employees from the student body. Dow Chemicals made napalm. Which meant their own university was colluding in the war, in the burning of Vietnamese villages.

It was a full-scale riot and it was on the news – which meant Glenn's parents got to see. Protection. Privilege. His father had phoned up Wisconsin and chuntered on about his son's background and prospects, how he wasn't some radical freak and how he'd been led astray. *Led astray* . . . Glenn had been glad to get in there, glad even to be beaten up if it would make a difference to what was happening in Vietnam.

If it weren't for his mother, Glenn would have stood up to be counted and, when his name appeared, he would have refused to fight. He'd heard of guys who faked mental illness, who held their breath so they'd pass out during the health check, who pretended to be deaf. There was a long list of tricks to get a 3-A status. But Glenn didn't want to dodge anything. He'd like to leave the false security of college – it felt like he was copping out. But no way was he going to war.

His mother, though, begged him not to give up college. It was hard to refuse her and even when he knew his grades were bad, he couldn't help noticing that he managed enough to stay on. Collusion. There sure was more than one way to make a protest. But he knew his time would come. By the time he left Wisconsin, draft exclusion for college students was no longer in operation, anyway. Now, they were all included. Now, the privilege of education couldn't save anyone. A few of the guys at college applied for conscientious objector status. But that still meant you'd be working for the war, Glenn realized – albeit in some civilian status. It still meant cooperation with the system, recognition that the war was legitimate. It wasn't a true objection. For Glenn, it wasn't what pacifism was all about.

So. He went home to wait for what he knew would come.

Glenn walked for a while along the beach, feeling the wind and the sand rough in his hair, and then at last he got hungry.

He went back to the riad. Bethany and the guys were still sitting around the table, looking a good deal more stoned than when he had left. They'd had dinner, and all that was left of the hash brownies Giz had made the day before were some dark crumbs on the table.

'Hey, man, where did ya go?' asked Gizmo.

'You all right, hon?' Bethany reached out a hand. 'I saved you some food.'

'I'm cool.' But somewhere inside him, Glenn knew. It wasn't the end, no way. But it could be the beginning of the end. And he had to think of something to stop it from happening, to protect what they had. And this time, he had to get it right.

CHAPTER 27

Amy hadn't known what to think when she saw him sitting there in the riad's reception room – so cool, so careless. She knew Nell thought she'd been unnecessarily hostile, but Nell was a soft touch and she didn't know Jake as well as Amy did. It wasn't that she didn't like him exactly . . . *Did* she like him? She wasn't sure. The question seemed far too complicated when it was applied to Jake. But this project had already been snatched away from her. Amy needed to be trusted. She needed to feel trusted. And it was plainly ridiculous for Nell to say that Jake Tarrant had come over to Morocco to see Amy. Why would he – when she was about to return to the UK herself? And hadn't he told her? He wasn't interested in personal stuff.

But he was good company. They'd eaten chicken tagine with sweet dates (Jake), sea bass with olives and lemon (Amy) and lamb with apricots (Nell), and shared a plate of steaming couscous and a dish of tomato and aubergine salad. And two bottles of delicious red wine. Jake had entertained them with stories of events he'd organized which had gone wrong – though, privately, Amy found that hard to believe – including the time he'd been travelling in Australia, worked for a club in

Byron Bay and dressed up as a fried egg for a moonlit beach barbecue. Nell had laughed like a drain and even Amy had finally felt herself begin to unwind. Jake Tarrant had surprised her. Not only was he charming, he was fun.

When Nell went off to find the bathroom, Jake leaned forward across the table. 'I'm not here to check you're doing your job properly, Amy,' he said. 'Believe me.'

Hmm. 'What about that list you gave me then?' She realized she was teasing, flirting almost. 'Weren't you dictating where I should go? What pictures I should take?'

'Not *dictating*.' He pulled a face. 'Suggesting. There's a big difference.'

'*Suggesting* that you knew best?'

'Amy . . .'

They both laughed. 'And what did you do with it?' he asked. 'Throw it away?'

How had he guessed?

After dinner, the three of them drifted to the square, where the music had already begun.

'I was here in June for the Gnawa Music Festival,' Jake said. 'The place was heaving. People dressed up in all sorts of outlandish costumes . . .'

'Like fried eggs?' murmured Amy.

Nell giggled.

'Much more outlandish than that,' said Jake. 'You should come here next year and see for yourself.' He shot her a look.

Was that some sort of invitation? Amy didn't want to think

about it – not at the moment. She was feeling full and contented from the wine and the food. Her one regret was that she'd been unable to get on the other side of that blue door this afternoon. She had been so hoping to find something out, she realized, something that would help Aunt Lillian come to terms with her loss, something that might help repay her for everything she had done for Amy's family.

But perhaps she *would* come here again. Amy could understand why Jake was drawn to the place. Standing in the crowded square surrounded by the colours and fragrances of Morocco and listening to its music, she could feel its magic. The musicians were dressed in bright robes and headgear and she recognized the instruments that she and Nell had tried playing in the music shop earlier that day. The haunting melodies were underlined by a chanting which was soothing to the ear and to the senses. It was oddly compelling. But Amy kept her wits about her. This might be trance music, but no way was she going into a trance – not with a man like Jake Tarrant around.

When they'd had enough of the music, Jake walked them back to the riad and, before Amy realized what she was doing, Nell had slipped off up to their room and she was alone with him, standing by the door.

'So,' he said.

'So.' She smiled. It had been a lovely evening. Perhaps she'd read him wrong, perhaps he'd never doubted her abilities and perhaps he wasn't here to check up on her after all. Maybe she shouldn't have been so mean to him earlier either.

'Perhaps you can tell me something, Amy Hamilton.'

'If I can.' She leaned against the door frame. And if I want to, she thought.

'What exactly are you afraid of?'

'Afraid of?' That took her by surprise. 'What makes you think I'm afraid of anything?' Though she was, obviously. And not just spiders. *Of being loved. Of being controlled. Of losing what she needed the most* . . . Amy blinked. Where had all that come from?

'Oh, you pretend to have your life sorted out,' Jake said. 'You can find your way around a new foreign city, you can run a gallery and take good photographs, you can have a fling with the boss and not let yourself fall in love with him . . .'

'What?' Amy was stunned. That was a bit below the belt.

'But you can't trust anyone, can you, Amy?'

Amy looked into his eyes. Even in the dim light from the lamp outside, they reminded her of rooibos tea. He seemed very serious suddenly; the light-hearted and flirtatious mood of the evening had completely dissipated. Here they were, just Amy and Jake Tarrant, and it seemed as if he were trying to see inside her very soul. 'Perhaps it's just you I can't trust,' she found herself saying. Why had she said that? Was it even true?

He gripped her by the shoulders. 'Why not?'

Because you're dangerous to my peace of mind. That was how she felt. But she said nothing. She just looked at him and she thought, He's not interested in personal stuff; he had said so. So what did he want from her? Was it like Duncan all over again?

'Amy?'

It was a moment when she could have closed her eyes and let him kiss her. She knew that. She even wanted that. But something stopped her. Some old piece of armour, some scrap of self-defence. She had to take control of the situation – otherwise, she would be lost. 'I'm going up to bed now, Jake,' she said. 'Goodnight.' And she leaned forwards, kissed him on the cheek, stepped inside the riad and, very firmly, closed the door.

CHAPTER 28

First thing in the morning, Nell and Amy caught another bus – destination this time the saffron farm. It was full of people of all nationalities and there was a general buzz of excitement in the air. Some seemed to have planned their entire trip to Morocco around the blossoming of the saffron. And Nell, more than anyone, understood why. It was a special time. A spectacle that couldn't last long. The flowers had to be harvested as soon as they bloomed and before the petals began to wilt; by that time, the saffron would have spoiled. Nell suppressed a shiver of anticipation. She had only ever seen their small saffron harvest in Cornwall. This would be a feast for the senses indeed.

Nell glanced across at Amy, who had recovered her good humour last night but had come upstairs far more quickly than Nell had expected, and with a determined look in her eye.

'What happened?' Nell asked her. She had been expecting a romantic interlude at the very least. Amy had confided that her relationship with Duncan was over, at least in the personal department, and Jake was eligible and seemed very keen . . .

'Nothing.' She had turned towards her. 'I just can't do it, Nell.' And the expression in her eyes told Nell all she needed to know. Amy, like Nell's mother, might seem strong but, emotionally, she was far more vulnerable than she liked to let on.

Nell transferred her gaze to the window of the bus. Already this pink and dusty landscape had become strangely familiar, almost as if she had lived here in some other life. She might be little more than a tourist, but in just a few days she felt as if she had come so far somewhere within herself. And she had made a decision.

'So are you hooked?' Amy asked her.

'Hooked?'

'Will you go on cooking Moroccan cuisine when you get back home?'

Nell smiled. 'Oh, yes.'

This course had reminded her how much she loved to cook with saffron, but it had done so much more than that. It had opened up the delights of all the other spices; of the precision and slow cooking of the tagine; of the Moroccan flatbreads and pancakes; of soups such as harira, a lamb and chickpea concoction traditionally served with dates after Ramadan; and of delicious pastries and desserts. Saffron had been so popular once. Perhaps she could play a small part in restoring that popularity. 'In fact . . .'

'Yes?'

'When I open my own restaurant, I'd like to specialize in

Moroccan cuisine.' There, she'd said it. It was real now. Not just her own fantasy, but shared.

'Honestly?' Amy gave her a searching look.

'Why not? Where is there a Moroccan restaurant outside of London?'

'I can't think of any,' Amy admitted.

'Every town has a Chinese, an Indian, a Thai . . . Why not a Moroccan?'

'Why not, indeed?' Amy drew back a little and smiled at her, as if she were seeing her for the first time in another light.

'And I could do other things, too.'

'Other things?'

'I don't know. Sell tagines and Moroccan ceramics? Serve *thé à la menthe*?'

'And grow saffron,' teased Amy.

'Yes.' Which had given her another idea.

'Yes?'

That way, the legacy would be intact; that way, she wouldn't stop hearing her mother's voice – although she couldn't quite imagine Callum's reaction to the news. 'I could call it The Saffron House,' she said dreamily.

'You mean . . .?' She saw the understanding dawn in Amy's eyes.

'Exactly,' she said.

As they drove closer to the foothills, the shape of the mountains became more clearly defined and, approaching the valley, the roadside mimosa grew more lush, the palms taller, the vegetation greener. There were terraces of almond, argan and olive trees, and a drift of thyme and gorse lay over the hillsides. They must be approaching the saffron farm now. The bus had slowed and the buzz of conversation from the people on board had changed tone as they rummaged for their possessions and zipped up bags and jackets.

When they arrived at the saffron farm, Nell wasted no time in joining the tour, but Amy lagged behind. Nell knew her well enough to know that tours weren't really her thing. The farm was, apparently, not large but it had joined a cooperative with other farms in the area to sell, and to protect their workers' rights and pay. Nell was glad to hear this. The mountains' dry climate was ideal for growing and discouraged parasites, so there was no need for pesticides or fungicides. Weeding was done manually, and the earth was ploughed regularly to break it up before irrigation and to limit the amount of water required. In fact, it was an organic concern, and only cow dung was used as fertilizer. Nell nodded. Her mother, too, had always advocated this as a fertilizer – she used to get it from the farm further down the lane in Roseland.

Nell thought of the climate in Cornwall. She knew that saffron had been grown all over Britain in times gone by, but most successfully in the eastern counties. So important had it been to Saffron Walden that the town had been named after the spice, and continued to honour it through decorative engravings which could still be seen on houses and public buildings, and by its street names and pub signs. Cornwall was generally considered too wet. The land around the farmhouse in Roseland, though, was a sunny and sheltered spot, and the walled field faced south and sloped slightly, so the soil was naturally well drained. Her mother had added sand and lime from time to time, saying that the crocuses preferred a slightly alkaline soil. Maybe their farm had a small microclimate of its own, thought Nell. Or maybe the soil was naturally just right . . . At any rate, their saffron had always thrived. Against the odds. Which somehow made it all the more special.

'All saffron shares the same genetic lineage,' their guide told them. 'It all comes from the same single bulb.'

It was a sobering thought. How had the saffron bulbs first come to Cornwall? Through trade? In the pocket of a Roman soldier, perhaps? Or hidden in the hollowed-out walking stick of a travelling pilgrim? Nell would love to know.

During the time of the harvest, they were told, whole families would work up to twenty hours a day in order to gather the flowers before the sun was too high. 'The rose of saffron blooms at dawn. It should stay in the plant for the least possible time. It withers quickly. The stigmatas lose colour and aroma.'

First the rose of Mogador, thought Nell, and now the rose of saffron. *Crocus sativus Linnaeus*, commonly known as rose of saffron.

Following the gathering of the flowers, they were told, groups – usually of women – would sit around a table in a dimly lit room, pulling the stigmata which would be dried to produce the secret spice. It took the threads from one hundred and fifty flowers to produce one gram of dried saffron.

Most people gasped. Nell already knew this.

They were taken outside, to where the crocuses were flowering. Nell stopped in her tracks. She stared at the vision before her. Wave upon wave of pale purple and green shimmering in the sunshine. It almost took her breath away. Some had already been harvested, others were being picked by crouching women even as they watched, although baskets were full and the sun was already growing too high in the sky. Other crocuses, she could see, were just about to bloom in a great sea of purple. She closed her eyes for a few seconds and shut out the guide, the people. The sweet and musty perfume filled her head with memories and made her fingers tingle.

'There is a strange excitement at the time of harvesting,' said their guide. 'Time stands still, and yet it is a race against time.'

Nell acknowledged this with another nod. She had experienced that, too. It was a grasping of the moment, for the moment would not come again.

Their guide pointed out the herbs planted nearby to attract bees – lavender, marjoram, mint and tansy – and showed them the channels of irrigation. The pathways between plots were lined with rosemary bushes still in flower, their heavy scent mingling with the bitter-sweet saffron, and there were mud and straw buildings for the animals scattered around the land nearby. There was an orchard of apples, apricots and sharon fruit and an olive grove in the field beyond.

'How often do they rotate the saffron crop?' Nell asked their guide.

'It is a five-year cycle,' he said. A field takes seven years of lying dormant for a full recovery.'

'And how many bulbs can you plant in one acre?' someone else asked.

Their guide frowned. 'An acre is, I think, about 40 per cent the size of a hectare. We plant seven tons of bulbs in one hectare,' he said. 'Four hectares will give us five kilos of saffron.'

Which was why, thought Nell, saffron was more expensive than gold.

Their guide was as knowledgeable about saffron as Marion was about Moroccan culture and food. He told them how saffron had been used by Persians, Egyptians and Arabs as a perfume and in make-up. He talked about the 'Saffron War' in Europe and the thieves to whom saffron was so valuable. And he spoke of its historical use as a dye. 'A cloth left in a vat of saffron dye will emerge a vibrant yellow,' he said. 'Golden and intense as the sun itself.' His voice was proud and full of reverence.

Nell wondered if saffron had been used as a dye in England, too. She suspected it had, thinking of the decorative golden ruffs, cuffs and bodices of Stuart England, when saffron was still in its heyday. If the colour was golden, then it would be fitting for the rich, for royalty. And even now, she suspected, in these days of wishing to return to more natural practices, there were probably artisans around who used it for this purpose. She would have to find out. For a single spice to be so admired, so revered, thought Nell, its qualities must be magical indeed.

There was a glorious view of the Atlas Mountains beyond the farm and Nell could see white egrets flying above the fields and groves, the waves of purple from the saffron fields washing the landscape with vivid bruises of colour. And when the rest of the party wandered further up the pathway towards another field and she was left alone, a tranquillity quite unlike anything she had felt before seemed to settle over her.

What had saffron meant to her mother, Nell wondered. Was it just a family legacy she had been taught to respect because it had been around for so long? Was it simply a spice that could brighten up a meal, add a distinctive taste and colour to the traditional bread she baked? Or was it something more?

As she stood gazing at the saffron fields, she felt small, unimportant and alone. But you were never just yourself. You were always part of something else, someone else. She was part of her mother and yet she didn't know everything about her and now she had gone. And she was part of her father, too. But who was he? Was he one of those men who had come to the farmhouse in Cornwall and left before autumn, before the harvest? Or was there a darker story?

Nell remembered her mother's face whenever she had asked her, the way her expression would close, her smile fade. *I don't want to talk about that time* . . .Her tone of voice would accept no argument. *It's not important. It's just us now, Nell. You and me*. But it was important. It would always be important. It was the time when there were no photographs to record any memories, Nell knew that much. It was part of the bad time. But even so . . . She had to know. She wouldn't feel complete as a person until she knew. And her mother should have respected that need, should have treated her as an adult woman who could cope with knowing . . . whatever it was. Instead of always – always – treating her like a child. She closed her eyes for a moment, tried to relax the tension in her body, let the anger go.

'I'm scared, too,' she had said to Amy last night. Was she asleep? It was ten minutes since she had switched off the bedside lamp, but she guessed that Amy had a lot to think about, too.

'What of?' Amy whispered into the darkness.

'That I'm the daughter of someone who hurt my mother,' she said.

'Hurt her? You mean emotionally?'

'Perhaps. Or . . .'

'Physically?'

'Maybe someone who forced her.' There: it was out, it was said. Perhaps the darkness helped. Nell had thought it so many times but never spoken the words aloud. If it had been a simple fling, her mother would have told her, surely? She wasn't a prude and she'd never pretended to be.

'Raped her, you mean?' Amy sounded shocked. Nell sensed rather than saw her raising herself up on to one elbow. 'For God's sake, Nell. Why would you think that?'

Nell had tried to explain.

'There are lots of other bad things,' Amy murmured, her voice soothing. 'It could be anything. Maybe your mother had a bad time with her parents or at work. Or problems with a boyfriend. You know.'

Yes, Nell knew. But . . . 'It was more than that.' Nell had been over and over it in her mind. She was almost sure she was right. 'If my father wasn't the bad thing – then who was he? How come I never knew him? How come she never even told me his story?'

Nell thought back once more to the men who had stayed at the farm. They hadn't been important to her mother, she'd always known that. They didn't matter. She enjoyed their attentions and then . . . Nell thought of the old saffron legend. Her mother was Smilax. But why hadn't she cared about any of them? Nell knew that there must be a reason.

CHAPTER 29

Morocco, 1977

The night before they were due to leave, Gizmo got out his guitar and started playing. He sure loved that Gnawa music; it was called trance music for a reason: the rhythm was so hypnotic it got you on to a different level somehow. It wasn't working for Glenn tonight, though. He was nervous and jumpy. He wished Bethany wasn't going. God knows he'd tried hard enough to make her change her mind over the past few weeks. He couldn't believe how stubborn she was. 'It's my life, Glenn,' she'd told him. 'I get the right to choose.' But if anything happened to her, he'd never forgive himself. And what was worse was that, if anything did happen, he was helpless to do anything about it. He wouldn't even be there. But Howard would.

He decided to lay his cards on the table. When Bethany left the group to make tea and Gizmo was softly crooning, Glenn went to sit on the pile of cushions next to Howard.

'Say, Howard . . .'

'What gives?' Howard took a languid drag of his cigarette.

'Gotta favour to ask you.' He put a hand on Howard's shoulder, but Howard didn't respond so he took it away again.

'What's that?' He exhaled slowly. The smoke rose in the warm night air.

'It's about Bethany.' Glenn looked to see if she was coming back yet, but there was no sign, no sound of her footfall on the stairs.

'Yeah?' Howard frowned. 'What about her?'

'She's a bit of an innocent.' Glenn took a deep breath. 'Look after her for me, will you?'

Howard took a final drag, sat up and stubbed the cigarette end in the full ashtray by his feet. 'Have you asked her to do the same for me, man?' He grinned.

'The same?'

'Have you asked her to look after me?' Howard laughed, an explosion of mirth that turned into a cough.

'Fuck off.' Why was he bothering? Glenn got to his feet.

'What're you so scared of, man?' There was a look in Howard's pale, glinting eyes that reminded Glenn of a rat he'd cornered once in the yard at home. 'Doncha think she can look after herself?'

'Who says I'm scared? And I know she can. She's my lady. I'm looking out for her, that's all.'

'Right.'

Howard didn't pursue it, but he didn't have to. This wasn't the first time he'd asked Glenn what he was scared of, not the first time he'd accused him of being chicken. And Glenn knew what he was thinking. Vietnam. The draft. It always seemed to be on Howard's mind.

Glenn sat back down on the other side of Gizmo. He closed

his eyes and felt the music wash over his frazzled senses. Would he never escape the legacy of Vietnam? He hadn't been injured or messed up by the war, but it had branded him all the same. He remembered how he had felt when he first left Wisconsin. How he had gone home, lived in a wired-up state of waiting, not even applying for jobs – he couldn't for the life of him think of possibilities for an English major. Not even possibilities of a future. Until the time came.

'What will you do?' his mother whispered the day the papers arrived. It was late afternoon, but Glenn had been out all day, down at the river, thinking.

'I won't fight,' he said. He had decided. How could he fight? It was wrong. But he knew what people would think of him. And it was never easy to set yourself apart, to go against the flow, to be sure of your own beliefs.

He saw a myriad of emotions pass over his mother's face. Fear, anxiety but, most of all, relief.

She pulled him to her. 'Where will you go? What will you do? Have you thought about it?' Her voice was low.

'I'll be arrested, I guess.' It was a frightening thought, at a time when all his high ideals and values were reduced to one sheer fact of life. Incarceration. Five years. He knew in his heart that nothing would ever be the same again.

'No.'

He looked into her eyes. Saw the bruising of the shadows around them. It had been a long time since he'd heard that kind of decisiveness in her voice. She had been ground down, he could see that now. It came to him with a certainty that was shocking. Ground down by events, by the domination of his father, by a life that had not been the life she'd been expecting when she came over to America as a young GI bride-to-be. And yet here she stood, shoulders straight, looking him in the eyes and telling him 'No.'

'No?'

'I've thought about it. You must leave the country.' She reached out, held his hands in hers. Her voice was urgent.

He shook his head. 'No, Mom. I don't wanna run away. I want to stand up for what I believe in.' He was scared, though. He had to admit he was scared.

Something that looked like anger flared briefly in her eyes. 'Be realistic, Glenn. What use is it to throw your life away for a cause?'

'I'm not a coward, Mom.' But he felt like one. Because her words had sent a rush of adrenalin through him. The adrenalin of a possible solution. Be realistic, she had said. Could she be right? Was it possible that he could go away, leave America, go to Canada like lots of others had already done, find work, wait for it all to die down? For the war to end. Because surely it would end. And yet . . .

He eyed her warily. There was something in her – some quiet desperation that was beyond his understanding, beyond his control. He'd never seen her like this before.

'It has nothing to do with being a coward, Glenn.' Her hands were on his shoulders now. It was as if she were trying to instill her own certainty into him. But it wasn't working.

Wrong, Mom, he thought.

'And everything to do with what you believe in.'

He blinked at her. Perhaps, he thought now, he had just been waiting for her to convince him. It was his way out, his escape route.

'Just think what you can do for the anti-war movement if you're free,' she murmured. She looked down, perhaps waiting for her words to sink in. And her voice was so quiet. His father would be in from work soon. It was as if she was already anticipating his presence.

'Protest, you mean?' Glenn felt himself clutching at the straw of freedom.

'Of course.' She made a little shrug of her shoulders, as if the sense of it was obvious. 'You can work against the war. Challenge people with new ideas. Be heard, Glenn.' Her breathing was rapid and shallow. 'What could you do if you were behind bars?' she said. 'Or worse? What voice would you have then?'

Or worse? Glenn wasn't sure there was a 'worse'. Freedom was everything to him. The thought of having it whipped away was like a fist in his gut. 'I don't know, Mom.' Still, he wavered.

'You must.' She held his face in her hands now. 'You must.'

There was a noise from outside and she turned around, fear in her eyes. But it was a false alarm. The neighbour's cat perhaps, someone else's screen door slamming.

'But —'

'Listen to me, Glenn. Trust me. You can't just waste five years of your life.' Her eyes were calm, her grip strong. He could feel her willpower, the intensity of her. He'd underestimated her, he realized. She'd always just been his Mom – not this force of nature.

'Go upstairs. Pack your rucksack. Take only what you need.' She crossed the room swiftly, took down a tin from the back of the cupboard. She withdrew a packet of tea and plucked a wad of notes from underneath.

Glenn stared at her, stared at the money.

'It's mine,' she said, as though he'd questioned it. 'And now it's yours. It's all I have.' She thrust it into his palm, forced his hand to close around it. 'And now you must go – quickly, before your father comes home. Before . . .'

She grabbed the draft card from the kitchen counter just as he made a lunge for it. 'I'm keeping this.' She shoved it in the tin.

'But I want to –'

'No grand gestures, Glenn. That isn't the way.' She put the tin in the cupboard, turned around again, defiant. 'Go while you can. Before anyone knows. It won't be long before you could be arrested on sight. Listen to me. Take this chance. Go.'

And then she was pushing him away and up the stairs.

Instinctively, he did as she'd told him, packed a few necessities, a change of clothes, some sneakers, a rain mac, his copy of *Catcher in the Rye*. Because maybe she was right. Maybe he could do more as a free protestor than he could from inside a prison cell. His mother had given him the motivation, but Glenn had the legs to run.

Downstairs, he heard his father come home from work, the rise and fall of their voices. He sounded angry. Glenn strained to hear what was being said.

'Where is he?'

'Upstairs.'

'Has he heard?'

'I don't know.'

'He has, hasn't he? I can see it in your goddamn face, woman.'

Glenn stopped his packing, appalled at the tone of his father's voice. He'd heard it before, of course. But there was something different about it today, something crueller. He left the room, stood at the top of the stairs, frozen.

'You're hurting me.'

Glenn picked up his rucksack and took the stairs two at a time. At the bottom, he let the rucksack fall to the ground. In the kitchen, his father was holding his mother's wrist, twisting it. Her jaw was clenched but, otherwise, she showed no fear, no pain.

'Let her go.' He could see a bruise on her wrist, another on her arm, already yellowing around the edges. For Christ's sake. How long had this been going on? How come he hadn't noticed before now? Glenn took a step closer. He wanted to hit his father. He was a pacifist and yet he raised his hand and only the sudden look of warning in his mother's eyes stayed him. His arm dropped, useless, to his side.

'Ah.' His father let go of her, swung around to face him. Glenn saw her rub her wrist with her fingers, saw the small shake of her head and the clasp of her hands. *No, Glenn.*

'No son of mine is gonna stand under some peace banner because he doesn't have the guts to fight for his country,' his father said.

'No son of yours will have the choice,' Glenn snapped back.

His father frowned.

'The draft has taken away our right to choose.' But Glenn did have the right to say no. He had the right to refuse to do the bidding of the politicians of his country – most of whom were probably corrupt, in any case. That was taking a stand – for democracy. Glenn fingered the wooden peace sign that hung on a leather thong around his neck, inside his red-checked shirt, next to his chest. This war was immoral. Using war as an instrument of national policy was immoral. Refusing to fight was the only active protest he could make.

'This is the defining event of your generation,' his father said. 'Hell, you should be glad to go. Show your country what you're made of.'

'Did war define you, Dad?' Glenn really wanted to know. How long had he been treating his mother that way?

'It'll make a man of you.' But his father didn't answer the question. Perhaps he didn't know the answer.

'But what sort of a man?' Glenn whispered.

'It'll be the death of him. That's what it'll be.' Glenn's mother was holding on to the edge of the sink. 'Can you blame any of our boys for choosing life?'

'Women don't understand war. They're too damned emotional.' His father stomped out of the room.

Glenn's mother waited until the door closed behind him. She grabbed Glenn's arm. 'Come with me.' He followed her into the hallway and grabbed his rucksack.

She opened the front door. 'Do as I say.' And that's when he realized. She had it all planned.

'Hey, Mr Dreamboat.' Bethany was beside him, snuggling in.

Glenn thought he could sense Howard watching them from the other side of the courtyard. He could see the glow of his cigarette in the dark. 'Let's go inside.'

'What's up?'

'Nothing. I need to talk to you.'

In their room, they got undressed and climbed into bed.

'What is it?' she whispered.

'Whatever happens on this trip,' he said, 'stay cool. Act like you're just a traveller, just passing through, happy-go-lucky, you know? Don't look worried or anxious.' He stroked her hair as she nestled closer. 'You're less likely to be stopped that way.'

'And if I am stopped?' Her voice changed.

Glenn sighed. 'You'll have to play it by ear. I did warn you what might happen. But be careful, Bethany. You're important to me.'

'Then why are we doing it?' She leant on her elbow and looked down at him. He could see her dark, almond-shaped eyes but couldn't read their expression.

'For Christ's sake.' He couldn't believe he was hearing this. 'I've tried to stop you. I never wanted you to do it. I've tried everything to keep you out of it. Every night for almost a month I've tried to get you to change your mind.'

'I know.' She looked away.

He had no idea what she was thinking. It was infuriating. She was infuriating. Why now?

Abruptly, she pushed back the worn satin coverlet and got out of bed.

'What are you doing?' He sat up. 'Where are you going?'

She pulled on her cotton robe and lit the lamp. Turned towards him. 'I'm scared, Glenn.' Her voice was husky. And now he could see it in her eyes. All her bravado had left her. 'I don't want to do the run.'

'Bethany . . .' He tried to take her hand, but she moved further away. She paced the room. 'Are you saying . . .?' He had tried to protect her but she hadn't wanted to know. She'd said she had the right to choose. And now this.

'I'm not going to do it,' she said. 'I've decided.'

'Right.' It surprised him how angry he was with her. Christ knows, he didn't want her to do the run, he never had. But why had she left it till the last minute? They'd made all the arrangements now. Howard would be mad – and no doubt he'd blame Glenn for talking her out of it.

'I can change my mind.' She was defiant now and close to tears, he could see.

For a moment he wavered. Part of him wanted to take her in his arms, tell her it would be OK, that he'd go in her place as he'd originally intended to anyway, that he could keep her safe, protect her. Howard would go crazy, but what the hell did that matter compared to Bethany's safety? Howard would have to lump it. And then Glenn and Bethany could maybe go away someplace together – away from Howard and his taunting. Howard had been right to say Glenn was scared. He wasn't scared for himself, though. He was scared for Bethany. The other part of him thought of his mother – protecting him, not letting him take responsibility for his own actions and beliefs, his own life. And he just felt mad with Bethany again. Why hadn't she told him before? 'Go, tell Howard, then,' he said. 'Tell him you're not going. Tell him now.'

'I can't.'

'Then you can't not go,' he said softly. 'You can't back down. Not now. It's too late. You have to take responsibility for the decision you made.'

'You did.' She shot the words back at him so quickly that he realized they must have been there, in her head, the whole time.

'What do you mean?' But he knew.

'You backed down. You didn't stand up for your beliefs in the end. You changed your mind and you ran away.'

For a long moment, Glenn looked at her. And then he

turned his back and faced the wall. At least now he knew what she really thought. She and Howard both. And they were right.

She came back to bed, but they didn't make up. They spent the night not touching, not talking and not sleeping and in the morning she left, early, with just a long look and a touch of his hand. It was another step, he thought. And there was nothing he could do about it.

CHAPTER 30

Amy had never enjoyed listening to speeches; she'd yawned or giggled through school assemblies and avoided people who adored the sound of their own voices. She didn't enjoy being herded around – she always longed to go in the opposite direction – and she resented being organized. So after five minutes of listening to the guide droning on about the history of saffron, she slipped away from the group to explore a different pathway. No one seemed to notice that she had gone.

The path she took led her away from the saffron fields and through an orchard of fruit and almond trees; the fruit had been harvested, but some of the almonds were still on the trees. There was no one about, so she dawdled down the path, soaking in the peaceful atmosphere, the scent of the earth, the dry grass, the lavender that was still flowering among the trees. They had only had a little light rain in this, the start of the Moroccan rainy season, and the land seemed to be parched and waiting. By the time it came in earnest, she and Nell would be gone.

It had been a good trip, Amy thought. And a thought-provoking one. She had more photos than she knew what to do with and she had made a special friend. As for Jake . . . She wasn't ready to think about him. He had crept under her skin with his searching questions. But so what if Amy was scared? Didn't she have good reason? Acknowledging her fears didn't mean that anything should change.

She sat down on a bench under an almond tree for a moment and closed her eyes. What she was most sorry for was that she didn't have anything to tell her aunt, not even a reassurance that someone had seen her son, had known him. Just that Glenn had probably been visiting the town of Essaouira when he sent her that card all those years ago. It wasn't much, but maybe it was something . . .

After a while she got up and walked on until she reached a wooden gate. It didn't look like private land beyond, though she could see sheep and goats grazing the rough land. She unlatched the gate and walked through. There was a dusty track, which she supposed served as a road – of sorts – and a few buildings randomly scattered around and in the distance. They weren't houses, though, and she knew the settlement lay on the other side of the farm. These were more like huts, maybe for shelter for the workers or for animals, the same colour as the land, probably made of straw and the pinkish-brown mud. There wasn't another soul around.

Perfect. She walked up the track.

'Hello.'

The voice was soft, but still Amy jumped. She had imagined herself so completely alone. He appeared from the back of one of the huts, a young boy of around twelve or thirteen, with tobacco-coloured skin, black eyes and a mischievous smile. 'Oh, hello.' She hesitated. Should she apologize for being here?

'You are lost?' he enquired politely.

'No.' She shrugged. 'I was just taking a look around, getting some pictures.' She indicated her camera.

'You can take one of me if you like,' he said proudly. 'My name is Malik.'

'Well, thank you, Malik.' She considered. 'Could you stand just there, by the door of the hut, please?'

He repositioned himself and Amy took a few shots. 'Thank you.'

'Are you visiting the farm?' he asked. 'They have a tour. It is very good. It tells you all about saffron.' He preened himself. 'When I am older,' he confided, 'I will lead the tour. *Insha' Allah.*'

Amy nodded. 'You should do. Your English is excellent.'

Malik smiled his agreement. 'I have a good teacher.'

'And you live in this village?'

'Yes. Can I make you some tea, mademoiselle?' His brow furrowed. 'Is it correct to call you that?'

'Yes, it's correct, but you can call me Amy.'

'And the tea?' he asked.

'Well . . .' She had wanted to have more of a look around, but she'd developed rather a taste for mint tea and she couldn't resist the boy's impish arrogance. 'Yes, thank you. That would be lovely.'

'I have everything here.' He disappeared inside the hut. 'It is good for me to have English conversations.' He seemed particularly proud of that last word.

'It's the best way to learn,' Amy agreed.

He reappeared. 'Were you bored with our tour?' he asked sternly.

She smiled. 'A little.'

He stood up straighter. 'When I am doing the tour, people will not be bored.'

'I should think not,' she said.

'Many people care about saffron.' He shot her a faint frown of disapproval.

'Yes. I came with a friend,' she said. 'She's probably loving every second of it.' Amy felt slightly guilty about escaping so quickly. But at least she'd come here with Nell, that was the important thing.

Malik went inside to make the tea, and returned with two small glasses crammed full of mint leaves, hot water, sugar, and probably plenty of insects, too. But Amy thanked him and took a tentative sip. At least she was experiencing a taste of the real Morocco out here in the foothills.

'You are interested in our country?' Malik asked her.

'I am, yes.' It certainly had a pull.

Malik nodded, as if this was only to be expected. 'You can ask me anything,' he said.

So she asked him about school (yes, he had lessons, but not every day) and about his parents. His father grew vegetables and sold them at market and his mother looked after the younger children and worked on the farm when they needed her. It sounded as though – with the exception of Malik's English-language skills – the family existed pretty much in the traditional way they always had.

'And do you like the taste of saffron?' she asked him.

'Of course, yes.' He straightened his back. 'It is our life.'

Their livelihood, too, Amy thought. 'My friend's family also grows the saffron crocus,' she said, hoping Nell's passion would excuse her own failure to come up to scratch in the saffron tour department. 'They have done for generations.'

'Generations?' He frowned.

'First the grandmother, then the mother, then the daughter . . .' Suddenly Amy saw a small and distant figure waving. She could make out the frizz of blonde hair and the bright-blue jacket. 'That's her.' She stood up and waved back. 'Would you like to meet her, Malik?'

'Yes, please,' he said. 'Conversation with two people is more better.'

'Just "better",' said Amy. She beckoned Nell towards them. One minute a solitary landscape with just the goats, the sheep and the Atlas Mountains for company, and now a tea party.

She turned back to Malik. 'You don't help with the picking?' She had rather got the impression from the guide that it was all hands on deck at this time of year – children, too, although this scrap wasn't exactly a child; he certainly had his wits about him.

Malik looked rapidly around as if he expected someone to appear and drag him off to the fields. 'I was picking since just past dawn,' he said. 'It is too late now. Look at the sun.' He pointed, but Amy didn't follow his suggestion; it might be November but she'd still be blinded by the light. And it must be at least twenty-two degrees.

They watched Nell draw closer.

'Has the tour finished already?' Amy asked innocently.

'Not quite.' She looked at Malik. 'Hello.'

Amy introduced them.

'You are interested in saffron?' Malik enquired politely.

'Oh, yes.' Nell's face lit up. 'I love it. The look of it, the smell of it and, well, lots of things really. But most of all I love cooking with it. It's curiously captivating.' Nell flashed him her wide smile and Amy could see that even though he might not fully understand, he was captivated, too.

'I know a man . . .' he began. He looked further up the track past a lone jacaranda tree, but although Amy followed his gaze she could only see sheep and goats and rough pasture-land. 'He is expert.'

'*An* expert,' Amy corrected automatically.

'In?'

'In the uses of saffron.' He nodded energetically. 'I can take you to him, but . . .' He frowned. 'He sees few people these days.'

'Who is he?' Nell asked.

'He is English.' He laughed delightedly at their surprise. 'Yes, it is true. He is very old and very wise. And he knows how to use saffron to heal, like medicine.'

'How come he knows so much?' Amy was sceptical.

Malik shrugged. 'He has been here many years. He has learnt it. He has made it an interest, a pastime, a . . .' He seemed to be searching for the right word. 'A passion.'

Amy glanced at Nell. He had found the right word for her all right.

'I'd like to meet him,' Nell said decisively. 'He sounds like the perfect person to talk to.'

Malik held up a hand. 'He perhaps will not agree,' he warned. 'And his hut is thirty minutes' walk across the foot-hills.' He waited, head on one side, for their decision.

But Amy knew Nell had already made it. 'You can show us?'

'Yes.' He looked very serious. 'I will be your guide.'

'And you think he might talk to us?'

He sighed dramatically. 'I will try. But I do not know.'

They exchanged a glance. 'Nothing to lose,' said Amy.

'Nothing to lose,' agreed Nell.

CHAPTER 31

Morocco, 1977

They got back later than planned. Gizmo had gone out to listen to some Gnawa music that was on in the square and Glenn was alone, lying in the upper courtyard on the mattress watching the swallows begin their pre-sunset acrobatics. A delicate swoop here, a high arc there. They dived down so low, almost skimming the rooftop, then peeled off and back, up and up, their rasping whistle filling the air. Even when he closed his eyes he could still see the black markings of the birds embroidered on the clear blue sky as it paled and reddened into sundown. Then he heard the car engine as the old Seat grumbled down the street – his brain was tuned into its individual voice. He jumped to his feet and clattered down the stairs.

The car was parked half up on the pavement at a rakish angle, the paintwork so dusty you could hardly make out its original colour. They were both inside, Howard in the driving seat. Glenn paused for a moment, watched Howard lean across to Bethany – a bit too confidentially for his liking – and say something. She nodded. Then Howard looked back, clocked Glenn still standing in the shadows of the doorway to the riad.

He loped towards the car. She was back. She was safe. That was all that mattered.

As he approached, Howard pulled his skullcap further over his forehead. He opened the driver's door and swung himself out with a yawn and a groan as he stretched his muscles. Bethany was still just sitting there. Glenn frowned. Was she OK? He nodded at Howard. 'How did it go?'

'Like a dream.' Howard tugged at the boot, pulled out his bag, gave Glenn a thoughtful look and strolled away in the direction of the riad.

Glenn opened the passenger door. 'Bethany.' She looked weary. Her dark hair was matted, her lips were chapped with the heat and there was a film of perspiration on her forehead. But she was safe.

She climbed out without taking his hand, met his gaze briefly and leaned closer. He felt her soft kiss lightly graze his cheek. 'Hello, Glenn.' He barely had a chance to inhale the musky scent of her before she had moved away and was pulling her bag from the open boot.

'Are you OK, baby?' He went to take the bag, but she brushed his hand away as if it were a fly.

'I'm fine. I can do it.'

He'd done that, Glenn realized. He'd stopped protecting her. His shoulders slumped. 'How was it?'

'All right.' The curtain of her dark hair hid her face from him. 'Tiring. Scary at times. But don't worry – we got the money.' She laughed, without meaning it.

Glenn nodded. Of course she was tired. He had felt the

same when he got back from a run. Exhausted from the pretence, from the fear lying in the pit of your stomach that you'd be stopped, questioned, that something would go wrong. And it would. He knew it would someday.

She turned to him. 'I don't want to talk about it,' she said. 'Not yet. I just want a hot bath. And some tea.'

'I'll get the water on.' He wanted to *do*. He felt bad now that he'd told her she couldn't change her mind about going. He'd had plenty of time to think about things while she was away. Things he wanted to be different. Things he wanted to change.

In bed that night, Glenn held her. But when he tried to touch her, she grasped tight on to his hand to stop him. 'I'm too tired, baby,' she said. 'I'm just too tired.'

'Sure, I understand.' He stroked her hair. He didn't ask any more questions, though. Let her talk in her own time.

Just when he thought she must have gone to sleep, she stirred against his shoulder. 'I'm sorry, Glenn,' she said. 'For what I said about you and the whole Vietnam thing.'

'I'm sorry, too,' he soothed her. 'I shouldn't have made you go.'

He felt her tense. 'I do get it,' she said. 'I understand why you didn't fight. I get why you walked away.'

'It doesn't matter now.' She'd washed her hair, and it was silky to the touch. He'd like to bury his face in it and breathe in the scent of rosewater and musk. But it was Bethany who'd been through a bad time and who needed to be comforted, not him. And despite their physical closeness, he could still sense it – a new distance between them.

'I understand how you feel about it,' she continued in a whisper. 'I know what Vietnam did to people.'

And what it did to America, he thought. It was his birthplace. He wanted still to think of it as home. But when he discovered the darker side of the war – the devastation that American troops had brought with them, the corruption that ensued, the prostitution, the drug addiction . . . it was hard, after that, to think of America as home. He could still picture some of the newspaper images. Helicopters hovering over peasants in fields, close-ups of their shell-shocked faces, their wounded bodies, the emptiness in their eyes. The war had fucked up America's armed forces, its economy, its image, its national unity and its morale. It had divided families – including his – and it had divided generations.

Nixon had finally got them out but, Christ, he'd taken his time. People talked about how many Americans had died. People always talked about that. But how many Vietnamese had died in the conflict? Two and a half million out of a population of thirty-two million. And many of them were civilians. A country decimated, indeed.

But now wasn't the time to be thinking those kind of thoughts. Not in the darkness of the night. Not now that Bethany was back. Glenn shifted slightly. He realized she was asleep. Had Howard talked to her about Vietnam? he wondered. Hell, of course he would have. He wouldn't have lost such an opportunity to put Glenn down.

Was he a coward? Yes, because he had left rather than be sent to jail. Was he a pacifist? Yes, but not at first. He had become one. But he wasn't afraid to fight. He refused to serve in Vietnam because America had no right to be there. No right to bring suffering and destruction to that country. No right to act like the bully of the world, using a vast military might against a small nation of peasants. He hadn't let his country down. America had let him down. There had been an alternative to his legal obligation to slaughter politically incorrect Vietnamese and their families and neighbours – and he had found it.

Glenn gently withdrew his arm and turned to face the wall. He must sleep. Tomorrow, or maybe the next day, he'd tell Bethany his plans. The two of them would be OK. He'd make sure that they were OK. Otherwise . . . But he wouldn't think about the alternative. Not here. Not tonight. No way.

CHAPTER 32

Malik maintained a string of inconsequential chatter as they walked. He was interested in everything British, it seemed. He wanted to know it all, from what kind of houses they lived in to what kind of shops they shopped in to what they ate for breakfast.

Amy paused for a moment to take a swig from the water bottle. It was all rather surreal, talking about things like that, given their current circumstances. 'How much further?' she asked him. They must have been walking for forty-five minutes at least since they turned off by the misty-blue jacaranda tree. She wondered vaguely what time the bus left for Essaouira and what exactly they thought they were doing, wandering over the foothills of the Atlas Mountains looking for an eccentric Englishman who lived in a shepherd's hut. Because he must be eccentric, surely?

'Almost there,' said Malik, looking as fresh as when they'd set out.

Even Nell was soldiering on oblivious. Any mention of saffron, Amy had noticed, and she was like a woman besotted.

Amy shrugged and followed them. The land was much

more desolate now, the earth bare and parched, and there were no plants or trees, apart from the odd bristly cactus. Malik had said that this man saw few people. She doubted that many people would venture out here, so that was hardly surprising. But when she turned around . . . In the distance behind them the purple crocus fields were bathed in afternoon sunshine. She nudged Nell. 'Look.'

'Amethyst fields,' Nell murmured.

It was a stunning sight – the pinks and browns of the foothills, the waves of mauve. Amy got out her camera. After she'd taken a few shots, they walked on.

At last, Malik stopped. 'There,' he said.

Amy squinted into the distance. She could see a hut now, and an old man outside, sitting in what looked like a cane chair. He was motionless – perhaps he was sleeping?

'I go ahead first,' said Malik. 'I ask him.'

Amy shot Nell a dismayed glance. She didn't want to intrude where they weren't wanted. But the thought of walking all the way back again without even getting to talk to this old man . . .

Nell put a hand gently on her arm. 'It's OK,' she said. 'We'll wait.'

And it struck Amy that Nell had found some new inner strength these past few days. From somewhere.

They watched Malik walk towards the hut, at about twice the speed he'd been walking before. Would this old man tell them to clear off? He must have isolated himself here for a reason. He didn't want to see people, he wanted to be alone.

She could make out the building more clearly now. It appeared to be made of mud and stone but had a proper wooden door and a makeshift porch of bamboo.

They waited as Malik approached him. Presumably, they were having a conversation, though the man didn't seem to have moved a muscle. Eventually, Malik turned around and beckoned Nell and Amy forward with an enthusiastic gesture of his skinny brown arms.

'He'll talk to us,' breathed Nell. Her eyes were bright. Amy hoped she wasn't going to be disappointed.

They approached the hut. Malik was coming back to meet them. He was grinning.

'He say he sees no one,' he said. 'But I, Malik, make him change his mind.'

'Well done, Malik,' said Nell. 'How on earth did you manage it?'

She just had that way about her, Amy thought; the way that men liked. She wasn't conniving at being flattering; it was perfectly natural. It was just Nell's way. She had got on well with Jake, too; she had none of Amy's awkward prickliness. If Amy were more like her . . . But she shrugged the thought away as soon as it appeared. She was who she was. And if that was why she was single, then so be it.

'I told him your family grow saffron in England,' he said proudly. 'This is when he decides to talk to you. It is unusual, he says, to grow saffron there.'

Amy looked ahead, to where the old man lounged in the cane chair. She could make out now that his eyes were closed, his lined face raised to the autumn sunshine, the faintest shadow of a smile on his lips. He wore a red turban swathed around his head and had a grey beard. He wore a loose shirt of rough hemp-like material she'd seen the locals wearing with baggy Arab trousers, and his feet were bare. His skin was tanned and weathered. It was impossible to guess his age. He could be anything between fifty-five and eighty.

When they reached him, his eyes were open and he was staring at Nell. Another one, thought Amy. He wasn't smiling and his eyes were a very fierce blue.

'Thank you for talking to us,' Nell said. 'We really appreciate it.'

He didn't reply, just continued to look calmly back at them.

'I fetch cushions?' Malik indicated the inside of the hut. Amy could see a faded piece of carpeting on the stone floor and a kettle and some cooking utensils set on the top of a small stove.

The man nodded and Malik darted inside.

He reappeared with three cushions, which he carefully placed on the ground. 'Please sit.'

Amy and Nell did as he asked.

'Will I put water to boil?' Malik asked him. He moved restlessly, shifting his weight from foot to foot. Amy wondered if this was the man who had taught him English. If so, it was a miracle, since he didn't seem to say very much.

Again he nodded, and Malik darted back inside the hut.

'You would like saffron tea?' he asked at last. So he did

speak, thought Amy. His voice was low and soft and she couldn't quite place the accent.

'Saffron tea?' Nell's eyes lit up. Amy noticed that the man was still watching her appraisingly. 'I've never tried that. It sounds good.'

He smiled, and Amy was astonished at the transformation. 'Saffron has many healing properties,' he said. 'But in tea it needs a little cinnamon and honey, I think, to taste good.'

'What sort of healing properties?' Nell sat hugging her knees. She looked like a child. Amy made herself more comfortable on the cushion. Mint tea, and now saffron tea . . . What next?

'Since ancient times it has been used to help with a variety of maladies,' he said, 'from skin problems to depression.' He paused, as if to gather energy.

It must be strange, Amy thought, to barely speak from one day to the next and then to have to expound the virtues of saffron to a couple of unexpected visitors from England.

'Can you tell us more?' Nell asked gently.

He gave her an intense, somewhat disquieting look. 'It has long been used medicinally to reduce fevers and to calm nerves,' he said. 'The Persians scattered it over their beds at night to induce a restful sleep and to ward off melancholy.'

Goodness. Perhaps in those days, Amy thought, it wasn't more costly than gold.

'And the colour?' Nell whispered. 'What about the colour?' Already, she seemed to be under this man's spell. Amy supposed this encounter in the foothills of the Atlas

Mountains would be a bit like Amy meeting David Bailey at a photo shoot for *Vogue*.

'The colour of saffron comes from crocin, a chemical component in the flower,' he explained.

'Crocin?'

'It's an antioxidant. It's even used as an alternative cancer treatment. Some say it can help prevent the onset of blindness.'

'That's quite a claim,' said Amy softly. She thought of her Aunt Lillian and the macular degeneration which she now suffered from. Perhaps they could all learn something from the past, from the natural world, from ancient ways of healing.

The man shrugged, and this time fixed her with his penetrating gaze. Amy felt unnerved. It was as if this man knew things about her that she didn't even know herself. 'Sometimes it is wise to be cynical and cautious,' he said, 'but many of the ancient wise men believed in the healing properties of saffron even if they didn't understand why it worked.' He got up and followed Malik into the hut.

Amy blinked. 'Cynical and cautious'. She felt chastened. Was that what she was? Was that what Jake thought she was? But she supposed the old man was right. Why not believe in something you didn't fully understand? Wasn't that what faith was?

When he reappeared in the doorway, he was carrying an old tin tray with four glasses on it filled with a yellowish liquid. Malik held a small cable-roll holder, which he upturned for a table.

'May I ask you another question about saffron?' Nell asked.

'Yes, of course.' He stooped to place the tray carefully on the makeshift table and sat back again in the old cane chair. He moved stiffly and awkwardly, as if perhaps he was in pain.

'Has saffron ever been used . . .' She hesitated. '. . . in a spiritual way?'

The old man closed his eyes for a long moment and Amy thought at first he wasn't going to answer her. But: 'It has,' he said at last. 'People rub it on their brow chakra to induce enlightenment and increase energy flow.' He leant forwards and reached out his hand.

Nell shifted closer, and he rested his fingers on her brow. She closed her eyes. For a moment they were both still, almost as if something invisible were passing between them. Then Nell opened her eyes again and he leant back, nodding as if satisfied.

It must be powerful stuff. Amy decided to break the spell. 'I'm Amy, by the way,' she said. 'And this is Nell.'

He bowed his head. 'My name is Hadi. I am pleased to meet you both.'

'Hadi?' That didn't sound a very English name. He didn't sound very English either, come to that. He must, she concluded, have done a great deal of travelling.

Nell smiled and held out her hand. 'I'm pleased to meet you.'

He hesitated for a moment and then took it.

'Why Hadi?' Amy asked. She couldn't stop herself.

'It means "quiet and calm",' he said.

And Amy had to admit that he was. 'But . . .'

'It is how I am now known.' He handed them one each of the glasses, which were beautifully decorated in green and gold. They made Amy smile. Such decorative glasses didn't seem to go with a man living alone in a hut in the foothills of the Atlas Mountains.

'Do you live here all year round?' she asked him. It must get terribly cold in the winter.

He nodded.

'And you've been here a long time?' He had certainly adopted the dress and manner of the locals. He even sounded a bit like them.

He sighed. 'You ask many questions.'

'I know. Sorry.' He wasn't the first person to tell Amy this.

'I have lived here for many years, yes.'

She wondered what had brought him here in the first place. But what took anyone anywhere? Circumstances? Fate, Nell would probably claim, what with her Tarot cards and her search for inner meanings. Amy hoped she had more of a say in her own particular pathway.

You must be lonely. But she didn't say it. Some people chose to be alone, to retreat from the world; some people liked it that way.

'I'm not lonely,' he said after a moment, as if he had read her mind. 'I have the fields and the sky.' He smiled. 'And at this time of year I have the view of the saffron.' They all gazed back at the farm and the fields of purple in the distance. There would be no one picking now. But at dawn they would be back for the next wave, continuing the job each day until every last crocus had been harvested, Amy supposed.

'This is delicious.' Nell was beaming. She raised her glass. 'The cinnamon offsets the bitterness of the saffron beautifully. And it needs the honey. Only . . .'

'Only?' Once again, he was watching her intently.

'Have you tried adding something else? Like cardamom, for example, or ginger?'

Amy smiled to herself. She picked up her glass and took a tentative sip. It was slightly bitter and spicy. But there was something else. A lightness, a delicacy, which she couldn't describe.

Hadi raised an eyebrow. 'Interesting,' he said. 'I will try it.'

'Was it hard to retreat from the world?' Amy asked him. She knew that she was asking too many questions again and this was probably why the poor man had retreated from the world in the first place. But she couldn't help being curious.

'At first, it is not easy.' He sipped his tea, a slight frown on his face. 'You miss your old life, the ways of others, the way they expect you to be . . .'

What was his old life? Amy longed to ask, but she didn't want to intrude any further on his privacy. 'How did they expect you to be?' she asked instead.

He eyed her for a moment without speaking. 'Everyone has expectations,' he said. 'When you retreat into yourself, you only have expectations of yourself, not of others. You have no other guide.'

Unless you had a religious faith, Amy thought. Then you

had a different sort of guide. Although her own parents had never had strong religious beliefs, her first primary school had been Church of England-orientated and she had gone there simply because her family lived in the catchment area. But it hadn't suited her to have strong beliefs pushed into her; it had only made her want to question, to argue, to resist even more. And since then she had remained agnostic rather than atheist. There might be a god, there might be something else. She had no idea. She was ready to believe nothing and anything. It wasn't so much that she was cynical. She just took a bit of convincing.

'And does it become easier after a while?'

'Yes, it does,' he said. 'After a while it becomes the only way to be. A man must be happy in the shoes that he is wearing.'

She eyed him curiously. 'You mean you wouldn't want to go back – to civilization?' At that moment she couldn't think of a better word.

He smiled. 'I couldn't,' he said. 'I've gone to a different place.'

Amy was intrigued. 'A different place?'

'Inside.'

'But you need all this . . .' She gestured to the land, the sky, the mountains, '. . . to achieve it?'

Again he gave her a long look. 'For someone who talks so much, you're very perceptive,' he said. 'And you're right. You must find a place in which you can be at peace. *Insha' Allah*.'

They had all finished their tea, and Malik took the tray and the glasses back inside the hut. He seemed almost protective of the older man. Amy wanted to ask Hadi if he had ever visited Essaouira and if he had by any chance come across an American there called Glenn Robinson, but she decided against it for now. She had asked far too many questions already. This was supposed to be Nell's part of the deal.

'And why have you come here?' Hadi directed this question at Nell. His eyes were searching. 'What is it you seek?'

Amy saw her take a deep breath and her cheeks flush. 'We came to the farm to look at the fields,' she said. 'To do the tour, and to find out more about saffron.'

'And did you?'

Nell chuckled, and Amy noticed Hadi flinch. Perhaps he had been on his own for so long that he hadn't heard laughter for years. 'It was very interesting,' she said politely, 'but . . .'

'But?'

'But it wasn't telling me what I really need to know.'

'And what do you really need to know?'

His voice was quiet, and either that or his penetrating look had quite an effect on Nell. She seemed about to speak, to brush the subject away, as she often did anything that got too close, but then she changed her mind. 'I need to know what saffron meant to my mother,' she said.

He bowed his head for a long moment. 'And you can no longer ask her?'

'No, I can't.' She hesitated. 'And that's not all. There was a darkness in her life. A bad memory. Something she never spoke of . . .'

You could cut the tension with a knife. Amy didn't like it. She was always the one who would gabble at dinner parties to break the ice or talk to strangers next to her in a queue. All this talk about darkness just didn't seem right somehow. And who was this old man, anyway? How did they know he wasn't about to whip out a knife and cut their throats as they sat here? She held on to her camera a little tighter.

'Where does your family grow saffron in England?' he asked softly. 'Is it in Norfolk?'

Nell was eyeing him steadily. 'My family's saffron is grown in Cornwall,' she said.

'In Cornwall, you say?'

Nell leant forwards and clasped her hands in that way she had. Amy had thought at first it was a nervous gesture but now she recognized it as earnestness, a desire to get a thought across, a worry that she wouldn't be understood.

'Yes,' she said. 'It's unusual, I know. And it's a very special place. Roseland.'

'Roseland.' His lips shaped the word. 'I see. But where did your mother experience the darkness you speak of? Did she ever come out here to Morocco?' He seemed to be trying to help her, Amy conceded. He seemed kind.

'I don't think so,' she said. 'She never mentioned it.'

What could anyone say to help her? Her mother had committed suicide, and Nell believed that she herself was the daughter of a rapist. Nothing this man could tell them would make any difference to that.

Amy glanced at her watch. 'We should be leaving.' She got to her feet. 'We came here by bus. We don't want to miss it.'

Hadi didn't speak. He seemed almost dazed. His eyes half closed and Amy wondered if they'd tired him. He didn't seem well and it had been a long conversation for someone who didn't want to talk very much, for someone who had retreated from the world. But he opened his eyes and scratched at his grey beard. 'I have something to give the young woman who cares so much about saffron,' he said at last. 'Wait here.'

He got up and shuffled into the small hut. Amy and Nell looked at Malik, who only shrugged. He had been practically silent throughout the whole visit, but no doubt he had been taking it all in.

When he re-emerged from the hut, Hadi was carrying a thin and worn tubular canister. Carefully, he pulled out a rolled-up sheet of some sort of manuscript. He spread it out on the table top. It wasn't big, but it was certainly old, a sepia parchment, probably an aged and dried-up animal skin. It was wrinkled and the writing above the drawing was in a fine and spidery black script in what looked like some ancient Arabic language.

Nell gasped.

Amy realized what she had seen. The colours had faded, but there was no mistaking it. The drawing was of a woman with long tresses of dark hair. She was dressed in a flowing white robe with a yellow veil and was bending forwards slightly at the waist, caught in the most natural and uninhibited of poses. Her eyes were dark and her lips were red. Her slim hand was outstretched, her gaze expectant. She was picking a saffron flower. It was unmistakable from its shape, though the purple had faded to a pale lilac. On the woman's lips was the faintest of smiles.

'Where did it come from?' breathed Nell. She put out a hand as if to touch the parchment, but didn't seem able to dare make contact.

Hadi seemed pleased by her response. 'There was a man who worked on the farm. His family once owned the land,' he said. 'He was very kind to me. I helped him, too, I think. We became friends. I learnt a lot from him.' He paused. 'Before he died, he gave me this. He said that it had been in his family's care for centuries. For as long as they had grown saffron.'

She frowned. 'What does this say?' She pointed to the script. '*Zafaran*,' he said.

'And . . . who is she?'

They all looked again at the woman in the ancient drawing. She looked rather regal, thought Amy. 'A goddess?' she ventured. There were, after all, lots of stories about saffron in Greek and Roman mythology, so everyone kept telling her.

'Ancient frescoes showing goddesses and saffron have been found in many places,' Hadi said. 'In Greece, for example. It is possible . . . And it was the tradition of many cultures to use saffron to colour bridal veils yellow.'

Nell put her head on one side. 'She doesn't look like a goddess,' she said. 'She looks . . .'

'Like a bit of a tease,' Amy added.

'She's yours,' said Hadi. 'Please take her. Let her be on show again, as she once was.'

'But I couldn't possibly . . .' Nell was getting agitated now, Amy could see. 'The parchment's very old. It's too much. It might even be valuable, and . . .' She looked to Amy for help.

'We hardly know you,' Amy said.

'It has nothing to do with money,' he said. 'I would not sell it and you will not sell it. It is what it is.' He spread his hands. 'And I have no one.'

Amy glanced at Malik. The old man had him in thrall, that was for sure. But she supposed he wouldn't be interested in an old drawing of a woman and saffron – he'd barely bothered to come closer to take a look.

'Perhaps,' said Hadi to Nell, 'the sunshine that your mother found in her saffron helped dispel the darkness she had experienced in her life.'

Nell's hands were again clasped in front of her. She was still for a moment as, steadily, she looked back at him. 'Perhaps,' she whispered. She didn't seem able to turn away. 'Can I write to you here?' she asked him. 'Will a letter reach you somehow?'

He seemed surprised. 'Yes, if you use my name and if you send it to the farm. Malik will bring it.'

'All right. And I'll give you my address, too.' She scrabbled in her bag for pen and paper.

'Yes.' He seemed to expect this.

'Thank you.' Nell dropped to her knees and took hold of

his hands. Amy watched the tableau, which was strangely moving. And there was something else, though, for the moment, she couldn't quite grasp what.

They said goodbye and Malik led them back along the same route, Nell now holding the old metal canister tight under one arm. She glanced at Amy. 'What an amazing man,' she breathed.

Amy nodded. It had been quite an experience. She felt almost shell-shocked. And as they retraced their steps to the misty-blue jacaranda tree, she turned back one last time. Hadi was still standing there, staring after them.

CHAPTER 33

Morocco, 1977

He never even heard her leave. He just woke up one morning and she was gone. No kiss goodbye, no note.

He thought at first she was making tea. He yawned and stretched and waited. Nothing. Finally, he pulled on his *kurta*, slipped on his *babouches* and padded to the kitchen. No one. He went up to the terrace. Sometimes, one or other of them slept up there, especially in the summer. That felt so good, sleeping under the stars, a light breeze keeping you cool, although the mattress was narrow for two. But now that the nights were getting chillier, it seemed unlikely. Maybe she'd gone up there to watch the sunrise, Glenn thought blearily. But there was no one. Just the remains of last evening. Empty beer bottles, an ashtray crammed with roaches and cigarette butts, a plate with a few remaining sticky dates. Glenn surveyed the debris, couldn't face it, turned away.

He clattered back down the spiral staircase to the upper courtyard. Three doors, his wide open. He went back inside. 'Bethany?'

She must have gone out for a walk. It was early, but she could have gone to the beach to practise her yoga on the sand.

Only, Glenn remembered that she hadn't been doing much yoga lately, that she'd been quiet and preoccupied and not the same girl he'd brought back to Riad La Vieux Rose four years ago. Not the same, in fact, since she'd come back from that run. She was unhappy. He knew that she was unhappy, and this scared him.

He opened their wardrobe. Inside hung one of his shirts – denim – and a pair of jeans. Her side of the wardrobe – usually spilling into his, with patterned paisley dresses and patchwork skirts, white cotton smocks and cheesecloth shirts – was bare. Her T-shirts were not on the shelf. He opened a drawer. Her underclothes were gone, too. He spun around. No jar of Nivea on the top of the chest of drawers, no make-up bag, no bottle of musky rose perfume. No hairbrush or toothbrush balanced precariously by the sink. Nothing. It seemed that not a trace of her remained. How the hell had she cleared all her stuff out without him even hearing her?

Glenn swiftly got dressed and left the riad. Where would she go? The waterfront? The hotel? The harbour? She couldn't have left town, could she? Not just like that. Every year she took a few weeks off from the hotel and helped with crop-picking at a place just outside of town, but she would have told him if she was going there.

He went to the hotel. They hadn't seen her. No, they weren't expecting her in today. Tomorrow, yes. No, she hadn't said anything about leaving.

She wasn't at the waterfront, nor in the artisan quarter, where she often used to stand and watch the craftsmen at work on their leather and *thuya* wood. She wasn't at the harbour watching the blue fishing boats return from sea with full baskets of fish, glittering and gleaming in the sun; she wasn't having coffee in the square.

And if she had left town . . . Glenn surveyed the long road out that led to the Atlas Mountains and the city of Marrakech. She certainly would have gone by now.

Back at the riad, Howard's door was open.

'Hey, man,' he said. 'What gives?'

'Have you seen Bethany?'

'Yeah.'

'This morning?'

Howard seemed to consider. 'Yeah.'

'When, exactly?' Glenn felt a lurch of hope. He looked around, half expecting her to materialize from behind him, to laugh, to spin around, to say it was all a joke.

Howard shrugged. 'Some time before seven. I got up to make tea. Couldn't sleep. Seems I wasn't the only one.'

'Did she say anything?'

'You mean did she tell me she was leaving?' He paused. 'Nah.'

Glenn frowned. 'Then how d'you know she was? Leaving, I mean.'

Howard lounged against the door frame. For once, he wasn't wearing his skullcap. His hair was matted and looked as if he hadn't washed it for weeks. 'I saw her bag, man. It was crammed full. Not just for an overnighter, if you get my meaning.'

Glenn felt a pain like a blow to his gut. His head was spinning. He loved Bethany. What had happened? Why had she left? 'Why the hell didn't you come and tell me?' he shouted. 'For fuck's sake!'

'None of my business, man.' Howard shrugged.

'What's up, guys?' A bleary Gizmo appeared from his room, stark naked except for his bandana.

'Jeez.' Howard shielded his eyes. 'Spare us the drama.'

'What?' Gizmo spread his hands. 'The human body is a natural thing, man. You need to loosen up a bit, relax, hang loose.' He must have caught Glenn's expression. 'What?'

'Bethany's split,' said Howard. 'Didn't even have the guts to tell us she was going.'

Glenn turned on him. 'She had guts.' He felt his fists clench.

Howard's mouth twisted into a grin. 'Yeah, right,' he said. He turned away. 'Whatever you say.'

Glenn found the note in the kitchen, propped against the kettle. She'd written his name in blue felt-tip pen on the envelope and the childishness of it just about brought tears to his eyes. How come he hadn't seen it before? Guess he'd been looking for a girl at first, not a goddamn letter. He ripped it open.

'Darling Glenn,' he read. 'It's not working out and it's my fault. I'm going back home. I've had a great time – please don't think I haven't. But maybe I'm not cut out for this kind of scene after all. And like you've always said – we've got to know when it's time to move on. So don't try and follow me or anything. It was great. But now it's over. I'm so sorry.

'My love, Bethany.'

His love, Bethany. Glenn stared and stared at it, but the words didn't change and they still made no sense. If it wasn't working out, couldn't they at least have talked about it, tried to sort it out? He looked around him for a clue. Anything. Why would she have left like that? His guts were churning. He didn't know what to do with himself. He couldn't stand it – the thought of losing her.

Why hadn't she even given him a chance to change her mind?

CHAPTER 34

Lillian decided to take a walk along the waterfront at Lyme. Today it was cold and crisp, but at least the sun was shining. It was also a good day because today Amy would be back from Morocco. She'd rung briefly before her flight and promised to call in later for hot chocolate, and Lillian couldn't wait to see her. Had she found out anything? Lillian wasn't sure what Amy could do that a private detective could not, and she had long ago accepted that she would never discover what had happened to Glenn. But . . . in her mind, in her heart, there always remained a 'but'.

Lillian put on her warm coat – never be deceived by sunshine. She had learnt long ago about truth and illusion. Hadn't she fooled herself for years? She thought of all those letters she'd written to Ted Robinson in America, never knowing if he was alive or dead, pouring out all her innermost thoughts and feelings as if the letter were a diary. Poor little fool. What must he have thought when he finally got back home and read them?

Lillian left the house and set off. She'd go past the town mill, she decided, and through to the clock tower that way. She was old, but she wasn't decrepit; one had to at least try and stay fit and healthy. After that, it was up to God, or the Fates, or whatever else you believed in. Lillian wasn't sure she believed in anything – but love.

And he had read those letters. He was alive, he had returned to America and he had read them, every one. He could have ignored them. No doubt, in time, she would have grown bored with writing to a ghost. She would have met a young lad like Johnnie Coombes, she would have married and become a farmer's wife. But she didn't. She saw her sister married and she kept on writing, and then one day . . .

Lillian reached the pink house with the bay windows at the waterfront. This row of buildings rather summed up Lyme Regis, she'd always thought. Pretty cottages with white shutters, quirky houses with elaborate drainage pipes and carvings around the doors, bright and breezy villas reminiscent of the beach huts on the lower prom, and sombre Gothic monstrosities that made Lillian think of a Victorian lunatic asylum. Together they were an eclectic mix; they were Lyme.

She remembered the day she saw the postman at the gate and he'd said, 'One for you, I reckon, young lady.'

'For me?'

He'd handed it to her and she thought for a moment she'd stop breathing. Because it was a letter from America in a blue airmail envelope. She had gasped, examined the writing – for surely it must be from some relative of Ted's telling her please not to write any more letters to a dead man – and turned it over in her hand. She had gone inside the house before she opened the seal, unfolded it, examined the neat writing.

There was plenty of it – which was a good sign. Her heart almost stopped. She searched for the signature. 'Yours, Ted.' He was alive. She let out the breath she didn't even know she was holding. He was alive, after all this time. She held the letter close to her heart, ran upstairs to read it in the privacy of her bedroom. She devoured every word. Remembered the flash of his smile, the twinkle in his eye. He was alive.

'Hey, kiddo,' he had written. Not a good start. Lillian didn't want to be thought of as a kiddo. She was seventeen years old. Old enough to date, to fall in love, to be courted. She was a woman. She was not a kiddo. 'Thanks for all your letters. They mean a lot. I sure do treasure my time in Dorset, and it was good to be reminded.'

But did he want to be reminded of Mary? Lillian wondered.

He didn't write of the war. He wrote of what it had been like to return home, what home meant to him and what he was going to do next. And Lillian wrote back.

Soon they were regular correspondents. Lillian wrote about her plans to go to secretarial college, how she intended to go to London and make her life there. She wrote about films she had seen and books she had read. And she wrote about what she really felt. How her family simply didn't understand her, how parochial and ordinary the people around her seemed to be, how dull their lives. She wrote of how she felt walking alone along the street in the dark under a moonlit sky, how she felt strolling through the fields on a summer's day when the lambs were gambolling in the sun, and how lonely she felt in the dead of the night.

'What do you want, Lillian?' he asked her in the letter – for now, he no longer called her kiddo. 'What I want,' she wrote back, 'is to feel alive.'

Lillian walked as far as the Cobb before turning back. She paused for a moment and felt the wind in her hair. Did she feel alive now? she asked herself. Some days, yes.

And then one day, another letter came. Lillian was eighteen. It was a letter that came as a surprise, but the best surprise in the world; a letter she had longed for and dreamed of but never dared to hope would become a reality. A letter in which he asked her to come over to America. A letter in which he asked her to be his bride.

'You may think this has come out of the blue, Lillian, my sweetheart,' he wrote. His sweetheart? Could she really be his sweetheart? 'But you see, I've got to know you from your letters. Truth is, I've fallen head over heels in love with you. I want to marry you. Will you come over here? Will you be my bride?'

Would she? Lillian was still only eighteen years old, but she knew her own mind.

The next months had passed in a blur of discussions, packing and purchasing. Her parents reacted in much the way she'd expected and then gave in, as she'd known they would. And Mary . . . Well, Lillian hadn't really thought of Mary. She was married now, of course, but . . .

Lillian walked more slowly on the way home. She had her stick – after the fall, Amy had insisted she use one – and she leaned more heavily on it. She'd get back, make herself a nice cup of tea.

America hadn't been what she had expected. It was bigger, blander and terribly conventional. And Ted . . . It was gone in a moment. But she remembered the look on his face when he first laid eyes on her so well, as if it was branded into her.

'Hey, Duchess,' he'd said. Already, the look was gone. 'Good to see you again.' He took her in his arms and he held her, but the hug lacked the enthusiasm she'd envisaged. There was none of the romance, none of the passion, no twinkle in those warm brown eyes. Had the war changed him so much? Or had he been deluding himself – was that it? And that had been her problem, too, Lillian thought now. An overactive imagination. He didn't behave like the man she remembered, he didn't even look like him. Could he be thinking what she was thinking? *What have I done . . .?*

Ted, too, had tried to pretend they hadn't both made an awful mistake. He would never have made a promise and then sent her away. He introduced her to all his relatives – his parents, an uncle and aunt, a married cousin and her husband – and they welcomed her into the family with broad smiles and blueberry muffins. Really, they couldn't have been nicer. Ted had looked at her and smiled fondly. Was that why she'd come all these miles from everything and everyone she knew and loved? To be married to a man she barely knew – who was *fond* of her?

344

Lillian wanted to curl up in a corner and disappear. She wanted to get on the next boat home. She wanted to scream, There's been some terrible mistake! I don't belong here after all — I never did! But she didn't do any of these things. She took a deep breath and got on. She had made this decision and she couldn't unmake it. This was the life she had chosen. She went along with the family's expectations, meek and docile as a rice pudding, she thought now.

Ted went along with the family's expectations, too — in a daze, as if he thought one morning he might wake up and find Lillian metamorphosed into Mary, giggling over a ladder in her stocking or teasing him with a playful tap on his arm and the raise of a perfectly plucked eyebrow. But Lillian had never been her sister. She was nothing like her, she never had been. And she and Ted didn't talk of their letters, of the outpourings of emotions, hopes and dreams that had brought them to this. They didn't talk of what had happened in the war; what Ted had witnessed and what he had survived — which had also brought them to this. They didn't even talk of themselves and what either of them wanted. They just continued with their plans to marry.

And then it was done.

Lillian got her front-door key out of her bag and inserted it carefully into the lock. She pushed the door with her elbow and home jumped up to greet her, pulled her inside with a gush of warmth, welcome and cosiness. Home had never done that in America. It had never quite believed in her; perhaps it had known she wasn't the person she was pretending to be.

Lillian propped her stick in the umbrella stand. She took off her coat and hung it on the peg, resisting the impulse to greet her house verbally as she would a long-lost friend. She put her gloves on the hall stand and eased her feet out of her boots. Her slippers were furry and inviting. She slipped in each foot, let out a small 'ah' of contentment.

And so Lillian had become Mrs Ted Robinson. They lived in a little house in Pennsylvania. And she was a wife. She would make it work, she decided. She had to.

The first time he made love to her she knew she'd disappointed him again. There was something she should be doing, something that was missing which she knew nothing about. What was it? There was no one she could ask – certainly not his mother or his married cousin, and she had no friends here as yet. She could hardly write back home and ask Mary. And worse than this was what she felt – or, to be more precise, didn't feel.

When they had first met in Dorset, she would have done anything for a touch, let alone a kiss, from the handsome GI in the smart khaki uniform. But now . . . The man she'd known, the man she'd fallen in love with, the man who had courted her sister, had disappeared. He simply wasn't there any more.

She thought back to their early meetings, even recalled phrases from his letters, moments when he had allowed her to glimpse his heart. And she realized with a growing sense of horror that he had never been there at all. What she had fallen in love with had been a fantasy – her fantasy. Not a man.

346

What she had connected with when they had written to one another had been her own response to him, her desire to be needed, to be loved. The reality, lying on top of her here in bed, half suffocating her, repelling her with his thick breath, the dark, matted hair on his arms and chest, the lack of recognition in his eyes, was not someone she loved, nor was it someone who loved her. She didn't even like the smell of his skin. It was a man she had no connection with. A stranger.

What a fool she had been. Lillian clicked her tongue. She went into the kitchen to put the kettle on. But she had never considered leaving. Even then she had wondered – was this her punishment for what she had done to Mary?

When she'd found out she was pregnant, she'd longed for a daughter. This sounded disloyal and she fervently hoped Glenn had never suspected, but in her heart she knew that Ted would have accepted a daughter more easily, that a daughter would have slipped into position in their fragile family ensemble and kept it stable somehow. Everyone knew about fathers and their daughters.

But when her child was born . . . When that little bundle was placed in her arms, when she looked down into his blue, sightless eyes, when she had heard his cry and felt him rooting for her breast in a way that stirred some ancient and new longing deep within her . . . then, Lillian could never have regretted the fact that Glenn was a boy. Because everyone knew about mothers and their sons.

Despite what Lillian had done, Mary didn't break all ties.

After their mother died, she wrote short notes telling Lillian how the family were faring. And, of course, she wrote to tell her when their father died, but although Lillian desperately wanted to go to England for his funeral, Ted told her it was impossible, that they couldn't afford it, that her visit would have to wait. The fact was that Ted had no time for any of Lillian's family – perhaps, not even, any more for Mary.

When it came to it, of course, they did have money and they could have afforded it, but Lillian hadn't known that then. She only knew that she couldn't say goodbye to her father, just as she hadn't been able to say goodbye to her mother, and that this was her fault, because she had chosen her life, chosen Ted, chosen to move to America.

With the birth of Glenn, Lillian's life changed out of all recognition. Where before she had dulled her senses to the things she couldn't change, to Ted and to whatever it was that haunted him, to the aching loneliness of her life in a place where she didn't fit in, would never fit in . . . Now, she had a son and her life would be dedicated to him.

CHAPTER 35

On the flight back Nell closed her eyes and thought about what she had achieved on this trip. She'd at last found out something about her mother – perhaps not much that was tangible, but it had increased her understanding. She'd learnt a lot from Amy, too – about confidence and independence; two qualities Nell had always struggled with and which Amy seemed to possess in abundance. She opened her eyes, shifted in her seat and registered the approach of the steward with the drinks trolley. She'd made a friend, a good and trusted friend. They'd promised to keep in touch, they didn't live so far away from one another and Nell would definitely attend the Moroccan event in Lyme. It would be fabulous to see Amy's photographs, to relive their Moroccan adventure one more time.

Nell retrieved her purse from her bag. Even more importantly, she'd made a huge decision about her professional life. Running their own restaurant had been the ambition of most of her peers at catering college. Lucy had done all sorts in the past few years – she'd even tried selling crêpes from a camper-van at music festivals. Whatever, working for yourself had to be better than working antisocial hours for someone else in a demanding environment for very little financial return. But Nell had never felt brave enough to take it on – until now. Now, she had a clear idea of the project she wanted to pursue and where she intended to pursue it. She smiled up at the steward. She'd stay off the alcohol and stick to juice, she decided. She thought of Callum. She'd told him her flight details, but would he even be there to meet her? She had no idea. Whether he was or not, she had a lot she had to tell him, so she needed a clear head.

She bought her cranberry juice and set it up on the little table top. Thinking about all the positive things that had happened, she remembered one more. She had been given a strange but incredible gift by Hadi, the wise man in the mountains, a man who had found his sense of peace in Morocco, who brewed saffron tea and knew how it could be used in healing. Astonishing. Nell sipped her drink. She would have the parchment framed; it would have pride of place on the wall of her new restaurant, The Saffron House. She – Smilax – would be seen again, as he had wanted.

Nell stared out of the little porthole window and glanced at her watch. Had the old wise man been right? Had the sunshine of saffron helped dispel the darkness of her mother's memories? If so, then it was more important than ever that Nell continued to grow the saffron crocuses, that she kept her mother's legacy intact, whatever her own feelings about what her mother had failed to tell her and how her silence had let her down.

They would be landing in an hour. Her visit to the saffron

farm and her meeting with Hadi had made her even more determined not to give up the farmhouse. But she still had to face the estate agents and the prospective buyers. And Callum.

He was there. She saw him the second she came through the doors, standing stiff and upright, hazel eyes fixed straight ahead, not quite knowing how to be, what to say. And, despite herself, she felt a jump of pleasure, of relief.

'Callum,' she mouthed.

He saw her, an involuntary smile twitched at his mouth and then the stern look returned. She knew how much she'd upset him and she didn't know what was ahead or whether they could even move forwards. But . . .

'Hi.' She walked up to him, stood on tiptoe and kissed him tentatively. Lips or cheek, she was somewhere in between. Which kind of summed it up, she thought.

'Hello, Nell,' he said. He moved forward as if to hold her and then his arms fell to his sides.

It felt terrible. Nell leant against his chest, feeling the warmth of him, willing it to come back – the love, the closeness.

He backed off. Grabbed her case. 'How was it?'

She hurried after him. 'Good. Very good.' Apart from the painful bits, she thought. Apart from her anger, her fear of losing him.

'And who's this new friend, this Amy, who dragged you halfway across Morocco?'

'She's great. You'd love her. And she didn't drag me. I wanted to go. It seemed too good an opportunity to miss.'

'Why was that, Nell?' He was still waiting. They were almost out of the terminal, and heading for the car park. It was dark and it was cold.

Hadn't he heard anything she'd told him? Some of her pleasure at seeing him began to evaporate. 'Because I wanted to find out more about her,' she said. 'About Mum.'

'Nell . . .'

'What?' They had stopped by the ticket machine. So was this when she was about to find out for sure – how well he really knew her?

He sighed. 'How does visiting a saffron farm in Morocco tell you more about your mother? Just because she grew the same crop, it doesn't mean it was for the same reasons. Don't you think you're being a bit over-imaginative?'

Nell frowned. This wasn't what she'd wanted to hear. 'It's a kind of spiritual thing.' She wasn't expecting miracles. She knew Callum wasn't a mind reader. But *he* had understood. Hadi, the old man in the mountains. And she had the feeling that the man she'd met in Marrakech would understand, too. Rafi. She hadn't told Amy, but he had given her his phone number. 'Perhaps in the future,' he had said, his voice low. And she, Nell, had taken it.

Callum was scrabbling for loose change in the pockets of his jeans. He was wearing a thick fur-lined leather jacket and heavy boots. Nell shivered. Yes. It was a lot chillier here than in Morocco. In more ways than one.

352

'So what did you find out about her?' he said, after making the payment and retrieving the ticket. 'Or was it a wasted journey?'

Nell didn't like his tone. What *had* she found out? That saffron was much more mysterious and precious than even she had realized – which meant the legacy was even more precious, too. That her mother had been Smilax . . . She smiled; fanciful, she knew. But she had an old parchment in her bag that personified that image – at least as far as Nell was concerned. She had also discovered that saffron had all sorts of qualities and uses she'd never dreamed of. Her mother's secrets might never be truly discovered, but she must have had good reason to maintain that stubborn silence all these years. Nell sighed. She was still finding it hard to forgive her mother – but perhaps she would have to trust her on that one.

'It's hard to explain,' she told Callum. Would she ever be able to? Not until he was a little more receptive, she decided.

He pressed the button for the lift. They waited in silence for it to arrive. A week apart, thought Nell, and they had barely a word to say to one another. What was going to happen to them? Did she want to confide in him – ever? Did she want to hold him close and make love in the dead of night? Did she want to tell him everything that had happened to her – and more, besides? How well did she *want* him to know her?

The lift arrived and they stepped in.

'I've been thinking, Nell,' he said, as the door closed behind them. 'You may need help to get over your mother's death, you know.'

'Help?' she echoed. *Get over?*

'Some sort of grief counselling.' The lift winged them up two floors.

Nell blinked at him. I'm on the way, she thought. Not to get over it, but to find a path through.

'I understand that's why the idea of selling the farmhouse is so difficult for you,' he went on. 'It's bound to be hard. It's where you grew up.'

It's my home. But she didn't say it. The lift arrived and the doors slid open. Nell felt like staying inside. God knows where the metal box would take her to, but she didn't feel ready to face the world. Yet he was her husband and she followed him. For now.

'I realize you just couldn't face up to it.' He was warming to his theme. 'And that's why you said what you did about wanting to meet the buyers. All that stuff.' They reached the car and, at last, he met her eye. He unlocked it and swung the case into the boot. 'I can't pretend I wasn't upset with you.'

'That wasn't why I wanted to meet them,' she said, climbing into the passenger seat. 'I wanted to meet them to see if they were suitable.'

He let out a short and humourless laugh. 'Suitable?'

'But now I don't need to,' she said.

'Good.' Callum turned the ignition key. 'The sooner we get things sorted, the better. So you don't want to meet them now? That's such a relief.' He patted her hand. 'Well done,

354

darling. That's more like it. Oh, and I've booked us into a hotel, by the way. I don't want to be driving all the way back home at this time of night. It's only five minutes away.'

'I don't need to meet them now.' Nell clenched her hands together hard. 'I've changed my mind.'

'Yeah?' He was already heading for the exit.

She took a deep breath. 'You see, Callum, I don't want to sell the farmhouse any more,' she said. 'Because I want to go back and live there.'

CHAPTER 36

Morocco, 1977

Glenn couldn't decide what to do at first. He wandered around the town, still half looking for her, seeing the swirl of her skirt in the spice market, the sheen of her hair among the people in the leather bazaar, a glimpse of her floppety hat. He would hear her voice in a café and turn to look at some stranger, and once he followed a girl almost a mile along the beach because something about the way she walked reminded him of Bethany.

'Seems like you're pining, man,' Howard said to him one evening as they all sat inside, needing the warmth of the brazier, for it was the beginning of November and the nights were drawing in. 'What's up with you, for Chrissake?'

Glenn shrugged. Like the other two, he was wearing his rough llama wool jacket and, like the other two, he could never get rid of the smell. It wasn't warming him up very much either. It was true that he wasn't feeling too good. Tired, mostly. Perhaps he was tired of living this way. Perhaps he needed to think again about going home. And it was true that he missed her. Bethany.

'There are plenty more chicks in the sea,' quipped Gizmo.

'Though that lady was something else, man, I know it. Freaked me right out, her leaving like that.'

'Easy come, easy go,' said Howard. 'S'trewth, you of all people should know how simple it is to walk away, Glenn.'

Bastard. But Glenn wasn't interested in any other chicks and none of it was goddamn simple.

He'd move out of Riad La Vieux Rose, he decided that night as he lay in bed, strangely exhausted but unable to sleep. He had to. It wasn't just Howard – though Howard was part of it. It wasn't just the memories either. It was what Bethany had said in her letter. You know when it's time to move on. Right. Glenn guessed it was way past time.

When he slept he dreamed of Bethany. And when he woke he knew what he must do. He'd make his way to England. He'd find her. He'd talk to her. And maybe . . . Thing was, though, he couldn't get past that maybe.

The following morning Glenn still didn't feel right. It was as if the guilt were sitting in his head – his refusal to fight in Vietnam, leaving his mother alone with his father to face whatever consequences there might be, the guilt of Bethany leaving. He almost couldn't think straight. But he packed his bag, taking only essentials, giving the rest to Gizmo.

'D'you have to go, man?' Gizmo's brown eyes were big and sad.

Glenn nodded, though he hated leaving his friend. 'I'll send an address, Giz,' he said. 'We'll keep in touch.'

'Yeah.' Gizmo brightened. 'You can come back any time, man. Or maybe we'll meet up again somewhere on the road.'

357

'Sure thing.' But as Glenn left the Riad La Vieux Rose, he knew it was for the last time.

A Moroccan guy in his late fifties or so with strong, sculptured features and sun-weathered brown skin picked him up in his truck on the road out. He wore the usual *djellaba* and loose-fitting Arabic trousers. Glenn had been hoping for a lift as far as Marrakech. From there he'd make for Fez, then Tangiers.

'*Viens!* Come. *Asseyez-vous!* Sit down.' He spoke in French, but when he realized that Glenn had a smattering of Berber and Arabic, he reverted to what was probably his usual dialect, and Glenn could just about understand him.

'My name is Mustapha,' he said. 'How long do you stay in Morocco?'

Glenn introduced himself and told him he'd been living in a riad in Essaouira but that he was now travelling back to Europe, maybe to England. As they drove he caught his final glimpses of the sprawl that was Essaouira, the blur of olive-green sea and the distant dunes, windswept trees of pine and oleander. The wide road stretched out ahead.

'*Metsharfin.* I am pleased to meet you. And you like our country, yes?' Mustapha asked.

Glenn looked around him at the dry open plain, the brown desert, the drowsy pink mountains in the distance, the low slopes speckled with eucalyptus. 'Very much,' he replied.

'But now you leave.' Mustapha seemed puzzled. 'You English, yes?'

'American.'

'You travel many places away from home?'

'I have, yes.' Home seemed so far from here; sometimes Glenn felt he could barely remember it at all.

'There is a place for you somewhere,' Mustapha said. '*Insha'Allah*. If God wills it. What are you looking for?'

Glenn blinked. It was one hell of a good question. Had he been looking for love? Not really, though Bethany had come into his life and completely blown his mind. Had he been looking for spiritual enlightenment? Nope. India had been a good scene, but meditation had never been his thing. Or had he just been escaping, running away? Was Howard right? Was that all it was?

'Perhaps you look for something to believe in.' Mustapha nodded wisely.

Glenn considered. 'Yeah, maybe that is what I'm looking for.' This guy had Allah. Christians had Jesus Christ. What did Glenn have? He was an atheist. He didn't believe in God. Especially not in a God that allowed wars to continue, where innocent people suffered and died. So what could he believe in if not in love?

'*La. Shi bá má káin*. There is no harm in it,' Mustapha said thoughtfully.

After a while, the land became more agricultural; there were more plants, some groves of olive trees, a tractor in a field. And every so often they would pass a small village lined with palms, with roadside shacks selling fruit and vegetables from crates and baskets and dried beans and lentils from tin

359

bins; a café, small houses and the familiar copper-coloured mosque with green-glazed tiles. Cows and goats grazed by the roadside and donkey carts piled high with goods kept to the verges as they clattered along. They passed dried-up riverbeds, where some of the villages had been abandoned, and when Glenn asked Mustapha about this he said that people had left in search of work. It was November, but the sun still shone and Glenn could still smell the wild thyme that grew by the road and on the mountain, its scent of pepper and lemon carried on the breeze into the half-open windows of the truck.

'You have money?' Mustapha asked him. 'You need work? I could give you a week or two to help you on your way.'

'What kind of work?' He could do with some more cash, but now he'd made the decision to leave he just wanted to get on with it. He was hesitant.

'I live with Fadma, my wife, in a small village in the foothills of the Atlas Mountains,' Mustapha said. 'There is labour needed at our farm at this time of year. And Fadma and I would think it an honour if you would come to share a couscous dinner with us this evening. My wife, she loves to cook, and –'

'Thank you, but I must get on.' He shifted in his seat. He couldn't bear not to be on his way.

'As you wish.'

Glenn realized he had been abrupt, even rude. 'Pardon me, but . . .'

'I understand.' Mustapha bowed his head. 'You have no time. The young do not have the time, I think, not any more.'

Glenn stared out of the window into the pale, gritty dust of the plain, spiked with cacti and bamboo. Of course he had the time. He had more time than he knew what to do with. And he needed the money. He had said he was going to England, but what was the point? Bethany didn't want him to follow her; she'd told him so in her note. He could go and see his mother's sister, his Aunt Mary, but did he really want to? Was he ready? Right at this moment, with his head still pounding, Glenn didn't feel ready for anything. 'I would be honoured to visit your house,' he told Mustapha. '*Shukran*. Thank you. And I could do with the work. You are very kind.'

The man's eyes lit up. '*Wakha*. As you wish,' he said again softly, and he shot Glenn a gappy grin before turning his attention back to the road.

Glenn relaxed. What difference would a week or so make? Nothing when you were on the road. And perhaps by next week he'd feel more up for the journey.

'Soon the first snow will come to the mountains,' Mustapha told him. 'And the wind, it will sweep down to us from the summits.'

Winter. Glenn closed his eyes as they entered the powdery-pink foothills of the Atlas Mountains. He had no idea where they were going. He had put his trust in this man but God knows where he was taking him. He found himself thinking of a book he'd read in college in which a young traveller was befriended by a local in Cairo, given a sumptuous feast and had all his possessions stolen that night when he was in a drunken sleep. It wasn't exactly an original storyline. But it was a fable – and so, predictably, losing everything ended up being a blessing in disguise for the young traveller, because it forced him to undertake a different journey to the one he'd imagined. A more inspirational and fruitful journey. Glenn opened one eye. On the plus side, he was carrying very little of value, and that was probably obvious from the look of him – with his long hair, frayed jeans and worn desert boots, he didn't think he had anything to fear.

He must have drifted off to sleep for a moment because, when he awoke, the truck had come to a dusty halt outside a small house made of wattle and stone in a drowsy rural *derb* of similar houses, all the same pinkish hue as the mountains. A huge bush of rosemary was growing just outside the front door. A couple of stray chickens wandered across the street and in the near-distance a dog barked. 'Come,' said Mustapha. 'Come.'

Glenn picked up his rucksack and followed him up steps cut into the pink-brown earth. He ducked through the low doorway and was inside.

The house held on to the animal aroma he had noticed outside, of dung and sweet hay, but now it mingled thickly with the fragrance of cool mint and of meat cooking. The place was small and bare, with narrow windows and a wooden-beamed ceiling, and Glenn guessed it must be pretty primitive in winter although, now, already, there was a wood fire burning. The thick walls were roughly plastered and held wooden hooks for hanging a few decorative objects – Glenn saw a knife with a curved blade, a primitive musical instrument similar to the *guimbri* and a sheepskin rug – and in the living-room area there were cushions, a low table and a worn and faded rug on the stone and earthen floor. A small woman emerged from another room.

'This is my wife,' Mustapha said. 'She speaks only Arabic.'

'*Metsharfin.*' Glenn spoke in Arabic and bowed his head respectfully, not sure what was the done thing.

Fadma did the same, but did not speak – in Arabic, or anything else. Glenn had come across many such women here in Morocco; women seemed to be more wedded to old traditions, while their menfolk went out into the world and took on some of the changes they'd witnessed – though whose choice this was, Glenn couldn't say. She was clothed in the traditional full-length *djellaba* with the hood folded over her forehead so that only her kohl-lined eyes were showing, and she was almost silent, though she nodded a lot and beckoned him in and her dark eyes were friendly enough. She smelt of rosewater, too, which was disconcerting, as it reminded him of Bethany. Not that he needed any reminding.

Mustapha disappeared outside to wash – 'We must be clean to pray,' he said softly – and when he came back he laid out his mat and turned it towards Mecca to begin his prayer. Glenn hardly stirred from his position on the cushions. He had so little energy – he felt he might never get up again.

Fadma brought *thé à la menthe*, which she served in tiny cups and, later, a tagine of lamb, lemon and olives served in the conical clay pot that had now become so familiar to him.

Bethany had even bought a traditional terracotta Berber tagine to use in the riad. Bethany. It seemed that everything reminded him of her.

Mustapha muttered, '*Bismillah*' – thanks to Allah. And then '*Mangez, s'il vous plaît!*' – please eat. Fadma didn't eat with them. Glenn knew it wasn't accepted for her to do so. These women lived in separate, guarded worlds from the men, in the tradition dictated by custom and religion, the two inextricably linked.

The two men sat on cushions on the floor and ate with their fingers – of the right hand, Glenn remembered – and when they had finished, Fadma cleared the tagine and plates, whisked away the tablecloth on the low table to reveal a second underneath and brought out more mint tea and a tray of honey pastries and fudge.

Glenn thought he had never felt so full and sleepy. '*Shebaat*,' he said. '*Merci*.' Fadma appeared again, this time with water and towels. Glenn felt guilty. When was she going to eat?

'I will show you where you can sleep,' Mustapha said. 'There is room in our hearts for you and so there is also room in our house.'

Glenn didn't have the strength to object. Whether he was going to be robbed of everything he possessed or not, right at that moment, he didn't much care. He allowed himself to be led to the bedroom and shown where he could wash. After that, he remembered very little.

★

In the morning, Glenn woke in his narrow bed with a taste of bile in his mouth and a band around his head like a vice. 'Jesus,' he muttered. It felt like the worst hangover in the world, but he hadn't even had a drink. Could he have been drugged? Was it possible?

He tried to get up, but he couldn't summon the energy. And he must have gone back to sleep because some time later he woke again and Mustapha was standing at the bedside, his brown eyes concerned. 'You are ill?' he asked.

'No, no . . .'

Mustapha placed his broad, flat palm on Glenn's forehead. 'You are ill,' he pronounced. 'You cannot work. I will get Fadma.'

And Glenn realized it was true. He wasn't drugged – how could he have thought that of these kind people? He was ill. He'd never felt iller in all his life. He was hot and sweating, his head was pounding and he didn't think he could get out of bed. He remembered vaguely that he'd felt rough these past few days, but it was hard to remember anything; it made his brain hurt. He must have been building up to it, though. Shit. And now here he was in the middle of nowhere, unable to work as he'd intended, unable to reach Bethany and England, unable to move.

CHAPTER 37

'Live there? How can we live there?' Callum was clearly perplexed. His hands were still on the steering wheel, but he was looking from her to the road, then back again.

'I don't want to sell it,' Nell explained. 'I want to –'

'But what about our plans?'

Nell didn't know what to say. The reproach in his words hovered between them. Now, at one in the morning, was probably not the time to discuss it, she thought.

He had driven them out of the airport complex and to the hotel he'd booked for the night – large, disinterested, anonymous. Nell followed him out of the car and into the spacious and well-lit foyer, which seemed to want to think it was still daytime. The flight she'd been booked on before had arrived at three in the afternoon; this one had arrived at past midnight – another reason for Callum to be fed up – and it was a three-hour drive from Bristol to home.

'What about our plans?' he asked again, the minute they walked into the room. He pulled off his jacket and slung it across the back of a chair.

Nell sat on the bed and began to unwind her scarf. The room was clean and comfortable. And perhaps it was better to be having this conversation in the impersonal atmosphere of a hotel bedroom. 'I don't want to sell the farmhouse, Callum,' she said. 'It means too much to me. I want to live there.'

'But you want to sell our house?' His eyes were cold.

'I don't know.' That rather depended on what happened to their marriage. 'I thought, I hoped, I had the idea . . .' Her voice wavered. How would he take this? 'Of opening up a restaurant in the farmhouse.'

He stared at her. 'What?'

'I could specialize in Moroccan cuisine. I really loved it.' She could see that he thought it was a mad idea. And it did seem like a mad idea in this hotel room in the small hours in the middle of an English winter. 'And I could call it The Saffron House.' She gave a little shrug.

'A restaurant?' He took a step closer to the bed. 'But it's a house, Nell.'

'I was thinking of opening a pop-up restaurant,' she said uncertainly. She slipped off her jacket and folded it on the bed beside her. 'In the living room.' Of what would be her own home – or their own home. 'It's big enough.' Just.

'And what about our house?' he asked.

Nell bit her lip. 'We could rent it out?'

'For Christ's sake, Nell!' Callum paced over to the window. The blinds were still open and she could see the orange lights switched on outside the hotel, illuminating grey pavements still damp from the latest drizzle. There were no trees in sight, only parked cars, concrete and tarmac. It was a depressing view, very different from the one she'd left behind in Morocco. And very different from what she'd like to create in the farmhouse in Roseland.

Looking at Callum's angry back made her want to hold him. 'The rent would bring in an extra income,' she said. 'Until I got going.' She'd never considered him to be motivated by money – until recently. But perhaps he was only thinking of them. Of their future.

'What the hell's a pop-up restaurant, anyway?' he growled.

'It's non-permanent. It sort of just . . . pops up.'

He didn't laugh and she couldn't blame him.

'Lots of people are doing it, especially in London.' Nell tried to inject the enthusiasm she felt for the project into her voice – which was hard, when she wasn't sure whether or not her marriage was falling apart.

'We don't live in London, Nell.'

'But, in the catering industry, what starts in London spreads around the rest of the country,' she said. 'And it's not just professional chefs who are doing it either.'

'Really.' From his tone it was clear he didn't give a monkey's who was doing it.

'It's all sorts of people,' she told him, anyway. 'Foodies wanting to dip their toes into the catering industry. Anyone who fancies himself or herself a bit of a chef.' If they could do it, what was to stop a professional like herself?

'Hmph.' It was just a grunt, but she decided to take it as a positive one.

'There are supper clubs springing up everywhere and, let's face it, the internet's the best and cheapest advertising machine ever invented.' Nell had even had the idea of launching her little business on the back of Amy's Moroccan event in Lyme Regis. It would be a novelty. But once she'd drawn people in . . . The food had to be good enough for them to want to come back.

Callum's fists were balled. 'It's not what we agreed,' he said.

Nell got up from the bed and came to stand behind him. Tentatively, she wrapped her arms around him and hugged his back. 'I know,' she said. 'And I'm sorry.' But that was how life was. It evolved, developed and encouraged you to make new plans – constantly. It persuaded you – didn't it? – to leave old agreements lying in a pile of dust in the corner of an empty room.

'We said we'd sell the farmhouse. We said we'd buy something new.' She could still hear the anger there. But at least his voice had softened.

'I know we did. I thought I could do it, I really did. And then I realized . . .' Her voice was muffled into his sweater, '. . . that I couldn't.' It was her one remaining link to her mother. It mattered.

He turned around. He held her shoulders and looked at her, closely, in the way he always used to – but hadn't done for a long time, she realized. 'It's not so easy to turn a house into a restaurant, you know, Nell,' he said. 'You have to get planning permission. You have to think it through.'

'That's the beauty of opening a non-permanent restaurant,' she said. 'You don't need planning permission. You can just do it in the space you have available.' Suddenly she felt a surge of optimism. Perhaps it was crazy but . . .

'And imagine living in a place with people coming there to eat all the time,' he said. 'How do you expect to get a moment's peace?' He shook his head in despair. 'I've got a business to run, too, you know.'

'I know.'

'And it's in the back of beyond. Who do you think will come to eat there?'

Nell didn't point out the contradiction. She was just glad that they were having the conversation. 'It's not far from St Mawes and not much further from Truro,' she said. 'Once we build up a reputation, people will want to come to us.' She realized that somewhere in this hotel room, somewhere in this discussion – because, at last, they were talking, really talking – her 'I' had become a 'we'. She had to trust this, trust in her skills. And she had to remain confident. She'd learnt that from Amy. It was no good admitting defeat before you'd even started. As for not getting a moment's peace . . . She'd deal with that when the time came.

'I'm really not sure about this, Nell,' said Callum. But his gaze was searching hers as if he had started to believe in her again, at last.

'I know it won't be easy.' Clearly, there were obstacles to overcome before her plan could come to fruition, the main one being that Callum seemed almost to hate the farmhouse – as if it were a rival. How could she make him love it as much as she did? It seemed an impossible task. 'But isn't it at least worth trying?'

Nell felt his grip on her shoulders intensify. 'Perhaps,' he muttered.

'Do you mean it, Callum?' She lifted her face to his. 'Do you really mean that you're willing to give it a try?'

He released his hold on her shoulders and held her face in his hands. As always, his hands were warm and seemed to smell of the earth he worked with.

She shut her eyes and moved in closer. She could feel the strength of his body like a magnet and moved closer still, until she was pressing against him. *Please, please . . . Let it work between them.* She didn't want to lose him. She didn't want to throw it all away.

'If it means so much to you . . .' He bent his head. '. . . Yes. I'll give it a try.'

And then he was kissing her, really kissing her; mouth, lips, tongue. And the taste of him, the scent of him, was so dear, so familiar, that she felt something unlock inside her and click into place. A different place. She held him with a passion that might be born of desperation, but which was real enough. In seconds, they were tearing at each other's clothes, needing to be skin on skin. She wanted to feel him next to her, on her, inside her; part of her once again.

Later, they slept. It was almost ten when Nell awoke, and Callum was still sleeping beside her, his hair rumpled and dark on the white pillow, his face relaxed in a way she hadn't seen for so long.

Was it possible that this was all it took? Nell propped

herself up on her elbow to look at him properly. A short debate and then a frantic coupling? Because it had been frantic – and desperate, too. Emotionally painful – it had been so long – and yet strangely restorative at the same time. When Callum had finally rolled away from her, spent, he had held her scooped into his shoulder and Nell had wept.

'I thought you didn't want me any more,' he said, when he awoke. 'I thought you were blaming me.'

'What for?' She ran her fingers through his hair. Like Callum, it was softer than it looked.

'For making you leave the farmhouse in the first place. For your mother dying.'

'But you didn't,' she said. It was true that, if Callum hadn't come into her life, then she wouldn't have moved out. Or maybe she would. Maybe she should have moved out a long time before. And, hopefully, her mother would have willingly let her go. Smilax, she thought again. Poor Crocus trapped forever in a flower, the fiery threads of gold containing all that ardour. Smilax wouldn't have him, but neither would she set him free.

'I don't blame you for anything,' she told Callum. 'I'm glad we met when we did and I'm glad we moved in together and got married. And now, I need you more than ever.'

And when he kissed her again, when he held her in his arms and made love to her again, this time much more gently, Nell silently willed for all this to be true.

CHAPTER 38

'Amy!' Duncan got up from his chair and, before Amy knew what was happening, she was wrapped in his arms.

'Hi, Duncan.'

Finally, he let her go. Put his hands on her shoulders and drew away to look at her. 'When did you get back?'

'Last night.' She had called in to have a rushed supper with her parents. They were as busy as ever and her mother got up twice to answer the phone while they were eating. Her father looked well, although he skipped dessert and disappeared into his office to do some work on the computer instead. But at least she knew who they were, she reasoned. At least she didn't have any unanswered questions.

'And did you find out anything, darling?' her mother asked as she got up to leave. 'About Glenn?'

'Not really.' She hadn't found Glenn, but she had found something, and she had helped Nell find something, too. She kissed her mother and returned her hug. 'But it was an excellent trip. Everything went well. And I met this really nice girl.'

'A nice girl?' Her mother pretended to look disappointed.

'Now, Mum.' And she told her about Nell. How was she?

Amy wondered. How had things gone with Callum? Had she told him her plans? It was all very well having someone to share your life with, she reminded herself. But he also had to share your dreams. When one of you wanted one thing and the other wanted something entirely different, what did you do then? Compromise? Or walk away?

'Did you and Dad always want the same things? Dream the same dreams?' Amy asked her mother. They seemed to be quite a unit these days. And yet she remembered only too well those late-night arguments she'd overheard, when everything seemed to be going wrong between them. If you shared your dreams with the one you loved and things still went wrong, what hope was there?

'Yes.' Her mother seemed very sure. And her dark eyes got a faraway look in them that Amy hadn't seen there very often. 'Though we didn't always agree on the way to get it. And things didn't always go to plan.' She smiled. 'That's what happens in relationships, Amy, darling. There are ups and downs. It isn't all plain sailing. Sometimes it's as much as you can do to hang on.'

What was she thinking of? When Dad had to leave his teaching job? When the hotel didn't take off in the way they'd hoped? Or was there more that Amy didn't even know?

'But that's part of being a team.' She gave Amy another hug. 'It'll happen for you, too,' she said. 'When you're in a team, you both bring something to the table. That means you'll argue and you'll compromise. But your dreams . . .'

There was that look again. 'If you're lucky – they stay the same.'

'It's good to see you,' Duncan said, now. 'Sit down. Tell me all about it. Did you get some amazing shots in Morocco?'

'Not bad. I was a bit trigger-happy.'

'Been to your workroom yet?' The question seemed innocent enough, but Amy frowned.

'No. Why?'

'Ah, well, no reason really. Obviously, Jake's working in there and –'

'I can imagine,' she said dryly. She wasn't sure how she would react when she saw him. It was bad enough facing Duncan – who she supposed must know about Jake's spur-of-the-moment trip to Morocco. 'How are things progressing?'

Duncan sat down on the edge of his desk and straightened the cuffs of his white shirt. He was a nice man, but they had, she realized, only skimmed one another's surface. Amy hadn't a clue what he really thought about things, how he felt, what he was passionate about. She thought of what Nell had asked her – *how can you tell if someone really knows you?* Amy knew the answer to that one as far as Duncan was concerned. So much for shared dreams.

'It's out of my hands,' he said. 'I've started the planning for next summer's programme now.' He rattled off the names of various events and exhibitions, Amy nodding and letting most of the information go straight over her head.

'And about us . . .'

'Hmm?' This took Amy by surprise. She'd thought they'd dealt with that one.

'We were good together,' he murmured. He reached out and put a hand on hers.

'Up to a point,' she agreed. The point being: before any emotion set in. Jake had been right. Her relationship with Duncan had been the easy option for a woman who was scared of losing what she loved.

'We worked well together, too.'

'Yes . . .' Though it had never been an equal playing field. Duncan would always be the boss and she would always be his subordinate. Which wasn't good in a personal relationship – not when you wanted equality. Amy thought about Nell. And Francine. Sometimes, she couldn't help looking at Francine with her children and her husband, Mike, and thinking . . . what was she missing? Would it always be just her, Amy? Or would she, too, find someone who could give her what Francine had found? If you're ever brave enough, a small voice whispered.

'I didn't look after you properly.' Duncan pulled a glum face.

'I'm a woman, Duncan,' she said, 'not a BMW.'

They both laughed.

'Well, if you ever change your mind . . .' He put his arm around her shoulders.

'I won't,' she assured him. But at least they were both still smiling.

There was a light knock on the door, and it opened before Amy could extricate herself from Duncan's arm. Jake Tarrant's head and dark, spiky hair appeared in the opening. 'Am I interrupting something?' he asked mildly.

CHAPTER 39

Morocco, 1978

Glenn had never really been ill before. Oh, he'd had the usual childhood ailments, sure, and colds and coughs from time to time. Stuff you just shook off and then you carried on. He'd had some food poisoning in India, too – Christ, he'd had a sore gut for a while down in Goa. But he knew what it was and he knew it would go away. This was different.

The first few days, he didn't get up out of bed. He didn't know what it was and he couldn't imagine it going away. It was like it had already become part of him. He was sick, he had a vice of pain around his head and he felt more spaced out than he'd ever felt when he was high. His limbs were heavy, as if they'd forgotten how to do their job, and he couldn't think straight.

Fadma and Mustapha looked after him. Fadma made him tea – Christ knows what was in it, some countryside herb, he guessed – and though she sweetened it, the stuff still tasted foul. Sometimes he awoke to find her crouching by his bedside with sad, black eyes and a piece of flannel, bathing his sweaty forehead, though as soon as he woke up she would slip from the room as silently as a shadow. In the mornings and

378

evenings she brought him soup, a sort of bland harira without the meat, and although he tried to eat some he could usually only manage a few mouthfuls, and then he'd give up. It seemed too much effort somehow. Glenn knew that he was losing his sense of direction; his sense of time. And yet something was seeping into his consciousness — something else, something that he hardly understood.

'You must get strong,' Mustapha told him. 'You must eat. You must get well.'

'Don't worry. I'll be out of your hair pretty soon,' Glenn told him, every word an exertion. No way could he work for him, not now.

But Mustapha sadly shook his head. 'It is not that,' he said. 'We had one son, Fadma and I, and we lost him to God. If he had survived he would be the same age as you are now, I think. We do not want to lose another boy — even if he is not our own. Fadma knows you have a mother somewhere. She thinks of her.'

Glenn felt tears spring to his eyes. Christ, he must be weak. He wanted to ask Mustapha what had happened to his son, but he didn't have the energy. He thought about it, though, as he lay there in bed, sometimes dozing, sometimes staring at the beamed ceiling above as if it could tell him something, give him some truth. This was why Mustapha had been so kind to him on the road. This was why he had offered him work, invited Glenn to his house to eat. And then he had been taken ill. No wonder Fadma nursed him as well as she was able, given the conventions of her faith. No wonder he must get better. They were scared that he, too, was going to die.

Glenn had never thought about death. He knew guys from his hometown who had died in Vietnam. He knew others who had returned – and sometimes he wasn't sure which was worse. When a young guy went in there fighting – seeking adventure, maybe, looking for action – he didn't have a clue. He had no idea of that reality, of death, just waiting there on someone's shoulder in the shape of a rifle or a hand grenade. Boys' games, heroism, the thrill of the chase, of fighting, of victory. Geez, most of them had seen so many war movies that it must have seemed unreal, like a film set. Until of course they saw someone die.

Death. Glenn thought about it now and it brought him out in a cold sweat. He thought about his mother, too. Maybe Fadma wouldn't be so keen to nurse him if she knew what Glenn had done.

After a few days, he started getting up for an hour or two. He forced himself to drag his body out of bed. But he still felt rough. He didn't have a scrap of energy. He kept falling into a sleep that wasn't the least bit refreshing – except during the night, when he would just lie there awake and listen to the wind wailing. Something was occurring, though; he was aware of that. Something had changed. And then, one morning at dawn, he heard voices and more activity than the usual call to prayer.

'It is time.' Mustapha came into his room. 'You must come. You must see.'

'See what?' But Glenn allowed him to help him up.

Mustapha led the way on to the roof terrace, where there was a clothes line, a sink and an outdoor fire for bread. 'Look.' He pointed.

Glenn held on the balustrade and looked out past the clutter of rooftops, over the plain towards the mountains. Gently glimmering in the early-morning sun was a field of purple flowers. And then another. And another. Wave upon wave of them. The petals were opening to the sun, the red stigmas were fiery gold threads emerging from the heart of each flower to point to the sky. Glenn gripped the balustrade even harder. He knew what that was. He . . .

'Saffron,' said Mustapha. There was a suppressed excitement in his voice. 'We must leave you alone today, my son. We must harvest before the flower begins to wilt. Everyone is coming from the village to help.'

'I wish that I . . .' But his voice trailed into nothing. He could barely stand up, let alone help to harvest a saffron field.

'You must rest.' Mustapha took his arm. 'You must return to bed and rest. That is the way to heal. The body simply needs to rest.'

'But what's wrong with me?' Glenn turned to him in desperation. How long had it been? A week? More? He hated being dependent on anyone, let alone these kind people he didn't know from Adam. He needed to know when he would get stronger, when he'd be able to continue on his journey. He thought of Bethany. How could he not think of her now?

'I do not know.' Mustapha bowed his head. 'I cannot say.'

He patted him on the shoulder. 'But you will be well again. *Insha' Allah.*'

That night it was late when they returned to the house but Glenn sensed their satisfaction in a job well done, a harvest coming to fruition. He guessed that this was an important part of their livelihood. It wasn't just a farm, then. He had landed on a saffron farm. He couldn't help but smile.

It was four months later before he finally felt some vigour return. At last he felt a new possibility – that he would one day get better. He began to make plans. He thought of all the things he would do, how his life would change, where he must go and what he should try and achieve. He began to work with Mustapha, just for an hour or two a day to start with, doing jobs around the farm, working inside when it was cold.

'When spring comes it is said that God has forgiven the winter,' Mustapha told him. 'And that he has blessed us again with new growth, new shoots, the buds that will flower and bring forth the fruit, the thyme that will cloak the mountainside.'

Blessed them again with hope, thought Glenn.

The saffron corms, meanwhile, had continued to grow throughout the winter, developing their grassy leaves, storing up their energy. Many times in the past months Glenn had risen from his bed and watched their growth, looked out over the plains and the foothills of the Atlas Mountains and thought about what he would do next.

By spring, however, the foliage began to die; by May, the

saffron beds would be bare, Mustapha told him, the plants dormant until, once again in late summer, the shoots of the saffron, too, would grow strong, straight and green in the continuity that was Nature. All was as it should be, all was right in this world. And the saffron crocuses would grow sturdy until at last summer faded into autumn and they prepared to flower in that glorious swansong; the final burst of intense sunshine before the winter frost.

But that was to come. For now, there was more work at the farm. The corms had to be lifted, sorted, examined for disease; the earth had to be dug and fertilized. Glenn didn't do much at first. But he was determined to pay his hosts back for their care. At the start of each day he would wash in the basic shower cubicle made of concrete with a hook for the towel, a tin shower nozzle and a plastic bucket and then he and Mustapha would share a breakfast – of a dark and moist flatbread and honey.

Glenn noted that, when Mustapha walked, it was with an easy rhythm, his own rhythm, the rhythm of the day. Mustapha worked like this, too. He and his people kept to their own steady pace; they followed the movements of the sun, the moon, the wind; the time and rhythm of Nature, not the clock. Work was either done or not done. That was their way.

As they worked at the replanting together, making trenches and placing the corms twelve centimetres deep and twelve centimetres apart, in narrow beds with interlinking grass paths left between them for access, Mustapha often talked of their son, Simo. He had been taken from them as a child, Mustapha told him, by an infection that had spread through the village like a wild forest fire.

'Did you try to have another child?' Glenn asked him. Not that another child could be a replacement, of course, but it may have eased their sorrow a little and given them more to live for.

'God was not willing for us to have another child,' Mustapha said. 'We learnt long ago to accept this.'

'Uh huh.' But Glenn recognized the sadness on Mustapha's leathered face, and he wondered. Did faith enable a man to accept such grief? Did it never make him question it?

He also talked to Mustapha of his own feelings, of the dreamlike sensations he had experienced when he was ill, of the new sense of timelessness he felt, his immersion in the present.

'In submitting to these feelings, life may have an opportunity to find us,' Mustapha said. 'This is Morocco.'

One day in early summer when Mustapha did not need him, Glenn rose early, as dawn was breaking in a purplish veil, accompanied to the sounds of a dog barking and the *muezzin*, which began with a nasal whine creeping into the senses and became the slow, hypnotic chanting he was now accustomed to. He sat in his room and watched as trees and vegetation slowly became clearer and the silhouettes of the mountains seemed to come closer in the soft grey-blue light of early morning.

Later, he broke his fast alone, for the others were now

observing Ramadan, which had started with the new moon and which would last for twenty-eight days. It had taken Glenn a while living in Morocco to become accustomed to Ramadan; to accept that he could adapt to the changes in the rhythm of their lives that it brought, while not strictly observing its rules. In daylight hours throughout Ramadan work at the farm continued as usual, although at a slower pace, with a daytime nap and a general air of quiet weariness. But every evening seemed like a celebration. Once the swollen call of release came at sunset, the energy of the moment became almost tangible. The lamps would be lit, and Fadma would produce the traditional harira and honey cakes and the boiled eggs rolled in cumin. They would all enjoy the feast as a feeling of calm satisfaction descended on the people and the land. It was special; a time of sharing and satisfaction that was its own reward. And each dawn would signal a return to a day of fasting.

Today, though, felt like an extraordinary day, and Glenn decided to take the path to the waterfall. He had not gone there before, though one of the men had told him the way. Today, he wanted to be doing something. He wanted to smell the freshness of the earth, feel the breeze brushing his skin. He had been so shut up, so ill. He wanted to feel life.

Although he was stronger, he still sometimes felt the apathy in his bones, the pain around his head, the feeling of being spaced out and weary. Whatever it was hadn't simply gone away – he knew that much. Fadma knew it, too. He caught her watching him sometimes, her eyes dark and knowing.

Being hidden away from the world like that, closeted in her *djellaba* and her hood, must surely give her an inner wisdom, an access into the intuitive, the world of instincts, spirituality. Mustapha had an element of it, too – from the hours he spent praying, Glenn guessed. Whatever it was, he wouldn't mind some for himself.

The path among the rocks and coarse grass wasn't easy, and as he got closer and could hear the sound of coursing water the footholds became greasy, the balancing more difficult. Something inside his head had changed, he realized. Nothing was easy. He crossed a man-made, narrow wooden bridge and held his breath, unable to look down at the chasm below. Once, before his illness, he wouldn't have given it a second thought.

He couldn't yet see the waterfall, though he could hear it. He could even feel the occasional splash of water on his head as he climbed high above the river, sometimes stooping to climb on all fours. The rocks were hot and smooth. The mountains seemed to rise all around him, serene and utterly awe-inspiring. He was exhausted. After a while he stopped on a flat rock to catch his breath and take a drink from the water flask in his bag. Christ. A man could get lost up here in the mountains. He looked up into the ice-blue spring sky, listened for the birdsong, the rush of the cascade.

Finally, he got there. He turned a corner and it was in front of him. The waterfall, the surge, falling dramatically in a sheet to the rocks below. It was thunderous. It was something else. It was a force of nature. Glenn let out a whoop of delight.

This was life, all right. A rush of adrenalin came from nowhere. He took off the rough hemp shirt that Fadma had given him and climbed into the river, stood arms akimbo, freezing water raining on his head, his shoulders, his arms. And he screamed. It was numbing. The coldness of it almost took his breath away. But he could feel the purity of it, too. For God's sake . . . He was alive!

As summer went on, there was still plenty of work to do on the farm, and Glenn gladly threw himself into it. He had discovered something special up here in the mountains, and it wouldn't let him go – at least not yet.

'Will you stay?' Mustapha asked him one morning. 'Will you stay with us here?'

It was unlike him to enquire about the future, and Glenn was surprised. Perhaps Fadma had asked him about it. Or perhaps it was time he moved out of their house and got his own place to live. Most people, he guessed, would find it odd that he had stayed so long. But they had done so much for him; he felt that they had saved his life. And he was contented here; he felt no urgency to get on with his plans. But there was Bethany.

'One day soon I must leave,' he told him. 'I have to go to England.' He couldn't rest – not until he knew for sure why she had left him. He still loved her. She'd touched something deep inside him. He believed in her.

Mustapha rested for a moment and gave his wise nod. 'One path will lead to another and then another,' he said. 'Soon there will be a crossroads. Then you will know.'

This seemed like an echo of the fable he'd read about the young traveller in Cairo. Glenn hadn't been robbed. But he had lost something and gained something, too. 'I have to think of the future,' he said. He thought of his mother. She would be wondering what had happened to him, too. He couldn't go on living here, as if she and his feelings for Bethany simply didn't exist.

In the distance, a donkey brayed. 'In our faith we live in the present,' Mustapha said. 'We do not plan for the future like your people. When there is plenty in the present we take what there is, and if there is nothing in the future we do not take any. This is an Arab contemplation.'

Glenn smiled. It sounded simple enough. It sounded as if he were talking about peace of mind.

CHAPTER 40

After their first night back at home, Nell was determined to begin putting her plan into action. She needed to do a lot more research about pop-up restaurants – she could make a start on that later – and then she'd go over to the farmhouse, start measuring up, making decisions about possible layouts and design. She was so excited. And then there was the food . . . She couldn't wait to start building up a portfolio of Moroccan recipes.

'I'll contact the estate agent this morning,' Callum had said when they were having breakfast together, Nell still in her dressing gown, and no make-up, since she didn't have to get to work till ten-thirty. It was an early start as usual for Callum who was doing some winter land-clearing in a plot ten miles away. 'Leave that to me, OK?' He glanced across at her.

Nell smiled. *Leave that to me.* Her husband's motto. His life philosophy. 'But you have to go to work,' she said.

'I'll drop in. I'm going into Truro later to get some things anyway.' He got to his feet and came over to where she was sitting, rumpled her curls and bent to give her a quick kiss.

This was beginning to feel, Nell thought, like a second

honeymoon. Almost too good to be true. 'If you're sure,' she said. She had plenty of other things to keep her occupied.

'I want to do it in person.' He frowned. 'The bloke I've been dealing with – he won't be best pleased.'

'Sorry, darling.' Nell pulled a face.

'You're worth it.' He grinned. And he looked so like the old Callum that Nell's heart contracted.

And then he was pulling on his boots and his jacket and he was out of the door and off. She heard the truck rumble into life as he headed off down the lane.

Nell exhaled slowly. She had to admit to a sense of relief. She felt as if she'd been in the vortex of a hurricane; she needed space to breathe. But, on the other hand . . . She began to clear the breakfast things. It was good. It was all good.

When the kitchen was cleaned up, she went upstairs to take a shower. The water was hot, and soon the bathroom was steaming. It reminded her of being in the hammam with Amy. Cleaning the pores, cutting right through to the heart of things . . . Nell closed her eyes. She had thought then about her secret self and about whether she still loved Callum, still wanted him. And now it seemed that she had the answers. Yes, they still loved one another. They had been tested but they had come through. She lifted her face and felt the hot water rain down on her. And yes, she still wanted him, too. Her still-tingling body was the evidence for that.

She got dressed quickly and put on some make-up. She had

time to do a bit of restaurant research before she left for work, so she went into the living room, where they kept the computer they shared on a desk in the corner. But before she switched it on, she saw them – the sales details from the estate agents still lying there. Nell had seen these before, of course, when they had first sent them through. She picked up the single sheet of paper. 'Idyllic rural farmhouse for sale'. The grey stone and red brick farmhouse stared back at her reproachfully, the 'FOR SALE' sign nailed to the fence. Not any more, she thought.

Poor Callum. Why should he have to take all the flak from the estate agent? Nell sighed. It was her fault; she was the one who'd changed her mind and she should take the responsibility for it. She located the phone number on the details. She'd call them, she decided, now, before she went into work. She'd relied on Callum too much since her mother had died. And, before that, she'd relied on her mother too much. Wasn't it about time she started relying on herself?

They had spent the journey back from Bristol to Roseland discussing their plans – her plans. Callum had still found plenty of objections, but once he had realized how determined she was and how much the project meant to her, he gradually, with each mile they travelled, seemed to become a little more positive. Nell knew it would take time; she couldn't wave a magic wand. Her plan was to test the water and see how they got on.

'But it's your project, Nell, not mine,' Callum said as they left Bristol. 'I'm accepting what you're doing. But it's nothing to do with me. Not really.'

'OK.'

'And if the restaurant thing doesn't work out,' he had said. 'If after six months you're struggling to make it pay . . . and if I don't want to live in your mother's farmhouse any more . . .'

'Yes?' She knew what was coming.

'Then promise me you'll give it up.'

Nell could already hear their future conversation: 'Just give me three more months, Callum.' 'Three more months?' But she'd worry about that later. 'All right, darling,' she said.

'You promise?'

Nell crossed her fingers behind her back. Yes, she had learnt a lot from Amy. 'I promise,' she said.

She knew it wasn't what he had envisaged for them both. And that, although he had said they could give it a try, that this was just another agreement – but of the unspoken variety. What was he saying? 'If I let you do this, will you finally get over it?' Nell wasn't sure she liked this agreement any more than the other kind. She only knew that when you lost the person who meant the most to you in the whole world, all that was left to you, all that you could do, was try your hardest to find strength from within. Strength to carry on, that was. This was her way of doing just that.

Nell picked up her phone and tapped in the number. Was she so wrong to want to do this so much? She could only hope that, in time, Callum would become her partner in every sense of the word. And then . . . she smiled. They would be an unstoppable force.

The voice on the other end was female. Nell explained who she was. 'Can I speak to whoever's dealing with the sale of the farmhouse near St Just in Roseland?'

Callum had said it was a man. Nell realized she should have kept more tabs on this from the start. She could hardly blame Callum for taking over when she had just cried herself to sleep and allowed him to.

'Ah, that's my colleague, John,' said the girl. 'I'm afraid he's not in the office at the moment. Can I help?'

'Perhaps I should ring back later?'

'Hold on a sec.' She was probably getting something up on her computer screen. 'It looks like we're waiting for the solicitors' details. Can you help me with that? We'll pass them on the purchasers' solicitors.'

'Solicitors?' echoed Nell. 'Purchasers?'

'That's it,' said the girl. She must think Nell a complete idiot. 'That's right.'

'There must be some mistake,' Nell said. Where did they get these people from, for goodness' sake? 'I'm responding to an offer made last week on the property. We said that we wanted to think about it.'

'Hmm.' She seemed to be consulting her files. 'An offer was made . . . let's see . . . three weeks ago, according to our records.'

Three weeks ago? That was before she went to Morocco. 'Then your records must be wrong,' Nell said crisply.

Perhaps she should have let Callum deal with this after all. 'The offer came in last week. I was away and my husband –'

'Your husband accepted the offer and, as far as we are concerned, the sale is now going through.'

There was an awful silence. A silence in which Nell grappled with what she was hearing, struggled to make sense of it. But it wasn't hard. An offer had been made three weeks ago, Callum had found a last-minute holiday with a cookery course thrown in for Nell and whisked her out of the country, he had accepted the offer and now the sale was going through. Only it wasn't.

'Are you sure?' she said. She was gripping her mobile so hard she was surprised she hadn't crushed it. 'Are you absolutely sure?'

'Quite sure.' She rattled off some dates and times. 'In fact, your husband came into the office only last week and –'

'Thank you,' said Nell. 'But I'm afraid the farmhouse is no longer for sale and we will have to disappoint the purchaser.' She wasn't sure where the words were coming from or how she kept her voice so steady. 'The farmhouse was an inheritance from my mother and it's in my name. My husband made a mistake.' No understatement there. *Callum*. How could he have done that to her? How could he have deceived her like that? What had he thought? That if she was out of the country he could push things through? That by the time she got back it would be a fait accompli? That she would just *leave everything to him . . .?*

'I see.' Though the girl sounded as if she really didn't. And who could blame her? 'I'm very sorry about that. So do I take it you wish to withdraw the farmhouse from the market?'

'Yes.' Nell was finding it harder and harder even to speak now. How could Callum have done this? That was all she could think. How could he have pretended that he'd been so nice as to buy her a cookery course in Morocco when, in reality, he just wanted to get her out of the way? She remembered that elusive look. And then to call her and tell her that an offer had come in – *yes, Callum, almost three weeks ago*. How had he got to be such an amazing actor? Secret self? Her secret self was a pussycat compared to Callum's. No wonder he had been so angry when she was in Morocco. She had unknowingly scuppered all his plans.

There was an awkward pause. 'Perhaps you could call into the office and talk to John?' the girl asked her. 'I hope you understand. A phone call . . .' Her voice trailed off.

'Yes, of course.' She could, after all, be anyone.

Nell thought of the night before last in the hotel room. *Oh, Callum . . .*

She phoned work and told them she'd be late in. Johnson started rattling on and Nell cut him off. 'I'm moving,' she said. 'I have to pack some things.'

She filled a hold-all with some winter clothes and a few other necessities – she hadn't got round to washing her holiday stuff yet but she wouldn't be needing any of that for a long while. And she wouldn't bother to write a note – what was the point? Callum would go into the estate agents' office today and he'd find out what had happened anyway. He'd know they were finished.

She took her stuff out to the car and drove to the farmhouse of her childhood. She didn't want to think about it. She could still hardly believe it. But he had done it; it had happened. He had lied to her and betrayed her and Nell couldn't forgive that. Their marriage was over and she was heading back home.

CHAPTER 41

In less than an hour Jake Tarrant was peering over Amy's shoulder at the screen of her laptop. *Her* workroom had become *their* workroom while she was away. Amy supposed she should be grateful that he'd cleared his stuff from her desk. But somehow it didn't feel like her desk any more. Should she resign? Could one have an affair with the boss and then neatly extricate oneself when the time was up? Probably not. Duncan would always think he had the right to sling an arm around her shoulders or, heaven forbid, pat her on the bottom in front of clients. She'd never be able to go on working for him. And, besides, she reminded herself, her freelance portfolio was expanding; she could look for more work and take it from there. Perhaps it was just the push she needed.

'Brilliant colours,' Jake said as she flicked through. 'That powder yellow – it's so sharp you can almost taste it. And the blue . . .'

'Majorelle blue. It's intense, isn't it? He used it in his gardens and then trademarked the colour.' It had been obvious that the Majorelle Garden had been created by an artist. Every walkway, every bridge, every tree and every colourful urn had its place within the visual pageant of the whole.

'Stunning,' he murmured into her hair.

At first, she had felt uncomfortable. He hadn't alluded to what had happened in Essaouira – not yet. And what had happened? Nothing, she reminded herself. But there, Nell had been around most of the time to play chaperone. Here, they were alone. The workroom was small, he was intruding on her personal space and he didn't seem aware of it. And he smelt of leather and grapefruit – an unsettling combination.

But after a while, she grew absorbed in this, the pictorial story of her time in Morocco. She almost forgot about the proximity of him, focusing instead on the shots, deleting some more, selecting some for a long-list folder and noting with interest which ones Jake liked. He preferred the more technically proficient, the more structured, the more set up, while Amy was drawn to those that were more random, those which included great washes of colour rather than form, the ones she hadn't been able to take time over. Instinct versus technicality, she thought.

'What about this? And this?' She had taken this group in the souks of Marrakech. Grizzled faces, skinny arms, cartloads of mint, row upon row of Berber rugs. 'These have a good flow, don't you think?'

He frowned. 'I like the layout on this one.'

She'd captured some layered planting. In the foreground was a structural cactus and some *zellige* tiles and stonework; in the middle ground were palm trees and some vivid bougainvillea; all against a dark-blue, cloudless sky.

'It's pretty,' she said. And clever, she supposed. But it didn't shout out to her, it didn't have a strong message. It wasn't, she felt, one of her best.

'Did you get any of the weaving?'

'Weaving?'

'It'd be useful for the workshop,' he said. 'To see the origins of the skill.'

The stereotype of the old woman sitting at a loom in the home she was rarely able to leave, working the threads with her fingers and feet as she and others had done for centuries – because they'd never been allowed to do anything different? 'Sorry, no.'

'And what about the stories of the rug-making – the narrative of the weave?'

'Er, no.'

'Well, we can easily get hold of that kind of stuff,' he said. 'It's not important.'

Only, clearly, it was. She sighed. 'Well, if you don't like any of these, I'll just use them for my exhibition. I know what I'm looking for. You'll have to go elsewhere for the rest.' She switched off the laptop with a click. Now go away, she thought.

He pushed back his chair and leant back at a rather dangerous angle. Amy forced herself not to tell him to be careful. 'Amy, why are you always so defensive?' he asked.

'Am I?'

'Yes.'

'I don't know.' They stared at one another.

'And Jake? Why do you keep asking me those sort of questions?'

'Do I?'

'Yes.'

'I don't know.'

After a few moments his mouth twitched and he grinned. She grinned back at him. Dimples, she thought. And a crooked tooth. He rocked the chair even further back and laughed, and so did she. It was liberating.

'Let me show you what I've been up to while you've been away,' he said. He tore his hands through his hair until it was sticking up at odd angles. 'I'd like to hear what you think.'

It was going to be good, Amy was sure of that. She had a few ideas, though, of things that could be developed and at least he listened to them. But whatever her reservations, she could see that he was excellent at his job. He'd worked miracles in a week. He even had a Gnawa band coming to do a gig at the Marine Theatre — he'd spoken to one of the musicians in Essaouira the day she and Nell had gone off to the saffron farm and arranged it. As she'd suspected, he was the kind of man who made things happen.

It was 7 p.m. when they finished for the day. Duncan had long gone and she and Jake had to lock up the gallery. They had agreed to disagree about her photographs. Amy would have the creative freedom to choose the shots for her own exhibition and Jake could select whichever shots he liked for the rest of the event and for publicity material. It would work, she realized, as she finally got to her feet and grabbed her coat. They had compromised and they had both got what they wanted. Perhaps, after all, they could function well as a team.

'Fancy a drink?' he asked her when they emerged from the gallery into the darkness of outside.

It was chilly. Amy pulled her coat collar up higher and wound her scarf around her neck. Her body temperature was still half in Morocco. 'Well . . .'

'Or do you have a hot date?'

She laughed. Was he still wondering about Duncan? 'The only date I have is with my great-aunt. I promised to call in for hot chocolate later.'

He glanced at his watch. 'I don't have long either. So just a quick one? If I promise not to ask any awkward questions?'

'Deal.'

They walked in companionable silence down the street to the waterfront by the clock tower where the bay-fronted cottages and individually styled stone houses formed a terrace facing the sea, and along the higher promenade towards the Inn on the Shore. The wind whipped Amy's hair from her face. She listened to the groan of the tide below, the splash of the waves on the pebbles as they passed the brightly painted beach huts, almost indistinguishable from one another in the dark.

'Will you ever move away from Lyme Regis, d'you think?' Jake asked her.

Amy considered. She loved this town. Above them now were the terraced Jubilee Gardens, where you could stroll around the paths, play putting and look down on one of the best views in the world – at least, in Amy's opinion. Lyme Regis waterfront, harbour and Cobb. 'It would be hard,' she admitted. 'I might leave if there was a good enough reason to. But I'm pretty sure that one day I'd come back.'

They had reached the pub. 'Here we go.' Jake opened the door.

Amy was glad to get out of the wind. The pub was quiet tonight. But she'd always liked this place, with its view of the harbour and the little sandy beach. In the summer it was great to sit outside and watch the boats; in the winter it was fun to wave watch. And conditions were dramatic tonight; the swell was high and crashing against the Cobb. It was cloudy, so you couldn't see much by the light of the moon. But you could certainly hear it.

Jake went to the bar and she found a small corner table near the fire, pulled off her scarf and coat, sat down, relaxed.

'How much more do you think there is to do?' she asked as Jake returned with two glasses of red wine. 'Before you go back to Bristol?'

He sat down and stretched out those long legs of his. 'I'm almost done,' he said.

Although this would mean Amy could reclaim her workroom space, she wasn't as pleased as she thought she ought to be. She picked up her glass of wine. 'Cheers,' she said.

'Cheers.' He tipped his glass against hers and took a sip. 'But I'll be coming back as and when.'

'As and when?'

'As and when I'm needed.' He eyed her over the rim of the glass.

'I see.'

'And you?' he asked her.

'Me?' Not more awkward questions, she hoped. She took a sip of her wine, too. It was dense and slightly fruity, with an edge. Nice.

'Will you stay with the gallery?' He moved his glass to one side of the table.

Had he sensed what she'd been thinking earlier? Amy fiddled with the stem of her glass. The wine swirled around the base. Unusually for pub plonk, it had legs. 'I have been thinking it might be time to move on.'

'Look, Amy . . .'

She glanced up at his tone.

'It's nothing to do with me, of course. But you're a talented photographer.'

She raised an eyebrow. It was nice to be complimented. But what was he saying?

'I'm sure you could get plenty of other work. Freelance work. And you might find this event raises your profile quite a bit.'

'That would be good.' She nodded. 'Thanks.'

'I've got some contacts . . .' He let his voice trail. 'I could ask around.'

It was more than she deserved. She hadn't been very nice to him since he'd come here and put her nose severely out of joint. And here he was being kind. She wasn't sure she wanted that – it was an awful lot easier when they were sparring with one another. 'I'll be fine,' she said gruffly. There she went again. Being defensive. She picked up her glass and took another swig. He was right.

He shrugged. 'It's no trouble, Amy. I know you're independent. I respect that. But everyone needs a helping hand from time to time. Especially in this business.'

'All right then,' she conceded. 'Thanks.' If she was going to make a go of being freelance, she would have to accept help where it was offered, make use of networking opportunities; she couldn't be proud or prickly. He was right – again. How irritating. Amy sighed.

'And as for Duncan . . .' There was a note of curiosity in his voice.

'You're wondering why I got involved with him in the first place.' She took another swig. Why not tell him? There was nothing to hide. 'The classic mistake. The fling with the boss. He was kind, supportive, interested in my work.' And not just in her work, as it turned out. She took a deep breath, looked across at him and then quickly away. 'It was safe.'

He nodded. 'We all make mistakes.'

She glimpsed the sadness there again, the vulnerability. 'Even you, Jake?' Perhaps it was time she found out a bit more about him. He might ask searching questions, but he didn't give much away.

'Of course.' He smiled. 'I'm not immune.'

'What happened to you? What was your mistake?'

'Ah.' He drained the glass with one swift and decisive movement. 'My mistake was to fall in love with and marry a girl who had a thing for my best friend.'

'Oh.' She watched him, saw the bitterness in the twist of his mouth. Clearly, he hadn't got over it. 'What happened?'

'Like you said earlier. The classic. They had an affair and it ended in tears.' His mouth tightened. 'My tears. The two of them were fine. They went off together into the sunset. End of.' He looked across at her. 'I'm just relieved we hadn't got round to having any kids. I wanted them, though. She said she did, too. Christ . . .'

'I'm sorry,' she murmured. That must have been quite a blow. To lose your wife and your best friend. The disloyalty . . . In comparison, the disappointments of Amy's love life seemed minor. She'd never been seriously hurt – not like that. Her fears probably all stemmed from a lonely childhood. She finished her drink. The wine had given her a warm glow. She felt sorry for him – but touched that he had confided in her.

'It's old news. I should have got over it by now.' He got to his feet, but there was something harder about him, in the set of his mouth and jaw. It was almost as if Amy weren't even there. He looked tired and dishevelled – and not carelessly in control as he always had in the past. 'Another?'

She shook her head. There was more that she wanted to ask him, but she knew that the conversation was over for now. He'd let her see the more vulnerable side of him and he probably regretted it. Her aunt would be waiting for her, anyway. The best thing she could do was leave him on his own. 'I have to go.' It seemed abrupt, but . . . 'Thanks for the drink, Jake.' She got up and held out her hand.

He ignored it. Instead, he moved forwards and kissed her firmly on first one cheek and then the other. She felt the brush of stubble on her skin, smelt again the scent of leather and grapefruit, sensed the closeness of his lips to hers.

'It was my pleasure,' he said.

'Are you . . ?' She indicated the bar. 'Staying for a bit?'

He nodded. 'I'll have one for the road.' He touched her arm. 'Unless you need walking anywhere?' There was a caressing note to his voice that made her flush.

'No, I'm fine.' She grabbed her coat and scarf. She almost didn't want to leave him. That was what happened when people confided in you – you began to care about them. But he was a grown man. He'd be all right.

He nodded. 'I'll see you tomorrow then.'

'Yeah.' She glanced at him then quickly looked away. *For goodness' sake, Amy . . .*

And she walked out of the pub and into the darkness of the night.

Less than ten minutes later, Amy was knocking on the door of her great-aunt's Georgian cottage. It took Lillian a while to answer. Amy mentally traced her aunt's pathway as she got up from her cosy red-cushioned armchair, with maybe a glimpse through the net curtains to see who it might be, into the hallway, and . . .

'Hello, Amy, my dear. How lovely to see you back.' And she was enveloped in Great-aunt Lillian's scent of lavender, soap and face powder. Very different, she reflected, from leather and grapefruit.

'How have you been?' Amy said into the soft white hair.

'Just fine, my dear.' Her aunt drew back. For a moment there was a different look in those faded blue eyes. A question, a curiosity. Amy half shook her head. She knew she'd understand. Sometimes you didn't have to say a word.

In the lounge, where the gas fire was glowing orange and warm, Amy withdrew the postcard from her bag. It had been on another long journey, more or less a reversal of its first. She propped it up with the photographs on the bureau, just behind the fruit bowl. 'It's Essaouira,' she said. 'A town in western Morocco. On the coast.'

Her aunt nodded. 'He always loved the sea,' she said wistfully.

'And the flower emblem is the rose of Mogador.' Amy wished she could tell her more. But how could she?

'The rose of Mogador.' Her aunt seemed to linger over the sounds of the words.

'Lots of Westerners lived there at that time,' Amy said. 'It was a bit of a hippie hangout. He would have been happy there, I'm sure.'

407

'I hope so.' She let out a small sigh. 'Is that all, my dear?'

'That's all, I'm afraid.'

'I'll make the hot chocolate,' she said.

When she'd left the room, Amy picked up the photo of Glenn in its silver frame. So innocent-looking, but with that troubled expression that told you what he was like, what a deep thinker he must have been. She frowned. Then she put it back and glanced at the photo of her aunt and her sister in uniform, with their mother, Amy's great-grandmother.

'Auntie Lil . . .' Amy followed her into the kitchen. There was something that had continued to bother her, and it seemed like an evening for just coming out with it. 'Will you tell me what you did?' she asked. 'When you were unkind to my grandmother? To your sister, Mary? You said that you'd been unfair and that you wanted to make amends?' She looked at her aunt, who was standing by the cooker, where a saucepan of milk was coming to the boil. No microwave for her.

Her aunt turned to face her. She looked so sad.

Amy took a step towards her and took her hands. But she wouldn't let her off the hook. Like her mother always said – she couldn't let things go. 'What happened between you?' she asked. 'Will you tell me?'

CHAPTER 42

What had she done to Mary? It was a question that had always haunted her.

Lillian looked at Amy, at this girl – woman, really – who had become so special to her. And she realized that she deserved the truth. Lillian had thought that she was free, but you were never free until you told the whole truth; a tangle of lies could hold you in its power, as if it were a vipers' nest.

'Ted fell in love with Mary, not me,' she told Amy bleakly. 'Everyone did.'

It was a few weeks after their conversation about nylons and chocolates in Mary's bedroom when Ted was still a GI billeted in Bridport, that Ted came round to the house unexpectedly one day. Lillian's father and Mary were both out; her mother was in the kitchen cooking the evening meal. Lillian opened the front door and simply stared at him. He was even more good-looking than she remembered.

'Hi there, Duchess.' He grinned. 'Cat got your tongue?'

Lillian smiled back. He looked so pleased with himself, but she wondered if he even remembered her name. 'Hello, Ted.'

He glanced behind her into the narrow hall with the black, swirly wallpaper. 'Is that beautiful big sister of yours around?' He sounded eager, restless.

'Sorry, no.' Lillian hung on to the door jamb. She knew for a fact that Mary had gone off to meet Johnnie Coombes. Until Ted and the GIs had come along, he had been one of her regular admirers, but she'd given him the brush-off lately. 'He has no idea how to treat a girl,' Lillian had heard her say. 'He's just a boring old farmer.' Nevertheless, he was a farmer she'd known all her life and Lillian knew that he was a decent man. He was reliable, he was kind, he adored Mary and one day he'd inherit his father's farm and give some woman — though probably not Mary, she suspected — a good life.

'Will she be back soon, d'you know?' He sounded disappointed. His hand went to his jacket pocket as if to check that something — his wallet perhaps? — was still there.

Lillian shook her head. 'I shouldn't think so.' When she went up to Coombe Farm she was usually gone for hours.

Ted moved as if to leave, and then he turned back. 'Where is she?'

Lillian's eyes widened. She shrugged. But she hated having to lie to him. And she had the most overwhelming urge for him to know the truth about Mary.

'Lillian?'

So he *had* remembered her name. Lillian caught her breath. There he was, standing in front of her in his smart khaki uniform, cap in hand, looking like a film star, his dark-brown hair brushed back, shirt pressed, tie neat, brown eyes troubled. And there was Mary . . . Lillian took a deep breath. 'She's with someone,' she said.

'With someone?' He took a step closer.

'There's a boy. A local lad.' She couldn't meet his eyes. 'They have an understanding.'

'An understanding?'

'It might not mean anything. It doesn't usually. Not with Mary.' The words tumbled out. Suddenly Lillian had no idea of what she was saying or why. 'It's not just him. There are others. Anyone who's around, really. That's what she's like.' She stopped, appalled at what she'd said. It was the truth, but even so . . .

'Anyone who's around?' She couldn't work out if he was angry or upset or both.

'It's wartime.' Lillian spread her hands. 'There's no stability any more.' She had heard her mother saying this only yesterday, though she wasn't absolutely sure what she had meant. 'Some people have lost their sense of right and wrong.' Mother had said this, too. Lillian didn't know what she'd been referring to, but it might help explain Mary's behaviour. She wasn't bad. It was just . . .

'Yes, it's wartime all right, you're not kidding me there.' There was a deep frown on Ted's handsome face. His hand moved again towards his jacket pocket and then his arm dropped to his side. 'But, hell. What about emotions, Lillian? What about love?'

Lillian looked at him helplessly. She was only fourteen and she knew so little. But if only he could see her as she really was, or wanted to be. If only he could read her heart. She would show him about emotions, about love.

'Tell me the truth, Lillian.' To her surprise, he came closer, put his hands on her shoulders. She felt mesmerized by him. She gazed into his brown eyes, which seemed to burn into her. His breathing was shallow. 'Girls like Mary don't give a damn about love, do they?'

Girls like Mary . . . Lillian thought about her sister and the attention she'd always craved. She thought about Johnnie, Michael, Tristran and all the rest. And she thought about Ted. Most of all, she thought about Ted. 'I don't think they do,' she whispered.

He swore softly. And then he let go of her shoulders, turned on his heels, walked down the road and was gone.

'Who's that, dear?' Lillian's mother called.

Lillian realized she was shaking. Her shoulders felt as if they'd been seared by his touch. 'A friend of Mary's.'

In the kitchen her mother was wiping down the wooden draining board and cleaning the white Belfast sink with Vim. It all seemed so terribly ordinary. Lillian felt faint. Her mother was still wearing her green WVS uniform with her flowery pinny over it. On the little gas stove stood the steamer and a pan full of vegetables. Her mother pushed the checked fabric aside and got the casserole dish out of the cupboard. 'Fetch the meat from the larder for me, will you?' she said to Lillian.

Everyone knew that Americans were having flings with English girls; some were even getting married. How serious had it been between Ted and Mary? She hadn't known that – not then. All she knew was that Ted was right about Mary. She was with Johnnie Coombes. She didn't give a damn about love.

Lillian paused in her story and watched the girl in front of her. How would Amy react? Mary was her grandmother. Would Amy forgive Lillian for what she had done all those years ago? Especially when she knew the rest of it . . .

'What happened next?' Amy asked her. She seemed interested, but she wasn't giving the impression that she thought Lillian had done anything really bad – not yet.

'Mary came back from Coombe Farm much earlier than usual.' She was subdued the next day and the next. Lillian tried to talk to her, but she just told her to shut up and go away. 'What do you know?' she had shouted. 'What do you know about anything?'

And Lillian thought that she was right. She didn't know anything. What was happening? Had Mary tried to see Ted? Had he confronted her with what Lillian had told him? She had to know. And so she asked her one night when they were about to go to bed.

'I haven't seen him for ages, since you ask.' Mary had washed the make-up from her face; she looked young and vulnerable. She turned to Lillian in a rare moment of sisterhood. 'You know what these Yanks are like,' she said.

'No.' Lillian shook her head. What were they like?

'They take advantage of a girl. If you let them.' Her face hardened. She pushed Lillian away. 'Now, shoo, time for bed.'

Lillian thought about this. Ted, she concluded, had simply dropped her sister after what Lillian had told him. Which should feel good. But it didn't.

'So they broke up and you started writing to him?' Amy went and sat at her aunt's feet, took her hand, squeezed it.

Lillian felt somewhat reassured. 'I did. I didn't hear back from him, of course, not then . . .' He was still fighting. Omaha hadn't been a beach as much as a killing field. And she still didn't know what it had done to him – to see his friends and compatriots gunned down around him, to have to crawl over the wounded and dead, to witness that bloody carnage while desperately trying to get off the beach before he was killed himself.

'And then he got back from the war and proposed to you?'

Amy looked as if she found this hard to understand. And in a way it was. Ted had barely known Lillian. Why had he turned to the young English girl who poured out her heart to him in letters rather than to a woman he really knew in his own home town? Had he confused her with Mary somehow in his troubled mind? Had he believed that Mary's sister could give him something that he needed and desired? And why had Lillian said yes?

'Things are different in wartime, my dear.' Lillian patted Amy's hand. She had imagined herself to be head over heels in love with Ted since she was fourteen. She was desperate to leave Dorset. Any doubts, any anxieties she'd felt about going to a foreign country so many miles away to marry someone she hardly knew, had been swept away by the pure romance of it all. 'It was such an adventure.'

'What did your parents say?' Amy shifted her position and stretched out her legs in front of her. 'Were they shocked?' She grinned.

'Oh, they tried to dissuade me, of course.' Mother had been upset and Father had thought her quite mad. 'But Mary was their favourite.'

'And what did Mary say?'

Ah. Lillian took a deep breath. 'I always believed that she'd brushed off Ted's disinterest a long time before,' she said. 'That no harm had been done, and even that I'd saved him perhaps from being just another of the broken hearts Mary left behind her.' She smoothed the fabric of her skirt. She had to be honest with Amy now. She must tell her everything. 'But she hadn't brushed it off, my dear. She hadn't forgotten him at all. When I left England she kissed me on the cheek and she said, "Well, little sister, it looks like you got the man in the end, after all. Well done."'

'What do you mean?' Lillian had stared at her. She knew, but she didn't know.

'He dumped me when I was pregnant with his child.' Mary's indigo eyes were hard and emotionless. 'I was lucky Johnnie was there to pick up the pieces.'

'But you never . . .' Lillian had frowned, remembering back to the time a couple of months after Ted had left Bridport. The whisperings between Mary and their mother, the rushed wedding arrangements.

'I lost it. He never knew a thing.' And Mary had held her gaze for a long moment. Then turned and walked away.

Lillian stared into the distance and felt as if she could see her walking away from her even now.

'Oh, Auntie Lil . . .' Amy was holding her hand. She looked as if she understood. 'So she'd always cared for him?' she whispered.

'Yes.' Lillian shook her head, wonderingly. 'She'd always cared for him. It seemed . . .' She hesitated. '. . . that she had broken with all the others back then for him. That he was the one.' And that day when Ted had come round to the house, when she'd told him about Mary . . . Lillian had the strangest feeling — an instinct, really — that in his jacket pocket had been a ring.

'But you couldn't have known.'

'No.' But her mother had once let slip that Mary and Johnnie had split up for a while when the GIs were in town. That was why Mary had gone to Coombe Farm that day — to break up with him. Mary had fallen for Ted in a way she'd never fallen for any of her other admirers. He had been different.

'And it all turned out well in the end,' Amy said. 'My grandmother was happy with my grandfather. And you were . . .' Her voice trailed.

Had she noticed that there were no photographs of Ted here in this room? 'As you get older, my dear, you see the ironies of life more clearly,' Lillian said. 'I don't know whether Mary would have pleased him more, or if he would have pleased Mary.' She tucked a stray tendril of hair from her forehead. 'But whether they would or not, I did my sister a disservice. I spoke out of turn. I destroyed her relationship with the man she cared for.'

'But you came back to look after her when she needed you,' Amy said.

'It seemed the least I could do.'

Amy nodded. 'I can see how it all happened,' she said. 'But Mary shouldn't have been such a bitch in the first place.'

'Amy!' Lillian was shocked. 'She was your grandmother.'

Amy shrugged. 'I'm not saying I didn't care about her. But I understand why you did what you did. And you ended up with the raw deal, didn't you? With Ted?'

So she had noticed. 'He never talked about the war,' Lillian said, as if this answered Amy's question. 'I'm sure that he was a hero. Someone once said that all men who landed at Omaha were heroes. But . . .'

'It affected him for the rest of his life.' Amy finished the words for her. There was sympathy in her eyes – and love. Thank goodness, there was love.

'Perhaps you're right.' Lillian had often thought about this. 'I won't speak ill of the dead,' she said. 'But quite possibly, my dear, he never forgave me for not being Mary.'

CHAPTER 43

Callum brought the package round a week before Christmas. Nell hadn't been expecting to see him; she'd been upstairs in the front bedroom measuring for new curtains, thinking about it all. And Christmas – a daunting prospect.

Amy had invited her to spend it with her in Lyme Regis but, after everything that had been happening, Nell wanted to be at home. She tried to tell herself that Christmas here would be fine, that she could get through it, that it was a necessary challenge to take on and overcome. But it would be hard. Her mother's image was everywhere – laughing and wrapping presents in tissue paper, stringing cards above the old fireplace while she tunelessly sang 'The First Noel'. Stirring a Christmas cake crammed with fruit and almonds, the two of them decorating the tree with tinsel, gold chocolate coins and the fragile old porcelain angel.

Nell had to do it, though. So she went out and bought a tree that would bring the scent of pine into the farmhouse. She dug around in the boxes on top of the wardrobe in her mother's bedroom, which would, she decided, be her bedroom one day soon, and put the Christmas decorations up once again. She scoured nearby hedgerows for holly and ivy, she sent cards and she baked a cake. If she was going to live here and create her business here, she must be able to welcome in those memories every year, not let them destroy her.

Nell saw the red truck coming down the lane — unmistakably Callum's — and as it got closer, there, unmistakeably, was Callum at the wheel. Nell felt something shift inside her and she held on to the windowsill for support. He could still do this to her after everything, make her senses whirl, fill her head and her heart with regret. *They'd had such a chance* . . . She thought of the day they'd first met at the café, the first time they'd talked, the first time they'd made love in his small flat by the river in Truro. And they had thrown it all away.

He had thrown it away, she reminded herself.

After she had left the home they'd bought together that morning six weeks ago, after work when she had somehow got through the day and arrived back at the farmhouse once more, she had found him waiting for her. She'd been half expecting it, had been steeling herself for the confrontation all afternoon.

'Nell!' He'd jumped out of the truck, rushed over her, tried to take her in his arms.

But she'd fought him off, half crying. 'Don't touch me . . .'

'But I need to talk to you. It's not what you think.' He'd hung back then, his eyes pleading with her at least to acknowledge him, to listen.

'I'm not interested.' How could it not be what she thought?

'But at least —'

'Did you get an offer for the farmhouse before I went to

Morocco?' she snapped. 'And please don't lie. Not any more.'
She was scrabbling in her bag for the front door key and he
was following her down the path.

'Yes, I did. And I wanted to tell you. But —'

'But you decided it was too risky.' She found the key and
slotted it into the lock. Her hands were shaking, damn it.
'You thought I might say no.'

'Yes. No. It wasn't like that.'

She could hear the frustration in his voice. She opened
the door. Inside, the house was warm and it was waiting
for her. She felt as if she had never been away. She took a
deep breath.

'You couldn't get over your mother's death. I did what I
thought was right at the time. I thought that if I engineered
the whole thing it would stop you getting too upset, it would
help you get over it, help us to move on.'

Nell hung on to the stable door. 'Go away, Callum,' she
said. 'I don't want to hear it and I don't want to see you. Not
any more.'

'But —'

'No, Callum.' She couldn't believe that he was even bothering to try to explain. How could you explain lies, betrayal
and more lies? It wasn't exactly a strong foundation for a
marriage.

'Please, Nell . . .'

'No. I'm sorry, but there's no going back. Not for me. Not
for us. It's over.'

She saw his expression change to one of defeat. 'Sorry,

Nell,' he said. His shoulders slumped and he walked down the path. Climbed into the truck and drove away.

Callum . . . She had really hoped. And after that night in the hotel room she had done more than that: she had believed. There had been that evening in Marrakech with Rafi, but that had meant nothing; he had meant nothing. It was never going anywhere. It had been more like an awakening, a realization that she wasn't emotionally dead, after all. But Callum . . .

Nell had shut the door, leant her back on it and faced the truth. She was on her own now.

That had been more than six weeks ago and, in that time, she hadn't seen him. They'd had two polite conversations on the phone. During the first one, Nell arranged a time to go and collect all her stuff from the house and asked him please to be out. And during the second he told her he was putting the house on the market so that he could pay her back her share. She had no idea how he was or whether he was seeing someone. She hadn't done anything about filing for divorce because she couldn't bear the idea, not yet.

And now here he was walking down the path, a brown paper package cradled in his arms. A Christmas present? Surely not. He was standing on her doorstep. She realized she was holding her breath, waiting for the knock on the door.

But it never came. And now he was walking back down the path. He looked much the same as ever, dark hair a little longer perhaps, steps a bit more uncertain. And he wasn't carrying the package any more.

Nell had to stop herself from running down the stairs and flinging open the door. She watched him get into the truck, saw him glance back at the farmhouse – had he seen her? He didn't wave – and she watched him slowly drive away.

It was hard to lose both your mother and your husband in such a short space of time and, in the last six weeks, Amy had been her lifeline. Nell had rung her first on the night she had moved back into the farmhouse, and it had been a relief to talk things through.

'He did what?' Amy was shocked, she could tell.

'I had to leave.'

'Of course you did.'

'And now I have to get on with the rest of my life.' And Nell had looked bleakly around.

'Let's make a list right now while I'm on the phone,' Amy said. 'All the things you have to do to get ready for your project to become a reality. You were going to do it on your own, in any case. Now you still are – but without potential opposition.'

She had a point, and Nell had to smile.

And this was exactly what she had done. She had done her research about non-permanent restaurants and planned how she would do hers, where she would do it and when she would have her first night. She had made a list of recipes and ideas and she had cooked them – for two, putting the leftovers in the freezer for another time. She had visited Amy in Dorset and the two of them had pored over colour charts and fabrics and furniture until Nell felt as if her eyes were popping out of her head. They had discussed marketing, prices and menus. She had contacted suppliers and had arranged for necessary work to be done to the kitchen – she would keep the Aga but add a more commercial oven to make it easier to cook for large numbers. She had even applied for planning permission to turn the farmhouse into a real and much more permanent restaurant. She'd gone to see a planning officer, and he had said that there was no reason as far as he could tell that it would be refused. It wasn't a residential area; she didn't even need to have licensing to start with. Restaurants made a lot of their money out of sales of alcohol. But people were often attracted to places where they could park their cars and bring their own wine.

And, gradually, the idea of The Saffron House, her very own Moroccan restaurant, began to grow and take flight. And that wasn't all. There was plenty of land remaining; more than enough for Nell to cope with. In the spring she would be replanting the saffron.

'And what are you going to do about Callum?' Amy had asked her on the phone the night before.

'I haven't decided yet.'

'Well, don't leave it too long.'

Nell knew why she was asking and she knew what she was saying. *If you still want him back* . . .

And now he was here. Or had been here. Now, he was gone.

Nell went down the stairs and opened the front door. The package was on the doorstep. She bent to pick it up. It was thick and heavy. What on earth could it be? And then she looked at the writing on the outside and realized that it wasn't from Callum at all. It must have been delivered to the house and he had brought it round. It had been sent, she saw, from Morocco.

When she opened it, she found it was a thick journal bound with leather. The pages were covered with an untidy scrawl which looked vaguely familiar. She frowned.

Nell opened the accompanying letter. It was written in a childish hand, a different hand.

'Dear Madam,' she read. 'I send this because my dear friend is passed. He keeps your address you give him. There is no one else. Hoping you are well. Malik.'

Malik . . . Nell started reading the journal that day. At first she was vaguely interested, and then her interest grew. Every chance she got, she picked it up and read more. She finished it three days later. Once, she almost phoned Amy, and then she changed her mind. She'd have to tell her this in person.

By the time she finished, she was numb, shell-shocked. And there was something else. Something even closer to home.

CHAPTER 44

What Lillian had told Amy was true, Lillian thought now as she looked in her wardrobe. It was true, but not quite the whole truth. Sometimes, the whole truth could be a step too far.

She pushed aside jackets and skirts with increasing impatience. What on earth could she wear to the preview of Amy's photographic exhibition, the reception that marked the opening of the Moroccan event? Not her navy suit – it was too old-fashioned, not at all suitable for the great-aunt of a talented and probably soon-to-be-famous photographer. She sorted through the hangers. Not the lilac dress either – that was far too summery. Something long and floaty, she thought. Something discreet but elegant. She didn't want to be accused of trying to look younger than her years, but at the same time she didn't want to be a frump. There was really nothing at all appropriate. She frowned. She should have thought about this before. Was it too late to buy something new?

The *ratatat* on the door took her by surprise. It wouldn't be Amy – she was far too busy with the exhibition at the moment to come calling – and it was the wrong time for the postman. Who else was there?

She took the stairs slowly. Opened the front door. 'Celia.'

'Hello, Aunt Lillian.' Celia was smiling. She looked much more relaxed than the last time she'd seen her, too.

Lillian smiled back at her. 'Hello, my dear,' she said. 'How are you?'

Celia put her head on one side. 'I hope you don't mind me dropping by –'

'Of course not.' Only, of course, she didn't usually.

'But I know Amy's busy at the moment, and I wanted to have a chat with you about the reception.'

'Oh? Come in, my dear. Come in.' Lillian took her coat. 'Some tea, perhaps?' She wouldn't stay, she would be too busy, she'd have to get back.

But Celia smiled again. 'Why not?'

'You have enough time?'

Celia followed her through to the kitchen. 'I've taken the day off,' she confided. She sounded like a child playing truant.

Lillian chuckled. 'How pleasant.'

'Indeed.' They exchanged what was almost a conspiratorial look.

Lillian filled the kettle. 'Who have you left in charge? Ralph?'

'No fear.' They both laughed. 'Actually,' Celia said, 'I've employed a manager. I've been showing her the ropes for the past few days, but today's her first day on her own. Everything's quiet. I'm sure she'll be fine.'

426

'A manager?' Lillian put the kettle on the hob. 'What a marvellous idea.'

'Well, you did suggest it,' Celia replied. 'More or less.'

'Did I?' Delegate, she had said, if you want more time. And it looked as though Celia had done just that. Good for her. And good for Amy, she thought.

'I was wondering,' Celia went on, 'shall we pick you up on the way there? We've decided to order a cab and go in style.'

Lillian had been concerned about this, thinking she should call a cab herself. 'Oh, would you? That would be so kind.' She hadn't wanted to bother Amy.

'What are you wearing? Have you decided?' Celia got mugs out of the cupboard and dropped a casual teabag in each. Normally, Lillian would use teacups and make a pot, but she was so surprised at Celia even being here, let alone the fact that she was helping to make tea, that she bit her tongue. Mugs it would be. The world wouldn't stop turning.

'I have no idea,' she confessed. 'I was just looking through my wardrobe when you arrived. I've got nothing remotely suitable. I was even wondering –'

'I could take you shopping,' Celia said. 'If you'd like that. I'm looking for something to wear myself. We could go to Exeter. Have lunch there.'

Lillian stared at her.

'I've never thanked you, not properly.' And Celia took Lillian's hands in hers. 'For helping us so much when you came back to live in Dorset.'

Lillian's brain raced. That was such a long time ago. 'But I didn't expect you to, my dear,' she said. To tell the truth, she could hardly think straight. 'Your mother and I didn't always see eye to eye, you see, and there was the fact that I'd married Ted and —'

'I know about all that.' The kettle boiled and Celia let go of Lillian's hands and busied herself pouring water into the mugs. She gave them a quick swirl, added milk straight from the fridge — no jug — and yanked out the teabags so that they dripped on the counter. Lillian tried not to wince.

'I knew Mum had a grudge against you, and I thought I knew the reason why.' Celia glanced across at Lillian. 'But I didn't.'

'Oh.' Lillian wasn't sure what else to say.

'Until Amy told me what really happened,' Celia added.

For a moment Lillian was cross with Amy. She had told her the story in confidence. And yet she supposed it was Mary's story as much as Lillian's and Celia had a right to know. She should even, she supposed, have told her herself. 'I see.'

Celia picked up the tray and carried it through to the lounge. 'Mum never ceases to amaze me.'

Was that so? Lillian followed her. 'I hurt her, Celia,' she said. 'I really did.'

'Perhaps you hurt her pride,' Celia replied.

Rather sharply, Lillian thought. 'Perhaps,' she murmured.

'I loved my father very much.' Celia turned to face her. 'They were childhood sweethearts, he told me. He adored her, you know.'

'I know.' Johnnie Coombes had always worshipped Mary, this was true.

'Your husband almost broke them up, according to what Amy tells me. When they were courting, I mean.'

Lillian frowned. She tried to get a grip on this new, rather unexpected perspective on the situation.

'I knew there was something – someone . . .' She glanced at Lillian and suddenly Lillian knew. Celia had thought it was Lillian who had almost broken up Johnnie and Mary. When, in fact, in a funny sort of way, she supposed that she'd done the opposite. Because of what she'd told Ted, she'd kept Johnnie and Mary together. The baby might have made a difference. But Mary had miscarried Ted's baby. If it had even been Ted's baby.

'Oh,' she said again.

Celia smiled. 'But they came through. And they had me.'

Lillian blinked at her. Really, she'd never looked at it that way before.

'I owe you, Aunt Lillian,' Celia said. 'So we're going to Exeter and I'm going to treat us to lunch and help you find a gorgeous dress for Friday night.'

The dress that they chose was a mushroom silk, soft to the touch and elegant to the eye. 'It goes with your hair,' Celia said.

'It's perfect,' said Lillian. She could wear it with her cream court shoes – they had a slight heel but were comfortable.

'You'll be the belle of the ball.' Celia laughed.

'Go on with you. As if anyone would even notice an old lady like me.' But Lillian had drunk two glasses of Prosecco with her lunch and she couldn't help giggling.

'Nevertheless,' said Celia, 'you'll feel like a million dollars.'

The whole truth, Lillian thought, as she hung the silk dress up in her wardrobe, was indeed sometimes a matter of perspective.

She had come back to Dorset to care for her sister, not knowing what Mary had told her daughter, not knowing what she would find. But it hadn't, after all, been such a huge thing to do. Lillian had felt good about helping them. It had given her back the purpose missing from her life since Glenn had left it. And now she had Amy and, perhaps, in a funny sort of way, she had Celia, too. After all, she thought, as she closed the wardrobe door, it should be her thanking them.

CHAPTER 45

On Christmas Eve, Nell was in the farmhouse kitchen trimming fennel stalks flush with the bulb in preparation for her seafood in saffron broth. Just because she was spending Christmas on her own, she had told herself sternly, didn't mean she shouldn't make an effort. And, in a way, she didn't feel as if she was on her own. Her mother's voice was still here, in this kitchen, in this house, and Nell could hear it whenever she wanted to.

She began to chop the fennel and onion finely. It was funny, she thought, but she never grew bored of chopping onions. It always made her eyes sting and water, but it was so satisfying – the clean way the knife sliced through the neat multilayered segments and let them fall. Sometimes it was like that in an argument, she thought. And then afterwards you had the time to reflect, to think about what had been said. *I was trying to help you move on*, Callum had told her. And this had made her realize: Nell had been wallowing in her grief. It was true. She had allowed herself to lose sight of Callum and their life together. And he had taken desperate measures.

Nell looked out of the kitchen window into the darkness

that shrouded the kitchen garden and the saffron meadow. She would have to get her skates on in the spring if she was going to get all her herbs planted in time. And then there was the saffron; she might have to get help in for that. She smiled. Just like her mother had.

She had given Johnson plenty of notice that she'd be leaving in the spring. She'd miss Sharon, of course. Nell wouldn't be able to afford full-time help, not at first. But if she started doing well, maybe Sharon could come and work for her as a waitress. And in the summer she was hoping she could lure Lucy here for a few months. She'd need all the help she could get.

She began to deseed and chop the tomato. Then she minced the garlic. At least it was easy to get good fish and seafood here in Cornwall; she'd already found a supplier. She started scrubbing the mussels and removing their beards. Fish and seafood wasn't what first sprang to mind when you thought of Moroccan cuisine, but her experience in Essaouira had shown Nell that saffron and other spices and the slow, careful method of Moroccan cooking complemented fish and seafood just as well as it did meat. Lots of people were scared to cook shellfish – it didn't have a great reputation. So it was something people liked to eat in restaurants. She hoped.

She prepared the prawns and cut the fish. She was using a nice fresh piece of halibut but, really, any thick white fish would do the job.

When the knock came at the door, she looked up from her preparations, blinked. *Who on earth . . .?*

She wiped her hands on her white chef's apron and went to answer it.

Callum stood on the doorstep. He was smiling, but in that way people smile when they're not too sure of their welcome. 'Hello, Nell,' he said.

'Hello.' Nell found herself wishing she'd put some make-up on after her bath. She didn't want to appear wan, pale and distressed. She wanted to look as if she was enjoying life without him. *Yes, by staying in alone cooking seafood and saffron broth for one on Christmas Eve*, a small voice whispered.

'How are you?' He shifted his weight from one foot to the other. Fidgety and on edge, she thought.

'Fine.' She hesitated. It was Christmas Eve. 'Would you like to come in for a minute?'

'Really?' He brightened. 'Well, if you're not too busy.'

'It's cold out there.' She opened the door wider, gave him her most cheerful smile. 'I'm just cooking.'

''Course you are.' They both laughed.

She led the way into the kitchen, keeping a few steps away, aware of the proximity of him. It was strange. He was still her husband and they had spent so much time together. And yet, already, he seemed like a stranger. She felt apprehensive, unsure of him.

'I brought you this.'

'Would you like a drink?'

They spoke at the same time. Laughed.

'Yes, please,' he said. 'A small glass of wine, if you've got anything open.'

She nodded. There was a bottle of French Viognier in the fridge; she'd already had a taster and had been planning to have a small glass with dinner. She was using some in her recipe, too though the alcohol would evaporate. She fetched it and poured him half a glass; he was driving, so they'd both be on rations.

He handed her a small package wrapped in jolly Santa Christmas paper.

'What is it?' He shouldn't have got her anything. She shouldn't have let him in. Whatever his reasons, Callum had still deceived her. He had tried to control her and then excused his behaviour by saying he was protecting her. What was it with everyone she got close to? First her mother, and then Callum – both determined to shelter her from what needed to be faced. Was it something in Nell that made this happen? Was it . . . because she needed to grow up?

Nell ripped off the paper to reveal a small white box. 'Wishing on the Wind' was written in silver lettering. Be careful what you wish for, she thought. She opened the box.

Inside, a delicate silver necklace nestled on creamy fabric. It was a teardrop pendant on a silver filigree chain, a small hollow of glass with a silver cap. And inside the bulb of glass was a tangle of saffron, real saffron, gleaming threads of red-gold. Nell looked at Callum.

He took a slug of his wine and shrugged. 'So you can have it with you all the time,' he said. 'Saffron.'

'But where on earth did you find it?' Nell took it out of the box. Should you accept gifts from your ex-husband?

Callum looked suitably modest. 'I had it made,' he said. 'That jewellery maker we came across on the arts trail last May.'

Nell remembered. Happy days, she thought. Just after they were married. Before her mother's death. And a long time before Morocco . . . He'd had it made. She was impressed. They had both loved the jewellery, fashioned in hand-blown glass and silver. But to commission a piece like this, with saffron at its heart . . .

'Do you like it?'

'I love it,' she said.

'Let me.' And before she could stop him he was up and out of the chair, fastening the necklace, his hands almost touching her shoulders, but not quite. She could feel his breath, smell the faintly earthy scent of him combining with apple shower gel and the damp December night outside.

'Thanks.' She found her voice from somewhere. 'You shouldn't have. But thank you, Callum.'

She stepped smartly away to hide the tears in her eyes, held the saffron pendant between her fingers for a moment and smiled. 'I have to get on. Otherwise, the food will be spoiled.'

'Do you want me to leave?' He moved across the room, hovered in the doorway, awkward as ever.

She shook her head. 'Stay for dinner if you like.' She didn't want him to go, not yet. She had something she had to tell him. And she didn't want to be alone.

'Really?' His eyes lit up.

'Yes,' she said. 'We need to talk.'

She took a quarter teaspoon of crumbled saffron threads and stirred it gently into some white wine. This present that Callum had given her . . . It was as if he was acknowledging it at last. How important it was to her, this legacy of her past. Using saffron always gave her a thrill. It was the beguiling sharp scent of it and the intensity of the colour. It infused the wine immediately and turned it a glorious orange. Like sunshine.

'You can be the guinea pig,' Nell said. She put a generous glug of olive oil in the pan and put it on to heat.

'Sounds good to me.'

'Thanks for bringing that package round last week.' She began to cook the fennel and onion over the heat, stirring them with a wooden spoon. They would take about five minutes to soften. 'It was quite a revelation.' She would talk to Amy about it when she saw her in a couple of days' time. The Moroccan event in Lyme was starting on Boxing Day. She knew that they had wanted to squeeze the whole thing into December 2013, since that was the anniversary of the first Moroccan emissary to Britain, in the time of King John. But as Amy had said, Christmas had a way of always getting in the way.

'Is that what you wanted to talk about?'

Nell glanced at him, noted the expression in his hazel eyes. 'It's part of it.'

She added the garlic. She loved that pungent scent when the garlic hit the hot oil and onions. And the anise gave it an extra dimension. After a minute or two she added the saffron wine and left it to simmer. They would have the broth with crusty bread and fresh green salad.

She sat down opposite him at the old farmhouse table of her childhood. 'It was a journal,' she said. 'Written by an old man we met in Morocco.'

And while the saffron broth was simmering in the pan, the bitter fragrance of the spice mingling with the sweetness of the seafood and filling the kitchen, she told him about what she had read.

'Blimey, Nell,' he said, when she had finished.

'I know.' She got to her feet. The mixture had reduced nicely and she threw in the mussels, along with half a cup of her special fish stock. She covered it and set it to simmer. She had to stir it from time to time and then just wait for the mussels to open.

Callum looked across at the far wall, where Nell had positioned her parchment painting. It would go in the living room when the living room was the dining room of the restaurant. But until then . . . *Goddess, indeed* . . . That was no goddess. That was the nymph Smilax, with a flirtatious smile and a toss of her dark hair, or Nell was a Chinaman. She smiled.

'She looks a bit like your mother,' said Callum.

Nell laughed. She discarded a couple of unopened mussels, added the prawns, the fish and tomato and the rest of the stock and let it continue to simmer, nice and low.

'Saffron's your past,' Callum said. 'I always wanted to be your future.'

Nell turned around. 'But Callum,' she said, 'I'm made up of my past, my present and my future. We all are.' She thought of the Tarot cards, the endless layouts she'd done after her mother's death. *Past, present, future* . . . She rarely looked at them these days. For one thing, she had no time. For another . . . She'd learnt how to make decisions without them. 'You can't have one without the other,' she said.

'But what if the past threatens the future? Didn't the past destroy us?' His fists were balled.

'No.' She went to him and took his hands. Uncurled them gently. 'It wasn't the past, it was us.'

'Me, you mean.'

She shook her head. 'Us.' She'd been doing a lot of thinking. And she'd realized they were both to blame.

'The past isn't just a person, Callum. It isn't my mother.' Because that's what it was all about when you came down to it. Or who. She or what was left of her – her memory – was the threat he felt. And Nell had to accept that, to Callum, it was a genuine threat. Even now that she was gone.

'I know,' he whispered. 'I'm sorry.'

'And now,' she said.

'And now?'

'I'm pregnant, Callum.'

He stared at her.

It was hard to take in, Nell knew. She could hardly believe it herself. But she'd done the test and it was true, and it was a result, she knew, of their desperate and passionate coupling on the night she returned from Morocco.

438

Callum reached out. He put his large hands tentatively on her belly. 'Oh, Nell,' he said. And then his expression changed. 'And so you want us to try again? Is that it? For the sake of the baby?'

She searched his face. 'I want us to try again, yes.' She, more than anyone, knew how it could be, growing up without a father. Her mother had been the most loving, the most indomitable person she would ever know, but even she could not be two people. Even she couldn't make up for the loss, nor even explain the loss. And Nell didn't want that for her child. 'But not just for the sake of the baby,' she whispered.

She didn't have to explain any more because he seemed to understand. He took her in his arms and kissed her very gently.

I am not my mother, she told herself fiercely. *And I will not be trapped – by the past or the present.*

It was a few minutes before Nell was able to move back to the seafood broth simmering on the Aga. She tasted it and adjusted the seasoning. 'Smell it.' She held out the spoon. He sniffed. 'Taste it.' She waited. 'What do you think?'

He frowned. 'A bit salty. A bit sweet. It's really good, Nell.'

She smiled. He'd get there. One day, he'd taste the magic.

CHAPTER 46

Morocco, 1979

Glenn remained involved in life at the farm and worked hard, in the pendulous way in which all the other men seemed to work. Hours passed by very easily. Days, too. Glenn was shocked when he realized he had been there a year.

'I can't imagine leaving,' he said to Mustapha, 'but I must.'

'Even if you have found your place to be?'

Glenn thought of Bethany. Could it be that simple? And was it too late to go to England to try and find her? 'I have no choice,' he said. How could he live with never knowing the reason why?

Mustapha sent him a serene glance. It said that every man has a choice. 'If you are restless,' he said, 'why not come with me to Essaouira tomorrow? I have some business to attend to. There will be Gnawa music in the square. We will arrive at noon and leave around midnight.'

Glenn hesitated. He hadn't imagined returning there. But now he felt well and fit, and he was sure the virus — if that's what it was — had left his body. He had worked hard for

Mustapha and his family and now he must think of moving on. 'OK,' he said. 'Why not?'

It was strange to be back. The town was familiar and yet alien; Glenn could hardly believe he'd lived here for so long. In the square, he watched the musicians in their white robes. The music started with a slow beat and the pulse built. And just as it always had before, it crept into your head, hummed its way into your very soul.

'Hey, man.' It was a familiar voice. 'I thought you'd left town.'

Glenn turned to face Howard. He looked much the same. If anything, his face seemed browner and more weathered, though he wore the same crumpled skullcap that he had always worn. It was a peculiar thing. It had only been a year, and yet it felt so much longer. Glenn wondered if the journey he'd travelled had indeed been longer. It seemed more like a lifetime. 'I did.'

'Where'd you go? Fez? Casablanca? Marrakech?' Howard offered him a cigarette.

Role reversal, thought Glenn, thinking of the day they'd met. He took it anyway, just to be sociable, though he didn't smoke much these days. 'Just into the mountains.' He waved a hand. It would seem odd to Howard, but since his illness Glenn hadn't wanted to be around people so much. Even being here in this crowded square, rubbing shoulders with so many people wasn't easy for him. He was getting the heebie jeebies and wondering if he shouldn't have come. Only . . . It was the music that had tempted him. He'd wanted to hear it again. And he wanted to prove to himself that he could get out, that he could still leave and go to England to find Bethany.

'The mountains? S'trewth . . .' Howard shook his head. 'It really freaked you out, didn't it, mate?' He leant closer, his voice soft and strangely conspiratorial.

Howard was different, Glenn realized. He didn't seem so self-assured. His eyes were glassy. He wasn't the Howard Glenn had known. 'What?' He stuck his hands in the pockets of his jeans, tried to focus once more on the music. Though he knew.

'The way she left you. That chick, Bethany. The way she walked out that day.'

'I guess so.' Glenn wasn't sure he wanted to be having this conversation, and especially not with Howard. He'd thought many a time about why she'd left, and he still had no idea. Relationships broke up, sure; people went their separate ways. But why hadn't she just come out and said something? It wasn't like Bethany to be underhand. She'd always been open as a book. He supposed it was his own fault. It must have been. She'd been acting strange, yes. But maybe she'd thought the same about him. Hell, look at him. First getting that weird illness, and now living in the mountains, working on the farm, spending hours writing poetry or just staring out across the plain. Glenn looked around, but Mustapha was tucked away in some local eatery, and he wasn't meeting him till midnight on the waterfront.

'Always thought you'd followed her back to England.' Howard's eyes narrowed. 'Always thought you'd find out why she left.'

Glenn blinked at him. His words had shut out the music completely, the people, too. 'Why she left?' he echoed. But perhaps Howard didn't mean it like Glenn thought. Perhaps Howard, too, knew nothing. He shook his head. 'Nah.' Not yet, at least.

The song came to an end and the musicians grinned and bowed and announced they were taking a short break.

'What about Giz?' Glenn asked Howard. 'He still around?' He'd like to see him, just one more time. They'd had a laugh, the three of them, in that riad, then the four of them when Bethany had moved in. For a while it had been . . . Well, not perfect, nothing was perfect. But it had been a good scene. They'd worked well together, they had pretty much the same values, they'd looked out for each other, combined their resources. But nothing lasted for ever. Even the best communes had human beings in them, after all.

Howard shrugged. 'He left a month or so ago, man.'

'Where'd he go?'

'Search me.' He seemed uncomfortable. 'Wanna beer?'

Glenn hadn't been drinking up at the farm. No one did. He'd got out of the habit. But Howard wanted company and what he'd said about Bethany decided him. 'Sure.'

Glenn soon realized that Howard had already been half-cut when they'd met in the square. When he went for a piss after his second beer, he hardly seemed able to stand up straight. Or maybe he was on something other than his usual kif. His pupils were dilated enough and he was certainly acting weird. It was odd, though. All that time they'd lived in the riad, together he'd never seen Howard that way. Gizmo, yes. Glenn had often taken a blanket from his room and covered Gizmo wherever he had happened to pass out. But Howard . . . Howard had always seemed in control.

'I could tell you, man . . .' He leaned across the table towards Glenn.

'What?' Again, he felt uncomfortable. He wanted to leave. To get back to what he now thought of as reality. But it wasn't yet midnight, and something stronger was making him stay. He looked around at the other guys in the bar, half of them pretty much worse for wear, and he seemed to see them through different eyes – through his new eyes, he thought. The eyes of a guy who'd been leading a different kind of life.

'Why she left.'

Glenn straightened up. So he'd been right after all. What a bastard. What did he know? 'Why?' He kept his voice level.

Howard attempted to touch his nose with his forefinger, missed and jabbed at his cheek instead. 'She was pregnant,' he said.

Glenn's world spun. He stared at Howard. 'What?'

'She was pregnant.'

Pregnant? 'But . . .' Glenn tried to compute it. Could it be

444

true? That was a year ago. So what did that mean? That now she had a baby? Their baby? He had a sudden vision of Bethany; sad, vulnerable, pregnant, making her way home to England to have the baby back there alone. His baby . . . Why would she do that? Why hadn't she told him? Goddammit. Why hadn't she told him?

'She was gonna get rid of it,' Howard said.

'You bloody liar!' Why would she have told Howard and not him? It wasn't possible. It couldn't be possible. She wouldn't just . . .

'That's what she told me. She didn't want it, man. No way, she said. She was scared to tell you. Reckoned you'd go apeshit.' He looked at Glenn appraisingly.

Glenn realized that he was shaking. 'When? When did she tell you?' For some reason, this seemed important. Was it when they'd done the run? Was that why she had suddenly changed her mind about going on it? For Christ's sake. He put his head in his hands. Why hadn't she told him?

Howard took a slug of his beer. 'It was that morning.'

Glenn looked up. 'What morning?'

'Strewth, man. The morning she left. When I asked her why she was splitting.'

That morning. Glenn gazed into the square. But when had Bethany found out she was pregnant? He frowned, trying to remember some detail that might be a clue. The musicians were still playing, but the crowd had thinned. Those left were swaying to the beat or dancing, humming or chanting the lyrics along with the band. Lights glared out from the stage and all around the square. Beyond was the slow darkness of the sea. The music droned on.

Glenn couldn't believe he was so angry. So much for quiet contemplation and gentle living. It was a year ago. But he was furious. Bethany had left because she was pregnant. Bethany hadn't wanted his child. Worse, she hadn't even wanted him to know about his child. 'Why didn't you tell me?' he said at last.

'She made me promise not to, didn't she, man?'

Disloyal bastard. 'You still could have,' he muttered. 'You bloody should have. We were supposed to be mates, after all.' Though they hadn't been. Glenn recalled the jibes, the comments, the digs.

Howard laughed. 'Where were you all that time?' he jeered. 'You and me were never mates, man. We just lived together is all.'

True. 'You always had it in for me,' Glenn said. It was just a matter of fact. He had no idea why.

'Yeah, well.' Howard's eyes narrowed. 'You might have got out of it. But my brother – he fought in Vietnam.'

'What?' Howard was an Aussie. But, of course, they'd had conscription there, too, by 1966.

'Just like all the other poor idiots.' Howard rocked back on his chair, pulled a crumpled cigarette packet from the pocket of his jeans and some matches. 'He thought he'd be a hero.' He lit one, cradling the light in his palm to protect the flame from the breeze. 'He got sent in to help you bastards fuck up someone else's country.'

Glenn watched him take a draw, deep into his chest. So that was what it was all about. No wonder he'd given Glenn a hard time. Suddenly, it was all making sense. 'What happened to him?' Had he been killed in action? No wonder the guy was so bitter.

Howard shook his head. He took a swig of his beer. It dribbled down his chin and he wiped his face with the back of his hand. 'He came home. He was totally screwed, though. He didn't know what to do with his life before he went to war, and he sure as hell didn't know what to do with it after. The things he saw . . . man.' He glanced across at Glenn. 'Well, you wouldn't know, would you? Fucking draft dodgers.'

Glenn was silent. What could he say? Guilt was a useless emotion. It didn't help anyone.

'He suffered, man. Anxiety, stress, trauma, you name it. By the time I left, he'd become an agoraphobic and an alcoholic. He needed to be in control. But yeah, he wasn't fit for anything much after Vietnam.'

Shit. Glenn stood up. There was no point in saying anything. It was done. It was over. That's what they had all been protesting for. But he wasn't about to start debating the Vietnam War with Howard. Still, 'That's tough, man. No one should have to –'

'Yeah, you're right. No one should have to.' Howard stood up, too. 'She had to get rid of it, man,' he said. He grinned, and for a second he looked like the old Howard. 'After all, she didn't have a clue which of us was the father.'

Glenn swung the punch before he'd realized what he was about to do. He saw the surprise on Howard's face and then he saw him slump to the floor, blood oozing from his mouth. Glenn was a pacifist and yet he wanted to hit him again. He wanted to stamp all over him, grind his face into the floor, make him stop talking. That's how much of a pacifist he was. The anger was burning in his gut and in his throat; it was filling his head with a red flame.

He took a deep breath, closed his eyes for a moment and opened them again. Someone was helping Howard to his feet. His lips were bloody and he was staggering but that grin was still on his face. It must be midnight.

Glenn walked away.

CHAPTER 47

Amy took one last look around the exhibition. Everything was ready for the opening. There was nothing more that she could do. She had tried to arrange things so that entering this space was like coming through a doorway into the country of Morocco, beginning with the blues and yellows of the Majorelle Garden, then moving into the wide desert plains and dunes, towards the high pink haze of the Atlas Mountains. And, in the centre, underpinning the exterior landscape was the great swathe of the purple saffron field in full bloom.

The interiors, she had arranged differently, so that they were like separate rooms: the inside of an old Berber cottage, the dilapidated grandeur of the ancient riad in Essaouira, the souks with their carpets and neat rows of sequinned leather *babouches*. And the people: the girls with red-gold henna decorating their hands, the grizzled old fishermen with their nets and buckets of wriggling fish glinting in the sunshine, the brown-skinned kids playing football in the pink alleyways of the medina, the snake charmer with the long, white beard and hair plaited into his turban . . . It was all here. Well, most of it. Amy had chosen her favourite shots, but she had also created a story, a pictorial narrative of Morocco today. Which was what she'd called the exhibition. *Morocco Today.*

Jake had looked around earlier. She hadn't seen much of him lately, though he'd kept in touch by phone and email, and he'd passed her details, he'd told her, on to various contacts who were interested in her work. Several of them would be attending the exhibition. *So be prepared* . . . She knew what that meant. She had her CV and portfolio at the ready – and an envelope in her bag.

He had, however, dropped by once or twice. To see how things were progressing, he'd said. To see her? She had no idea. She'd always known before when a man was interested in her – they generally made it obvious. But Jake Tarrant . . . She knew something of his past, but she didn't even know if he was single at the moment. It was hardly likely. He was attractive, sociable, intelligent . . . Why would he be on his own? Back in Morocco, she had wondered, felt that he wanted something to happen between them. But now? All the signs told her he thought of Amy as just a friend. They'd gone out for drinks one night and spent a long time discussing the event, and little else. And when he walked her home and said goodnight, he had kissed her on both cheeks, as before, and simply walked off into the darkness. He hadn't lingered. Not that she wanted him to linger. Only . . . That smell of leather and grapefruit, that way he had of getting a little too close . . . She remained pretty sure she didn't want that in her life, pretty clear that she was better off as she was. But it had got to her. She knew that it had got to her. *More fool you, Amy,* she told herself.

'You've done a good job,' he'd said approvingly when he looked around the gallery this afternoon. 'I'm proud of you.'

She'd smiled. It sounded like something her mother would say – or Auntie Lil. She supposed she should mind – it inferred he'd had something to do with her achievement. But she didn't, not any more. She'd come to realize that she'd needed Jake to work with her on this project; she could never have done it alone. He was an accomplished man, even if a tad irritating at times. But she respected him. She *wanted* him to be proud of her, she realized. *Oh, dear.*

In the Turmeric Room (Jake had suggested naming the gallery rooms after spices used in Moroccan cuisine) was the weaving workshop, run not by an old woman for whom the practice had been a lifelong tradition but a young girl of twenty something called Jo. Jo, who sported bright-blue eyeshadow and vivid pink blusher, knew how to work a loom – Moroccan style – and, needless to say, her workshop was full.

In the Paprika Room, Jake had organized another exhibition of the work of Moroccan artists, loaned by various art centres and galleries in the UK and beyond. In the evenings, three films were being screened in the Ginger Room, and tucked into the gallery foyer (Cinnamon Lobby) was a Morocco travel information point manned by one of Lyme's travel agents.

In the Saffron Room – alias the gallery's kitchen – was the cookery workshop run by Jenny, who had written the book on Moroccan cuisine that was to be illustrated with Amy's photographs. It was due to be published in six months' time. They had had more than double the number of people Jenny could cope with in there, and Amy had suggested that Nell might run another workshop – if they could find a local venue. But Nell had insisted that she was still learning herself. And she was too busy, she said. She was in the process of moving home and setting up her new restaurant. But she was coming over this evening and Amy couldn't wait to see her again. She had put some of Nell's flyers advertising her new venture in the information point, in the cookery workshop and here on the glass table where people could sit down for a while and have a good view of some of the photographs. She was sure it would do well.

Jake came in, brandishing a bottle of bubbly and two glasses. His spiky hair was standing almost on end and there was a shadow of stubble on his jaw. He was tired, she realized. This was important to him, and he'd worked really hard to make it what it was.

'We should drink to our own success,' he said, in answer to her questioning look.

'What about the others?' Amy would have to find Duncan later – to give him the envelope in her bag. But she didn't think he would mind. Thing was, she thought, you can't go back. And, in this case, she wasn't sure there was a way forward either. Not for her and Duncan, at least.

Jake shrugged. 'This is our moment, Amy.'

Our moment . . .

He passed her the glasses. Eased the champagne cork until it popped and fizzed.

Amy laughed and held the glasses up. What was it about champagne? It was irresistible. It made you laugh before you'd even taken a sip.

He took a glass from her. 'To us.' And wound his arm around hers. Under the tan leather jacket she could see the cuffs of his pale-pink linen shirt. Whoever had thought that pink wasn't a manly colour?

'To us,' she murmured. *To us?* What was she saying? What was he saying? She couldn't bring herself to look at him. It must be just a work thing. 'And to the Moroccan event, of course,' she said brightly.

He raised a quizzical eyebrow. 'Of course.' And sipped his champagne. Watched her out of those tea-coloured eyes of his. Long lashes, she thought.

Once again, he had got too close. Amy wasn't sure what to say. She disentangled herself. They sat down at the glass table, and she, for one, was glad of the distance it put between them. Too much closeness could be disconcerting. 'So everything's ready for tomorrow?'

'We just need the people.' He smiled at her with such warmth that Amy felt it graze over her, like sunshine.

'They'll come.' There had been articles and pictures in the local papers and magazines and interviews on local radio – she'd done one herself. They'd even had a mention in the national press, as Duncan had shown her the other day, pleased as Punch, of course. Jake had sparked an interest at the right time. He had used the anniversary of the first emissary travelling from Morocco to Britain in 1213 as a pitch, and this had hit the perfect note with the public, it seemed. Timing was all. Interest in Morocco was on the up.

Jake glanced at his watch. 'And in an hour we have the preview,' he reminded her.

'An hour? I'd better go home and get changed.' Amy put down her glass. They had made up a small guest list for a drinks reception and preview; it included a few special friends – including her parents, her Great-aunt Lil, Nell and Callum (Nell had rung her yesterday on Christmas Day, no less, to tell her in a breathy voice that Callum was back in her life. And Amy was happy for her, of course), Francine and Mike – and the press. Jake had invited a few people, too, as had Duncan, and the workshop leaders and artists would also be there, about thirty of them in total.

Jake put his hand on hers. 'You look lovely as you are.'

Amy looked down at her hand, cocooned under the warmth of his, and then at her usual gallery uniform of long black skirt, white cotton blouse and close-fitting jacket. 'Thanks, but . . .' She wanted to look a little more glamorous.

'Amy . . .'

'Yes?' He hadn't taken his hand away. If she reached across the table she could brush off that tiny fleck of dust from the shoulder of his leather jacket. She wouldn't, though; of course she wouldn't.

'I may not get much of a chance to speak to you later.'

He seemed very serious. Why not? she wondered. Would they both be so in demand? And she felt a slight dip of disappointment. In her mind's eye she had half imagined going out somewhere with him afterwards. For dinner, perhaps. Maybe he might lean over the table and take her hand. Suggest that they dance − so it would have to be somewhere you could wear a long evening dress, have dinner and dance the night away to a big band. She would glide on to the dance floor, he would take her in his arms and she would inhale the scent − *that* scent − of leather and grapefruit; only not leather, because he wouldn't be wearing his leather jacket − and she'd relax into his hold, the two of them moving effortlessly with the music. At the end of the evening he would try to kiss her, but she would stop him with a tap of her fan − she must remember to bring a fan − and tell him. Tell him . . . No. You are just a fantasy.

'Amy?' He frowned.

'Yes?' She realized he had taken his hand away.

'Things have turned around for me lately,' he said.

'Turned around?'

'Everything's been going so well.' He sighed. 'What I said to you that night in the pub . . . I just wanted to tell you that it doesn't matter any more.'

She knew what he was referring to, of course. His wife running off with his best friend. But why didn't it matter any more? What could have happened? And what was he trying to tell her?

'Thing is, I'd like us to stay in touch,' he said. 'After all this has finished.'

She blinked at him. There was simply no sign. No drawing her closer. No smile. Nothing. He'd even taken his hand from hers. And what was that about his ex-wife? What kind of a turnaround? In what way was everything going better for him now? Had he met someone? 'I'm sure we will,' she said. 'Any time you need a photographer . . .'

It was meant to be a joke, but he didn't laugh. Instead, he got to his feet, and she did the same.

'See you later, then.' He gave her one last, long look, nodded and left the room.

For a moment, Amy felt strangely bereft. She picked up the half-empty champagne bottle and took it to Duncan's office. He wasn't around, so she left it on his desk, took the envelope from her bag and propped that next to it.

She was just about to leave when a sheet of paper caught her eye. A guest list, she realized. For the reception. Automatically, she ran her gaze down it. Most people she knew or had heard of; there were her personal guests and Duncan's. Jake Tarrant, Melanie Tarrant. *Melanie Tarrant . . .?* She froze. Who was Melanie Tarrant? A relative? Not his mother, she guessed, with a name like Melanie. Surely it couldn't be his ex? And yet she remembered his expression when he'd talked about her in the pub. He wasn't over her. Any fool could see that. What had he said just now? *Things have turned around for me lately . . .* What things? Could she have come back into his life? Was that it? He had told Amy he wouldn't be able to talk to her tonight. So why the champagne? What was he up to? Was it going to be like Duncan all over again? Was that what he was after? Or was it purely a work thing, after all?

She must go. She had to get home and get changed and be back here before anyone else arrived. But she didn't feel as if there was any hurry. Suddenly, Amy was not looking forward to the evening quite as much as she had before.

At the reception, Amy spotted Melanie Tarrant immediately. For one thing, she was stunning, with blonde hair artfully put up, a few delicate tendrils wisping around her graceful neck, simple and understated gold jewellery, an elegant black maxi-dress and a figure to die for. For another, Jake was standing close beside her, his hand on the small of her back, as he introduced her to Duncan. She couldn't be a relative – there was no family likeness. And there was a proprietorial look about Jake tonight in his dark, well-cut suit, cream shirt and maroon tie. This was his wife, she was sure of it. Amy, in the red silk vintage dress she had thought so stunning when she tried it on in the shop a week ago, felt a frump. She wished the ground would open up and swallow her whole. But instead she had to smile, chat, sip champagne and pretend she'd forgotten about that other bottle of champagne that had been opened only an hour and a half earlier.

And then Nell arrived. She looked so happy. Pregnancy suited her, thought Amy. Or something. She had been concerned when Nell confided in her just before Christmas; it wasn't the best to time to find out you were pregnant, when you'd just decided to split up with your husband. But even then, Amy had a strong feeling that it wasn't over between them. Nell was wearing a blue dress that fizzed with lace, high heels and a delicate silver teardrop pendant necklace and earrings, and there was a tall, good-looking, outdoorsy sort of man standing protectively by her side. Callum.

'Amy!' They hugged, and Nell introduced them.

'It's good to meet you,' said Callum. He had warm hazel eyes and a sincerity in his voice that Amy liked immediately. He seemed calmer than she'd imagined and more relaxed.

'And you,' she said. 'Welcome to the Moroccan event. Can I get you a drink?' She beckoned over the waitress who was working for them that night.

'Thanks,' he said. 'This is amazing. What you've done here, I mean.'

Nell nodded enthusiastically. She grabbed Amy's arm. 'Amy,' she said. 'We have to talk.'

'Yes, of course. It's a bit tricky now, though. Come and meet my family.'

Amy introduced them to her parents and to her great-aunt.

'Are you a relative, dear?' Auntie Lil said, peering closely at Nell.

Bless her. It had been hard to equate the Mary of her aunt's story with the grandmother Amy had known. And she knew that Aunt Lil had been worried that Amy would blame her, that she wouldn't understand. But Amy had felt immediate sympathy for the young Lillian who had lived in her sister's glamorous, golden shadow. She had never been close to her grandmother, not like she had to Aunt Lil. Her grandmother had suffered from ill health for as long as Amy could remember; she had died when Amy was still quite young. It was unfair. But she had never really known her, she supposed. As for her grandfather, he had died in a farming accident before Amy was born, and she knew her mother had taken this very hard. They had been close. No wonder her mother had thrown herself into work. She had been escaping, just as much as Amy had.

'Just a special friend,' Amy told her aunt, squeezing Nell's arm. 'This is Francine. And Mike.' She leaned towards Nell. 'Come on, I'll show you the Saffron Room.'

She saw Callum's fingers touch Nell's. 'I'll stay here for a bit,' he said. And he turned to Mike and Francine. Amy was glad they had made it; she knew it wasn't easy with young children, and that practically every social occasion required a babysitter. But Francine was a good friend, too.

'Are you OK?' Amy asked Nell as they squeezed through. 'Callum –'

'Oh, it's not about Callum . . .'

'I'm happy for you.' Amy gave her a quick hug.

'Thanks,' Nell whispered.

But the Saffron Room was full of people, too. The press were taking photographs, and Amy was pushed into posing with Duncan. When they discovered she was the photographer whose exhibition was in the main hall, back they went

459

in there to stand in front of the image of the saffron field. Francine, sleek and elegant in a figure-hugging black cocktail dress, was watching. She shot Amy a wink.

'Move in a bit closer, please,' the journalist requested. 'That's better.'

Duncan was grinning like the proverbial cat with the cream. He put his arm around her waist, and Amy glanced across the room to see Jake looking their way. He was frowning. Well, what was she supposed to do? Say, Sorry, I don't want to have a photo taken with my boss; he's also my former lover? It was hardly her fault that the press were giving all the kudos to herself and Duncan rather than to the events manager who had organized virtually the whole thing.

'What's happening with Jake?' Nell hissed at her when the photographer finally let them go. She was looking over to where he was standing. 'And who's that with him?' She seemed about to go over.

'Don't.' Amy put a hand on her arm. 'That's his wife.'

'His wife?'

'Don't stare.'

Nell's eyes were wide. 'I didn't know he was married.'

'She was his ex-wife,' Amy said. 'Until very recently.'

'Oh, Amy.'

'It's fine, Nell.' The last thing she wanted was sympathy. But she was almost surprised to discover that it wasn't fine – not at all.

'Are you sure you're not misreading the situation?' Nell asked. She looked over again, and waved but, thankfully, stayed by Amy's side. Amy didn't think she could bear watching Nell chatting to Mrs Melanie Tarrant, not tonight.

'How can I be? How can you misread a wife?' Either she wasn't there – or she was.

Duncan said a few words about this year being the anniversary of the first diplomatic links between England and Morocco, making a joke about King John promising to become a Muslim and how Morocco was partly responsible for the Magna Carta. People laughed politely. He talked of how Britain, intimately close to Morocco for the four hundred, if perhaps not quite all the seven hundred years before the First World War, was beginning to reassert its friendship in a new and very appropriate way. And he thanked Amy and Jake and everyone else who had helped in bringing the event to the gallery.

Somehow, Amy got through the evening, skipping a path between her guests and people who were interested in the photos, all the time managing to avoid Jake Tarrant and his glamorous wife. He had said it himself: *I may not get much of a chance to speak to you later.* Damn right.

By nine thirty there were only a few stragglers left at the gallery. Amy's family had gone home, but Jake and Melanie were still there. Loyally, Nell had stayed by Amy's side, but now Amy could stand it no longer. 'Let's go for a pizza or something,' she said to Nell. 'I'm starving.'

'In that dress?' Nell stared at her.

She shrugged. It was a long way from how she had imagined the evening might end, but that was the curse of a vivid imagination. Probably better to read a lot of books and live in your dreams.

Callum had to pick something up from the car, and then they walked around the corner to a small Italian place up the high street.

'So what did you think?' Amy asked, when the three of them were settled at a table by the window.

'It was wonderful,' Nell said. 'We were really impressed with the whole thing. Especially your photographs.' She looked at Callum, who nodded and smiled. 'And thanks so much for putting out my flyers.'

Amy squeezed her hand. 'I want The Saffron House to succeed,' she said.

Nell glanced at Callum. 'Thanks,' she said. 'Only . . .'

'Only?'

'Amy, there's something I need to tell you,' she said. 'Something I need to show you.' From the canvas bag Callum had taken from the car, she pulled a book. An old book, some sort of leather-bound notebook.

'What's this?'

'It's a journal,' she said. 'A true story.'

'Who wrote it?' Amy was confused.

'Oh, Amy.' Nell's face was a picture. She looked excited, puzzled, sad and happy, all at the same time. 'There's so much to say. I don't really know how to begin.'

CHAPTER 48

Morocco, 2013

Glenn had no idea where the years had gone. But he did know that he was dying. For some time now, he had felt something evil eating away at him from inside, a cancer. And, one day, he could no longer get up in the morning. A woman from the village came to tend to him; he wanted nothing more. Not a doctor or a hospital. That would kill him soon enough, all right. The woman made calming teas from her own recipes, and broth, which she spooned into his mouth, though he felt he could stomach nothing.

Malik came in to see him every day. He was a good boy. He would go far. He had no father and so Glenn had tried to instill in him some of the knowledge that Mustapha had given him, the wisdom of the world. He had taught him English, too – this would be useful. But Malik was bright; he, too, would find his own way.

Glenn would soon be able to depart the world in peace. 'God rest your soul,' he whispered to Bethany. And he hoped that, wherever she was, now, at least, she could hear him.

He had not gone to England to find her – how could he, after what Howard had told him that night? The thought that she had desired Howard, too, the pain of betrayal, hung heavy in his heart. Instead, he returned with Mustapha to the saffron farm, and he had made his life here. Mustapha had given him a hut to live in. It wasn't much, but it was shelter, and Glenn had learnt to be practical. He had mended the roof and patched up the walls. Fadma had given him some simple cooking utensils and a square of faded, frayed carpet. He had removed himself, he realized, from the materialistic world. How could he go back to America now? And what would he find if he did? Cowardice had always been his secret shame, but he had put that behind him here. Besides, he had made the break with his family so long ago, could the rift ever be mended? Could he ever return to America and know for sure he wasn't putting his mother in danger by reminding the old man of his existence?

Glenn had thought about this a lot in the early months. He had thought about his father and what he must have gone through in that war he used to talk of, in France, at Omaha Beach and beyond; what it might have done to him. Nothing could excuse him, but Glenn worked hard and reflected and finally found some forgiveness in his heart for his father.

He wrote to his parents, then. Separate letters. One to his mother, expressing his love and his regret. One to his father, seeking reconciliation. He appealed to his father's better nature: he was a war hero; he must have one, surely? His father had been his enemy and the clash between them had ripped their family apart. But perhaps the old man had mellowed with age?

Glenn waited and waited, but there was no reply. That was his answer, then. And perhaps it was for the best. He had run, and now it was safer to stay away, to make a clean break. To return would only cause pain. Apart from seeing his mother, he had no wish to go back – even for a visit. It seemed alien to him now; that entire world seemed alien. In truth, he was no longer Glenn. He had stopped being Glenn many years ago and stopped being American, too. It hadn't been an easy decision. But he had renounced the country of his birth for what they had done – to him, to countless men who had been sent to Vietnam, and to those who had not.

He had been living at the farm for twenty years when Mustapha's wife, Fadma, fell ill. Glenn had done what he could to help, and he was aware that Mustapha had begun to depend on him, treat him even more like the son he had lost. One day he had to go back to Essaouira on an errand for the old man, and that was the day he ran into Gizmo in the square. The weird thing was that Gizmo had hardly changed. As for Glenn – his old friend didn't even recognize him at first.

'Far out,' he kept saying, his brown eyes widening with delight. 'Far out. Didn't I always say we might meet up again on the road one day, huh? Didn't I?' And he clapped Glenn on the back.

'Yeah, you sure did.' This was hardly 'on the road', but Glenn let it pass. 'So you never left Morocco then, Giz?'

He spread his hands. 'Why would I, man? It's home, right?'

Glenn had to laugh. 'It is, yeah.' Or it had become so.

'But I thought you were heading to the UK,' Gizmo went

on. 'You and Bethany. You were the real thing, you know? What the hell happened to you two guys, anyway?'

Glenn wasn't sure he wanted to talk about Bethany. It had hurt him; she had hurt him. He was over it now, but what was the point of opening old wounds? 'Oh, you know . . .'

But Giz was waiting.

'Turned out she had a bit of a thing with Howard, too. So there was no point following her and making an idiot of myself.' He paused. 'What?'

Gizmo was staring at him like he'd gone crazy. 'No way,' he said. 'She weren't interested in Howard. He had a thing about her, yeah. But he was just jealous of you two dudes. He seemed cool, but the guy was bitter, y'know.'

'Yeah.' Glenn knew. 'So why did you leave the riad, Giz?'

Gizmo looked out towards the sea. 'I always liked Howard,' he said. 'But after you left it weren't the same. He kept losing it, man.' He shook his head. 'He was married back in Oz, y'know.'

'He was?' That was news to Glenn.

'He didn't talk about it much. She took the kids and most of his dosh. He was so pissed with her he even had the snip –'

'What did you say, Giz?' Glenn's head was pounding.

'He even had the snip, man. Said he weren't interested in any of that serious commitment stuff. Guess he changed his mind when he saw how happy you and Bethany were, huh?'

How happy they were . . . That's when it all fell into place for Glenn. That's when it all made sense.

It had been good to see Gizmo. *Bethany . . .* Was Gizmo

right? Had she never been interested in Howard? But Glenn was a different person now and he couldn't contemplate trying to find her after all these years. He couldn't leave Mustapha and Fadma – they relied on him – there was no one else – and Fadma's illness had left Glenn concerned not only for her but for Mustapha's mental health. And it was too long ago. It was done. Bethany had left him, whatever the reason. He had given up a lot. But at least here at the farm he had found that place to be that Mustapha had spoken of. Against all odds, this landscape in the foothills of the Atlas Mountains had given Glenn the peace he'd always craved. And he had learnt, of course, as so many had learnt before him, that true peace comes from within. *There is no other way* . . .

He glanced over at the papers piled on the makeshift table. He used to write poetry. What a romantic he had been. He smiled. But now he had written his own story, exactly as it had happened, or at least as he remembered it, because memories were wispy, insubstantial things, he had found. They blurred and changed with time. They could not be relied on. But there was a core within which *could* be relied on. Anyway, he had written this journal, because he had a story to tell.

Mustapha was left alone when Fadma passed, and when Mustapha died he bequeathed to Glenn what little he had. A few items of furniture from his house – though much had been sold to cover his debts, incurred when Fadma fell ill. And the parchment. But he had given him much more. He had taught Glenn the art of contemplation, the pathway to peace. And he had taught him about saffron.

Bethany. Once, there was a girl who loved saffron. She loved its secrets, its mystery, the way it flowered in November when most plants were fading. She loved the wave upon wave of soft purple and green in the field, petals delicate as butterfly wings. She loved the urgency of the harvesting, the pulling of dusty red threads of gold in dimly lit rooms, voices murmuring and low singing while the pile of threads grew higher. She loved the aroma of saffron drying; its bitter and surprising scent. She loved the way it brought something special to a plate of food, sunshine to the heart. And, best of all, she loved its hint of magic.

In Essaouira, Bethany often used to talk about the Phoenicians and their links with saffron. She had a thing about it. That was why she'd been so excited when she discovered that Essaouira itself was originally the site of an ancient Phoenician city called Mogador. It was the right kind of site for them, she said, lying near the outlet of a coastal estuary with a good natural harbour, a rocky promontory ideal for fortification and having access to stone for building material. The Phoenicians were sailors and explorers, eager to experience the unknown, born to roam.

'Like you and me,' Glenn said.

Her dark eyes glowed. 'Before the Phoenicians arrived in this coastal area of Morocco,' she told him, 'the indigenous people were made up of the Berber tribes.'

Glenn knew this already. They were people that kept to the interior, like the people that lived here in the foothills around the saffron farm.

The Phoenicians, though, were traders as well as explorers, Bethany told him. They opened up new routes and they even settled for short times with natives of other countries. She raised an eyebrow. 'Sometimes they had to spend the winter,' she said. 'So they would dock their boats, do any necessary repairs to the sails or the wood. Sometimes they would just wait for the wind to change.'

'How did the native people receive them?' he asked her. He had no idea how she knew all this, though he got the feeling that it was a story that had been passed down to her through her family.

'Perhaps they distrusted them,' she said. 'Perhaps they were envious that they could drop their ties with such apparent ease.'

'Mmm.'

'Or perhaps,' she said, 'they loved to see the goods they brought from exotic places which others could only dream of. Perhaps they were excited by them. I should think they loved to listen to their stories.'

Glenn loved listening to her stories all right. 'Maybe you have some Phoenician blood in your veins,' he teased her.

'Perhaps.' And Bethany looked back at him rather archly, as if, secretly, she knew this to be true.

'They went to Cornwall, then?' he guessed.

'They did.'

'And what goods do you think they brought there?' he asked her, knowing what her answer would be.

'Of course,' she said. 'Of course they would have brought

saffron. They took it everywhere, it was one of their most prized commodities. It wasn't heavy, it was highly valued, there were so many uses for it. Everyone would have wanted to buy it or barter with it.'

'So the Cornish bought the saffron from the Phoenicians?'

'Or exchanged it for tin. Possibly as long ago as 400BC.'

Glenn whistled. 'You don't say?'

Bethany nodded. 'I'm sure it's true.' And she winked at him. 'How else could saffron have come to be there?'

How else indeed . . .?

Bethany had plunged headlong into the ways of Morocco; she had taken it to her heart. One day she had visited a *shiwofa*, a woman who practised magic. 'Only good magic,' she had told him afterwards. '*Khait zinadi*. She used cards – like an ancient Tarot. A crystal. And the Koran.'

'The Koran?' he echoed.

After that, there was no stopping her. She got herself a pack of Tarot cards and she would sometimes burn incense and do readings, drifting into another world – her other world, he thought now. Come autumn, she would always get broody; watching the weather and the temperature. Then she would take off to a saffron farm near Essaouira for a few weeks to help with the harvesting. She did this every year, and she returned from her community crop-picking re-energized in a subtle way that he didn't understand – though he thought he understood it now. The family legacy of the saffron growing was in her blood – she might be far from home, but she could still be connected to the saffron trail.

When he had seen that girl . . . There was something about the way she walked that reminded him so much of Bethany. It was like a sharp pain in his chest, that reminder. And when she smiled . . . It was Bethany's smile. When she spoke, when she said that her family were from Cornwall and that they grew the saffron crocus, he had felt quite dizzy. How could it be? And yet, how could it not be?

Of course, he had asked her about her mother, and it seemed impossible to hear, to believe that someone as vital as Bethany had died. His Bethany gone . . . It was perhaps the final blow. *God rest her soul.*

He had examined her closely. There *was* a family resemblance to Bethany. Something even more than a walk and a smile – although Bethany was dark and tall and this girl was blonde and blue-eyed. Like Glenn. Like Howard, too, but Howard, he reminded himself, was out of the picture. *Was it possible?* Howard had said Bethany was pregnant and that she was getting rid of her baby. But Howard had lied about other things, too. Howard was a bitter and unhappy man. He had wanted to ask the girl how old she was. But you didn't ask young girls how old they were; he remembered that much of the ways of the world. So he stayed silent. Perhaps there were other families growing the saffron crocus in Cornwall. Perhaps he was looking for resemblances where there were none. And, in the end, if she was indeed Bethany's daughter, brought here by her love of saffron – by her mother's love of saffron – then this was enough.

Even so . . . 'Did your mother ever come out here to Morocco?' he had asked her, because he was unable to resist.

'She never mentioned it.'

She never mentioned it. But Glenn knew what was here in front of his eyes. It wasn't his imagination. He knew it, as well as he had ever known anything, deep within his soul. But why would Bethany never have talked of Morocco? Of him? Had he been so unkind? He sighed, felt the stab of pain that seemed to come with every breath these days. He must let this go, as he had let so many things go. Still, as soon as he recognized the young woman's passion for saffron, as soon as he was as certain as he could be that she was Bethany's child, if not his own, he decided to give her the parchment. She would understand it. Malik was not interested in an old drawing, he had told him. And who else was there?

He could tell that she appreciated the gift. That was his reward. She asked for his address, and that pleased him, too, that she might care to contact him in the future. Not that he had much of a future left, but he did not wish to tell her that. Neither did he know why he had not told her his given name. He didn't know what her mother might have told her about him, but this wasn't the reason. It was his need to stay hidden, his fear of what the world could still hold, his renunciation of everything he had once been. Even the fact, perhaps, that his life was almost over. Besides which, he hardly thought of himself as Glenn any more. Those days had slipped from him like gossamer. And he was happy to let them go.

He wondered sometimes what had brought him here to the saffron farm. Perhaps it was chance, perhaps it was a twist of fate that Mustapha, the man who picked him up in

Essaouira, should live on a settlement that was part of a saffron farm. Not so unusual, he supposed. There were many in these parts. But he had stayed. And it had always been reassuring for Glenn to know that, because he was close to saffron, he was close to Bethany.

The girl – Nell – told him that she had come to find out more about her mother. He hoped that he had helped a little. Everyone deserved the truth. Her mother had a lot of darkness in her life, the girl had said. A bad memory that she never spoke of. This saddened him.

And then, suddenly, it all made sense in the way that things sometimes do, like the click of a light switch illuminating the truth. Howard's swagger. His jealousy. His determination to pay Glenn back – and for what? The fact that he had not fought in Vietnam? That Howard's brother had fought there – and been fucked up by it? That Glenn had found a woman who loved him?

Other things made sense, too. The way Bethany was when she got back from that drugs run: cool, hurt, vulnerable; the distance she put between them, the way she turned away from their intimacy. What had happened? Had Howard forced himself on her? Had he tricked her? Seduced her when she'd had too much to drink or smoke? What? When she'd found out she was pregnant . . . Glenn closed his eyes and searched for calm, for the space that helped him find it . . . He could imagine how she felt then, too. And Glenn knew that this was the truth. He was only surprised that it had taken him this long to see it.

Could he have done anything differently? This thought had not plagued him for a long time. Perhaps he could have. And yet it was as Mustapha had taught him. You walk, you reach a crossroads, you choose which way to go. Not right or wrong but your pathway.

This girl, Nell, had a way of clasping her hands in front of her that made him try to remember. It was all such a long time ago. And then she had laughed. He hadn't heard it for so many years. But it was a distinctive, bubbling laugh – his mother's laugh, he knew. He looked again at her body shape, her height. And he froze.

He had written this down, too. It was the end of his story. *I believe that this young woman is my daughter.*

CHAPTER 49

'Are you honestly telling me that the old man in the mountains was your father?' Amy stared at her. Her pizza was left half eaten on her plate.

'Yes, I am.' It had been a shock to Nell, too. And she hadn't yet told Amy the other half of it.

'I can't believe it,' she said. 'It's such an incredible coincidence, Nell.'

'Not as much as you think.' Nell had thought a lot about this. 'He was in love with my mother. He met her in Paris and lived with her in Morocco for several years. She'd always loved saffron – she must have talked to him about our family's saffron in Cornwall – and, according to his journal, she worked for a few weeks in October and November on a local saffron farm all the time she was in Morocco.'

'So when he was taken to a saffron farm, he decided to stay?' Amy frowned. 'Just like that?'

'He went originally to help with the harvesting,' Nell told her. 'Just like she did every year. It was the beginning of November; it's always a busy time, and they probably try to get as many workers along as they can. And then he fell ill.' Having read the account, she suspected it was some sort of

475

post-viral illness, ME perhaps, maybe even brought on by the stress of her mother leaving him.

'But if he loved her so much, why didn't he come to England to find her?' Amy asked. She absent-mindedly began to chew the edge of her pizza.

Nell thought of the way Amy had been tonight, her obvious sadness that it hadn't worked out with Jake. Nell was sad for her, too. She'd find out what had happened – later.

'Why stay buried on a saffron farm in Morocco?'

It was a good question. Nell wondered how different her life would have been if he had come to Cornwall, to look for her mother. Nell had the distinct feeling that he had been the love of her mother's life, just as she had been his. So she would have been pleased, Nell was sure. She would have opened up to him – eventually. They would have worked things out between them and, probably, they would have been happy. What a terrible waste . . . And yet she couldn't blame Glenn for not going. 'As he got better . . .' She shrugged. '. . . he found out that his housemate in the commune – this Howard – had been involved with her, too. And he also found out that she was pregnant.'

'With you.'

'With me.' Somehow Nell wasn't surprised that she had been conceived in Morocco. The country had touched her so much on so many different levels, not least the cuisine. Now that she had read this story – her father's story – she could see how that could be. It had happened to both her parents, too.

'My mother was a pretty strong character,' she told Amy.

476

She glanced at Callum, who raised an eyebrow and smiled. 'He must have thought she meant it when she told him not to follow her.' She thought of Amy. That was the mistake you sometimes made with strong people. You failed to see their vulnerable side. You didn't see their need to protect themselves from hurt. 'And then there was Howard.' It must have hurt Nell's father deeply to find out that the woman he loved had been involved with another man – especially if that man was Howard. 'When he found out that she'd been pregnant and didn't know who the father was . . . he must have been devastated.'

'And so he stayed at the saffron farm,' Amy said.

'He found peace there. It made him feel close to my mother.' She remembered his wise words that day about finding strength from a different place. She may have only met him once, but he'd still had a profound effect on Nell, and now that she'd read his journal, she felt that she understood him, too. He had helped her, she thought, in his own way. He had given her the old parchment drawing of Smilax and her saffron and he had given her his wisdom, too. Most of all, he'd given Nell her father. How much, she found herself wondering, had the boy Malik known? How much had Hadi told him? Had he guessed that Nell was important to his old friend – from the fact that he'd talked to her and given her the parchment? Or was it because of the connection between them, of England and saffron? Had Malik really sent her the journal after Hadi had died because there was 'no one else'?

'And your mother could never bring herself to tell him

what had happened with Howard?' Amy asked. 'What he had done to her? When she got back to Essaouira, I mean?'

This was the most heartbreaking part of the story for Nell. She had wanted to know the truth about her mother's life and yet it had been hard to read this journal and to conclude – as her father had concluded – that her mother had been raped by Howard. But it confirmed everything that Nell had ever wondered about in her heart of hearts. It explained why her mother would never discuss Nell's father. There were several reasons. She couldn't be sure who he was; to relive the traumatic experience she'd had would be too painful; or she was sheltering her daughter from the knowledge that her father could have been a rapist. Or all three. It explained why she had never talked of Morocco and her life there. It filled in all the gaps in the photo album, the gaps in her mother's life that Nell had always sensed included a dark time, a bad time.

How had she felt, returning to Cornwall alone, pregnant, violated? Nell didn't really want to think about it. But she had to. Because this explained another part of her mother's life and character. Why she had clung to Nell, half afraid to let her go into the world, why she had overprotected her, why she had lived the way she had. Letting men come and go, never allowing them to get close. She had lost her trust. Lost a lot more than Nell's father in Morocco had ever realized. And although Nell had often been angry at her mother – for not telling her what she needed to know – she could certainly understand her reasons.

'And we all know why I was desperate to visit a saffron

farm,' Nell said to the other two. Callum was watching her closely. The past two days with him had been special – a Christmas she would never forget, and one which would sit comfortably in her memories with all those Christmas memories of her childhood. She had shown him parts of her father's memoirs, and she felt – she hoped – that at last he was beginning to understand Nell's compulsion to do what she had to do, to continue her mother's legacy. But there was one thing she hadn't told him.

'But how amazing that it should be that saffron farm,' Amy said.

'It's close to Essaouira.' Although Nell had her own, less logical theories. She wasn't her mother's daughter for nothing. She might not do the Tarot cards very often these days, but she still believed in their power. In Fate. In synchronicity.

'Essaouira . . .' Amy's expression changed. Nell knew what she was thinking about. Or who.

'Amy, prepare yourself for a shock,' said Nell.

'Another one?'

'That's where Hadi lived with my mother,' she said. 'In a small commune. In a riad. And he's only half British.'

Amy blinked back at her.

'He renounced America because of the Vietnam War. He was a pacifist. He refused to fight.' His memoirs had been honest on this subject, too. Nell had gone from not having the faintest idea who her father was to having his entire life, thoughts and feelings spread out in front of her. She understood why he had done what he did; she empathized with his values, his fears, his regrets. In some ways, although she had lived with her for more than twenty years, she had more of an insight into her father's life now than she had ever had into her mother's. Her sadness, though, was that she never knew him. That her father – like her mother – was now dead and lost to her.

'Hadi's father was American and his mother was English. He lived in the US until he was twenty-one years old. He left in 1969.'

Amy stared at her.

Nell took her hands. Her voice dropped to a whisper. 'Before he became known as Hadi,' she said, 'my father's name was Glenn.'

Amy was standing on the doorstep. And there was a young woman with her – the woman who had been with her last night at the reception. Lillian had thought for a moment that she . . . but. 'Come in, come in,' she told them. Was something wrong? Amy had a strange expression on her face – somewhere between a smile and tears. And her friend was looking rather emotional, too. Lillian blinked at them. 'Please,' she heard herself say.

'Come and sit down, Aunt Lil.' Amy had her by the arm now and, really, Lillian had no idea why she had felt as if she were about to fall. They hadn't said anything. And perhaps that was it – they hadn't said anything.

She allowed herself to be helped back into the sitting room and eased into her chair. Amy was fussing over her, and her friend – Nell, wasn't it? – was hovering by the door and looking concerned. Lillian smiled at her reassuringly. She was fine. But she wanted to know what this was all about.

'Aunt Lil.' Amy knelt by her chair. 'When I told you I hadn't found out anything about Glenn in Morocco . . .'

'Yes?' Lillian's senses were on the alert.

'It was true. Or I thought it was true.' She looked up at the young woman in the doorway, at Nell.

Lillian followed her gaze. She saw now that Nell was holding a leather-bound book, clutching it to her breast. She looked back at Amy, waited for her to go on.

'But, actually, we did find out something.' She hesitated, took Lillian's hand. 'We met him,' she whispered.

'Met him?' Lillian stared at her. 'But . . .'

'He was living under another name,' Amy said quickly. 'He was practically a recluse and he lived in a hut on a saffron farm.'

'A saffron farm?' Lillian was struggling to take it in. Amy had met him? But she had used the past tense. *He lived*. Did that mean . . .?

'Yes.' Amy squeezed her hand. 'I'm so sorry, Aunt Lil, but he's not alive, not any more.'

Lillian allowed the pain of this to seep into her consciousness. But she had lost him many years ago, of course. 'Why?' she asked. 'Why was he living on a saffron farm?' Although perhaps she was asking, *why did he never come home?*

'It's a long story,' Amy said. She sat back on her heels. 'I can hardly believe it myself. But Nell says it's all written down in his journal.'

At this, Amy's friend Nell came forward and held out the book she had been holding so close. 'I've read it,' she said. 'And perhaps now you would like to read it, too?'

Lillian nodded. But she felt as if she had been struck dumb.

482

His journal. She stared at the book which Nell had placed in her lap. This was his journal. Wonderingly, she picked it up. She held it to her lips, to her heart. Closed her eyes and whispered his name. 'Glenn.'

When she opened her eyes again Amy and Nell were both looking at her with concern,. Were they worried what the shock might do to her? 'Why did you read it?' she asked Nell. Why was it so important to her? Why had she been holding it so close?

The young woman's eyes filled with tears. 'It turns out that Glenn . . . that Glenn . . .'

'I'm going to make us some tea,' said Amy. 'I think we're going to need it.'

It took Lillian some days to read Glenn's journal. Once, she had been able to decipher his large, untidy handwriting very easily – she had witnessed its transformation from single letters into joined-up writing then into adult script, after all – but now her eyes were weaker and sometimes she needed a magnifying glass. She wouldn't skip anything. She wanted to read and understand every word.

The first pages were clearer. She could tell, perhaps with a mother's instinct, when his health began to deteriorate, when writing became difficult, and then when he could only manage a few sentences before he had to rest. By the time she finally got to the end of the manuscript she had wept so many tears; tears that she never thought she would weep for him.

Her son's story had taken her back, right back, to the start of her life in America.

She got up from the armchair with some difficulty. Her joints were stiff; she had been sitting there too long. She would make some hot chocolate, she decided. And then she would sit quietly and think. Thinking time was undervalued these days, when people spent so long looking at screens and talking on the phone. Glenn, though, had found his thinking time. His story proved that. And she was glad.

Lillian reached for her stick. The truth was that when Glenn had left their family home, Lillian had sensed she would never see him again. She had watched him lope off into the darkness, her tall, gangly son, the rucksack on his back, just one final wave. And it almost broke her.

She didn't cry, though. She returned to the house, acted as if nothing out of the ordinary had happened, closed her mind and her heart and did all the things she usually did. She cooked dinner, washed up, watched television with her husband. She went to bed and she lay there while he relieved his frustration. It wasn't making love. It had never been making love, even at the start. She hadn't been lying when she'd told Amy he had never forgiven her for not being Mary, because that was the way it had always felt. From the moment she'd first arrived in America and seen his face – different, touched by something he hadn't yet experienced when she knew him in England – she'd known that she disappointed him.

Lillian put her stick back in the umbrella stand on the way through to the kitchen. The first time he lost his temper she told herself he was tired; something had gone wrong at work. She hadn't put enough salt in the potatoes and the chops were overdone and this had been the final straw for a man who simply wanted a good dinner at the end of his working day.

'Jesus Christ,' he had said. 'Is it too much to ask?' His eyes had gone curiously blank.

Lillian tried to tell him she was sorry, but before she had the chance he pushed her roughly away from the table. She staggered slightly before regaining her balance. She was shocked. Her father had always been respectful towards her mother; he would never have treated her with such disrespect. Ted went off and out into the garden. He stayed there for half an hour and, by the time he returned, Lillian had calmed herself. It didn't mean anything. Of course it didn't mean anything.

He was calmer, too. He picked up the newspaper and went into the other room to sit down. Later, when he spoke to her to comment on an item of news, it was as if nothing had occurred. And that's how it was for him, she realized.

The second time was when she spoke out in front of his mother. She hadn't meant to show him up; she'd only been making something clear. He had got the dates wrong and she pointed this out. But she saw the anger flare – more than anything, he hated to lose face – and after they got home he grabbed her wrist and twisted it, hard. He was a big man. A strong man. He was ensuring that she understood. She looked him straight back in the eyes. He had that look again – that blank anger. So that was how it was. She understood all right.

She learnt how to deal with him. She learnt what made him angry and she avoided those situations if she could. What point was there in antagonizing a man like him; a man who was driven by something she had no experience of? She cooked what he liked to eat and she made his house comfortable. She took care of all the domestic chores and ensured he always had shirts that were cleaned and ironed. When they went out she let him choose where they should go. She didn't argue with him, she rarely wept, she learnt not only to control her emotions but not to show them at all. And, inside, she turned away from him. Completely and utterly away.

She had made a bad mistake, and this was her punishment. She had to live with it. She couldn't go back to England, not now. Lillian was not Mary. And neither had she meant to hurt Mary. This was not what she'd wanted and not what she'd expected. But it was all she had. So she would get on with her life. She had no choice.

Lillian fetched the milk from the fridge and half filled her mug. She poured it carefully into the pan and replaced the plastic container in the fridge door, trying to suppress the sudden yearning for one of the old glass bottles. Milk had always tasted better from a glass bottle; she remembered having the top of the milk on her cereal as a girl – but only when Mary didn't get there first.

Throughout her marriage, Lillian began slowly to carve out times when she could be herself – when she could walk and think of home and perhaps even cry a little. When she could write long letters to her mother and even to Mary. When she could read a book and immerse herself in a different world that was not of her own foolish making. This was almost enough. In bed, she closed her eyes and let her imagination swoop and soar and take her to some other place, and she remained dutiful and uncomplaining. She must, she thought now, have been the most boring wife in the entire world.

Lillian put the pan of milk on to boil and took the chocolate powder from the cupboard. She didn't hold with microwave ovens, never had. She spooned some powder into her mug and added a little of the milk for mixing. Leant against the cooker for support, half mesmerized by the pan on the boil, the steam rising.

And then there was the gift that had changed her life. Glenn. She had thought then that life would be bearable, even good. That life might, in the end, be more than good. The milk rose in the pan and Lillian got it off just in time. She poured it, stirring, into the mug, put the saucepan in the sink to cool, turned the tap on for a minute to stop it burning on. She put the mug of hot chocolate on her little tray and carried it carefully through, back to the living room.

But as his son grew older, so Ted became stricter, more set in his ways. And when Ted and Glenn began to argue, Lillian had a different battle on her hands. It was called keeping the peace. And it was a battle she was never going to win. Lillian put the tray on her little table and lowered herself back into the armchair. She had paid for her son's leaving. It was a few days later. Glenn had not returned home and Ted demanded to know the truth.

'Tell me, woman,' he snarled. 'Tell me what you've done.' He had her by the wrist and he slapped her hard with the back of his free hand.

Her teeth seemed to jangle inside her mouth. She thought she tasted blood. She knew that he wouldn't stop hitting her until she told him. Perhaps he'd never stop hitting her, anyway. So she told him. She looked into his blank eyes and she told him. By now, Glenn would be free.

He shook with anger. 'Why the hell shouldn't he fight?' he yelled at her. 'Stupid, interfering bitch. Do you want your own son to be called a coward?'

Was that all that mattered to him? 'I don't want him to die,' she cried. 'And I don't want him to be destroyed by war in any other way either. Like –'

'Like me?' His grip on her wrist tightened and stung.

In that moment, she knew he hated her. Perhaps he'd hated her from the moment she first set foot on American soil.

He put his hands around her throat. 'Like me?'

She looked into his blank eyes. She'd seen him so often just sitting, gazing into space, into the distance. Looking back, perhaps. Remembering Omaha Beach and the rest of his war? Or remembering Bridport and Mary? Did he have flashbacks? She knew he had nightmares sometimes, and she'd tried to help him, tried to hold him in her arms and comfort him. But he'd always resisted, always pretended, always told only stories where he was the brave one, where violence solved everything.

'Like you. Yes. Like you.' It was the closest she'd ever got. For a moment she saw it flicker in his eyes, the truth about war and killing and how he really felt, and then he blinked it away and it was gone. She'd always thought that if only she could get through to him, if only she could help him let go . . . But.

'I'll teach you.'

It was the only time Ted had really let rip, and it had left her battered and bruised. She had fought back – up to a point. She had struggled and kicked out at him, but it only seemed to inflame him more. He pinned her arms behind her and he slapped her again around the face. Her cheek stung. Her skin was on fire. He punched her in the stomach and she doubled up in pain; almost imagined she would never breathe again. And he half strangled the life out of her. Lillian had bruise marks on her neck for weeks. Finally, he left her crumpled in a heap on the kitchen floor and walked out of the house to drink the rest of his anger away.

Lillian put a hand on her neck at the memory. She could still feel that pain. She didn't regret what she'd done, though – not for a second.

Because Glenn hadn't fought. And Lillian was grateful that she had protected him from this. Perhaps it was even a good thing that Glenn hadn't returned home while his father was alive. How long would it have been before her son tried to protect her? How long before Ted turned on him? She shivered. She had saved them both from that, at least.

Lillian sipped her hot chocolate. For years she had not wanted to think of these times. But she was safe now, and reading Glenn's story had helped her review her own. People might wonder why she hadn't left Ted – especially once Glenn had gone. Lillian wasn't sure there was an easy answer. These days, relationships were different. In those days, if you'd made your bed . . .

It wasn't Ted's fault, what had happened, what had changed him, what he had been through. Lillian's sacrifice had protected Glenn from that. But what kind of a life had her son experienced instead? She had thought she would never know. She had told him not to contact her unless there was an emergency; she didn't want to risk Ted finding out, discovering his son's whereabouts, even informing the authorities, because she had no doubt he'd do this – and more.

But one day there was the postcard. She looked over to where it stood, propped against the shelf of the bureau. What a marvellous day that had been. She couldn't see it clearly from here, but she knew the picture so well; the blue door slightly ajar, the archway, the flower that Amy had told her was called the rose of Mogador. And on the back of the card – the Moroccan stamp. Essaouira, Amy had said. And just a few precious words from her son.

She had treasured that postcard, hidden it in a drawer, read it over and over in moments when she was alone, and thanked God that her husband had never seen it and that she'd been first to the post the morning it arrived. The postcard told her that her son was safe. It was all she needed. After the amnesty, she had hoped . . . Of course, she had hoped. But she had never received the letter Glenn had written later, nor known of one sent to Ted — according to this account. Had Ted destroyed his letter — and hers too? It was possible, probable even. He wasn't the sort of man to forgive.

Lillian paused as she remembered the afternoon she'd found him, the afternoon he died. She'd been out to the store to buy groceries and had left him mowing the lawn. He was obsessed with that lawn; it had to be kept as shorn and neat as his own hair had been, it had to be mown in straight lines and the edges clipped with shears. No matter how tired he was, if the lawn was anything less than perfect, then Ted had to see to it. That afternoon was no exception. 'You need to rest,' she'd told him.

'I know what I need to do,' he'd growled back at her.

Lillian had left him to it.

There had probably been a moment when he knew he should stop, when he was aware he was pushing himself too much. But he never would have stopped — so the heart attack stopped him instead.

Lillian finished her drink and put the mug back on the tray. Outside, the soft orange light from the street lamp was creeping through the gap in the curtains, along with the darkness of the night. It was late. She wondered what Amy was doing. She was a good girl, and Lillian hoped her great-niece would find what she was looking for. Amy now knew Lillian's secret. And, despite it all, she still loved her.

Lillian got up to take the tray back to the kitchen. She'd go to bed now, she decided. It had been a long day – and an emotional one. She thought that she probably loved Ted more after death than she had when he was alive. When he'd passed on – that's when she was free to remember the early days; in the war when she'd first laid eyes on the handsome GI in his smart khaki uniform, when he'd thrown her his address wrapped up with some chewing gum, when he'd called her 'Duchess' and when he'd written to her and told her all his hopes, his sadnesses and his dreams.

Lillian left the tray in the kitchen, made sure everything was switched off and headed for the stairs. Amy had mentioned a stair lift but she hoped it wouldn't come to that. Neither did she want to move again, though she could if necessary. A nice bungalow wasn't totally out of the question – if it wasn't too late.

She had been surprised to discover that Ted had left her comfortably off. Lillian had never had much to do with the finances of the household. She found out after his death that his parents had left him a decent financial legacy and that he, too, had invested wisely. So . . . Lillian smiled to herself. Six months after he died, she'd employed a private detective to try and trace her son.

He had found nothing. Lillian reached the landing, exhaled

and went into the bathroom. She stared into the mirror. Could this really be her – this white-haired old lady peering back at her with faded blue eyes? It had been as if Glenn had disappeared without trace, as if he were determined not to be found. But now . . . She felt as if he were right here with her at this moment. She leaned on the sink to steady herself. Right here. Thanks to this young woman, thanks to Nell – who was, she had told Lillian, her voice faltering, her blue eyes filling with tears, her granddaughter . . . She had been able to find out his story.

Even Mary had forgiven her – Lillian was sure of this, though they had never talked of it. Mary hadn't talked to anyone much; she had become a diminished woman; it broke Lillian's heart to see her. She used to watch Lillian sometimes, though, with those same dark eyes and, once, she'd squeezed her hand. Lillian wondered if she was thinking, if she was remembering. She'd had such a fizz of life, her sister. Had she been happy with Johnnie Coombes? Lillian thought of what Celia had told her. She hoped so.

Lillian finished in the bathroom and made her way to bed. Tonight, she would be happy to get between those sheets. She was glad that Glenn had found peace and a place where he could be. And she was glad, too, that he had given her a granddaughter. More than he could ever know. A part of him to love and to care for. A part of him that lived on.

She seemed such a lovely, such a caring girl. And she was expecting a child herself. Lillian would be a great-grandmother. She could hardly believe this. That morning, when they'd brought round the journal, when they'd told her about Glenn . . . She, Amy and Lillian had sat together talking gently and drinking tea. And then they had seemed to know that Lillian needed to be alone with her son. They had walked out of the front door and Lillian had taken a deep breath, opened his journal and begun at last to read his story.

CHAPTER 51

One day in early spring Nell went to the village to buy hyacinths and, coming out of the florists, she bumped into Tania, one of her mother's oldest friends. In the early days, she had avoided people like Tania. There weren't many; generally, her mother had been a solitary soul. But there were a few women she'd had time for and Tania was one of them. She was an artist – she painted watercolours, which were sold in the small gallery in St Mawes and in a shop in Falmouth. The paintings were sketchy and vague – a bit like Tania herself, who had been married to a potter and divorced and who tended to waft around the place like a lost soul, painting as she went. But she had always come up to the farmhouse for the saffron harvest. She was one of a small circle of women who knew Nell's mother, who hadn't just thought her strange with her field of saffron crocuses and her rather eccentric behaviour.

Tania stopped as though she'd seen a ghost. For the first time, it occurred to Nell that other people missed her mother, too.

'Nell, how are you?' Tania had long, pale hair and eyelashes that were almost invisible. She put her hands on Nell's shoulders, as if to pin her down and stop her from running away. 'I meant to come and see you.' Her eyelids flickered, and Nell knew that this wasn't quite true.

'Thanks.' Though Nell was glad she hadn't. 'I'm well, actually.'

Tania drew back to inspect her. Her pale artist's eyes narrowed. 'Are you –?'

'Yes.' She felt herself blush. She was always surprised that people could tell so soon.

'When's it due?'

'Late August. It's still quite early days.'

Nell felt herself enfolded in Tania's watery embrace.

'Ah. Your mother would be so happy.'

'Yes.' Nell could see her as a grandmother. She would get down on all fours and play with the baby, pull silly faces until he or she laughed and gurgled. She would make a rattle out of something she happened to have in the kitchen and knit a cuddly toy and she would keep him – or her – amused for hours with her songs and her stories and her games. She would sing lullabies and if the baby woke in the night she would rock him – or her – back to sleep under the light of the moon. She would laugh – loudly – and when the baby got older she would talk to him or her about the Tarot and saffron. She would defy every convention under the sun. She would be nothing like the grandmother Nell now had – tiny Lillian, her father's mother, who had lost her son all those years ago.

Nell had liked Amy's great-aunt on sight. Not least because

she knew how much Amy loved her. 'Are you a relative, dear?' she had asked in her sweet, rather wavery voice at the reception for the Moroccan event in Lyme. That made Nell smile now. Had Lillian recognized her somehow? Or had she just been confused?

'What made you think I was a relative?' Nell had asked her when Amy took Nell to her grandmother's cottage the following day, after she had given her Glenn's journal, as they sat drinking tea.

'You have the look of your father, my dear,' she replied. She might be old, but she definitely wasn't confused.

The look of your father . . . And Nell realized that's how it was with families. You had a bit of this and a bit of that. You could see a part of someone's ancestry in the slant of a cheekbone, a blink of an eye or a curve of a smile. She had a grandmother! Nell could hardly believe it. And she had other relatives, too – several of them, including Amy, who was now her second cousin, so she'd gleefully informed her. If two people were first cousins – in this case, Amy's mother and Nell's father – then their children were second cousins, apparently. No wonder they had been so drawn to each other in Morocco, no wonder they had become such great friends. Nell grew thoughtful. She had lost her parents and no one could ever replace them. But how wonderful was that, to have this new family?

'And what's happening about the farmhouse?' Tania's light-blue eyes grew troubled. 'I saw it was up for sale last autumn. I couldn't imagine –'

'We've moved back in,' Nell told her.

'Oh my goodness.' Tania shook her head. 'That's fantastic news. I was going to say I couldn't imagine anyone else living there. She'd be so pleased.'

'I think she would,' Nell agreed. 'But I'm doing it for us. Me and Callum. We're changing some things, of course.' She thought of her mother's Tarot cards wrapped in the purple silk scarf, still tucked on the shelf on the dresser. But not others, she thought. The cards had helped her hear her mother's voice, they had helped her make decisions when she'd been overcome with grief and unable to think straight. They were a prop. Perhaps she didn't need them any longer. But she'd keep them for ever. 'We have to look to the future. We're a family now.'

Tania nodded as if she understood.

'And will you still grow it? The saffron?'

It was, Nell supposed, a bit of a local legend. 'Oh, yes,' she said. That was another thing that wouldn't be changing. Only, this year, Callum would be in charge of the planting and the growing. He'd even said he was looking forward to it. 'I hope you'll still come and help with the harvesting, too?'

'Just like the old days.' Tania was wistful.

'We're going to open a pop-up restaurant,' Nell said. Which was not remotely like the old days.

'In the farmhouse?'

'Yes.' Nell scrabbled in her bag to find a flyer. She handed it to Tania. 'We're calling it The Saffron House. Moroccan food will be our speciality.'

'Gracious.'

'I hope you'll come over one evening?'

'Oh, I definitely will.' Tania looked thoughtful. 'Your mother came to see me, you know,' she said. 'The night she died.'

'Did she?' Nell felt a shiver of foreboding. Would she want to hear this? She had put her mother to rest in her mind. She didn't want to open any wounds, not now. 'How was she?' What was she asking exactly? *Did she seem as if she might be about to throw herself off a cliff?* She had come to accept so much. But she still couldn't quite accept this; it still seemed like such a selfish act.

Tania looked into the distance, towards the sea, as if this might help her answer the question. The baker who sold saffron buns came out of his shop for a moment and waved. They both waved back, as if everything was fine, really fine, and they weren't having this conversation. 'It was a weak moment,' Tania said.

'Yes.' Nell's voice sounded clipped to her own ears. But at the same time she wondered. Did Tania know something? At the very least she must have sensed her mood. She had been with her.

'We had a glass or two of wine. She wanted to talk. That wasn't like Bethany.' She looked at Nell. 'Well, you know.'

'What did you talk about?'

'She made me promise not to say anything to anybody.'

'Oh.'

'And I thought at the time . . .'

Nell waited.

499

'That it wasn't fair. For you not to know. For her to do nothing.'

'Nothing?' Nell stuck her free hand in the pocket of her coat. She was cold. Even the blue hyacinths wrapped in brown paper seemed to be shivering. She was a bit scared, too – of where this conversation might be going.

'She was ill.' Tania put a hand on her arm. 'I'm telling you now because it may help you to know, Nell. She was ill.'

'What was wrong with her?' Nell whispered. It wasn't what she had been expecting.

'I have no idea.' Tania spread her hands. 'She didn't say. But she didn't want surgery, she said. Doctors prodding her around.'

'No, she wouldn't.' Her mother had distrusted doctors at the best of times. Nell thought of how she had refused to re-plant the saffron that year, how she'd wanted to sell off some of the land. She and Callum had even wondered if she was punishing them for Nell moving out. But what if she really couldn't manage it alone any longer? What if she knew her time was running out, just like Nell's father had known his was? It was a chilling thought. But it would explain a lot.

'Are you all right, Nell?' Tania looked worried. 'You do understand why –?'

'No, you were right to tell me. Thank you.' Nell turned away. Who would know what was wrong with her? None of her other women friends; she was so proud. As Tania had said, she'd only told her in a weak moment. Their local doctor? This was even more unlikely. Could her mother have caught some disease while travelling when she was younger? Was it something that could have been cured – if she'd gone for help? But, in the end . . . Nell sighed. What did it matter now? She could get upset over it, she could berate herself for not noticing, for not being there for her, but, ultimately, it had been her mother's decision, and the responsibility for it was hers. If it had been a decision, Nell reminded herself, and not an accident.

She got in the car and drove to the end of the lane, near to the spot where her mother had died. She climbed out of the car and walked to the exact place, the blue hyacinths in her hand. She took flowers whenever she could. Bulbs were best; they lasted longer, and these were planted in a shallow brown pot. She looked down at the ground. The last bunch of flowers she'd left had wilted now. She picked them up and replaced them with the hyacinths, taking the brown paper away and crumpling it into her coat pocket. Her mother had loved the scent of hyacinths. Nell hoped that the fragrance would rise in the wind and that, somehow, it would reach her. *Wishing on the wind.* She touched her saffron and silver necklace, which was nestling under her coat.

Saffron had been her mother's sunshine. Just as Nell was. Her mother had made mistakes. She had overprotected Nell. But how could she blame her when she'd done it for all the right reasons, for love? And the important part of her mother . . . Nell had known that all along. It had filled her childhood every day. It was about love and sunlight and healing. And no one could take that away from her.

Nell stood on the edge of the cliff, almost as close as her mother had. Below her, the waves were crashing on to the rocks. No one could fall – or jump – and survive. It was impossible. The sea was olive-grey, its winter shade, almost merging into the damp mist of the horizon, the leaden grey of the sky above. But on that night her mother wouldn't have seen the ocean – unless there had been a full moon and a cloudless sky. She would have heard it, though – the roar and the rush of the tide, the crackle of water breaking on stone. She would have seen only darkness and the oily, liquid gleam of the ocean below. She would have jumped – or fallen – into an inky nothingness, a deep void of cold air and wind tunnelling around her. Until she hit rock bottom.

Why? Nell felt the tears hot on her cheeks as she turned her face to the wind. She had come to see that her mother was more emotionally fragile than she had ever realized. She was ill. She was in pain. Maybe she was even dying? Was that the reason why?

'Nell!'

She spun around in surprise. Callum's truck was parked next to her car and he was striding towards her. 'Nell! What the hell are you doing?'

'Nothing!' She yelled back. Well, not nothing. She was bringing flowers. Seeing how it felt to be on the edge. Had it felt like that for her mother? Had she jumped deliberately? Or had she simply lost her way?

'Be careful.' Callum was breathless. 'Come away from the edge.'

'I wanted to feel what it was like for her.' Her words disappeared in the wind.

'But not for you.' He was by her side now. 'Not for us.'

'Of course not.' She smiled. Held out her hand.

'You're not unhappy?' Gently, he took her hand and pulled.

She stepped away from the edge. She really had been awfully close.

'About us? About the baby?' He rested a hand on her stomach.

'Oh, Callum. Of course not.' Things were different between them now. And the baby was a gift. It was astonishing. With death came new life; it was the way of the world.

'But we didn't plan it.' He frowned. 'And . . .'

Nell laughed. 'Life takes no notice of plans.' Like agreements, really. Life made its own decisions.

'And the restaurant. You had so many ideas . . .'

'*Have* so many ideas,' she corrected him. 'The baby doesn't change a thing.' *The baby*. A real, live he or she, growing in her womb. A death, or two deaths, and now, this life. It was a good thought to cling on to.

'It doesn't?' He blinked at her.

''Course not.' It was hard for Callum, with his well-ordered way of doing things. She knew that. She took his other hand. 'I can delegate. You've heard of house husbands, haven't you?'

'Nell . . .'

She reached up on tiptoe to kiss him. 'I'm joking.' Fingers

crossed behind her back. 'But since when did having a baby stop a woman from working? I might have to take a few months off, that's all.'

'That's good,' he said.

'It's very good.'

Nell let go of him. She moved forward again, bent to touch the hyacinths on the clifftop grave. 'Bye, Mum,' she said. 'Happy dreams.'

She and Callum linked arms and walked back along the cliff. The wind was tearing at her hair, stinging her cold lips. 'This is a new start for us, Callum,' Nell said. How did you get to know someone anyway? You fell in love with them and then you talked. About everything. Callum hadn't known her because she hadn't given him the chance to know her; she had kept too much inside – she'd never let him in. There were other things, too. You gave them top priority in your life – which she'd never really done before. You spent time with them. You shared. You grew up. You fell in love with them all over again.

'I know.' He sounded very sure.

'And for the baby,' she whispered.

Had she walked over deliberately, or had she lost her way? Nell thought she knew the answer. Because perhaps she would always hear her mother's voice – from somewhere deep inside her; that part of her they shared. And, like her father had said in his memoir, her mother always knew when it was the right time to move on.

CHAPTER 52

Amy was driving to Cornwall in her Renault Clio to take some pictures of Nell's first night as a restaurateur in The Saffron House. Another first night. She thought back to the first night of the Moroccan event. Pushed the thought away. Focused instead on the road as she left the motorway after Exeter and took the familiar route to Cornwall on the A30. There was no point, she told herself, in brooding.

It was the beginning of March and the first spring flowers were visible in the hedgerows; cow parsley and celandines, even the occasional tuft of primroses in bud. Although there was still a definite chill to the air, there was also a sense of spring, of promise. Beginnings, she thought. For Nell's restaurant venture, for their new child. And for Amy's freelance photographic work. Amy was pleased with how this was developing. Duncan had been understanding about her leaving the gallery; he could see that he needed a full-time personal assistant and that she needed to focus on her career. He had no intention of holding her back, he'd said, a faint gleam of reluctance in his eyes.

She passed Launceston and checked her watch. There was plenty of time. It took about two and a half hours to get to

Roseland from Lyme Regis. And it was still light, though the sun was dipping in the sky. Once she got started, most of Nell's clientele would be holidaymakers, Amy supposed, so it was important for her to get her flyers into all the tourist information offices, campsites and hotels. As for tonight, Amy wouldn't have missed it for the world. Nell was family now. She and Callum had offered her a bed for the night, so once she'd taken the necessary publicity shots she could relax, eat, have a few drinks and enjoy.

It started to drizzle and Amy switched on her windscreen wipers. Typical Cornwall. But, hopefully, it would be nice tomorrow and it would be good to spend some time with Nell – her second cousin. She grinned at the thought. She'd been working hard lately, and she could do with a few days off. The Moroccan event had been as much of a success as Jake had promised and had brought in quite a bit of work.

Jake . . . Amy found herself gripping the steering wheel just a fraction tighter. He still contacted her from time to time – emails passing on contacts' names and addresses, and even some work he needed doing himself. And she was grateful for that. He had really helped her. But she never saw him. Once she even went to his office in Bristol to pass on some material. She'd taken a deep breath, waited for her heart to stop hammering . . . Knocked on the door. And he hadn't been there. OK, she was over an hour later than she'd said she'd be – which had been unavoidable. Even so . . . She couldn't help feeling let down.

But it was for the best. The rain eased and Amy put her

foot down. It was a Saturday afternoon, so there wasn't too much traffic. It was for the best, because she had been shocked at how she'd felt when she'd seen him with Melanie Tarrant. Upset, jealous, angry. Try as she might, Amy couldn't stop the memories creeping in. But, most of all, she'd been hurt inside. Because there had been a small part of her which had foolishly hoped . . .

She was driving through Bodmin Moor now, one of her favourite places. Bleak, desolate, windswept – and today was no exception. The way she had felt should have reinforced the patterns she had created in her life; to be well guarded, to insure yourself against hurt and loss, to depend on just one person alone – yourself. It could just sneak up and wrap itself around you in moments. Emotion. You could start to care, you could be rejected. And it hurt. As she'd told Nell back in the hammam in Marrakech, it seemed almost impossible to live with a man and yet keep your own identity, your own dreams. She didn't want to lose herself. Not for anyone. So she had done the right thing. But if so . . . why did she feel that she had missed out?

Apart from Jake's contacts, work had come directly from her exhibition of *Morocco Today* and also from her illustrations for Jenny, the cookery writer. In fact, the publisher had already commissioned her for another job. Amy took the turning for Truro. So far, then, she was on course to making a living as a freelance photographer. And that was what she'd always wanted.

It was past six when she arrived at The Saffron House. The

sun was setting, a chilly dusk had moved in and there were already a few other cars in the yard. She had first visited a few weeks ago and she noticed that Callum was getting on well with the landscaping of the front garden and terrace. Nell had told her that they were planning to create an outside space for eating al fresco – Cornish weather permitting – in the summer. But it was one step at a time at the moment, especially with the baby coming.

Amy got out of the car, retrieved her photographic equipment from the boot and made her way towards the front door. She was wearing a cream maxi dress with slashes of purple, lavender-stone drop earrings and a cream silk wrap borrowed from Auntie Lil. Amy's aunt would have liked to have been here herself, but she hadn't been feeling very strong this week so, instead, Nell had invited her grandmother to a quieter family celebration in a month's time.

Amy shifted her camera on to a shoulder and decided to take a few exterior shots. The farmhouse itself was old and rustic. It was built from what was probably a local grey stone, she guessed, and had red brick around the door and windows and a black slate roof. It had been decorated with fairy lights and there were tubs of spring flowers – narcissi and white and purple crocuses planted in tubs that echoed the acid yellow and Majorelle blue of the gardens in Marrakech. A sign hung outside. 'The Saffron House,' she read, the artwork of the background made up from Amy's original photograph of the saffron field in the foothills of the Atlas Mountains.

She rang the doorbell and a slightly harassed-looking Nell

came to open it. 'Amy!' She let her in and they hugged. 'I'm so glad you've arrived. Can you take some photos before everyone sits down to eat? I spent forever on those tables.'

'Of course I can. You look great, by the way.' Pregnancy suited Nell. Her eyes and skin were positively glowing. She was wearing a blue dress with a white chef's apron tied over it and a white cap holding back her blonde curls. 'How are you feeling?'

'Exhausted.' Nell swept a stray tendril of hair behind her hat. 'But happy. Come through.'

Nell and those working with her – an assistant chef, Callum, and a waitress, Nell's friend Sharon, who used to work with her – were putting the final touches to whatever was being created in the kitchen, Nell told her. It certainly smelt good.

'You get on, I'm fine.' And Amy ushered her gently back while she went through to the restaurant area, previously Nell and Callum's living room.

'Wow.' She looked around. Somehow, Nell and Callum had captured the spirit of sunlight and sunset in the colour of the walls; the niches of terracotta where they had stored tagines and bottles of wine, the painted wood panelling and the furniture. The room seemed to Amy to hold the very essence of Morocco. It was a good size and they'd cleverly fitted in six tables each seating four, with some extra seating in the corner. Here they had built a two-sided bench piled high with gold, crimson and mustard-coloured cushions within the nook on one side of the fireplace where a log fire was now burning. Amy took a few shots. The floor was solid oak with a Berber-style patterned rug in the centre and this was echoed in the oak of the dining tables and chairs. Two walls were painted in a deep sienna, two in ochre, while the nooks on either side of the fireplace were a warm and dusky terracotta. For the place mats Nell had used an eclectic mix of Moroccan tiles in startling colours and patterns, and rose petals had been scattered on each table.

Amy looked around. It was perfect. The lighting seemed to create just the right atmosphere of opulence and repose. There were Moorish lamps and lanterns of metal and coloured glass throwing a gentle glow on to the walls. And in the centre of the room hung a delicate silver Moroccan lantern with intricate, geometric shapes cut into the metal, casting long shadows on the tables and the floor. On the wall above the fireplace, framed, was the parchment, the drawing of the woman in the white robe and yellow veil picking the saffron flower, given to Nell by Hadi. Nell's father. Glenn.

Amy shook her head. She could still hardly believe it. The story reminded her of the labyrinthine passageways of the medina itself. It was a maze, but somehow, if you kept going, you could find your way to the inner core, to the truth, to the heart of things.

More guests began to arrive, including Nell's friend Lucy, whom she'd told her about back in Morocco, and Amy photographed them all as they stood around chatting and drinking the straw-yellow Moroccan Sauvignon Blanc which Sharon had brought out on trays. 'I hope you like it,' Sharon whispered to Amy. 'It's from the Atlas Mountains. Nell was looking for some Moroccan fizz, but it was really hard to find.'

Amy took a sip. 'It's delicious.' It tasted of anise and apple and Morocco, she thought.

'Do please take your seats.' Callum had come out to direct proceedings. 'There is a seating plan.'

Amy was glad to note that he was looking cheerful. Good for him. As Nell had told her on the phone, he had at last fully embraced the idea of The Saffron House and had flung himself into the project with his characteristic energy. Nell must be glad to have him onside. She was lucky, thought Amy.

'You're over here, Amy.' Callum was at her side, steering her to the corner nook of wooden benches and scarlet and gold cushions illuminated by a coloured Moorish lamp on the wall. 'It's a better vantage point.'

'Great.' She sat down and he topped up her wine glass. On the table was a basket of Moroccan flatbread and argan oil for dipping.

Callum glanced at his watch. 'Not everyone's here yet,' he muttered. 'But Nell says we should get on.'

Amy shrugged. 'Go for it.'

But just as he was about to speak the doorbell rang once more and Callum hurried to open it.

Amy picked up her camera. Scanned the room and focused on the door. And the tall, lazy figure of Jake Tarrant appeared in the viewfinder.

Oh, my . . . Her hands were trembling, for goodness' sake, and she was glad that at least the camera was shielding her face. What in God's name was he doing here?

And, of course, he was sitting at her table. He would be. Thanks, Nell, she thought. She put down the camera.

'Amy. Hello.' He bent to kiss her on the cheek. She was assaulted by the scent of leather and grapefruit, as if it had never gone away. 'Sorry I'm late.'

'I didn't even know you were coming,' Amy hissed, because Callum was just calling Nell out of the kitchen.

'Oh, didn't you?'

'My wife would like to say a few words,' Callum said. Everyone clapped.

'No. What are you doing here anyway?' Amy eyed Jake warily.

Nell came out, pulling off her white chef's cap so that her blonde curls sprang free.

Jake raised an eyebrow. 'As friendly and polite as ever, I see.'

'Hello and welcome,' said Nell, smiling at the assorted diners. 'Thanks for coming along to our first Moroccan evening at The Saffron House. The first of many, we hope.'

Someone gave a loud whoop, and everyone laughed.

'Before we begin, I'd like to say a few words about Moroccan cuisine,' Nell said. 'Morocco, partly because of its situation on the north-western edge of Africa, has been a crossroads of cultures for centuries. And its cuisine is therefore among the most diverse and flavoursome in the world, expressing the historic influences of the Romans, the Arabs, the Moriscos of Spain, of Sephardic Jews – and, of course, its native Berbers.' She smiled. 'The land is fertile and the climate is good for growing.'

Nell paused. 'As some of you already know, we grow our own saffron here at The Saffron House and I've taken the liberty of serving some endored biscuits with your first course. This is to remind us that saffron was once grown throughout the UK and that many people kept a small plot for their own use, as we do today. Endoring is a medieval technique – it uses a glaze of saffron and egg yolk to make the biscuits golden. It's not Moroccan, but . . .' She shrugged and picked up a tile from a nearby table. '. . . the foods of Morocco are as robust and colourful as a Moroccan tile,' she said, and chuckled. 'And dozens of spices and herbs are used in the cooking. I've just provided a small sample for you today. I hope you'll come back and try more.'

Everyone clapped. How she had grown in confidence, Amy thought, from the person she'd met in Riad Lazuli last year. Nell put her cap back on and returned to the kitchen as Sharon appeared with the first course. According to the menu in front of Amy, this was marinated aubergines with tahini dressing. It looked and smelt delicious – as did the small plate of endored biscuits placed in the centre of their table.

'Sorry.' Amy addressed this to Jake. She smiled her thanks to Sharon as she put the plate in front of her. 'But I didn't know Nell had invited you.' She picked up her fork. How did Nell even know his contact details? Amy certainly hadn't told her.

'She contacted me through Duncan.'

Amy frowned. Why would she have done that?

'And I met Callum at the event.' He gave her a look. *As if you could forget.*

'Did you?' Amy hadn't noticed that. She could only remember Jake telling her he wouldn't have time to talk to her, Jake ever attentive to his guest, Melanie Tarrant. Amy tried the aubergine. It was rich and silky on the tongue and she could taste garlic, chilli and coriander. The tahini was lemony and fresh and the two made a perfect combination. A bit like Jake and Melanie, she thought grimly.

'How's Melanie?' she asked.

'She's fine, thanks.' He put down his fork. 'She's working with me now.'

When they were finished, Sharon efficiently whisked their plates away.

'How lovely,' Amy said. She picked up her camera and took a shot of the diners. From their facial expressions, they seemed pretty impressed by the first course.

'We've always got on very well,' Jake added.

'That must be useful.' If you were married to someone. So why was he here? she wondered. To taunt her?

The main course was a tagine – chicken and almond with a honey saffron jam, served with couscous. Amy sniffed. It smelt wonderful. And she wasn't going to let Jake Tarrant spoil her appetite. She dug in. It tasted good, too. The chicken had obviously been cooked slowly in tomatoes and spices and the honey saffron jam had caramelized and been scattered with toasted almonds. Nell had captured that sweet and sour aspect of Moroccan cuisine with this dish, that way of combining meat, fruit and nuts that made it unique.

Callum had brought out some red wine to accompany the main. It was a Tandem Syrah, he told them, and it was certainly full-bodied and fruity enough to complement the spicy chicken. 'Some well-established French growers have teamed up with Moroccan estates,' he told Amy and Jake as he poured them both a glass. 'We don't have a licence to sell wine at the moment, but when we do, I'll be working on a wine list.'

Amy smiled at his enthusiasm. Between them, they'd make it work, she was sure. Now that they were a team.

Over the main course Amy felt herself begin to relax as she enjoyed the food, the wine and the atmosphere, and she and Jake began to chat more easily, much as they used to, about an event Jake was organizing in a seafront hotel in Sidmouth, about Amy's work and Glenn's memoirs.

'I never thanked you properly,' Amy said.

'What for?'

'For the contacts you've provided me with. For supporting my work. For all your help with the event.' There, she'd said it – at last.

He seemed surprised. 'It was my pleasure, Amy,' he said. 'I . . .' But even as he spoke, his mobile bleeped with a message and, distracted, he murmured, 'Sorry.' He glanced at it and switched it off.

'. . . it doesn't matter.' But she couldn't help wondering what he had been about to say.

Sharon came to clear their plates. Amy was feeling pleasantly full. Jake had been difficult to work with, she reminded herself, and they had clashed constantly. Any romance between them would have ended in disaster. She'd had a lucky escape.

Dessert was served. It was fig and sesame tart with cardamom orange cream. Amy stared at it. It was a beautiful thing. And it looked delicious. She took a small spoonful, then another. The flavours of the orange zest, the figs, the cardamoms and the sesame were so good that she didn't want it to end.

Jake was watching her. 'There's something I wanted to ask you,' he said. 'Nell thought it was the kind of thing I should ask face to face.'

'Oh, did she?' Nell and Callum had come a long way in their relationship since Morocco. They'd worked it through. Amy, too, had realized what she needed. Not a meaningless relationship or an affair that would never come to anything. She wanted a partner. An equal. A friend. Someone who could understand her and let her be the person she wanted to be. Was that too much to ask?

They finished dessert, and fresh *thé à la menthe* was served. Now, this really took her back to Morocco. Fresh mint tea after a day exploring the souks and the gardens. Fresh mint tea for breakfast and fresh mint tea for tea.

Jake picked up her hand and started playing with her fingers as if it were the most natural thing in the world.

'What was it?' She stared at him. She should pull away, she knew that. Only . . .

'Hmm?'

'The thing you wanted to ask me.'

'Ah.' He looked into her eyes. Rooibos tea, she thought. 'Amy. Is there anyone else? Are you seeing someone?'

'Anyone else?' Why would he be interested when he had his wife, the lovely Melanie, the woman of his dreams? She shook her head.

'In that case, would you consider –?'

They were interrupted by Sharon clearing the dessert dishes.

Amy was suddenly suspicious. She snatched her hand away. 'Why did Nell ask you here?'

'I think she felt that we were missing an opportunity.'

'An opportunity?' Amy frowned. He was definitely coming on to her. When he was married! She took refuge in her *thé à la menthe*. It was fresh and calming. 'What do you want from me, Jake?'

'Isn't it obvious?'

Amy considered. 'Are you trying to pay her back – is that it? And you think I'd be the right kind of person to –?' How could she explain? She felt tears starting somewhere in her upper chest. She wouldn't cry, of course. She never cried. That was one thing she didn't do. But she hated that he thought this about her. Duncan had been a mistake. She had been feeling low and Duncan had been there at the right time, encouraging her, supporting her work, telling her that she should have faith in herself. *Faith* . . . And in a way it had made her life more uncomplicated. She could forget about men and concentrate on her photography. Until Jake Tarrant came along, that was. She glared at him. For one thing, she had no intention of explaining anything and, for another, it made it easier not to cry.

'Amy? Pay who back? What are you talking about?'

Through her tears his face was a blur. She took a large gulp of mint tea, swallowed hard, pushed the tears back to wherever they'd come from. Or tried to.

'Melanie.' She gulped. 'Your wife.'

'Melanie?' He frowned as if trying to make sense of it all. He watched her for a moment. And then he grinned, damn him. And damn those dimples. And that crooked tooth. It really wasn't fair. 'Oh, I see,' he said.

'Please don't.'

'Sorry. It's just that –'

'It isn't funny.' She got to her feet.

'Amy.' He pulled her back again, to his side of the bench, and this time he kept hold of her hand. 'Melanie isn't my wife.'

Melanie wasn't his wife. This made no sense at all. 'Then . . .?'

'She's my sister.'

She blinked at him. 'But . . .?'

'I told you Emma left me for my best friend.'

'Yes, but . . .' He hadn't told her his wife's name was Emma.

'And that I'm over it. Over her.'

'You didn't say that. You said what she'd done didn't matter any more. That things had turned around.' She thought of that conversation in the gallery that afternoon when he'd brought the champagne and they'd shared a toast. *To us*. 'I thought it was because she'd come back.'

He moved closer to her on the bench. She realized that was another advantage of this seating plan. You could get very close to someone on a bench. 'It didn't matter anymore . . .' He was whispering urgently into her ear. '. . . Because of you.'

'Me?'

'Things had turned around for me because I'd met you. And because you're crazy and deluded and stubborn and defensive and you drive me mad.'

Amy trusted herself to look at him. She breathed in the fragrance of leather and grapefruit. 'And is that a good thing?'

'It's a good thing,' he said.

What was it Nell had said that day in the hammam when Amy had asked her how she could keep her identity, her career, when she was married? Something about there being different parts of her. And different parts needing different things. Amy reckoned that there was quite a big part of her that had been waiting for Jake Tarrant to come along. *Faith* . . . She might as well admit it.

'Does Nell know?' she asked him. 'Is that why . . .?'

He shrugged. 'I introduced Callum to Melanie that night at the event. He certainly knew.'

519

But he wouldn't have necessarily thought to mention it to Nell. Unless, one day, Nell had said, 'Poor Amy, it's a shame about Jake Tarrant getting back with his wife like that.' And then . . .

'Nell said that there's a full moon tonight,' he said. 'If you fancy a stroll outside?'

Nell seemed to have been saying rather a lot, thought Amy. But: 'Why not?'

The dinner party was breaking up and people were once more standing around and chatting. Amy and Jake slipped out of the front door and walked round the back towards the kitchen garden where Nell grew all her own herbs, and the walled field, where she would be growing the saffron this year. The ground was bare and ready. Waiting. Amy looked back at the farmhouse and, just for a moment, she thought she saw Nell's face at the window, before she smiled and turned away.

'I always thought we'd make such a good team,' Jake murmured into her hair. 'I'd really like to give it a try.'

Amy thought of what her Great-aunt Lil had told her. 'It doesn't matter if you go about it in different ways,' she said, 'as long as you want the same things in the end. As long as you share the same dream.'

Jake had his hands on her shoulders. He was looking into her eyes. 'We made the Moroccan event a huge success, Amy,' he said.

'Mmm.'

'So . . .' He bent towards her.

Amy put her arms around him. He felt pretty much as she'd expected. Familiar and yet unknown. And then, all Amy was aware of was the rustling of new leaves in the trees, of the full moon shining down on them and the touch of Jake's lips on hers.

'Why do you always smell of grapefruit?' she muttered.

But already he was kissing her again and he didn't even seem to hear.

ACKNOWLEDGEMENTS

I should like to thank all the team at Quercus for their continuing hard work and support, including the team at the time of writing this book: Caroline Butler, who helped me get to grips with social media back then, Margot Weale for PR and, most especially, Stef Bierwerth, for being the most lovely editor. Thanks to Laura Longrigg, too, for her editorial support and advice. These two helped me get this novel into shape and I really enjoyed that process . . . (Laura has since retired and I am delighted to now be represented by Broo Doherty at DHH). Thanks to Juliet Lewis for the way she once talked about slicing onions and to Stuart Innes for his poignant recollections of Vietnam. Thanks to my early readers: Alan Fish, Sarah Sparkes and Holly Innes. They all – especially Alan – gave me a lot of useful feedback.

I went on a bit of a saffron trail myself when I was researching for this book, starting with Pat Willard's excellent book *The Secrets of Saffron*, discovering saffron recipes, learning about the growing and the myths and history associated with the spice and generally just falling in love with it, really. Thanks, Pat! Mark Starte at the tourist information centre in Saffron Walden was also very helpful, especially in putting me in touch with Norfolk Saffron, England's first modern-day commercial saffron producer. Invaluable help was given to me by the clever and generous botanist Dr Sally Francis who runs this saffron farm in Norfolk (www.norfolksaffron.co.uk) where one can buy top-quality, delicious saffron, learn about the history of the spice (and recipes) from Sally's book Saffron, taste her award-winning liqueur, King Harry, and even attend a workshop or two. Sally is an expert on the subject of saffron and any mistakes in this novel are, of course, my own. Other books were very useful, among them *Zohra's Ladder and Other Moroccan Tales* by Pamela Windo, *Hideous Kinky* by Esther Freud, *Border Crossings* by Daniel Peters, *Amazir* by Tom Gamble, *Called to Serve*, a collection of stories edited by Tom Weiner from men and women confronted by the Vietnam War Draft, *The Drifters* by James Michener, *Cinnamon City* by Miranda Innes, *Awakening* by D. Johns, *A Year in Marrakech* by Peter Mayne, as well as other reference books on Moroccan cuisine and design. Finally, the brilliant *Vietnam 1945–75* by Vivienne Sanders. All were inspirational.

I'd like to give special thanks to all my lovely readers who enjoy the books. I know it's been said before – but this novel wouldn't be here without you! Finally, thanks to my late mother, Daphne Squires who loved this book so much; my son and daughter-in-law Luke and Agata Page; my daughters Alexa Page and Ana Henley; and my husband, Grey Innes, who are all intrepid supporters of my writing, who listen to me, are there for me and who help spread the word. Thank you, Family. I love you.

**Discover more breathtaking escapist
stories from Rosanna Ley**

The Villa

When Tess Angel receives a solicitor's letter inviting her to
claim her inheritance – the Villa Sirena, perched on a clifftop
in Sicily – she is stunned. Her only link to the island is
through her mother, Flavia, who left Sicily during
World War II and cut all contact with her family.

When Tess goes to Sicily, Flavia realises the secrets from
her past are about to be revealed and decides to try to
explain her actions. Meanwhile, Tess' teenage daughter
Ginny is stressed by college, by her blooming sexuality and
filled with questions that she longs to ask her father,
if only she knew where he was . . .

Out now in paperback, eBook and audio

QUERCUS

Bay of Secrets

Spain, 1939

Following the wishes of her parents to keep her safe during the war, a young girl, Julia, enters a convent in Barcelona. Looking for a way to maintain her links to the outside world, she volunteers to help in a maternity clinic. But worrying adoption practices in the clinic force Sister Julia to decide how far she will go to help those placed in her care.

England, 2012

Six months after her parents' shocking death, 34-year-old journalist and jazz enthusiast Ruby Rae has finally found the strength to pack away their possessions and sell the family home. But as she does so, she unearths a devastating secret that her parents, Vivien and Tom, had kept from her all her life.

Out now in paperback, eBook and audio

QUERCUS

The Little Theatre
by the Sea

Faye has just completed her degree in interior design when she finds herself jobless and boyfriend-less. While debating what to do next, she receives a surprise phone call from her old college friend Charlotte who now lives in Sardinia and is married to Italian hotelier, Fabio.

When Charlotte suggests that Faye relocate for a month to house-sit, Faye wonders if a summer break in sunny Sardinia might be the perfect way to recharge her batteries and think about her future.

But then Charlotte tells Faye that there's something more behind the sudden invitation: her friends Marisa and Alessandro are looking for a designer to renovate a crumbling old theatre they own in the scenic village of Deriu.

The idea certainly sounds appealing to Faye, but little does she know what she's letting herself in for if she accepts this once-in-a-lifetime opportunity . . .

Out now in paperback, eBook and audio

QUERCUS

The Lemon Tree Hotel

In the beautiful village of Vernazza, the Mazzone
family have transformed an old convent overlooking the
glamorous Italian Riviera into the elegant Lemon Tree
Hotel. For Chiara, her daughter Elene and her granddaughter Isabella, the running of their hotel is the
driving force in their lives.

One day, two unexpected guests check in. The first,
Dante, is a face from Chiara's past, but what exactly
happened between them all those years ago, Elene wonders.
Meanwhile, Isabella is preoccupied with the second guest,
a mysterious young man who seems to know a lot about the
history of the old convent and the people who live there.
Isabella is determined to find out his true intentions and
discover the secret past of the Lemon Tree Hotel.

Out now in paperback, eBook and audio

QUERCUS

From
Venice with Love

With her marriage in danger of falling apart, Joanna
returns home to the beautiful but dilapidated Mulberry
Farm Cottage in rural Dorset, where her sister Harriet
is struggling to keep the Farm afloat and cope
with their eccentric mother.

When Joanna discovers a bundle of love letters in the attic,
written by a watercolourist named Emmy, she is intrigued
and sets out to discover Emmy's true story. Emmy's letters
take Joanna to the picturesque alleyways and bridges of
Lisbon, Prague, and the most romantic place of all:
Venice – where a whole new magical world seems
to unfold in front of her.

Meanwhile, back at Mulberry Farm Cottage, a mysterious
prowler adds to Harriet's problems and interrupts her search
for a perfect partner. Will she ever find true love? Where will
Emmy's mesmerising pathway lead? And more importantly,
will Joanna and Harriet be able to rescue the cottage and
finally be able to re-discover their sisterly bond?

Out now in paperback, eBook and audio

QUERCUS

The Orange Grove

Holly loves making marmalade. Now she has a chance to leave her stressful city job and pursue her dream – of returning to the Dorset landscape of her childhood to open Bitter Orange, a shop celebrating the fruit that first inspired her.

Holly's mother Ella has always loved Seville. So why is she reluctant to go back there with Holly to source products for the shop? What is she frightened of – and does it have anything to do with the old Spanish recipe for Seville orange and almond cake that Ella keeps hidden from her family?

In Seville, where she was once forced to make the hardest decision of her life, Ella must finally face up to the past, while Holly meets someone who poses a threat to all her plans. Seville is a city full of sunshine and oranges. But it can also be bittersweet. Will love survive the secrets of the orange grove?

Out now in paperback, eBook and audio

QUERCUS

The Forever Garden

Amid the sun-soaked hills of southern Italy lies the Romano family olive grove, where Lara lives with her daughter Rose and her granddaughter Bea.

Lara has spent a lifetime trying to forget the traumatic events that led to her desperate escape from Dorset seventy years ago. But when she sees Bea – a passionate horticulturalist most at home in nature – being swept off her feet by Matteo, a handsome and charismatic restaurateur, Lara fears her granddaughter is in danger of making the same mistake as Lara did all those years ago.

Remembering a promise she once made, Lara asks Bea to travel to Dorset to restore her family's long-lost garden. Bea is torn. She would love to find out more about the mystery of her beloved grandmother's past. But if she leaves Italy, will Matteo wait for her? And when she arrives at the house in Dorset – what will she find?

Meanwhile back in Italy, an old flame from Rose's past reappears, threatening to expose a secret that could tear the heart out of the Romano family for good.

Out now in paperback, eBook and audio

QUERCUS